SUSPECTS

By *William J. Caunitz*

ONE POLICE PLAZA

SUSPECTS

SUSPECTS

WILLIAM J. CAUNITZ

CROWN PUBLISHERS, INC.
New York

Copyright © 1986 by William J. Caunitz

Published by Crown Publishers, Inc., 225 Park Avenue South, New York, New York 10003 and represented in Canada by the Canadian MANDA Group

CROWN is a trademark of Crown Publishers, Inc.

Manufactured in the United States of America

Library of Congress Cataloging-in-Publication Data

Caunitz, William J.
    Suspects

    I. Title.
PS3553.A945S8   1986   813'.54   86-13427

ISBN 0-517-55864-5
Design by J. Victor Thomas

10 9 8 7 6 5 4 3 2 1
First Edition

"But if the while I think of thee, dear friend
All losses are restored and sorrows end."
Shakespeare, Sonnet 30, line 13

William E. Farrell, journalist,
the *New York Times*
Joseph I. Grossman, sergeant, NYPD

SUSPECTS

1

The old man walked unnoticed into the park. His face was badly wrinkled and shaggy gray hair covered the tops of his ears. His clothes were old, his shoulders stooped; in his right hand was a large shopping bag brimming with rags and newspapers.

It was Thursday, a slow June day. The summer was not yet in full bloom; the heavy wet heat of July and August lay ahead. Mothers had gathered their children inside the play areas while teenagers hung out, listening to boxes playing hard rock at full volume. Several joggers slapped around the park's block-wide perimeter; a lone skater boogied along a pathway with his cassette earplugs affixed and his cosmic antennae bobbing. People with Slavic features sat on benches speaking Polish.

At the end of the parkway the old man came to the monument that had been erected to the heroes of the Great War. He paused and looked up at the statue with the human body and the birdlike face. Turning away, he moved to a nearby bench and sat, his wary eyes taking in the indifference around him. A woman sitting nearby hefted a baby playfully. She glanced at him and smiled. He scowled back. She quickly looked away.

The newcomer pulled the shopping bag onto his lap and reached inside. The peanuts were on the bottom, wedged under the cold barrel of a shotgun. He worked out the bag of nuts, put the shopping bag on the ground, and locked it between his legs. Leaning forward, he began tossing nuts into the quickly swelling flock of pigeons. There was nothing for him to do now but wait.

McGoldrick Park, a wide expanse of trees and forgotten monuments, was sandwiched between Driggs and Nassau avenues in the Greenpoint section of Brooklyn. It had once been named Winthrop Park but that name had been changed in order to honor the eighteenth-century cleric who had built St. Cecilia's Church on Herbert and Henry streets.

Across from the park, on Russell Street, the Lutheran Church of the Messiah was squeezed between two renovated town houses. Some of the row houses and the brownstones on that block had small patches of tended grass in front, and some had blue-and-white Madonnas.

The peanuts were gone. Most of the birds had strutted away. Some lingered. The pigeon feeder looked at his wristwatch, reached down and took hold of the shopping bag, and got up. Directly in front of him were two one-story buildings that were connected by a colonnade of Ionic columns. He examined the decaying facade of the most grandiose public toilet in the Borough of Brooklyn. The structure was enclosed within a high wire fence that was topped by loops of vicious concertina wire. Its cornices were festooned with signs: Danger—Under Repair.

Passing the lavatory on the women's side, the old man wandered over to the Antonio di Felippo statue, a bronze man hauling on a rope around a capstan. As he strolled around the monument he glanced beyond the park to the A&P supermarket on Driggs Avenue. His friend was not there. Had something gone wrong? His stomach churned.

Gazing up at the massive bronze figure, he noticed the cupid heart that someone had painted on the right buttock: KB loves KS.

The old man turned his head and looked again in the direction of the supermarket. This time he saw his friend standing there, a wan smile fixed on his face. The hairs on the old man's neck bristled. His hands were suddenly clammy, and a sense of isolation engulfed him. He began a slow walk toward Driggs Avenue, his shopping bag firmly in hand.

One block away from McGoldrick Park, Joe Gallagher was backing his dented '71 Ford Fairlane into a space on Pope John Paul II Square directly across the street from St. Stanislaus Kostka Church.

Leaning forward in his seat, Gallagher looked out at the traffic signs. No Standing 8 A.M. to 7 P.M. He took the vehicle identification plate from behind the visor and tossed it onto the dashboard. NYPD Official Business.

He got out of the car, leaned back inside, and slid a cake box off the front seat. With palms firmly planted under the box he crossed Driggs Avenue, heading for the open telephone booth on the corner. He was dressed in tan slacks over which hung the tails of a gaudy Hawaiian shirt that covered his potbelly and the holstered gun tucked inside his trousers.

He slid his parcel onto the skinny ledge, holding it in place with his stomach, and lifted the receiver off the hook. Dialing, he noticed a woman leading a Chihuahua, and watched her bend to place a sheet of paper under the squatting dog's behind.

Yetta Zimmerman's candy store was on Driggs Avenue, one block west of McGoldrick Park and across the street from St. Stanislaus Kostka Church. It was six stores in from where Joe Gallagher was making his telephone call. The shop was a long, narrow place that blossomed in the rear into a good-size storage area where Yetta stacked cases of soda and where two video games stood. A row of bare light bulbs hung from grimy chains fastened to a tin ceiling. An old-fashioned soda fountain was to the right of the entrance, and next to it was a rotating rack of paperbacks. Behind the soda fountain there was a large wooden display cabinet with sliding glass doors, crammed with cheap games and toys.

Yetta was a hulking woman with sad gray eyes and a thick jaw that sprouted scattered gray whiskers. Pussy jaw, some of the neighborhood boys would tease.

Yetta's was a local landmark. She had been operating her candy store for more than twenty-five years. It was where the neighborhood women held their morning coffee klatch to gossip about the neighborhood men. And it was where the neighborhood men came to borrow a five till payday.

Most of the people in this section of Greenpoint were of Polish ancestry. They enjoyed their daily visits to Yetta's, where they could argue in Polish over events in their native country and discuss the pros and cons of gentrification. On this Thursday afternoon Yetta was wearing a faded housecoat buttoned down the front and white socks and sneakers. Her newsprint-stained right ring finger bore only a plain, worn gold band.

She had just slid out change to a customer when she remembered that the fountain was nearly out of soda. She shambled out from behind the counter and went to the rear of the store, where she picked up the top case of soda. Lugging it past the video games, she glanced at the three boys playing the machines and thought that they should be saving their money instead of squandering it on such nonsense.

She had just about finished replenishing her stock when Joe Gallagher appeared in the doorway. "Here's your birthday cake." He beamed.

Yetta bustled out to greet him. She pulled him into a bear hug, forcing him to hold the box out to his side to avoid having it crushed. "You're a good boy, Joe. Ol' Yetta appreciates you going out of your way for her."

A harsh voice barked from the doorway. "Hey you!"

Turning to look, they slowly backed out of their embrace.

The three boys looked away from the video games to see who had called out.

The pigeon feeder was framed in the doorway, his right hand deep inside his shopping bag.

Gallagher slowly measured the stranger, instantly sensing the presence of danger. There was something about that voice. Something in those eyes. The irises were white and had little specks of gray and the pupils were a deep . . . No! That was not possible. He knew those eyes. He took several steps toward the door, looking, making sure.

The shopping bag slid to the floor. Bottles and rags and newspapers scattered about. A Coke can rattled across the bleached wood floor and hit against the soda fountain, making an eerie clatter in the still, cool, dim interior of the shop.

Gallagher saw the shotgun coming up at him and blanched with fear. He lunged to one side and frantically reached under his shirt with his right hand, grappling for his gun. He was too late. The blast severed his right arm, spinning him around. The second explosion turned his face into a grotesque, bloody mask and hurled him backward, a look of horrible disbelief forever frozen in his one remaining eye.

"No! Not like this. Not after all that I've been through," Yetta Zimmerman shrieked. She tried to scream but the sounds would not come out. They were clogged somewhere in her throat so that only a frenzied gurgle came forth.

She wanted to run, to flee to safety, but her feet would not move. And then, when she saw the barrel being swung toward her, she closed her eyes and threw up her hands to cover her face.

2

---

ony Scanlon sat at the end of Monte's long bar playing liar's
poker with Davy Goldstein and Frankie Fats, the bartender.
The Mets game was on the tube. It was a little after two P.M.
Most of the lunch crowd had departed, so the waiters had begun
to set up for the evening rush. A few of the neighborhood regulars
were scattered along the bar.

Scanlon sipped Hennessy as he studied the palmed bill. He was
holding four sevens. His long, narrow face was complemented by
black eyes and jet-black hair graying at the temples. He was a
handsome, well-built man of medium height, who at forty-three
had a still-youthful face, a quick mischievous smile, and a cleft in
his chin that formed the inverted apex of a ragged triangle. If El
Greco had painted a cop, Scanlon would have been a perfect
model.

Davy Goldstein was an owl-faced man in his mid-fifties who had
a fondness for Havanas. He liked to smoke them from a cheap
amber plastic holder. Nodding his head in concentration, Goldstein bid four threes.

The other players reexamined their hands.

A customer at the other end ordered a Martell.

Frankie Fats slid off the bar stool and waddled down the length of the bar. He was wearing a white-on-white shirt with the collar opened and his tie wrapped but unknotted, the broad half rolled over the top.

Monte's was on Wither Street, a small side street one block from the elevated highway of the Brooklyn-Queens Expressway, which separated the Polish section of Greenpoint from the Italian section. The houses in the Italian part were mostly one- and two-story dwellings of wood and clapboard. The streets in both parts were clean, and the buildings, unlike those in other parts of the city, were graffiti-free. On every Monday, Wednesday, and Friday an array of neatly tied green refuse bags lined the curbs of Greenpoint awaiting the garbage pickup.

Frankie Fats returned and draped his considerable rump over the top of the bar stool. He glanced at his hand and bid six fours.

Scanlon bid seven sevens.

Davy Goldstein called him.

They showed their bills. Scanlon's sevens had won it. He raked in the other players' bills. They were all folding new bills when the private line under the bar rang. Frankie Fats reached under, pulled out the receiver, and grunted into the mouthpiece. When Scanlon saw the bartender's tiny, piglike eyes dart to him, he knew that the plans he had made for the remainder of his day had just been changed for him.

That Thursday had begun for Tony Scanlon when he opened his eyes and reached out to shut off the buzzing alarm. Turning back onto his side, he inched his bulk across the queen-size bed to the other form. He began to rub his body against hers. She made a small catlike sound and moved with him. When it was time, she turned onto her stomach, snatched a pillow down, stuffed it under her, and spread her legs.

He mounted her, doggie-style.

Sally De Nesto could always tell when a man was ready to finish. She thrashed her head over the bed, miming sleepy ecstasy. "Come, Tony. Come with me," she moaned moments before his orgasm.

Scanlon lay on top of her, catching his breath, permitting himself the pleasure of leaving her body naturally. Her backside felt warm and nice, and he rubbed himself into the wetness of her.

Sally De Nesto reached her hand up and ran it through his damp hair. "You're one of the best, Tony."

He rolled off her onto the bed. "Sure I am," he said with sudden annoyance. He moved to the edge of the bed and sat up, reaching out for the prosthesis on the nearby chair. He pulled it over and rested it across his lap. He rolled the stump shrinker off the stump of his left leg, folded it, and put it down on the bed beside him. With both hands he kneaded his stump. The edema wasn't so bad this morning. He took the stump sock out of the socket of his prosthesis and rolled it up over his stump. He tilted back on the bed, elevated his stump, and slid the socket of the prosthesis over it. He stood, pressing his weight down on both legs, ensuring that the patellar tendon rested firmly on the patella bar of his artificial leg.

He moved into the bathroom and sat on the lip of the tub. He removed the prosthesis and the stump sock, put the sock inside the socket, leaned the leg against the wall, and slid around into the tub.

A few minutes later Sally De Nesto sat up in bed with a sheet across her chest, watching him get dressed. She wondered why she was so hung up on this one-legged man. Why the hell did she feel so much compassion for this one? After all, there were worse handicaps. And he certainly did handle his affliction well. He walked without a limp, had a good job, a cute cleft in his chin, and a subtle animal aura about him that made women pay attention to him. As he sat on the bed and slid into his trousers, she asked herself what it was about him that made her want to know more about him, and she decided that it was the simple fact that he didn't seem to give a rat's shit about her. There were other reasons too: the way his lips pulled back to form the cutest dimples, and there were those magnificent eyes that were so full of sadness. Many times she wondered about the woman who must have put the sadness there. Hookers are real connoisseurs of sadness.

At ten o'clock that Thursday morning Detective Lt. Tony Scanlon parked his car on Freeman Street, in the space in front of the Nine-three Precinct that was reserved for the squad commander. He walked to the candy store on the corner and bought three packets of De Nobili cigars. He left the store and went half a block on Freeman Street until he came to the end, the western tip of the Borough of Brooklyn. His gaze went across the East River to the shimmering towers of Manhattan. South, to the Twin Towers, they were in the First. North, to the Citicorp, that was in the Seventeenth. To the Empire State Building, that was in Midtown South. That's how a cop remembers prominent locations, by the precincts within which they are located. His forlorn stare fixed on the distant skyline. Manhattan. The same job, a different job. The Tenderloin. He used to work there. But then, that was ancient history.

Six minutes later Scanlon walked into the Nine-three Precinct and asked the desk officer what was doing. The gray-haired lieutenant with the half-glasses and heavy brogue lowered the *Wall Street Journal,* peered down at Scanlon from behind the high desk, and said, "And what could be doing here, Anthony?"

Scanlon walked behind the desk. He moved to the long green clerical cabinet and picked up the teletype message book. He paged through, scanning the latest messages. He turned his attention next to the Arrest Record. No arrests had been made in the Nine-three for three days. Going through the Unusual Occurrence Folder, he saw that the last Unusual had been prepared eight days ago when a car had exploded on the Brooklyn-Queens Expressway, killing the five occupants.

He saved the Personnel Orders for last. They would give him the pulse of the Job. Tell him who was transferred where. An inspector transferred out of the big building, as the cops called police headquarters, to Manhattan South was tracked for promotion. The same inspector transferred to Brooklyn North was being given a message to put his papers in.

As he looked over the latest orders he sighed in disgust when he saw that Inspector Sean O'Brien had been promoted to deputy chief and transferred from Support Service Bureau on the tenth floor of the big building to Management Analysis on the twelfth floor. They never go far from the breast, he thought, walking out from behind the desk. He crossed the muster room, heading for the curving staircase.

The Nine-three was considered one of the best houses in the city to work in. There were few crimes, plenty of available women, and many good restaurants where the man on post was always welcome.

The caseload of the Detective Squad did not warrant a lieutenant assigned as the Whip. But Scanlon had been put out to pasture after he lost his leg in the Adler Hotel payroll heist. "Take it easy, Tony. Go over to the Nine-three and enjoy the good life. You've paid your dues," retired Deputy Chief Kimmins had told him after his year-long recuperative leave was up. That was four years ago. And today Tony Scanlon was a man bored out of his tits.

Sipping coffee from a mug with the words "Slave Driver" painted across it, Scanlon crossed the squad room and entered the cubicle that was his office. Moving behind his desk, he glanced down at the Sixty sheet, the chronological record of all the cases that the Squad had caught for the year, and was pleased to see that the night team had closed out two more cases. Although he was out of the trenches, he still had a Detective Squad to run. And he, and every other detective commander in the city, knew that clearances were the only real standard by which they would be judged.

Stuck into the corner of his desk blotter was a slip of paper with the present whereabouts of two of his detectives. Detective Hector Colon was at his Polish girlfriend's apartment undergoing horizontal therapy, and Detective Howard Christopher was at the Y, swimming laps. Detectives Maggie Higgins and Lew Brodie were out in the squad room, holding it down.

After he read the *New York Times* and worked the crossword puzzle, Scanlon signed the few reports that were in the basket and then leaned back in his ancient, squeaky swivel chair to plan out the remainder of his tour. Looking out of his office he could see Maggie Higgins fast at work typing her term paper on human infanticide. Maggie was a senior at John Jay College and hoped someday to go to law school. She was a big woman with short brown hair and a willing smile. She favored loose-fitting tops that concealed her heavy bosom and offered her some protection against the endless stream of snide remarks from male detectives.

Maggie Higgins was a lesbian. Three years ago she had come out of the closet in order to testify before the City Council on the gay-rights bill. The bill was shelved for the ninth time and Higgins was flopped from the prestigious Bond and Forgery Squad to Greenpoint. The Nine-three Detective Squad had become a dumping ground for fallen angels.

Whatever reservations Scanlon had had about Higgins soon

disappeared. She had turned out to be one of his best detectives when there was work to be done, which wasn't often. The other members of the Squad liked her too. Cops like an underdog. Especially one who has guts. It *had* taken guts to do what she had done, to come out. But the way the other members of the Squad felt about her did not prevent them from exercising their male egos at her expense. A cop's machismo knows no bounds.

It was a little after twelve forty-five in the afternoon when Scanlon strolled from his office and dragged a chair over to where Higgins sat. Lowering himself, he glanced over at Lew Brodie, who was at the next desk with his feet up, reading an old issue of *Soldier of Fortune* magazine. "I'm going on patrol, Maggie," Scanlon said, leaning forward, reading the page in the typewriter. In the lexicon of the Job, "going on patrol" meant that the Whip of the Nine-three Squad was off to his favorite watering hole, Monte's.

Higgins looked up at him and smiled. "I've got the number, Lou," she said, addressing him with the diminutive of "lieutenant" that was regularly used in the Job.

It had been Maggie Higgins's hurried telephone calls that had sent Tony Scanlon running from Monte's to the double-parked department auto in front, and had sent Hector Colon fleeing from his girlfriend's apartment, and had caused Howard Christopher to rush from the Y without showering.

When Scanlon arrived at the crime scene he found Driggs Avenue clogged with police cars, many with their turret lights still whirling and splashing red and white light on the faces of bystanders. The wail of sirens continued to fill the air. Units were responding from adjoining precincts. 10-13, Assist Patrolman; Report of an Officer Shot.

A sergeant stood by the open door of his radio car shouting into the radio, "Call it off! No further. No further."

Two lengths of cord had been hastily stretched from the entrance of Yetta Zimmerman's candy store to the handles of two radio cars. Police officers stood behind the barrier holding back gawkers. The forensics station wagon was parked on the sidewalk. Technicians were sliding out black valises, preparing for their grim but essential tasks.

Traffic for a five-block radius around the candy store was at a standstill. Scanlon had to double-park three blocks away and run the rest of the way. When he arrived at the scene, he straddled the cord barrier with his right leg, pushed the rope down with his hand, hefted the artificial leg over, and ran into the candy store.

Maggie Higgins rushed over to meet him. Her face was drawn and shocked. "It's Joe Gallagher," she shouted, as though unable to believe her own words.

Scanlon was stunned. Not Joe Gallagher! Not the Joe Gallagher who was the past president of the Holy Name Society. Not the Joe Gallagher who was the chairman of the Emerald Society. Not the same Joe Gallagher who acted as the unofficial master of ceremonies at department promotion and retirement rackets. Not Lt. Joseph P. Gallagher, NYPD. Not *that* Joe Gallagher. That one was immortal; everyone in the Job knew that.

He brushed past her and rushed into the store, recoiling from the carnage. Shards of bone and gray globs of brain were splattered about. An eye was attached to a bloody optic nerve. Chunks of body parts plastered the walls and the tin ceiling. A severed arm lay in a pile of whipped cream. Fragments of cake and raspberry filling had settled into the gore.

Yetta Zimmerman's body was sprawled over the top of the soda fountain, her arms stretched unnaturally over her head. In the rear of the store, detectives had corralled the three boys who had been playing the video games. The detectives were trying to calm them down and get statements.

Scanlon bent down next to the corpse on the floor. The face was gone. The body was the same size as Joe Gallagher; it had the same strong frame. He looked around the scene. Higgins came over to him and bent and began to search the body. Scanlon looked at her and said, "Whaddawe got?"—automatically lapsing into the dialect of the Job.

She looked up from her grisly task. "Two DOA by shotgun." She passed him the leather shield case she had just removed from the body. He snapped it open. Stared at the photograph on the laminated identification card. That familiar face. That familiar grin. The man standing before the red backdrop wore a blue uniform shirt and a black tie. His commanding presence could be felt even in the photograph. Scanlon visualized him walking into the monthly LBA meeting. Tall, proud, his brother lieutenants rushing to shake his hand.

Lt. Joseph P. Gallagher, NYPD . . . Postman, Return Postage Guaranteed.

Higgins raised the dead man's shirt to reveal a .38 Colt Cobra secured in an in-trouser holster. "He never had a chance to get it out," she said.

"What do we have on the woman?" Scanlon asked Higgins, looking over at the corpse.

"Yetta Zimmerman, age sixty-three, according to neighbors. Been operating this store for about twenty-five years."

"Physical evidence?"

"Three shell casings were found near the entrance. We also found a shopping bag that we think was used to conceal the shotgun," Higgins said.

Scanlon looked to the store's entrance and saw the evidence technician putting a shopping bag into a plastic evidence sheath. Standing a few feet away from the technician was a familiar face from the Ballistics Squad, Frank Abruzzi.

Scanlon went over to the ballistics detective, who was wearing plastic gloves and examining the base of a shotgun shell through a magnifying glass.

"Hello, Frank, whaddaya got for me?" Scanlon said.

Abruzzi looked up from the glass. "Howya doin', Lou? Long time no see. For starters, your perp used an automatic shotgun and sixteen-gauge shells." He held the glass over the base of the shell. "Take a look."

Scanlon bent and looked through the round glass.

"That mark that you see at three o'clock is from the firing pin. And the one at one o'clock is from the ejector. The mark at twelve o'clock is from the extractor."

"Which all means?" Scanlon said, looking up from the glass.

"I can't be positive," Abruzzi said, "but there is a good shot that your perp used a Browning automatic, Sweet Sixteen model. The Sweet Sixteen makes an unusual configuration like that. In most shotguns the firing-pin mark is closer to the center, and the extractor and the ejector marks are more dispersed."

"Could it have been concealed in a shopping bag?"

"Yes. The Sweet Sixteen breaks down. You turn a screw and

push the barrel down. It takes seconds to break the weapon down."

Yetta Zimmerman's housecoat was shredded; her right breast was gone, in its place a scarlet patchwork of puffy black holes. "What notifications have been made?" Scanlon asked Higgins, who was standing a few feet away.

"Command and Control and the borough have both been notified," she said, moving up to him and handing him the wallet she had just finished tugging from Gallagher's back pocket. "Temporary headquarters has been established across the street, in the rectory."

Scanlon rummaged through the compartments in the wallet. The driver's license and the car registration were tucked in behind a wedding picture. Scanlon moved to the door and stood in the entrance. The crowd had grown. Reporters shouted questions at him from behind the rope barrier. Ignoring their racket, he carefully examined the streets for Gallagher's car. A homicide victim's car was important physical evidence. People keep things in their cars, important things, telling things. He spied a car fitting the description on Gallagher's registration parked on Pope John Paul II Square.

Stepping into the street, Scanlon took a sergeant by the arm and led him aside. He described the car and its location. "If the plate checks out, call department tow and have it brought into the house. Store it in the garage and have it safeguarded for prints," Scanlon told the sergeant.

Lew Brodie was a tough-minded detective with a poorly repaired harelip, broad shoulders, hooded eyes, and a drinking problem. He had been flopped out of the Manhattan North Homicide Task Force eighteen months ago because of what the department perceived to be his persistent and unnecessary use of force on minority citizens. Lew Brodie had been classified as Violent Prone. The department shrink had recommended a less demanding assignment. There were no blacks living in Greenpoint. And Lew Brodie had quite a different idea on the whole subject: he was a good cop who was conducting his own urban renewal program.

Brodie came up to Scanlon, looking down at his steno pad. "According to the three kids, Gallagher walked in and Zimmerman rushed out from behind the counter to greet him. Shortly thereafter the perp appeared in the doorway and shouted, 'Hey you,' and then proceeds to produce a shotgun from inside the shopping bag and starts blasting. The kids take a dive onto the floor. Job done, perp flees. We came up with two housewives who were on their merry way to the A&P and were passing the candy store as the perp ran from the store to a waiting blue van. License number eight eight Henry Victor Robert."

"Description of shooter," Scanlon demanded.

Brodie read: "Male. White, between five-five and five-nine. Wearing old black pants with paint stains on both legs, a white pullover under an army fatigue jacket. He had long gray hair, a wrinkled face, and a scruffy beard." He checked his notes. "That's it, so far."

"Age?" Scanlon asked.

Brodie shrugged. "There we got a problem. None of the witnesses can agree on this guy's age. The three boys say he was old, maybe in his sixties. One of the women says in his forties, and the other late thirties."

Detective Hector Colon came up to Scanlon and Brodie, who were standing over Gallagher's body, and without prelude read from his steno pad. "Lieutenant Gallagher had twenty-two years in the Job. Married with two kids. Lived in Greenpoint, 32 Anthony Street. He was assigned to the Seventeenth Narcotics District. He ran one of the buy-and-bust operations and worked out of the One-fourteen. He worked a ten hundred to eighteen hundred yesterday and swung out. His next scheduled tour was Saturday, an eighteen hundred to oh two hundred." Colon lowered his pad. "The PC and the borough commander have been both notified. The CO Labor Policy and the Catholic chaplain are on their way to notify Gallagher's wife."

Scanlon sighed. "And the Zimmerman family?"

"She was widowed with two grown kids," Colon said. "The son, a doctor, lives on East Seventy-ninth Street in the big city. The Nineteenth is going to make the notification."

Scanlon asked Brodie if they had come up with anything on the van.

"The driver was a male, white," Brodie said. "We ran the plate through NCIC and it came back not stolen. Then we checked for the registered owner and discovered that the owner ain't on file. We figure that it's probably a new registration. It takes Motor Vehicles about ninety days to get the new ones into the system.

Biafra Baby is across the street in temporary headquarters calling Motor Vehicles in Albany on the department tieline. They should be able to tell us something."

Scanlon took out a De Nobili and lit it, carefully inserting the dead match between the back cover and the bottom file of matches and putting the matchbook back into his pocket. He shifted the cigar to the other side of his mouth. "Anything on the murder weapon?"

"Among the missing," Higgins said, working the wedding band off Yetta Zimmerman's lifeless finger.

Sucking on the cigar, Scanlon surveyed the crime scene. First impressions were important; some overlooked point could later prove vital. Too many bad guys walked because some detective failed to do what he was trained to do during the preliminary investigation. He recalled the DOA that had been discovered last month on Crown Street in the Seven-one. The radio car team first on the scene reported back that the DOA appeared natural. The detective who responded to the scene found nothing suspicious. The ME in his not unusually casual fashion endorsed natural causes. The undertaker had the gall to report that he had discovered a tiny hole behind the left ear that later proved to have been made by a .22 short. There were a lot of red faces and a lot of excuses in Brooklyn North over that one. It pissed Scanlon off when a case went bye-bye because of police ineptitude. So he moved all around the crime scene, satisfying himself that what was supposed to be done was done.

He examined the glass fractures that the stray shotgun pellets had made in the doors of the display cabinet. The radial and concentric fractures formed cobwebs with holes the shape of volcano craters. Looking inside the opened door he noticed numerous flakes of glass in the guiding tracks. Some of the shot had embedded itself in the wall of the cabinet. He motioned to one of the forensics technicians. Moving out from behind the soda fountain, Scanlon went up to Hector Colon and told him that he was going across the street to the rectory.

According to the *Patrol Guide,* a temporary headquarters will be used to coordinate police resources at the scene of an emergency when the circumstances of the occurrence indicate that the police operation will continue for a period of time and when direct telephone communications and record keeping will improve efficiency. The green police standard and lantern were on station outside the rectory to indicate to members of the force that temporary headquarters was located inside that building. Scanlon took the rectory steps two at a time.

The NYPD had commandeered the waiting room to the left of the large foyer. The walls were done in mahogany paneling, and there was a heavy oak desk with ornate scrollwork edging its borders. A large crucifix hung on the wall behind the desk, and long lace curtains covered all the windows. Two elderly priests were sitting on a carved wooden bench watching with muted amazement as their serene residence was converted into a message center for a murder investigation. A sergeant with dirty-blond hair sat behind the desk manning the Headquarters Log, entering a chronological record of personnel and equipment at the scene, listing specific assignments.

Linemen from the Communications Division were busy installing additional lines, the numbers of which had already been telephoned to Command and Control, Patrol Borough Brooklyn North, and the Nine-three Desk.

Scanlon signed himself present in the Log. He went over the list of assignments with the sergeant. From the corner of his eye, he spotted Detective Simon Jones elbowing his way through the crowd. Scanlon shouted to Jones, "What's with the van?"

Simon Jones had a long thin frame and a tiny potbelly, and a head of untamed kinky hair that looked like a beehive undergoing constant electric-shock treatment. His long bony arms appeared to reach down to his knees. His skin was coal-black and he had a voice laced with a heavy Mississippi drawl. Ten years ago a detective in the Fifth Squad had commented that Jones looked like one of the starving Biafra babies. The nickname stuck.

Jones came over to Scanlon. "Just got off the phone with the owner of the van," he said, patting down his hair. "The man done told me that he bought the van one month ago off a lot off Ocean Parkway in Brooklyn. He parked it last night three blocks from his home and when he went to get it this afternoon, the mother was gone. He was on his way to his local precinct to report it when I telephoned. The owner's name is Frank Lucas. He resides at 6890 South View Lane in Bath Beach."

Scanlon cursed under his breath; he had been hoping that the van had been stolen from someplace in Greenpoint. He had markers out in Greenpoint. He turned to the sergeant manning the Log and told him to telephone the precinct concerned in Bath Beach and have detectives dispatched to do an immediate canvass of the area where the van had been stolen. He picked up the receiver of one of the recently installed telephones and dialed the One-fourteen. He spoke briefly to the desk officer. He signed out in the Log, and he and Biafra Baby returned to the crime scene.

Higgins met them just inside the entrance. "Their property," she said, holding the victims' personal property in two separate evidence bags.

Scanlon turned to Biafra Baby. "I want you to transport the witnesses into the house. Make sure they're kept separated. I don't want them talking to one another about what they saw, changing their minds."

Biafra Baby nodded and made his way to the rear of the candy store. A short time later he reappeared leading three frightened boys. They came in single file, the witnesses looking away from the bodies, their feet attempting to avoid stepping on pieces of the two bodies.

Lew Brodie brought up the rear of the staggered column. Scanlon called to Brodie. "The witnesses agree—the perp yelled 'Hey you' and fired?"

"That's how it went down," Brodie said over his shoulder.

Parallel shafts of sunlight speared through the candy store's open facade, reflecting on the dead woman's matted hair and diffusing a shimmering hue of yellow through the pools of blood.

Higgins looked down at Gallagher's body. "Then it wasn't a robbery."

Scanlon's voice took on an edge. "It was a hit, Maggie. But on which one?"

3

Tony Scanlon stood back and watched the sergeant slip the steel jaws around the shackle of the black-faced combination lock. The sergeant's intense face was a sunburst of broken blood vessels. A cigarette that was one quarter gray ash dangled between his thin lips. Gripping the handles, he pressed the arms of the bolt cutter together and the lock fell apart.

Scanlon had wanted to be present when Gallagher's locker was broken into. A cop's locker was a secret place; it was a place to hide things. He had told Higgins where he was going and why, and then had left the crime scene. He knew that he wouldn't be missed for a while, not with all the commotion connected with a cop killing.

The drive from Greenpoint to the One-fourteen in Astoria, Queens, had taken Scanlon twenty minutes. The precinct was located on Astoria Boulevard, directly across from the sunken highway that leads onto the Triboro Bridge.

Many of the city's seventy-two patrol precincts provide space for "overhead" units, units whose responsibilities encompass entire borough commands, unlike patrol precincts that must operate within

19

set boundaries. Queens Internal Affairs, Public Morals, and Narcotics were quartered in the One-fourteen.

When Scanlon arrived he had found the flag at half-staff and policemen standing on ladders hand-draping the mourning purple over the entrance. A group of grim cops stood bunched on the steps, talking in angry tones. Walking into the station house, Scanlon had overheard snatches of their conversation. It had been a robbery attempt, one said. Joe Gallagher had taken police action, another maintained. Cocksuckers, groused a third.

The foul smell of old sweat permeated the cramped space of the locker. Uniforms were pinched together; a gunbelt hung from a rear hook; several nightsticks were clumped together. The blouses and jackets had gold bars on the shoulders. The sergeant complained that the overhead units should have their own locker rooms instead of being grouped in with the precinct's. This was the fourth locker that he had had to break into during his twenty-two years on the Job. The sergeant pushed uniforms aside, looking around, searching.

Scanlon focused his attention inside the locker. If there was anything there to be found he wanted to find it before word leaked out that Lt. Joe Gallagher might not have died a hero. Things have a mysterious way of disappearing whenever a cop is jammed up. It had happened recently in the Three-six. IAD was set to arrest the sergeant in charge of the precinct's gambling car. The complaint alleged that the sergeant had a pad going with the numbers men along Lenox Avenue. Word was leaked to the Three-six's PBA delegate by a cop who used to work in the Three-six. The precinct's Residence Known Gamblers File, and the Arrest Record, and three years' worth of roll calls vanished. Overnight. IAD called it a concerted conspiracy to obstruct justice. The cops in the Three-six called it an obvious act of God.

The sergeant began his disagreeable task. As each article of uniform was taken out it was searched to ensure that there was nothing in the pockets that might prove embarrassing to the family. SOP. Scanlon watched everything the other cop did. A rosary was draped over the locker's face mirror, and stuck into the frame were the photographs of three smiling women. Scanlon pushed the sergeant aside, removed the pictures, and put them into his pocket. The sergeant saw him do this but said nothing.

Gallagher's helmet was on the floor inside its carrying case. Scanlon bent and felt with his hand around the inside of the case. It turned out to be the repository for several flashlights and packets of used memo books that were bound together by rubber bands.

On the top shelf there were winter and summer uniform hats stacked one inside the other, two boxes of ammunition, a slapper, three blackjacks, and an assortment of knives, razors, and ice picks. A Chuka stick was lying next to Gallagher's shaving things.

The sergeant thrust his hand into the inside pocket of Gallagher's cloak raincoat. "Look at what we got here," he said, removing a Turkish Kirikkals 7.55 pistol.

"Is it on his Ten Card?" Scanlon asked, knowing that it wouldn't be. The sergeant picked up Gallagher's UF 10, Force Record Card, from the bench that ran along the aisle between the row of lockers. He turned the department pedigree form over, to the section at the bottom that listed the description and serial numbers of all the weapons that Lt. Joseph P. Gallagher, NYPD, was authorized to possess. The sergeant glanced over the card. "It's a throwaway," he said, tucking the unauthorized pistol into his waistband.

They were beginning to find things.

While the sergeant was busy searching the pockets of a winter blouse, Scanlon reached up into the locker and pushed the hats aside. A shoe box lay on top of a multi-use envelope. He took them both out and stepped away from the locker, sitting astride the narrow wooden bench. He lifted the lid of the shoe box. His eyebrows arched with surprise when he saw the double-headed dildo lying on a stack of amateurish pornographic pictures. He shuffled the contents about, searching. One of the photographs showed a woman on a bed laughing as she inserted a dildo into her body. In another, a woman's hand was guiding a penis into her vagina. He replaced the lid on the shoe box. Picking up the multi-use envelope, he unwound the red string on the flap.

"Whaddya find?" asked the sergeant, searching a summer blouse, not bothering to look.

"Just some papers," Scanlon said, studying the rent receipts and utility bills for an apartment in Jackson Heights. He reached behind and picked up the Ten Card. Gallagher's official residence was 32 Anthony Street, in Greenpoint.

The NYPD's Catholic Man of the Year for 1978 was fast becoming an interesting person.

A short time later Scanlon helped carry the uniforms and equipment downstairs to the Desk, where a blotter entry would be made of the forced entry into a member of the force's locker and the property that had been removed would be invoiced.

The uniforms were folded into a neat pile on a desk in the clerical office to await a member of the immediate family, whose unpleasant duty it would be to select Gallagher's burying clothes. It was then customary for the family member to donate the remaining uniforms to the precinct, where they would be stored in the "saver" locker. Whenever a cop needed to replace a torn or worn article of uniform he would go to the locker and search for a "saver" his size. Uniforms were expensive.

No record was made of the throwaway that had been found in Gallagher's raincoat. That too would be "saved," awaiting the proper police emergency.

Watching the desk officer make the entries in the blotter, Scanlon lit up a De Nobili, picked up the desk phone, and dialed temporary headquarters.

Higgins answered.

"How's it going?" he asked, passing the cigar under his nose.

"This place is a madhouse. The PC and his entourage have arrived."

"Are the witnesses in the house?"

"Yes. Brodie just called. They're being interviewed and are pretty much sticking to their stories."

"Anything back on the van?"

"Jacob from the Six-two Squad called. They did a canvass and came up dry. I transmitted a fifteen-state alarm."

Scanlon turned his back to the desk officer and said in a low voice, "Anybody looking for me?"

"Naw. All the brass are running around preening for the television cameras and trying to think up a synonym for 'perpetrator.' We have things organized and the worker ants are all out knocking on doors."

"Maggie," he whispered, "get to the PC and tell him not to go out on a limb on this one. There's a *problem*."

"What did you find?"

"We'll talk when I get back."

Eight minutes later Tony Scanlon left the station house and made his way along the side of the gray stone building to the walled-in motor pool. He wound his way around parked department vehicles to his own, which was near the gas pumps. He slid in on the driver's side, tossing the shoe box and the multi-use envelope onto the seat. He started the car. Remembering the photographs that he had taken from the rim of the face mirror in Gallagher's locker, he glanced down at the shoe box. He flipped off the lid and removed several of the pornographic pictures, spreading them out over the seat, separating them by actresses. He slid the pictures from the face mirror out of his pocket and began to compare faces. They matched.

"Lt. Joe Gallagher exemplified all that was good and decent within the police department. He was a hero who died as he lived, serving the people of this great city." Roberto Gomez's voice cracked. He turned away from the microphones, covering his face with his hands, slowly counting to twenty. A hush fell over the reporters as they waited for the police commissioner to regain his composure, to continue his impromptu news conference.

Bob Gomez was the first member of a minority group to become PC. He was himself a hero to the city's Hispanic community. To them it did not matter how the press and the public at large anglicized Gomez's name. He was their Roberto, their Bobby.

Gomez had started out in the police department as a real street cop, walking a beat in the Eight-one. He had worked steady six to two on a gambling post so that he might attend Brooklyn College during the day and later St. John's Law School. He was the first member of the Hispanic community to be promoted to the rank of captain. He had retired from the police department several years ago to head the city's Department of Social Services. When the present mayor had been accused three years ago by the city's black community of insensitivity to the needs of minorities, the mayor squelched the rising controversy with the appointment of Bob Gomez as PC. The blacks weren't happy about getting a Hispanic consolation prize, but they shut up. A master political stroke, the appointment was called in the press. The mayor was delighted. But there were many of the mayor's advisers who had counseled him against the Gomez appointment. It was an open secret within the city administration and particularly within the police department that Bob Gomez had developed several bad habits over the years. Habits that could hurt an ambitious mayor.

Bob Gomez dropped his hands and sighed deeply. He faced the reporters, ready to continue his performance. He immediately lapsed into his favorite homily on the need for more police, on the need for a judicial system that did not mollycoddle criminals, on the right of every citizen to be secure in his person and property, on the need for the abolition of concurrent sentencing.

With his arms stretched out at his side, Bob Gomez once again proclaimed that Lt. Joe Gallagher had died a hero.

When Scanlon arrived back at the crime scene he saw the PC answering reporters' questions. Gathered around the commissioner was the top echelon of the Job, grim men all in their late fifties. Conspicuously absent from the group was Chief of Detectives Alfred Goldberg. Scanlon spotted the CofD standing about twenty feet away from the PC surrounded by a loyal coterie of subordinates from within the Detective Division. Goldberg was glaring at the PC. It was no secret inside the Job that the two men hated each other. Goldberg had expected to be named PC, and when the job went to Gomez, Goldberg flew into one of his famous temper tantrums and proceeded to wreck his tenth-floor office, sending subordinates fleeing from his wrath.

Gomez had inherited Goldberg and would have replaced him with his own man if he could have. But he couldn't. The CofD was the darling of the Jewish real estate interests, the garment district, and the city's shadowy diamond industry. Neither the mayor nor the PC had the political clout to dump Goldberg. The CofD was entrenched and he damn well knew it.

As Scanlon paused on the rectory steps to take in the gathering of police brass, he noticed detectives scurrying through the crowd of onlookers canvassing for witnesses. What a way to run a job, he thought, entering the temporary headquarters. Scanlon moved directly up to the Log. A fifteen-block area around the crime scene had been divided into quadrants. A sergeant and ten detectives had been assigned to each quadrant. The occupants of every house and of every business would be questioned. People on the street would be stopped and questioned. Mailmen and bus drivers would be questioned. Emergency service units had been dispatched to search sewers and refuse cans for discarded physical evidence. Every assignment was listed in the Log; every assignment required a detailed report on a Five—a DD 5 Supplementary Complaint Report.

Scanlon found Higgins leaning over the rectory's ornate desk collating Fives and stuffing them into the Gallagher/Zimmerman case folder. "I just saw the PC making with a press conference," he said, coming up to her. "Didn't you give him the word?"

She looked up at him. "I most certainly did. But in his infinite wisdom Bobby Boy chose to ignore your advice. So up his." She went back to her task.

"Did you tell him yourself?"

"Detectives do not personally tell the PC anything. I relayed your message through the first deputy commissioner and he passed it on to Bobby."

Scanlon looked around at the crowd of policemen gathered inside the temporary headquarters. He turned back and asked her what she was doing. "I'm fastening Fives inside the homicide folder so that they coincide with each quadrant."

"Leave that for now," he said. "I want you to bang out the Unusual."

Howard Christopher was a tall, lean man who was always impeccably dressed in the latest Sears, Roebuck fashions for men. He had a pasty white face with an overlarge forehead. He was a gentle man with a warm smile and an addiction to soap operas and health food. As a major in the National Guard and a staunch believer in military courtesy, Christopher would never have thought of debasing the rank of lieutenant with the diminutive. He came up to Scanlon with his steno pad held out in front of him and began his report. "Lieutenant, it looks as though we're beginning to develop an outline of how this caper went down." Christopher went on to report that the killer's movements prior to the murders had been backtracked. There was a butcher in the Danzig meat market on Driggs Avenue who stated that he had seen a man who answered to the killer's description walk past the store a few minutes before the time of occurrence. And there was this A&P stock clerk on a coffee break. He had been leaning against one of the loading bays having a smoke when he noticed an old man with a shriveled face walk out of McGoldrick Park clutching a shopping bag. And there was a mother who had been sitting on a bench in the park playing with her baby. A creepy old man with an unfriendly glare had sat down on the next bench, she had told detectives.

Christopher reached into the pocket of his brass-buttoned light brown sport jacket and removed a glassine evidence bag containing peanut shells. He dangled it before Scanlon. "Lieutenant, I'm sending these to the lab. You never know, we just might get lucky."

Deputy Chief MacAdoo McKenzie, the CO of Brooklyn North Detectives, was an oversize fireplug of a man, a nervous type who wore ill-fitting clothes that never matched. Every time Scanlon saw him he was reminded of a bin full of used parts.

McKenzie pushed his way through the crowd inside temporary headquarters and came up to Scanlon. In his customary caustic tone, he said, "Whaddaya got on this one, Scanlon?"

Scanlon led the chief away from the others and calmly confided the results of the preliminary investigation. "A hit!" growled MacAdoo McKenzie. He began to sweat. He yanked a dirty, snot-encrusted handkerchief from his pocket and wiped his hands. "Joe Gallagher murdered? I can't believe that. Not him. It just don't seem possible. I can't believe that he's gone."

"That's the trouble with death, Chief. Everybody wants to go to heaven but nobody wants to die."

McKenzie gave him a dirty look. "Gallagher must have been into something he shouldn't've been into. Nobody ups and whacks a police lieutenant for nothing. Maybe Joe went into the junk business for himself?" He wiped the back of his neck. "If the press gets hold of this they'll have a field day with it."

"It doesn't always have to be the cop who's the bad one, Chief. Zimmerman might have been the mark."

McKenzie's face flushed. "That's bullshit and you know it. It's always the fucking cops, sergeants, and lieutenants who are forever getting jammed up. I'll tell you this much—this Job can't afford too many more scandals. Six cops and a sergeant were just arrested in the Tenth for riding shotgun for coke dealers. And another five in the One-ten went down the tubes for wheelin' and dealin' with Colombian juice joints. If we're not careful, we're going to get ourselves another Knapp Commission. And this time when the politicians are through with us we'll find ourselves with total civilian control over the Job." McKenzie looked uncomfortable. He was shuffling his weight from one foot to the other.

"Chief, I'm a team player. You know that. But you tell me how we're gonna play it didn't happen."

"Dunno. But I do know that you're going to sit on this one until we do know what happened inside that candy store. And as far as the rest of the world is concerned Joe Gallagher died a hero interrupting a holdup."

Watching MacAdoo McKenzie lumber away, Scanlon thought, How quick they are to always brand the cop the bad guy. Typical Palace Guard mentality. It's always the guys below them that screw up.

Scanlon moved around temporary headquarters making sure that everything was being done correctly. He noticed Howard Christopher pondering the bag of peanut shells and went up to him and asked him if there was a problem. Christopher looked at him with questioning eyes and said that he wasn't sure if a Letter of Transmittal was needed with the Request for Laboratory Analysis. Scanlon told him that it was and went on to remind him that the Letter of Transmittal preserved the chain of evidence. He patted Christopher on the shoulder and moved off. Higgins was busy folding copies of the Unusual into white department envelopes. Scanlon went up to her and read a copy of it. When he finished reading the report he folded it in the prescribed manner, in three equal folds parallel with the writing with the top fold folded toward the back of the letter, so that the entire heading could be seen without unfolding the communication, and handed it to her.

After she had addressed the last of the envelopes he told her to grab her pocketbook. They were going to take a little trip over to Jackson Heights. A cop's splash pad was a most secret place, and Scanlon was sure that he would find things there.

Scanlon pocketed the keys that Higgins had removed from Gallagher's body and pulled the door closed behind them. They were in a dark, musty place, apartment 3C. A narrow hall connected the front room and a kitchen. Higgins turned on her small pocket flashlight, found the wall switch, and flipped it on. A cheap redwood veneer covered the walls; five spotlights shone down from recessed fixtures. As they stepped into the apartment they saw a bathroom directly in front of them. Higgins went into it and switched on the three-bulb fixture over the sink. Cockroaches scattered into cracks.

Scanlon moved into the front room, went over to the gold-and-white drapes, and reached behind them. Finding the cord, he pulled. Late-afternoon sunlight came through the filthy windows. He looked around the room. Cobwebs were on the ceiling around the steam pipe. Carpet remnants covered the floor in a quilt of colors. A tweed convertible sofa was up against the far wall, and next to it was a three-legged serving table on which sat a telephone and an address book. He went over and picked up the address book and began to flip alphabetized tabs. The name Harris was listed under H. It had a 516 telephone number that had been crossed out and replaced by a 718 number. In parentheses next to it was "Luise" and a 212 number. The book also contained police department numbers, direct unlisted numbers. He found the telephone numbers of police benevolent organizations and police fraternal organizations. When he had gone through the entire book he discovered four additional names: Donna, Valerie, Mary, and Rena. The remainder of the numbers were all connected in some way to the Job.

The address book in a cop's splash pad would only contain a few numbers that were all connected to his secret life. And police department numbers; the Job was the bridge that connected both lives. The people in Joe Gallagher's other life would all have to be interviewed. He heard a noise and turned. Higgins was framed in the doorway. "What a dump."

"I'm sure that it served its purpose," he said, placing the address book on the sofa. "Find anything in the bathroom?"

"A few rusting blades and a rolled-up tube of toothpaste. No woman ever called this place home."

"What made you reach that conclusion?"

"Because a woman would keep certain things in any apartment that she was using as a rendezvous—cleansing lotions, a hair dryer, napkins, extra panties."

He rose effortlessly from the sofa and caught her watching him with the same astonished look that he had seen on so many other faces, a look that said: He moves and acts as though both his legs were real.

A pair of sliding doors enclosed the closet built into the wall directly to the right of the tweed convertible. He slid the right side open. A few articles of men's clothing hung from wire hangers. There was a movie screen leaning up against the wall, and on the floor next to it was an 8mm projector. The closet contained three shelves on brackets. The first one acted as the bar, and the second contained a stereo tape deck, record player, and AM/FM receiver. The top shelf was crammed with movie tins. He took out a handful and read titles aloud: *"Annie Can You Come? Big Cock Harry. Andy Hardy and the Nuns. Come Again Sweet Lips."*

"Do you think the precinct CO might like to show a few of them at the next Community Council meeting?" she asked.

He burst out laughing. "Some of those biddies would drop their store-bought teeth." As he said this, his gaze fell to the bottom of the closet, to the department storage carton. He dragged it out and over to the sofa, where he sat and flipped off the cover. He spilled the contents onto the floor. Nipple creams and prolong creams, and joy jellies, and emotion lotions, and edible panties in many different flavors, piled up in a bizarre heap. He sat rummaging in the pile. Ben Wah balls, anal love beads, dildos, vibrators.

He glanced over at Higgins. She clasped her hands to her chest and with fluttering lids said, "What is this world coming to?"

He picked up one of the vibrators and read aloud: "'A clitoral vibrator. This unique machine may be worn during intercourse. It is excellent for masturbation and for facilitating orgasm during intercourse. Luv-Joy Manufacturing Company, Brooklyn, New York.'" He dropped it back into the pile and picked up a set of Ben Wah balls. Turning them over in his hands, he glanced up at Higgins, a silly expression curling the ends of his lips, showing his teeth.

"Don't look at me," she protested. "I don't use them."

Before entering the apartment, they had canvassed the tenants in the four-story walk-up and found that none of them knew the occupant in 3C. A retired postal worker in apartment 1A had stated that he used to see the man in 3C entering and leaving from time to time in the company of different women. "It looked mighty suspicious to me," the toothless old man had confided.

During the drive into Manhattan, Scanlon noticed Higgins looking at her watch and saw the concern seeping into her face. "You pressed for time?" he asked.

"Gloria and I moved in together. She's making our first home-made dinner tonight." Gloria Lufnitz was a twenty-nine-year-old music teacher at Music and Art High School and Detective Maggie Higgins's lover.

"What made you decide to move in with her? I thought you were happy the way things were."

"She wanted to. I was perfectly content. We'd spend weekends together and a few nights a week and everything was great. But Gloria wanted to play house, so I went along."

"Good luck."

She smiled her thanks.

Higgins parked the department auto at the bus stop on Worth Street and went to telephone Gloria to tell her that she was going to be late. At five-thirty Scanlon hurried into the huge, empty lobby of the telephone building.

Two massive steel doors confronted him when he stepped off the elevator on the thirty-seventh floor. One of the four armed security guards stationed there asked to see his police credentials. After he handed them to the guard, and the credentials were scrutinized, he was permitted to sign in the Visitors Log. Then he was required to stand before a Polaroid camera that was mounted on a desk and have his picture taken. This done, a button was pressed and the steel doors opened, and he was permitted to enter Ma Bell's secret security service headquarters.

When Scanlon emerged from the building thirty minutes later he was in possession of the names and addresses of the subscribers whose telephone numbers had appeared in Joe Gallagher's most private address book. Sliding into the passenger seat, he said, "Did you make your call?"

Higgins drove out of the bus stop. "She was pissed off. Said that she cooked a roast and that it'll be dried out by the time I get home."

"Your girlfriend is going to have to get used to your being on the Job."

She smiled bitterly. "That's easy for you to say." She glanced at the list of names he was holding. "Are we going to pay the ladies a visit?"

"We'll let them stew awhile."

* * *

30

They lugged the carton of sexual paraphernalia and the address book into Scanlon's office and put it on top of one of the file cabinets.

Christopher walked into the Whip's office nibbling sunflower seeds. He brought Scanlon up to date on what was happening at temporary headquarters. He began his report with "Lieutenant" and went on to say that forensics technicians were still at the crime scene conducting tests, and that some of the detectives who had been "flown in" from other commands to assist with the preliminary investigation had been sent back to their own commands. Some of the buildings around the scene were still being canvassed.

Lew Brodie came into the office and handed Scanlon a long sheet of four-ply paper. "Thought you might wanna take a look at the Incident Log," Brodie said.

Scanlon took the paper from him and detected the faint odor of alcohol. He gave Brodie an annoyed look and then scanned the computerized printout of all the radio transmissions connected with the double homicide. He let his eyes sweep over the neatly arranged columns of computer symbols and abridgments. After one fast read-through, he went back to the beginning and started over, this time taking his time translating the symbols.

The initial call had been received at 911 by operator 42 at 1404 hours. The anonymous caller had reported that a police lieutenant had been shot at 311 Driggs Avenue. Operator 42 had typed the address into her queue and a display peeled onto the lime-green screen that had shown 311 Driggs Avenue to be within the confines of the Nine-three Precinct, sector Boy. RMP 1704 was assigned to that sector this tour, and the display showed that that radio motor patrol car was currently not on assignment. Operator 42 transmitted code signal 10-13, Assist Patrolman, Officer Shot.

Scanlon read the verbatim transmissions of the responding radio cars: "Boy, on the way. Sergeant going. George going. Frank going. Crime, responding from the other end."

Whoever had made that call to 911 had *known* that Gallagher was a police lieutenant. How? Gallagher had not been in uniform. Scanlon looked up at Christopher. "Where are the witnesses?"

"The women are upstairs in the Community Relations office with the department artist," Christopher said.

"Who interviewed the first team on the scene?" Scanlon asked.

"Colon," Brodie said.

"Where is that team now?"

"They're waiting downstairs in the sitting room," Brodie replied.

"I'm going upstairs," Scanlon said to Brodie. "When I come back I want to see those cops waiting for me."

"You got it, Lou," Brodie said.

The walls of the third-floor Community Relations office were covered with posters that were designed to address public fears: Be a Block Watcher; Vertical Patrol, the Answer to Residential Burglaries; The Auxiliary Police—Our Eyes and Ears.

A PR hand job, Scanlon thought, glancing at the posters as he plunged into the office. The department artist was a bald middle-aged detective who wore thick horn-rimmed glasses. The artist glanced up from his drawing board and nodded recognition to Scanlon. They had worked together on the Rothstein homicide, six years ago. Cops remember their unsolved cases. Two women sat on either side of the artist. The one on the right was Mary Cilicia, a woman of thirty-six or so who had a round plump face. She wore what appeared at first glance to be a bathing cap covered with blue plumes. Many women in Greenpoint wear such hats. She wore a blue polyester pantsuit with a diamond design. The other woman, Mary Adler, was twenty-eight; she had a tiny mole on the right side of her nose with two long hairs sprouting from it, and she had a potbelly and sagging breasts.

Scanlon walked up behind the artist and looked over his shoulder. "How's it going?" he asked, studying the charcoal drawing of a killer's face. A face with wrinkled skin and hair that covered the tips of ears.

"Okay, Lou," the artist said, making an erasure and blowing the residue away. "The ladies have been a big help."

Scanlon smiled at the women. They smiled back. He noticed that they both wore dentures, a not uncommon sight in his area. Poor people can't afford good dental care. "Do either of you ladies know who telephoned nine-eleven to report that a policeman had been shot?" He stared into their innocent faces.

Mary Cilicia didn't know who had made the call; the first they knew that a cop had been killed was when they were being driven to the station house. One of the detectives had told them.

There were two policemen waiting when Scanlon swept back into his office fifteen minutes later. He went up to his desk and wrote himself a note on the department-issued tear-off calendar: "Get tapes and do round robin on G." He turned his attention to the two policemen who were lounging on green department swivel chairs. Lew Brodie was leaning with his back against the wall, his left foot braced on it and his left arm draped over the top of a filing cabinet. Brodie introduced the cops to Scanlon. Stone and Trumwell.

Scanlon nodded at the cops and said, "Where were you two when the initial thirteen came over?"

Trumwell had a badly pockmarked face and red hair. "Apollo and Bridgewater streets," he said, stretching his legs out in front and examining the tips of his scuffed shoes.

"When you arrived at the scene, what did you see?" Scanlon asked, lowering himself onto the edge of his desk, wondering what Trumwell found so interesting about his shoes.

Stone had a bulbous nose and a receding hairline. It was he who answered the question. "A large crowd had developed. We got out of the RMP and pushed our way into the store. We found a woman sprawled over the soda fountain and Gallagher on the floor. There were three kids screaming in the rear of the store."

Trumwell continued, "I frisked the man and came up with a gun and shield. I got on my portable and told Central to have the Squad and the duty captain respond forthwith."

"Didn't you make an attempt to rush them to the hospital?"

"Lou?" Stone protested, spreading his arms. "There wasn't any doubt. They were both DOA. The ambulance arrived shortly after us. The attendant took one look and pronounced them both."

"Boy your regular sector?"

"Yeah," Trumwell said, still engrossed with his shoes.

"Did you both know Gallagher?"

"We knew 'im," Stone answered. "We used to see him hanging around Yetta's. He'd park his car in the restricted zone in front of the funeral home and put a PBA card, an LBA card, or his vehicle ID plate on the dashboard. One day we decided to check him out to make sure he wasn't some cop's relative using a hand-me-down card. He tinned us and then we both recognized him. We'd both seen him MC a couple of retirement rackets."

Staring past the two cops, Scanlon asked casually, "Yetta take any action in that candy store?"

The two cops exchanged nervous looks. Scanlon understood why. The NYPD had a strict policy of covert omission in its war on crime. The enforcement of narcotics and gambling laws was forbidden to the cop on post or in the sector car. The smoldering embers of Knapp and Serpico had made the Palace Guard paranoid about the corrupting influences of these crimes on the patrol force. The result was a proliferation of narcotics bazaars, juice joints, and gambling dens about which the cop on post could do nothing but submit a report which did nothing. Corruption Prone Locations were off-limits to the patrol force. But! Every cop in the Job knew that if any serious problem ever developed concerning one of these locations, it would be the cop on post or in the sector car who would have to take the weight. The Palace Guard would deny any policy of nonenforcement.

Trumwell sat upright in his chair and folded his arms across his chest, chin down. "I don't know anything about no gambling violations."

"Me either," Stone said.

A flicker of disgust creased Scanlon's face. "Hey, you two. A police lieutenant has been murdered. I'm on your side, remember? Anything that you say to me stays with me. You got my word."

Stone looked at his partner, shrugged shoulders, and said, "I guess he's a right guy." He looked at Scanlon and said defensively, "We ain't allowed to take gambling collars. We can't do dick about them."

"I know that," Scanlon said.

"Yetta'd book the ponies, numbers, and some sports action," Trumwell said with some reluctance.

"Who'd she lay off her action with?"

"Walter Ticornelli was her man," Stone said.

"Did you happen to notice him when you first arrived on the scene?"

Trumwell responded, "Not when we first arrived. But when I left to use the telephone on the corner to call the desk officer, I saw Walter across the street leaning against the church fence."

A cagey little smile. A remembrance. He'd had both his legs then. "I know Walter."

Inspector Herman the German Schmidt was a big man with a strong angular face and puffy discolored eyelids. He had powerful hands with wide thick nails. For the past forty-six months Herman the German had been in command of the Queens Narcotics District. He had recently been promised by the powers that be that he was next in line to be promoted to deputy chief. Everything had been going real good for him. His unit's arrests were up; the Inspection Division had recently issued an above-average evaluation of his stewardship; his youngest daughter was scheduled to graduate from Brooklyn Law School. Gallagher's death had suddenly changed all that. There was a chance now that he could end his glorious career by being demoted back to captain and losing his command. He'd end his thirty-two years as a fly captain who'd spend late tours responding to barroom brawls involving off-duty cops. Probably in Manhattan North, the dumping ground for defrocked inspectors.

Herman the German was a very worried man. The grapevine had whispered that Gallagher's death might not have been clean. And if that was the case, there would be an IAD investigation into Gallagher's background to determine why he was killed, to see if his death was in some way connected to his official life. If any hint of corruption was discovered, it would reflect on his leadership. The favorable Inspection Division evaluation would be forgotten. He had seen many fallen stars in the Job. Men who had been shunned by former friends and peers as though they had AIDS.

Herman the German had left the crime scene at about 1800 hours and driven directly to the One-fourteen. He wanted to comb through Gallagher's records for any clue to irregularities that might shed some light on why he was killed. He found none. It was a little after eight that night when he telephoned Scanlon at temporary headquarters and asked if he could meet him in Gallagher's office. He hoped that the Whip of the Nine-three Squad might be able to tell him what had really happened in that candy store.

The Seventeenth Narcotics District was quartered in a suite of six interconnecting offices on the third floor of the One-fourteen Precinct's station house. Scanlon arrived a little before nine and found Herman the German in Gallagher's office, partially hidden behind a cloud of cigar smoke. "Hello, Inspector," Scanlon said, making for the old wooden swivel chair.

Herman the German was not a man to mince his words. "I hear that you left the crime scene to personally break into Gallagher's locker."

"SOP whenever a cop is killed. You know that."

"It's not SOP for the squad commander to leave the scene of a double homicide in order to break into a goddamn locker. You could have directed a subordinate to do it."

"Joe Gallagher and I were brother lieutenants. I wanted to make sure that things were handled discreetly, that there wasn't anything mixed up with his personal property that might prove embarrassing to his family."

Herman the German frowned, leaned forward, resting his thick chin on a steeple of fingers. "If I want a hand job, Lou, I'll jerk my own prick. I don't need you to do it for me."

There was a strained silence. Scanlon was outside Herman the German's chain of command and was tempted to get up and leave. He decided to wait, to see what was on the inspector's mind. He watched Schmidt staring at him, chewing the tip of his cigar. A dark brown sediment coated the inspector's teeth. "You find anything in his locker?" His tone was low, inquisitive, and casual.

"Nothing interesting. A throwaway and some old memo books."

"A bird whispered in my ear that Gallagher was hit." He fixed Scanlon with a hard stare. "Any truth to that?"

Scanlon's stump hurt. "At this point we don't know for sure what went down inside that candy store. It might have been a holdup or it could have been a hit. But on who? Gallagher? Zimmerman? We just don't know."

"I have a personal interest in this case, Lou."

"I can understand that, Inspector."

"I don't want to end my days on the garbage heap. Joe Gallagher was one of my lieutenants, and I want his killer caught. So don't misunderstand what I'm about to say. But if he was into anything he shouldn't have been into it'll be my ass. Failure to supervise, they'll say in the big building."

Scanlon nodded his appreciation of Herman the German's position. "I had planned on stopping by to see you tomorrow to ask you some questions about Gallagher. Mind answering them now?"

Herman the German removed the cigar from his mouth, purposefully knocked the thick ash into a clean ashtray, and began tamping it with the glowing end of the cigar.

"I'll answer your questions," Herman the German said. "Most everyone in the Job knew Joe Gallagher. The *public* side of him."

"I need to know what he was really like," Scanlon said.

Herman the German thought a moment, rolling the tip of his cigar over the crushed ash. He let the cigar fall into the ashtray and heaved himself up onto his feet and started pacing restlessly. "What kind of a guy was he? He was the kind of a guy that they name streets after—one way, and dead end."

Scanlon's gaze followed him around the office. Large pin maps covered the walls. Narcotics Prone Locations were designated in green; buy locations, red; wiretap locations, white; surveillance locations, blue. A large map of the Borough of Queens had the five precincts that composed the Seventeenth Narcotics District outlined in black. Herman the German paused in front of the Queens map and let his hand move over it as though searching for a specific location. His back was to Scanlon. "What do you know about the Narcotics Division, Lou?"

"Not very much, Inspector. Most of my time in the Job has been in the Bureau."

"Each borough command is divided into narcotics districts, which are made up of a certain number of patrol precincts." His hand stopped. He turned abruptly to face Scanlon. "Each district gets buy money to run their operations. In our buy-and-bust units it's SOP for each undercover to have a backup whenever he or she makes a buy. Each district also runs operations that attempt to penetrate the top of narcotics networks. Those kinds of operations deal in kilo weight and take time, patience, and a lot of money. Joe Gallagher's assignment was to run this district's buy-and-bust unit, mainly nickel and dime bags. The men and women of this unit were his people. But they seldom saw him. Gallagher was a big star, the Job's unofficial master of ceremonies. The big man in the Holy Name. Joe Gallagher, superstar. But I'll tell you what he wasn't. And that was a leader. Whenever I or another boss paid this office an unannounced visit, Gallagher was among the missing. On patrol, they'd say, covering for him. He never went into the street with his people, never supervised any of his operations. He let the fucking office run itself. He couldn't tell you what operations his units were running. I tried on several occasions to get rid of him. But he had too much weight. I gave him bad evaluations. Recommended reassignment to less demanding work. I got telephone calls from the chief of Organized Crime Control suggesting that I reevaluate my evaluation of Gallagher. I raised his rating from below standards to above standards." His face flushed and the veins in his neck grew pronounced. He leaned his back against the map of Queens, waiting for the next question.

"Who ran the shop?"

"Nobody. His paper was a shambles. There was no record of the disbursement of his buy money. No documentation of overtime. His Eleven Cards were barely touched. There was no supervision of buy operations. The place was a goddamn mess." He punched his leg in anger. "Around two years ago Gallagher asked me to give him a Second Whip. He wanted to pick up Sgt. George Harris, who at the time was the Second Whip of the Two-eight Squad. They'd come on the Job together and had worked together in the Manhattan South Robbery Task Force and a few other assignments. I put in a Forty-nine requesting Harris, and a week later we picked him up in orders. In a week! Can you imagine that? It usually takes a request for transfer three months before it's acted upon. Gallagher made one phone call. That was the kind of weight he had in the Job."

A Harris was in Gallagher's address book. His original number, with a 516 area code, had been crossed out and replaced by one with a 718 code. The name Luise had been written beside it in parentheses. She had a 212 number. "What's Harris like?"

"A bit of a maverick. But the guy knows how to run a shop. He wasn't here three weeks and the paper was all up to snuff and the office running the way a narcotics district should."

"And Gallagher?"

"He continued to be the darling of the Job. He was doing talk shows on the radio and television. Big narcotics expert. The silly shit couldn't find a junkie in Needle Park. Gallagher was more than content to let Harris run his shop for him."

"Where does Harris live?" Scanlon asked, taking out a De Nobili.

"Huguenot, on Staten Island. He recently moved back into the city from Port Jefferson. Taxes and commuting got too much for him."

"Do you know his wife's name?"

"Ann, I think. Why?"

"I knew a Harris on the Job. His wife's name was Geraldine."

Herman the German began to shake his head. "It might sound funny, but for all of Gallagher's faults there was something about the guy I liked. He was alive, never down. No matter how pissed off he made you, he'd always leave you with a smile on your face."

"He was that kind of a guy, Inspector." Scanlon lit his De Nobili. "Has Harris been notified about his boss?"

"He's with the family now. They were pretty close. Used to socialize together."

"If you have no objections, Inspector, I'd like to take Gallagher's personnel record with me. There might be something there that could help me with the investigation."

A suspicious expression came over Herman the German's face. "Department records may not be removed from a command except by due process or with the permission of the PC, a deputy commissioner, or a ranking officer above the rank of captain."

Examining the tip of his De Nobili, Scanlon said, "Inspector is above the rank of captain."

"True," Herman the German said. "But why don't you tell me why I should give that permission? After all, if there should be anything in his record that's important to the investigation and it should disappear from his folder and IAD or some other hump unit looks and can't find it, I'm the one who'd have to take the fall. So you tell me, Lou, why should I play Mister Nice Guy?"

Scanlon brushed lint from his knee. "Because one of your people got himself killed. And because if during the course of the investigation I should come up with anything that might reflect negatively on your stewardship of Queens Narcotics, I'll personally send a little bird to whisper in your ear."

By ten-fifteen that night Scanlon arrived back at the Nine-three Squad carrying Gallagher's personnel record in several folders wrapped in twine. Hector Colon was sitting in front of a yellow makeup mirror trimming the thick black mustache that he liked to lick every time Maggie Higgins looked his way. Colon was a trendy dresser with a handsome Latin face, an Irish wife, and two sons in Massapequa Park—and an unmarried Polish girlfriend who had her own pad in Greenpoint.

Scanlon put the package on top of the cabinet next to the carton that he and Higgins had removed from Gallagher's Jackson Heights splash pad. Colon came in and told Scanlon that he had just been notified that temporary headquarters had been secured. The Log, flag, and lantern were back in the property room. Higgins, Christopher, and Brodie had signed out for the day and would be back on deck early in the morning. Colon motioned to the carton atop the cabinet. "You goin' mention that stuff in any of the reports?"

Scanlon hung his jacket on the department-issued coat rack that was next to the barred window. "No," he said, moving back to his desk.

"*Señor Teniente*, the Palace Guard is gonna be highly pissed off if they find out that you held out on them."

Scanlon knew that every DD 5, Supplementary Complaint Report, that was used to report additional phases of an investigation was supposed to be confidential.

"Every Five that we send down to Crime Coding ends up in some reporter's hip pocket. Every civilian clerk there is some newshound's stool, for a price. And I have no intention of seeing Gallagher's reputation smeared so that those parasites can sell more newspapers. He had a family, and it's our job to protect them."

"Ten-four, *Teniente*," Colon said, turning to leave the Whip's office. "See you in the ayem. I'm spending the night with my lady friend, if you should need me."

When Colon had gone and Scanlon was alone, he turned and looked wonderingly at the carton. Joe, he thought, what kind of shit did you get yourself into this time? I owe you, Joe, so I'll do whatever I can to save your miserable reputation for you. You crazy son of a bitch.

Scanlon pulled over the homicide case folder and began to separate the reports into two piles. He put the forensics reports in one and the canvass results and the witness statements in the other. From the squad room outside he could hear the scratchy cadence of the radio calls mixed with the hunt-and-peck sound of a typewriter. He leaned back in his seat and stared up at the decaying ceiling. He had been on a high since he first received Higgins's urgent telephone call at Monte's. Now he felt drained. His day had been one that was filled with sadness and a strange feeling of personal satisfaction. During the time he had been the Whip of the Nine-three Squad the office had caught the usual assortment of residential burglaries, payroll robberies, a few muggings, about a half-dozen vehicular homicides, and a dozen or so husband-wife or boyfriend-girlfriend assaults. Nothing that a detective could dig his teeth into. And now the Squad had a mystery on its hands. Person or persons unknown had done a double murder, and in so doing had released Scanlon's dormant predatory instincts. He was a predator stalking urban prey. He was back in the only game that really mattered; his time in purgatory was over.

He leaned forward in his seat and pushed the start button on the cassette tape recorder next to the tear-off calendar. Earlier in the tour he had dispatched the Biafra Baby to the Communications Unit to sign out the original tape of the call to 911 that reported the double homicide. All calls coming into and out of 911 are recorded and held for ninety days before the tapes are erased and reused. "You'd better get someone over to 311 Driggs Avenue. A police lieutenant has just been killed." It was a man's halting voice with a deep, throaty resonance. The operator's calm, professional voice followed. "Is there a callback number where you may be reached, sir?"

"Cut the bullshit, lady. Have someone get over here right quick. I told you, a cop has been shot."

When the recording ended, Scanlon arched a finger down onto the stop button. He had wanted to hear it one more time, to be sure. He knew that voice. It belonged to Walter Ticornelli.

It was after midnight when Tony Scanlon walked into Monte's. The dining-room crowd had thinned out, but serious drinkers were still three deep at the bar. Carmine, the maître d', came up to him. "Would you like to eat, Lieutenant?"

"I didn't come to play boccie," Scanlon said, flashing a warm smile. Carmine led him into the dining room and offered him a choice of tables on either side of the room. He selected a small table under the hanging plants and had begun to slide into the banquette when the maître d' bent forward and pulled out the table for him. A tuxedoed waiter appeared, placed a menu down, and then backed reverently away to await his pleasure. Scanlon looked over the fare and gave his order. A busboy came over and deposited a basket of warm bread and filled his water glass. "That was something about them murders. You gonna break the case, Lieutenant?"

Scanlon looked into the grinning Latin face and winked. "We break 'em all, Julio." The busboy left with a big smile on his face.

Angelo Esposito, the barber from Hess Street, came over and sat down, uninvited. "Goodta seeya, Lieutenant," the barber said. "Who would have thought such a thing could happen in this neighborhood?" He leaned across the table to confide, "It was probably some nigger or spic from Flushing Avenue."

Scanlon answered the barber with friendly banality. "We have a few leads, Angelo. But nothing that I can discuss. You understand." He tossed the barber his best confidential wink, and was greatly relieved to see Julio approaching with his salad.

The barber saw Julio coming and got up.

Later, lingering over the dregs of his espresso and the last of his wine, Scanlon stared ahead at the grouping of plaques commemorating the Monte family's civic achievements. Sitting across from him was a distinguished-looking man who appeared to be a well-preserved sixty. Clinging to his arm, listening attentively to each pronouncement, was an attractive woman with glistening pink lips and long black hair, who appeared to be in her middle thirties. You never see them with poor old men, Scanlon thought.

He leaned back and lit a De Nobili, enjoying its rich taste and aroma. He reached into his breast pocket and pulled out the round robin that Biafra Baby had brought back with him from police headquarters. He reread the internal record check on Joe Gallagher. The units of the department responsible for internal security reported that they had no disciplinary record on Lt. Joseph P. Gallagher.

Fifteen minutes later when he walked from the dining room out into the bar area, Joe Bite, the night bartender, called him over and asked him if he'd like a nightcap. "Hennessy," he said, sliding his real leg onto the rail.

Joe Bite slapped down a cocktail napkin and set down the pony glass.

Swirling the brandy around, Scanlon spotted his waiter at the end of the bar, caught his attention, and with his free hand scribbled on air to indicate that he wanted his bill. The waiter came over to him and discreetly whispered that Angelo Esposito, the barber from Hess Street, had done the right thing. Scanlon nodded, took out a roll of money, palmed a twenty, and shook the waiter's hand, a cop's way of saying thanks.

Joe Bite came over. "One for the road, Lieutenant?"

What a Job! Christmas every day of the year, he thought, reaching for the half-filled pony glass.

Distant traffic sounds rumbled across the night. An airplane skimmed low on the horizon. Scanlon drove his car into Mill Street between Herkimer and the Newtown Creek. There were no buildings on the north side of the street, only a vacant lot filled with rubbish and ugly construction scars. Polker's Bar and Grill was on the south side of the street. Attached to the bar's southern extremity was a stucco-and-timbered house with a mansard roof. Flush against the house on its other side was a one-story, flat-roofed factory building.

Gretta Polchinski owned all the land on Mill Street between Herkimer and the Newtown Creek. The people in that part of Greenpoint could never seem to agree on the exact date that Gretta first appeared on the scene and opened her establishment. But everyone in the neighborhood did agree that Gretta's brothel was run very discreetly.

It was one-forty in the morning when Scanlon drove up into the curb cut, honked the car horn twice, and waited for an eye to peer out of the elongated peephole that had been cut into the steel door. A metallic click, surprisingly loud in the quietness of the street, was immediately followed by the churning of the heavy door upward.

Once the door was fully open, Scanlon was directed inside by a pop-eyed black man. He parked his car between two foundation columns and got out. He became conscious of garage smells as he looked around the building, searching for a particular car. Spotting the one he was looking for, he walked over to the attendant, slipped him a five-dollar tip, and made for the four steps that led into the cinder-block passage that emptied into the basement of the house. He inserted his plastic key into the slot in the metal-sheathed door and waited a few seconds until the door clicked open.

The dominant motif was knotty pine. A carved bald eagle was over the bar, and above it two crossed flags. The Stars and Stripes and the Polish Imperial Banner. An old-fashioned jukebox outlined by a rainbow of moving lights stood against the wood-and-glass partition that separated the bar from the small dance floor.

Scanlon moved slowly, looking for Gretta in the crowd. He did not see her. He went up to the outer edge of the dance floor and looked into the darkness beyond. He saw her sitting alone at one of the small tables that ringed the dance floor, her face dimly visible in the faint light from the bar. She was dunking a silver tea egg into a porcelain cup.

"Looking for a good time, handsome?" she said as he approached her.

"How's business, Gretta?" he said, pulling out a scroll-back chair.

Gretta Polchinski was a short, squat woman with a high, flat forehead, a sagging chin, and a wild head of platinum hair that resembled brittle straw. She was fond of wearing low-cut dresses that displayed her wrinkled cleavage and the rows upon rows of gold chains around her neck.

She laid her bejeweled hand on the top of his and confided, "Tony, I have just taken on the most magnificent creature you have ever seen in your life. A Vietnamese. With a body that is not to be believed. And because I like you so much, you can have her for the night, on the arm."

"I'm here on business, Gretta."

She pulled her hand quickly off of his and leaned back into the shadows, causing a veil of darkness to descend over her face. She picked up her cup with both hands and sipped tea the oriental way. "Oh?" she said, watching him warily over the brim.

"I have to talk with Walter Ticornelli."

"Walter's not here."

"His Ford is parked in your garage."

"I let a lot of people store their cars in my garage when they go on trips."

He exhaled a sigh of disappointment. "Gretta, my love, did I ever tell you about my rule?"

"No, love, you didn't."

"When I ask a question of someone who operates in the gray area of life, they have to answer me, or else I get mad at them."

Her face jutted out of the shadows to challenge him. "Walter ain't here."

Scanlon assumed the benign expression of a disappointed teacher. "Gretta, I just can't tell you how shocked I am to discover a house of ill repute in this most Catholic of neighborhoods. And so shockingly close to the church."

"The monsignor is a regular, and he don't pay either."

"Be that as it may, my child, I'm afraid that it's my duty to hand you a collar for Promoting Prostitution as a D Felony in that you did manage, supervise, control, and own a prostitution enterprise involving the activity of two or more prostitutes."

She slammed her cup down, and tea splattered on the table. She half rose from her seat. "You peglegged, shit-on-a-shingle fuck! Just where the fuck do you think you're coming from? You sashay your ass in here whenever the mood strikes you, take your pick of the litter, and sashay out without it costing you a nickel. And now you got the balls to bust in here like fuckin' J. Edgar Hoover and lean on me. Well, fuck you!"

"Gretta?" he said in a hurt tone. "Is that any way to talk to your neighborhood good guy? Mr. Nice. I'm really surprised at you."

A babble of shouting came from the bar, causing her to look momentarily away, watching the crowd of longshoremen at the end of the bar. When the angry voices were replaced by slurred laughter she lowered herself back into her seat and glared at him.

An uncertain silence separated them.

At length he flashed a smile and blurted, "C'mon, Gretta. I only have to ask Walter a few nothing questions. Be a friend."

"Damn you, Scanlon," she said, breaking into a reluctant grin. "Walter's on the third floor."

He leaned up and kissed her nose. "Thanks, lover."

"Up yours."

Scanlon lit a De Nobili and blew the smoke into the surrounding darkness. "What do you know about the sexual paraphernalia business?"

She threw him a sharp look. "You thinking of changing occupations?"

"A friend of mine asked me to pick her up a vibrator. Seems her husband has lost interest."

She guffawed. "Most do. A few years ago women used to have Stanley and Tupperware parties in their homes. Today they're into Fuckerware parties where the hostess shows off her wares and the ladies fill out order forms and then seal them so that nobody knows what their pleasure is."

"Is it a big business?"

"Sex is always a big business."

"Are the wise guys into it?"

"Do a hobby horse have a hickory dick? Of *course* they're into it. They're into everything."

"You said the third floor," Scanlon said, standing.

"Let me go with you. I don't want you walking into the wrong room."

She led him through the lounge to the two-person elevator that she had had installed four years before to accommodate clients who had had bypass operations and did not want to trudge up stairs.

A mincing transvestite in a long yellow robe trimmed in marabou greeted them as they stepped off the elevator. The prostitute daintily kissed Gretta on both cheeks, whispering, "Is he for me, darling?"

"He's not your type," Gretta said, then asked, "What room is Walter in?"

"The Teak Room, darling," the transvestite said, staring at Scanlon and sucking on his bottom lip.

Scanlon threw open the door and entered the room.

"Can't a guy get any privacy around here?" Walter Ticornelli shouted. He was sitting up in a king-size bed with a brass headboard, his arm draped over the shoulders of a black transvestite.

"I need a word with you, Walter," Scanlon said, motioning for the prostitute to leave.

Ticornelli patted his lover's leg. "I'll catch you later."

The transvestite slid ladylike from the bed and snatched a thin white robe from a nearby chair. His female features, silicone breasts, and exaggerated female movements contrasted sharply with his limp penis and flouncing balls.

He slid on the robe, bunched it at the throat, and huffed past Scanlon on his way out of the room.

"Your friend is kinda cute," Scanlon said, sitting on the edge of the bed, glancing up at the mirror set into the bed's gold canopy.

Ticornelli folded his hands across his chest. "She's going into the hospital next week to get her plumbing altered."

Scanlon winced at the thought of castration. He noticed the five-carat diamond ring on Ticornelli's right pinky. Street talk said that it had been a gift from Joey "the Nose" Napoli when Ticornelli went through his candle-and-blood initiation into the Genovese crime family.

Ticornelli fixed his hooded eyes on Scanlon. "What's on your mind, Anthony?"

"I see that you still got the hots for black transvestites. Do the wife and kids that you got stashed out in Munsey Park know about your peculiar life-style?"

"What's a guy going to do, Anthony? We all got our hang-ups, right? Take you, for instance. You smoke them guinea stinkers of yours as a protest. You want the world to know that you're Italian even though you got an Irish name." He leaned forward, black ringlets falling over his forehead. He spoke in Italian. "You and me, we go way back. To the old days on Pleasant Avenue when you were a wild neighborhood kid with a drunken Irish cop for a father and an Italian mother who only talked to you in Italian. Tell me, Anthony, how many of your cop friends know that you speak Italian? How many of them know how much you hate their Irish guts? Not many, right? You're still a little bit ashamed of being Italian, aren't you?"

Scanlon rammed his hand into Ticornelli's groin, squeezing. He said, "*Come ti piacerebbe diventare uno castrato?*"

Color drained from Ticornelli's face as it furrowed with pain. "Let go," he said in Italian.

"What's the magic word?" Scanlon said in English.

"Please," he gasped.

Scanlon released his grip. He noticed the beads of sweat at Ticornelli's hairline. "I don't like to be talked to like that, Walter. It shows disrespect. You wouldn't open a mouth like that to one of your capos, so don't try it out on me." He playfully slapped Ticornelli's cheek. "Okay, paisan? Now, taking care of your padrone's gambling and usury interests in Greenpoint, you get to meet a lot of people, see and hear a lot of things. You have your hand on the pulse of the community, so to speak."

"Why don't you get to the point?"

"I heard your voice on a tape today, Walter," Scanlon said, smoothing down the edge of the sheet.

"What tape?"

"All calls coming into nine-eleven are recorded."

Ticornelli beamed. "So? That just goes to show what a public-spirited person I am."

Scanlon nodded in agreement. "This is so, Walter. What I would like you, as a public-spirited-type person, to do for me is to tell me exactly what you saw go down inside that candy store."

Ticornelli licked the sweat from his lips and reached for the pack of Camels on top of the night table. He shook one out, lit it, sent a stream of smoke through his nostrils, and leaned back and relaxed.

According to Ticornelli, he had been standing across the street from the candy store talking with Father Rudnicki about the problems in Poland when he heard three explosions in rapid succession. He heard squealing tires, looked in the direction of the blasts, and saw a blue van blocking his view of the candy store. Walking slowly away from the priest, he started to cross the street. He saw that the driver of the van was a white man who had on sunglasses and a brown hat pulled down over his head. He saw the driver reach across the seat as if to open the door on the passenger side. Someone rushed into the van on the passenger side, and the van sped off. He rushed across the street into the candy store, saw the bodies, and called the police. He knocked the ash of his cigarette into his palm. "That's it. The whole story."

"Did you know Gallagher?"

"From the neighborhood."

"Did you see him enter the candy store?"

"Like I told you, I was bullshitting with the priest."

Scanlon got up off the bed and went over to the chair that was next to the window. Ticornelli had carefully laid out his clothes on the chair. Scanlon picked them up and threw them on the bed. "Putcha clothes on, Walter. We're going into the station for a little chat."

Ticornelli began to gather up his clothes, a look of bewilderment plastered across his face. "Why are you doing this to me, Anthony? You got no call to lean on me this way."

"Gallagher's own mother would not have recognized him. His face was gone. But you knew who he was. Howdya do that, paisan? You clairvoyant?"

The gambler sat with his clothes bunched between his legs, pondering his situation.

Scanlon continued to press him. "Because you're a big money maker your puritanical friends on Mulberry Street overlook your sexual idiosyncrasy, as long as you're discreet. I wonder what they're going to say when I drag you in in cuffs? How are they going to react when they read the headlines in the *Post*? 'Genovese soldier discovered in homosexual tryst.'" He snapped his fingers miming error. "I'm sorry—'alleged Genovese soldier.'"

Ticornelli flushed with anger. "You're a first-class Irish scumbag, Scanlon."

"This is true, Walter." He leaned over the bed, bracing his palms on the mattress. "Walter, my old friend from Pleasant Avenue. Why don't you make it easy on the both of us? Tell me what I want to know, now, here."

Ticornelli punched the mattress in frustration. "Gallagher was into me for five large," he blurted. "He was supposed to meet me at Yetta's to make a payment."

A tremor of disbelief shook Scanlon's head. "You lent a police lieutenant five thousand dollars?"

"Whatsamatta, their money ain't the same color as everyone else's?"

"What was the vig?"

"Three points. And that was only because he was a cop. It shoulda been five points. But you know that I'm a soft touch when it comes to you guys."

"A hundred and fifty dollars a week interest on a lieutenant's salary? Ain't no way, Walter."

"Gallagher'd been into me before and he always anted up."

"Was he behind in his payments?"

"A little. The bread that he was supposed to give me today woulda brung him up to date."

"How much, paisan?"

"A week's vig and two large off the principal. He telephoned me last night at the club and asked me to meet him at Yetta's."

Scanlon tried to recall what was listed on the property voucher that recorded the personal property that had been removed from Gallagher's body. If he remembered correctly, item one had been sixteen dollars and something in U.S. currency. If Ticornelli had just told him the truth, where was the money? Trumwell and Stone were the first cops on the scene. If a score was to be made, that was when it would have had to be done. He dismissed the idea. Cops don't score other cops, particularly dead ones. "What was Yetta Zimmerman into?"

"The old broad wasn't into nothin' except her lousy candy store and bookin' a little action on the side. She didn't have an enemy in the world, and for that matter, neither did your Irish friend Joe Gallagher."

Scanlon wanted to say that one of them sure as hell did. But he said nothing. Smart cops know when to keep their mouths shut.

4

Tony Scanlon walked into the squad room a little before 0800 the next morning and found it in disarray from the night's activities. A half-eaten pastrami sandwich had attracted flies; three slices of curled-up pizza lay in a white box; empty beer cans threatened to overflow the waste barrel. The television blared: on the screen a woman with oversize glasses was recapping the morning news: the President had warned a Miami audience of the dangers inherent in the Soviet-Cuban-Nicaraguan axis. Here we go again, Scanlon thought, snapping off the set. It was much cooler inside the station house than outside, where the morning air was already promising a really hot day.

Settled in behind his desk, he reached for the first folder. As he did he glanced at the early-bird edition of the *Daily News* that had been left on his desk. The headlines told of Joe Gallagher's death. A hero, killed in the line of duty. There was another story inside the paper that told of a man who had murdered six people because he liked the way it felt. One of the victims had been shot dead because the killer had been full of the Christmas spirit. Scanlon read the stories, rolled up the newspaper, and threw it into the basket at the side of his desk. He wondered if the criminal justice system in this country was workable. How can Anglo-Saxon law be applied to savages? Might not Islamic law be the answer, an eye for an eye? There were entrepreneurs in the city who had already recognized that as a profitable truth. Grieving relatives now flocked to the gangs of Chinatown and Ninth Avenue seeking retribution against those who had murdered, raped, and maimed their loved ones, knowing that justice would not be forthcoming from the courts of this state. And who the hell can blame them? he thought, flipping open the folder.

The ballistics report detailed the gauge of the shells and the size and weight of the shot. Numerous latent prints had been found at the scene. They would be useless unless a suspect was found to match them up against. The place of occurrence was a public place; all that the fingerprints could do was connect a suspect to a scene, not tell when he was there. Fingerprints had been discovered in the tombs of the pharaohs. There is no way to tell when a fingerprint was left.

The crime-scene sketch had been done by the polar coordinate method. Triangulation had shown that the perp was between five feet five and five feet seven and that he had fired from a distance of sixty-two inches. The autopsy protocols were done on gray onionskins. They stated, in the impersonal language of the forensics pathologist, the causes of death. Cross projections of the human body were printed in the margins. Dotted lines traced each entry wound; narratives detailed the destruction each intrusion made. Shotgun wadding had been found in the wounds. Both victims had suffered cadaveric spasms at the times of their death. Scanlon recalled from one of his police promotion courses that cadaveric spasm was the immediate stiffening of a body after death. It was caused by great fear at the time of death or by severe damage to the central nervous system.

When he finished the forensic reports he turned to the investigative reports. The narratives typed under the details of the case were done in familiar police prose: At T/P/O, the time and place of occurrence, the undersigned personally interviewed Mary Hollinder F/W/22 of 1746a Nostrand Avenue, Brooklyn, who stated that she is employed as a waitress at the Warsaw Restaurant located at 411 Driggs Avenue, Brooklyn. Witness stated that at T/O she observed a male, white, who answered to the description of the perp walk east on Driggs Avenue moments before the crime occurred. Hollinder further stated that when the perp passed her he had a shopping bag clutched in his left hand. Hollinder stated that she was engaged in conversation with a friend whose identity is known to this department (statement 60# 897-86). Hollinder stated that she heard three loud reports and turned to see the above-mentioned perp running from the place of occurrence carrying what appeared to be a rifle. She stated that she saw the perp get into a blue van. Witness told the undersigned that she would recognize the perp if she saw him again and that she would make herself available to view a lineup.

He read the statements of storekeepers and pedestrians, reports of the emergency service crews who searched for physical evidence, reports of the detectives who had conducted the canvasses. All of them ended with the same capitalized letters, NR—negative results.

When he came to the Five on the three boys who had been present in the candy store at the time of occurrence he noticed that they had been identified only by their pedigrees. That was because department regulations forbid the identification of children who have been the victims of or the witnesses to crime. The report reiterated what Lew Brodie had told him at the crime scene. It was the last sentence that caused his lips to pull together into a thin, frustrated line: Witnesses state that they would not be able to identify perp if they saw him again. The parents of the foregoing witnesses state that they refuse to allow them to view photos or to attend lineup. Scanlon knew he had just lost his only eyewitnesses to the killings.

A noise in the squad room caused him to look up from the reports. He saw Christopher putting the filter into the top of the Dial-a-Brew machine. After he poured in the water, Christopher reached down and measured in the coffee. He ripped open the bag of bagels and bialys he had brought in with him. Since he was catching the first three hours of the tour, it was his responsibility to make the morning coffee and pick up the bag of goodies that was waiting at Wysniewski's Bakery. Tradition.

Soon the air was filled with the aroma of freshly made coffee. The day team began to arrive. To a man they shambled over to the coffee pot. Eric Crawford, an overweight detective with sagging shoulders, shuffled out of the four-double-decker-bed dormitory in his underwear, yawning and scratching his behind. He glanced at Maggie Higgins, who was standing in front of the urn buttering a bagel. "Hey, Maggie," he called out, hefting the front of his underpants into the palm of his hand. "Take a look at what I got for you."

Higgins glared her disdain at him. "Whaddaya hear from your head these days, Crawford? Nothing, I bet. You just get a steady dial tone."

Shaking his organ, Crawford said, "I bet this'd make you whistle 'Dixie.'"

She sauntered over to him. "Break it out, numb nuts. Let's see what you got."

He took her dare, spreading the fly of his underpants, revealing himself.

She took a few steps backward, looking in at the shriveled organ, shaking her head in pitying disbelief. "There's not enough there to fill a thimble. Thank God I'm gay." She went back to the urn. The other detectives laughed at the chunky detective in his oversize checkered boxer shorts.

Scanlon got up from his desk and went over and kicked the door closed, a signal that he did not want to be disturbed. His stump throbbed and his phantom leg was receiving messages. That happened whenever he did not get enough sleep. He took a pad from the bottom drawer of his desk and made notes. He recounted his conversation with Gretta Polchinski and Walter Ticornelli. He reread a Five that he had gone over last night. Something about it bothered him.

At T/P/O the undersigned personally interviewed Sigrid Thorsen F/W/27 of 2347 Avenue Z, Brooklyn, who stated that at T/O she was sitting on a bench in McGoldrick Park playing with her eight-month-old daughter when a man who answered to the description of the perp sat down on the adjoining bench. Witness states that the man fed pigeons peanuts. She stated that she looked over at him and he gave her a nasty look and she turned away. Witness further states that there was something peculiar about this man, but when pressed by the undersigned to state what, was unable to do so.

He pushed the Thorsen statement aside and after a brief search

54

through the case folder came up with the statement of another witness, Thomas Tibbs. A M/W/32 of 1 Pinkflower Drive, Scarsdale, New York, who stated that he was the manager of the Gotham Federal Savings Bank located at 311 Wall Street, New York City. Witness stated that at T/O he was walking east on Driggs Avenue when he heard three loud reports that sounded like gunfire. He looked in the direction of the reports and saw a man running from a candy store toward a blue van that was parked at the curb. This man, stated the witness, was carrying a single-barrel shotgun in his right hand. Tibbs stated that he would make himself available to view photos and that he would recognize the perp if he saw him again.

"Why Tibbs on Driggs Avenue at that time of day?" Scanlon wrote.

After filling seven pages with notes he turned to the department envelope containing the photographs of the crime scene. He untied the string and removed colored 8x10s. He studied each one, searching for some telling piece of overlooked evidence. In the end, he thought, raw meat always looks like raw meat. He slid the photographs back into the envelope and turned his attention to the composite sketch of the perp. Studying it, he thought, Who are you, pally? What was your motive? He had become painfully aware of the scarcity of physical evidence and hoped that the lab boys would come up with something that he could hang his hat on.

As he restudied his notes, he mentally reviewed his conversation with Walter Ticornelli. A week's vig and two large off the principal, the shylock had said. He reached back into the pile of department forms and pulled out the property clerk voucher. As he had thought, Higgins had invoiced sixteen dollars and thirty-two cents in U.S. currency. If Ticornelli had told him the truth, and if his calculations were correct, Gallagher should have had twenty-one hundred and fifty dollars on him at the time of his death. So, he asked himself, where was that money? After thinking about that for a minute or so, he heaved himself out of his chair and left the Squad.

Police Officer Kiley O'Reilly had never read Interim Order 11 dated March 4, 1983—Early Identification and Referral of Employees with Alcohol Problems.

O'Reilly had been on the Job sixteen years, and as close as his peers could figure, he had been drunk for the last eleven. Despite all the publicity about its modern management techniques, the NYPD protects its drunks.

O'Reilly had become part of the Job's folklore. At one time he was the scourge of the bars of Manhattan North. His frequent toots often ended with him using the terraced bottles of booze behind the bar for target practice. Miraculously, no one had ever been hurt during one of O'Reilly's toots, and he became a legend. But, alas, the day came when the borough commander of Manhattan North lost his sense of humor with Kiley O'Reilly. It all happened on a November evening, a payday, on or about 1800 hours. Police Officer O'Reilly found himself swaying in front of the rectory of the Church of the Redemption, stewed to the mickey. In his stupor, he associated the clouded second-floor window with instructions that he had received during his firearms training in Recruit School— aim for the gray area. And that was exactly what Kiley O'Reilly did. He put six standard-velocity lead bullets through the second-floor bathroom window. When the first of his bullets thundered through the window, Msgr. Terence X. Woods was seated upon the throne enjoying his nightly bowel movement and paging through the latest issue of *Playboy.* The right reverend monsignor leaped howling from the toilet seat, with his trousers gathered at the ankles, and made a desperate hop for the door in an attempt to escape the fusillade. He had made one good hop before he stumbled upon the cold floor, unable to control his bowel movement.

Within the hour, Kiley O'Reilly had his guns removed, and was transferred into the bow-and-arrow squad, and banished to the Nine-three, where he was assigned as the Broom, which meant it was his responsibility to keep the station house clean. He was most diligent in performing his daily chores, meticulously ensuring that the green Second World War–vintage window shades on every window were pulled down to exactly thirty-two inches from each sill. Duties finished, O'Reilly would retire to the garage and hide inside one of the two morgue boxes that were stored in every patrol precinct so that bodies found in a public place and offending public decency could be removed to the station house without having to wait for the meat wagon. Squirreled inside the morgue box was O'Reilly's "flute," a Pepsi bottle filled with whiskey.

Scanlon hurried out of the station house, passed under the two huge green globes that were affixed to the entrance of the fortresslike stone building, turned right, and made for the garage.

He pushed in the walk-through door and stepped into the garage. The interior was military-clean, with everything in its assigned place. Red buckets filled with sand were next to the two gas pumps; the portable generator was oiled and ready for the next blackout. The snow blower was next to the generator; the emergency string lights were strung over the brick wall.

Joe Gallagher's Ford was parked inside a rope barrier that had a single crime scene sign attached. The surface of the car was smudged with white fingerprint powder. Scanlon lifted the rope and ducked under. He peered inside the car and was relieved to see that the glove compartment was closed and that no personal property was strewn about. The precinct scavengers had not been at the car.

He climbed back out over the rope and went over to one of the morgue boxes. He flipped down the top lid. Kiley O'Reilly was stretched out with his feet crossed at the ankles and a Pepsi bottle at rest on his stomach. "Howya doin', Lou?" O'Reilly singsonged.

"You see anyone messing with this car?"

O'Reilly swung his legs out over the side and sat up, legs dangling over the edge. "That car belonged to the dead, Lou. Ain't nobody going to mess with it."

Scanlon took in the half-filled Pepsi bottle and went back to the car.

Scanlon entered the car on the passenger side and stretched his hand under the seat, searching. NR. Then he stuffed his hand between the front cushion and the back of the seat and inched along, slowly making his way across to the driver side. NR. Kneeling on the front cushion, he reached into the back of the car and yanked out the rear cushion. NR. Fascinated, Kiley O'Reilly watched him, taking short pulls from his bottle.

By now the seats were askew and all four doors open. Scanlon stood with his foot on the rear bumper, trying to guess where the money could be. After a few contemplative moments, he slapped his foot down and left the garage.

He returned within a few minutes twirling a key ring that he had just removed from the property clerk folder that contained Joe Gallagher's personal property.

Kiley O'Reilly took a long pull, anticipating.

Scanlon opened the car's trunk, leaned inside, and began poking around, moving tools and other things. When he didn't find what he was looking for, he unthreaded the wing nut that secured the spare tire in the well. Nut off, he hefted the tire out and set it down on the rim of the well. He spotted the department multi-use envelope on the bottom of the well. He reached in, removed it, opened the flap, and fanned twenty-one hundred-dollar bills and a brand-new fifty into the palm of his hand. Ticornelli told me the truth, he thought, looking down at the spread of money. But why had Gallagher been so cautious? Why hide money in his car? The gun and shield that cops carry usually give them a sense of invincibility.

The Gotham Federal Savings Bank had a glass facade. Bank executives could be seen at desks earnestly discussing things with customers. Higgins parked the department auto in the crosswalk and tossed the vehicle identification plate onto the dashboard. Scanlon started to slide out on the passenger side, hesitated, and reached back into the car and removed the radio handset from the black rubber cradle and laid it across the dashboard. "Now let one of the meter maids say she didn't know it was a department car that she hung one on."

"We should carry M&M candy wrappers with us and put them on the dash. That's how the parking enforcement people identify their private cars to each other," Higgins said, locking the door. They walked over to the bank and asked to see Mr. Tibbs.

"I told my story a dozen times to the other detectives." Thomas Tibbs was a man of medium height who wore his thinning black hair plastered down and parted on the side. He wore a three-piece gray business suit and had the obligatory college ring on his right hand.

"I'm afraid that you are going to have to tell it one more time," Scanlon said.

The banker came out from behind his desk and motioned the detectives over to a grouping of chrome-and-canvas chairs that had been arranged around a chrome-and-glass table. It was a large airy office with its own bathroom. As Scanlon lowered himself into the chair, he took in the precisely arranged photographs of bank executives that lined the nearby wall. They were all stern men with the look of acute constipation etched into their scowls. He looked away in time to catch the banker's gaze caressing Higgins's body. She had perched sideways on her chair, the fall of her blouse accentuating her healthy bosom. She too had noticed the banker's interest and had shifted in her seat and crossed her legs, ensuring that the hem of her skirt rode up above her knee, revealing some thigh. The witness stole a quick look and returned his full attention to Scanlon.

Higgins said, "We appreciate your seeing us, Mr. Tibbs." She used her best saccharine tone.

Tibbs looked at her and smiled. "It's my pleasure, Detective Higgins."

Scanlon leaned back and relaxed. This was going to be Maggie's show.

"Mr. Tibbs," she began, "you stated that the man whom you saw running from the candy store was carrying a single-barrel shotgun in his right hand."

Tibbs began to rub the stone of his college ring across his lips. "That is correct," he said, trying to make eye contact with her.

"The time sequence was in seconds," Higgins stated flatly. "How can you be so positive it was a shotgun that you saw and not a rifle or a stick, or a piece of pipe?"

Tibbs lowered his hand from his lips and responded smugly, "What I saw, Detective Higgins, had a ventilated-rib barrel and a plated breechblock. Only shotguns possess those characteristics."

Cocky bastard, thought Scanlon.

"There might come a time, Mr. Tibbs, when you will be asked to testify in court. If that time should come you are going to be asked what qualifies you to make such technical observations concerning firearms."

A confident smile caught the edges of Tibbs's lips. He sneaked another look at Maggie's thigh and said, "I'm an avid hunter, Detective Higgins. And when I was in the army I was trained as an armorer."

She started to ask the next question but he interrupted her and said, "Please make it Tom," so she continued, "Tom, did you notice if the stock or the barrel was cut down?"

"The stock was cut way down."

"In your previous statements you mentioned that you noticed

something odd about the killer as he ran for the van. At the time, you were unable to say what it was. Now that you have had time to think about it, can you tell us?"

"I've racked my brains and I just don't know what it was about him that bothered me. But I do know that it had something to do with the way he ran. It was unnatural."

"Could you be more specific?"

"I'm afraid not."

"Would you recognize the killer again if you saw him?"

"Absolutely."

Before they'd left the squad room Scanlon had taken several composite sketches that were connected to other cases and the one that the artist had prepared in the Gallagher/Zimmerman case and had laid them out on a desk. He'd taken the Squad's Polaroid one-on-one camera and photographed the layout. He now picked up the envelope from his lap and opened it, hoping that the witness would pick out the correct one. Leaning up out of his seat, he passed the layout to Tibbs. "Would you please take a look and see if you recognize anyone?" Scanlon said.

Tibbs scrutinized the layout. "This is the man I saw running from the candy store," he said, tapping the fourth sketch.

Tibbs had selected the correct one.

Higgins looked at Scanlon with an expression that said, He's going to make one helluva witness.

Juries tend to believe bankers and priests; it's the veracity of cops, lawyers, and doctors that they hold in disrepute. Scanlon was bothered. At one time cops didn't concern themselves with the credibility of witnesses. That was the DA's job. That was no longer the case. And Scanlon had learned that the hard way. Several blown cases had taught Scanlon to learn everything there was to learn about potential witnesses.

Higgins broke his private reverie. "Got any questions, Lou?"

Scanlon cupped palms over kneecaps. Arched his back. "You're married, live in Scarsdale, and work in Manhattan. Correct?"

A kernel of apprehension crept into the witness's bland expression. "Yes."

"How do you get to work, Mr. Tibbs?"

"The seven-sixteen from Scarsdale. It gets me into the office . . ." The witness stopped in midsentence, his eyes dilated with sudden concern. Scanlon nodded knowingly at him. He knew his secret and he wanted him to know that he knew. Scanlon would not press the issue, at least not yet. Scanlon pried himself up off the chair. "Thanks for your cooperation," he said, shaking the banker's limp hand, staring into his worried eyes.

Sigrid Thorsen lived on the southern edge of Brooklyn, in Bath Beach, the Six-two. When she answered her door she was holding a baby and her hair was turbaned in a white towel. While Scanlon displayed police credentials and explained the purpose of their unannounced visit, Higgins reached past him into the two-bedroom apartment and playfully grasped the baby's tiny fist.

The witness opened the door for the detectives. Higgins walked at the witness's side, admiring the baby and cooing at her. Thorsen led the detectives into a large comfortable living room with a black folding room divider that separated the room from the dining area. There was a terrace that overlooked other apartment houses and terraces.

Sigrid Thorsen was a Nordic beauty: tall and thin with clear white skin that emphasized her wide umber eyes. Thin crescent lines were visible around her lips. She was wearing fawn-colored shorts and a white short-sleeved cotton top. Her nipples were evident through the soft cotton. She offered them seats and excused herself; it was time for her baby's nap, she explained. As she moved toward the bedroom Scanlon took in her long legs, tight calves, and round behind. Higgins, who had sat next to him on the long white couch, leaned close. "Nice," she whispered.

"Competition I don't need," he said, watching the legs disappear into a distant room.

When the witness returned some time later, Scanlon noticed that she had applied makeup and had brushed her hair out. It was long and had a soft yellow hue and flowed smoothly past her shoulders.

She sat in a low leather chair. "How may I help you?"

Scanlon led her through the statement she had given the other detectives. She listened attentively. At appropriate places during the narrative she would nod or say yes. She stared down at the shaggy carpet as he talked. "You told the other detectives that there was something strange about the man who sat on the next bench, that he frightened you. Can you tell me exactly what it was about him that made you feel that way?"

Sigrid Thorsen looked up at him. "There was something odd about him, but I can't put my finger on it."

"Anything else?"

She shook her head.

Watching her closely, he asked, "Would you be willing to submit to hypnosis, Mrs. Thorsen?"

"Hypnosis? Why?"

"Because you're the one person who got a good look at the killer. Under hypnosis you might be able to recall some bit of information that could prove important." He leaned forward to emphasize the importance of what he was going to say next. "I assure you, it's perfectly safe, and we'd provide you with transportation and a policewoman to baby-sit."

"I would have to discuss that with my husband. I'll let you know." Scanlon picked up the envelope containing the sketches. He removed the layout and handed it to her. "Would you mind looking at this and seeing if you recognize anyone?"

She took it and laid it down on her lap, studying the grouping of composite sketches. After a while she looked up and said, "It's number four. That's the man in the park, the one who sat on the next bench and fed the pigeons."

She had identified the same composite as Thomas Tibbs. Scanlon let his hands fall between his legs, rubbing his palms together. "Mrs. Thorsen, there is a question that I must ask you."

She tensed.

"What were you doing in McGoldrick Park?"

"I thought that was obvious, Lieutenant. I was sitting on a bench with my child, enjoying a beautiful June day."

"I see," Scanlon said, looking into her beautiful eyes. "Mrs. Thorsen, what is your relationship with Thomas Tibbs?" He watched her fight to keep her composure.

"Who?" she said.

"Thomas Tibbs," he repeated. "I believe that you drove into Manhattan and picked him up, and then drove to Greenpoint to spend some stolen moments together. You couldn't find a parking space, so you and your baby got out while he searched for a spot."

She said nothing; her gaze was unflinchingly fixed on him; her hands squeezed the cushion of the chair.

He continued. "You and Tibbs have stumbled into a homicide investigation, and until it's put to bed your lives are in the public domain. The only reason I bring up Tibbs is to advise you that at some point in time someone else might ask you about your relationship with Tibbs. And if that time should come, I'd like you both to be prepared."

"Thank you for your concern, Lieutenant." She got up. The interview was over.

"Will you discuss the possibility of being hypnotized with your husband?" he asked, walking with her to the door. "I'd really appreciate it if you would."

"I will discuss it with my husband," she said, reaching for the doorknob. "My husband and I discuss everything together—we have no secrets."

"I'm glad," Scanlon said. "That's how it should be."

Watching oncoming traffic for an opening, Higgins said, "How'd you know?"

"Their statements," Scanlon said. "She lives in Bath Beach at the ass end of Brooklyn and turns up in Greenpoint with her baby. He works in Manhattan, takes the seven-sixteen from Scarsdale, and then he shows up in Greenpoint in the middle of a business day. You don't have to be Holmes to figure that one out."

A bus passed, enveloping their car in a cloud of carbon monoxide and other noxious fumes. "Will we be able to use them in court?" Higgins said, driving from the space with a scrunch of tires.

"By the time this caper gets into court, if it ever does, they'll have their act together."

5

All the ladies had one thing in common: they'd all committed adultery with Lt. Joseph P. Gallagher.

Scanlon had Higgins telephone them at their homes and ask them to come into the Squad for a chat. Each of them sounded nervous about being associated publicly with the dead police hero. Higgins had assured each of them that they wouldn't be embarrassed. One of the best ways to secure the help of hostile witnesses is to instill a sense of security, eliminate the fear of exposure. Policemen lie a lot. After about forty minutes of not so gentle coaxing, Maggie Higgins had gotten each of the ladies to agree to come into the Squad and be interviewed. She had scheduled their appointments so that none of the ladies would meet.

Donna Hunt was a diminutive woman in her early forties. She brought to mind the phrase "pocket Venus." Her figure was beautifully proportioned and her green eyes perfectly made up. But her clothes and jewelry were just a bit too loud and emphatic. She was obviously nervous and wore a paper-thin smile when she appeared at the squad-room gate and asked to see Detective Higgins. She stood behind the carved gate wringing a lace handkerchief while Christopher went to get Higgins out of the property room.

After a quick introduction, Higgins led the witness across the squad room and into Scanlon's office. As soon as the door to the Whip's office closed behind her, Donna Hunt threw herself into a chair and cried hysterically. Without being asked a question, she blurted out her story.

Donna Hunt had been married for twenty-six years to Harold, who was an accountant, a good provider, a loving father, and the only man she had ever gone to bed with. At fifty-two, Harold had lost interest in sex. Whenever she initiated lovemaking Harold would inevitably demur on the grounds that he was too tired or not in the mood. She stopped trying. With her two children away at college, Donna Hunt found herself alone more and more. Harold worked late most nights. Clients, he said. But she was beginning to have her doubts.

One day while she was driving through Astoria on her way to meet her sister for lunch a police car pulled alongside and the driver motioned her to the curb. It was on Steinway Street, she remembered, across from the new Pathmark shopping center. Through her sideview mirror she saw a policeman get out of the car and swagger up to her. He had been polite. She had run a stop sign, he said. She protested that she hadn't. At some point during the exchange a man in civilian clothes got out of the police car and came over and told the policeman he was in a hurry. The man in the civilian clothes asked her her name and smiled. "I'm Joe Gallagher," he said, smiling again, and walked back to the police car.

Around noontime the next day her telephone rang at home and she was surprised when the voice at the other end announced that he was Joe Gallagher. He was a police lieutenant and had gotten her home number by running a make on her license plate, he told her. He was conducting an investigation into a payroll robbery that had occurred around the time she had driven past the Pathmark. Would it be possible for him to interview her concerning this crime? Perhaps they could meet and have a cup of coffee?

Six days after that first meeting, Donna Hunt went to bed with Joe Gallagher. It was the sort of experience she had fantasized about many times. She remembered lying beside him exulting in herself. A man had wanted her; had pursued her; had enjoyed her. She was a woman again. The affair gave her empty life meaning.

She had been surprised at how guiltless she had felt. She had loved every moment of it—at first.

During one of their noontime rendezvous in Jackson Heights he had gotten out of bed and returned with a vibrator and a pair of anal love beads. Do you like to experiment? he had asked, gently pushing her legs apart. She had been shocked by the ferocity of her newly discovered passion.

Three days later Gallagher telephoned her at home. Never call before ten A.M., she had warned. Would she be interested in a threesome? he asked. He had a friend who had a friend.

Donna Hunt looked pleadingly up at Scanlon, who was perched on the edge of the desk staring down at her. Her eyes were swollen, her cheeks streaked black with mascara. Her sobs had turned to heaves, and she was fighting for breath. Higgins, who had been standing against the wall, came over and handed the witness some sheets of Kleenex. The witness smiled weakly and took them.

Hector Colon, who had slipped into the office while Donna Hunt was talking, left the office and returned with a glass of water.

After drinking the water, she began to make glass rings on the desk. "I did it," she whispered.

"Did what?" Scanlon asked gently.

"I participated in the threesome. It was with Joe and another woman. I'd never been with another woman that way. I realized that I was out of control. Like being in quicksand, being dragged deeper and deeper. When he called again I told him that it was over. That I'd never see him again. He telephoned several times but I held firm. Finally he stopped calling."

"When was the last time you heard from him?" Scanlon asked.

"Seven months ago." She looked up at Scanlon. "Harold is an unforgiving man. He'd leave me if he ever found out."

Scanlon felt sorry for her. A woman puts a lot on the line every time she spreads her legs, he thought. "Your husband will never know anything from us, Mrs. Hunt. Whatever you tell us will remain confidential." He didn't tell her that someday she might have to testify in court. Policemen have to lie a lot. She gripped his hands. "Thank you."

He picked up a photograph from the desk, one that he had found in Gallagher's locker. He held it up to her. "Is this you, Mrs. Hunt?"

"Oh, God!" She looked away. "He asked me to pose, and I did."

"Mrs. Hunt, what was the name of the other woman who participated with you in the threesome?"

"Luise Bardwell."

Scanlon looked at Higgins. The name Luise had been written in Gallagher's address book in parentheses next to that of George Harris, the sergeant friend of Joe Gallagher who had been brought into the Seventeenth Narcotics District to run Gallagher's unit for him.

"Was Gallagher an active participant in the threesome?" Scanlon asked.

Donna Hunt looked down at her hands. "Joe knelt on the bed watching and masturbating. He, he ejaculated over my breasts." She craned her head and looked at Higgins. "Is there a ladies' room?"

Higgins banged on the bathroom door and hearing no response pushed the door open and stuck her head inside.

Donna Hunt stopped just inside the doorway and took in the urinals. There was one doorless stall with a lot of crushed cigarettes and newspapers, and girlie magazines strewn around the base of the bowl. A large cardboard sign was on the wall: Female POs are to throw their sanitary napkins in the waste barrels and not in the toilet. Auth. C.O. 93 Pct.

Higgins saw her aversion. "Pretty disgusting, isn't it?"

"Don't you have a ladies' room?"

"The newer station houses have. We have to put up with unisex johns."

"But aren't they ever cleaned?"

"Every morning. But they don't stay clean long."

She looked around in disgust. "Men are such pigs."

"You've noticed," Higgins said, leaning her back into the door, preventing anyone from intruding.

"We wondered why we didn't find any personal things of yours in his apartment," Higgins asked her while she was still in the toilet stall.

"Joe wouldn't permit it," she responded. "He said that he didn't want me to leave anything incriminating. Not even in his medicine cabinet." The toilet flushed and the witness walked out of the stall, heading for the sink on the other side of the bathroom.

"Did he ever mention his wife?"

"No," Mrs. Hunt said, taking a handful of brown paper towels from the shelf above the sink and cleaning off the sink and the soap-splattered mirror. "I asked Joe if he was seeing any other woman and he assured me he wasn't. I was concerned with catching something." She balled up the towels and tossed them into the cardboard waste barrel next to the sink. Then she washed her face and hands.

Higgins remained on guard duty. "Did Joe ever mention any of his business dealings?"

Donna Hunt applied lipstick. "Nooooo."

"What ever possessed you to pose for those photographs?"

Donna Hunt lowered the stick from her lips, studying her reflection in the mirror, pondering the question. "I really don't know. He asked me to do it and I did. I never thought of the consequences."

Mary Posner was the next witness. She arrived thirty minutes after Donna Hunt had left. Posner was elegantly dressed in a white linen suit and heavy summer jewelry. She had short chestnut hair and a mature face that had retained much of its former beauty. Scanlon put her in her early fifties.

"Why the hassle?" Mary Posner said, crossing her legs and tucking her skirt under.

"No hassle," Scanlon said. "We'd just like to ask you a few questions concerning your relationship with Joe Gallagher."

Mary Posner reached into her leather pocketbook and removed a box of foreign cigarettes and lit one. "I don't like men very much. I wonder sometimes why I keep going to bed with them."

"It has something to do with the genes."

Mary Posner chortled. "You're cute for a cop." A look of concern came over her. "Before I answer your *fercockta* questions I want to know if you found a photograph of me in Gallagher's home-away-from-home."

"We did."

"I want it back."

"That can be arranged."

"Arranged my ass. No pitchee, no talkee." She flipped ash off to the side.

He watched her, not talking.

She took another drag on her cigarette and coughed. "I take it back, you're not cute."

He waited.

She tapped her foot, annoyed. At length she said, "Look, Lieutenant. I got a problem and I can use your help."

"We all have problems, Mary. A police lieutenant and a candy store lady have been murdered. That's a problem."

"I sure as hell didn't kill them."

"No one said you did."

She leaned out of her seat and reached for the brown department-issue ashtray on his desk. Thoughtfully stubbing out the cigarette, she said, "Sy Posner is my husband. He's one of the biggest factors in the garment district. Sy finances a lot of the rags that are made there. He's my last shot in life. I've been married three times before Sy and have been knocking around since before the Boer War. Sy and I have only been married three years. His first wife died five years ago. They'd been married for thirty-seven years and in all that time Sy had never been unfaithful." A disbelieving smile parted her lips. "Sy was probably the only faithful Jew on Fashion Avenue. Sy never had a big sex drive, and now that he's older . . ."

"I understand," Scanlon said. "Tell me about you and Joe Gallagher."

Mary Posner sighed in resignation and began to recount her first meeting with the dead police lieutenant. Gallagher had used the same old traffic-stop ploy to meet her, the one that many cops use to meet women. But unlike Donna Hunt, this witness was no novice at infidelity. She had played the game from both sides of the street, as the wife and as the girlfriend. Her relationship with Gallagher had been brief. "I don't like kinky men."

"What do you mean by that?"

She told Scanlon of Gallagher getting up out of the bed and returning with the vibrator and anal love beads, and asking her if she liked to experiment. "I looked him right in the eye and said, 'Listen, kiddo, I've done all the experimenting I intend to do. The only thing that gets into my behind is suppositories.' I told him that if he was so hot on anal love he could string the goddamn beads up his own ass."

"What was his reaction?"

"He laughed and claimed he was only kidding. But I saw that

tense look he was wearing. Your dead lieutenant was a sicky, a weirdo in blue. He proved that later."

"What happened later?"

She looked at her hands, examining brown spots. "We made love and then he dozed off. After a while he awoke and we went at it again. But this time when he was ready he withdrew and dirtied my stomach. Then he went down between my legs and licked up his own mess. I've been with a lot of men and none of them ever went in for anything like that. Your dead hero was a fag."

Scanlon exhaled. He looked over at Higgins and Colon, who both shrugged.

"Can you tell me anything else?" Scanlon asked.

The witness told how Gallagher had slid from the bed and gone to the closet and taken out a Polaroid camera and snapped her picture. She told of leaping naked from the bed trying to get the camera away from him. He was too strong for her. She never saw him again after that. She half expected him to try to blackmail her, sell the photograph back to her. But she never heard from him again.

"How long ago was that?" Scanlon asked, watching her face for the lie.

"Seven, eight months ago."

"Did you always go to his Jackson Heights apartment?"

She scoffed. "Some dump."

"Did he ever ask you for money?"

"I don't give men money. It usually works the other way around, presents and stuff."

Scanlon opened the top drawer of his desk and took out one of the Polaroids that he'd found in Gallagher's locker. He held it up to her. "You?"

"Me," she said in a disgusted tone. "Look at those thighs and that flab. I'm going on a diet."

"I can't let you have this back now. But I promise you that as soon as the case is over, I'll get it back to you."

"Are you going to have to use that photo in court?" she asked with a worried tone.

He held out a calming hand. "No way. I promise you that." He saw her relax and wondered why Donna Hunt had not asked him to return her photograph.

C. Aubrey White was one of the legal carnivores who show up each morning before the start of court to prey on the distressed relatives and friends of prisoners who were arrested the night before and were scheduled for morning arraignment. The arresting officer was the usual shill. He'd introduce the relative or friend to the lawyer and then discreetly leave to draw up the complaint, giving the lawyer time to discuss his fee. After being retained and extracting as much money up front as he could, the eminent member of the bar would then be most punctilious in his adherence to the most sacred of judicial ethics: bleed 'em and plead 'em. During one of the numerous defense-requested adjournments the arresting officer would be slipped his fifteen percent finder's fee, in cash, of course.

Scanlon was taken aback when he saw the silver-haired lawyer, accompanied by a woman in her early twenties, enter the squad room. He did not like C. Aubrey White or the rest of the legal carnivores, or the cops who did business with them, but like so many cops Scanlon realized there was nothing that he could do about it. The practice of "steering" had been going on for years, a practice that every judge and every district attorney in criminal justice was aware of and deplored, a practice that enhanced the contempt that honest cops felt for the system.

C. Aubrey White gripped his silver-topped cane and shifted his considerable weight forward, resting on it. "Tony, ol' friend, comrade in arms, this child is my dear sister's daughter, Rena Bedford. She asked her uncle Aubrey to accompany her to the Bastille in the hope of straightening out whatever minor unpleasantness might exist concerning her relationship with the departed hero, Joe Gallagher."

Rena Bedford was a pretty young thing with long hair the color of almonds. She had brown eyes and the bemused look of eternal virginity. Scanlon found it hard to imagine her getting it on with Joe Gallagher.

The lawyer was talking. "What's it about, Tony?"

"A few ends need tidying, Counselor."

A thoughtful smile set on the lawyer's lips. "Is my niece the subject of a criminal investigation?"

Scanlon's answer was forthright. "No."

"Might my niece be the subject of an accusatory instrument?"

"I cannot envision such a possibility." Scanlon noted that there was a faint smile on Rena Bedford's lips.

The lawyer waved his hand in front of him, making circles. He had the look of a man ready to expound life's mysteries. "Permit me, if you will, the opportunity to paraphrase a few recent decisions. . . ." Scanlon raised his hand in an effort to stop the legal harangue but instead dropped it in defeat, resigned to listening. Cops learn early not to interrupt lawyers when they are giving a performance for their client; it makes the lawyer uppity and hostile.

C. Aubrey White droned on. ". . . during a criminal investigation, a subject who has an attorney may not be interrogated about the case even though he has not been arrested and is not in custody, after the subject's attorney tells the police not to question his client in his absence, *People* versus *Skinner*."

Scanlon's nerves were sending strong signals to his phantom leg. Lew Brodie was sitting on a chair with the back turned front, listening and punching his palm with his fist. His eyes were bloodshot, his shirttail on the left side was hanging out, and the veins in his temples were throbbing.

Howard Christopher, who considered all lawyers to be communist, with the sole exception of Roy Cohn, was standing by the wall, glaring at the lawyer and munching julienne carrot sticks. A bad sign.

". . . when a defendant is represented by an attorney in a criminal matter, the policeman may not question him about any unrelated matter without the defendant's lawyer being present, *People* versus *Rogers*."

Scanlon wondered why it was necessary for lawyers to always put their legal prowess on display. He glanced up at the department clock, which had the day divided by civilian and military time, and decided the time had come to end the performance. Other witnesses were scheduled after Rena Bedford, and he didn't like the look on Brodie's and Christopher's faces. A shouting match between his detectives and the lawyer was most definitely not needed, so he let the lawyer say a few more things and then held up a pleading hand. "Counselor, spare us, please. We all read the legal bulletins. If your niece would prefer not to talk to us, that's okay. I'll just subpoena her before the grand jury. You of course realize that in that case, I'll not be able to guarantee confidentiality. You're aware of the tendency of grand juries to leak testimony to the press." He sketched a gesture in the air. "'Coed in love nest with hero cop.' The mothers'll sell an extra fifty thousand copies at your niece's expense."

C. Aubrey White gripped the cane with both hands, pouting. "No big megillah, Tony." He glanced sideways at his niece. "You don't mind talking to these gentlemen, do you, dear?"

"Of course not, Uncle Aubrey," she said, casting her modest eyes downward.

Rena Bedford was a graduate student in Social Work and Human Development at the New School. A year ago she had taken a course in Urban Art. One of the requisites of the course was a visit to a subway train yard on Pennsylvania Avenue in East New York to study how urban Rembrandts profane public property with graffiti. It had been an elective course.

While driving her blue Porsche 944 along Linden Boulevard on the way to the train park, she had been stopped by policemen in an unmarked car. They had placed a flashing red light on their dashboard and motioned her to pull over. Two policemen in old clothes got out of the police car and came up to her. They told her that her car matched the description of a car that had just been used in a bank robbery. She protested and showed them her license and registration. An older man got out of the police car and came up to them. He was tall and had a commanding presence. He told her his name was Joe Gallagher, and they began to talk. He was an interesting man, and before she realized it they were discussing city planning. The other two policemen drifted back to their car. She liked the sound of Gallagher's voice, and thought he was cute, and since she was into getting it on with older men, she gave him her telephone number. From that point on, Rena Bedford's story paralleled those of the other witnesses. Only she was more graphic in her details of their sexual encounters.

Watching her sparkling face, Scanlon realized that she didn't wear makeup and had the kind of look that advertising people called country-fresh.

Rena Bedford had not shied away from Gallagher when he approached her with the vibrator and anal love beads; nor did she hesitate to pose for him, or join in the threesome. "A woman should experience all that there is to experience before she settles down," she said calmly, staring at Scanlon with her wide, modest eyes.

When she had finished her tale, Scanlon asked casually for the name of the other female participant in the threesome. "Luise Bardwell."

"Did Gallagher ever discuss money with you or tell you anything about his job, or his personal life?"

"No. The only thing we ever discussed was doing it. He was really into that." She tilted her head, as though trying to recall a faint memory. "Once he told me that one of his buddies had come into some money and that they were thinking of going into business together."

"Did he tell you the name of his buddy, or mention the kind of business?"

"No, he didn't."

Valerie Clarkson was the fourth witness scheduled to appear. She never showed. Repeated telephone calls to her home went unanswered. Scanlon sent a Telephone Message to her resident precinct, the Ninth, requesting them to dispatch an RMP to her home. The notification that the Nine-three Squad received back ended with the initials NR. Valerie Clarkson was not in her residence. A neighbor on the first floor of her six-story Manhattan walk-up stated that he had seen her leaving her apartment about midday. She was carrying an overnight case. She seemed to be in a hurry, the witness had stated.

At 1500 that afternoon the detectives gathered about a desk in the Nine-three squad room to eat lunch: three large pizzas, two six-packs of Miller Light, and a diet 7-Up for Higgins. Christopher was off in a corner watching his favorite soap, "The Guiding Light," and eating plain yogurt mixed with raw cashews. Biafra Baby was leaning against a desk arguing with his wife over the telephone. Higgins waved a crust at the detectives gathered around the desk. "Joe Gallagher was a perv."

"Women and the ponies are expensive vices on a married lieutenant's salary," Christopher joined in, intensely watching the screen. (John was about to confess his infidelity with his sister-in-law.)

Lew Brodie nibbled a strand of melted cheese. "Maybe Gallagher had a main squeeze who was picking up his tabs?"

Colon joined in: "And maybe this main squeeze didn't cotton to him two-timin' her and when she found out she got pissed off and had him whacked." He began to slowly lick the end of his crust, staring pointedly at Higgins's breasts.

"She'd know," Higgins riposted, looking away from Colon and folding her arms across her chest.

Biafra Baby slammed down the receiver and stalked over to them, mumbling curses. He threw himself into a chair, grabbed up a slice, and sat shaking his head.

"Wassa matter?" Brodie asked.

"That damn woman!" Biafra Baby said. "She spends half my salary givin' my kids lessons tryin' to turn them into bionic black people. I pay for piano lessons, and ballet lessons, and elocution lessons so they can learn to speak like white folk. But this time she has gone too far. She's givin' my son basketball lessons! He's the only black kid in the whole country who pays to learn how to play basketball."

Lew Brodie nodded thoughtfully. "That's what happens when you take 'em out of the ghet-to."

A contemplative silence was broken by Brodie peeling off the top of a beer can and tossing the tab into the wastebasket. "I still think one of his lady friends had him whacked," Brodie said, reaching down the front of his trousers to scratch his testicles.

Higgins looked away.

Biafra Baby reached in for another slice. As he did he lifted one buttock up to one side and passed wind.

Higgins heaved out of her seat. "You're disgusting!" she said, leaving the squad room.

"Where you going, *señorita?*" Colon called to her back.

"To a restaurant, to eat with normal people," she said over her shoulder.

They watched her storm out of the squad room and slam the door behind her.

Folding a slice, Biafra Baby said, "They never shoulda let women in the Job."

Scanlon pondered talking to them about their deportment in front of Higgins. The personnel and management texts said he should, but his instincts told him not to. It was something they were going to have to work out among themselves.

Higgins walked back into the squad room twenty minutes later. The other detectives were cleaning up the lunch mess. She hurried over to the ringing telephone and pushed down the flashing button.

"Nine-three Squad, Suckieluski." The fictitious Detective Suckieluski was a cop's equivalent of an answering machine. There was one such phantom in every squad. Higgins listened. Covering the mouthpiece, she signaled Scanlon with a glance and mouthed, "It's Dr. Zimmerman, the son."

Scanlon took the receiver and said, "Hello."

A deep voice at the other end demanded to know what progress had been made on his mother's murder. Scanlon was told that many family members were distressed that no police official had taken the time to come and inform them of the details of his mother's death.

"We thought it appropriate to wait a day or two before contacting you," Scanlon said.

"We are sitting shivah at my home. I'd appreciate it if you would come by tomorrow."

Saturday was his regular day off. Scanlon had nothing planned except to do his laundry and some vague inclination to spend some part of the evening with his hooker friend, Sally De Nesto. He plucked a pencil from the empty coffee can and wrote down the address and told the doctor that he would be there tomorrow afternoon, about one.

When he hung up, Colon gave him a bewildered look. "Tomorrow's your RDO."

"*Noblesse oblige*," Scanlon said, walking into his office.

"What's this *noblesse oblige?*" Colon said.

"It means that you don't gotta be a fucking putz all your life," Brodie said, arching a dead soldier into the wastebasket.

Sgt. George Harris had applied for and was granted four successive tours of emergency leave with pay. He was going to stand by the coffin in his dress uniform, with white gloves, and a mourning band stretched around his gold sergeant's shield.

All the members of Gallagher's buy-and-bust unit would be in attendance. They were authorized by the *Patrol Guide* to wear mourning bands on their shields when they were in uniform from the day of death until 2400 hours on the tenth day after death. Other members of the force were permitted to display their grief from the time of death until 2400 hours on the day of the funeral. As the dead lieutenant's friend and close colleague, Harris had incurred traditional responsibilities. It would be he who would greet the grieving members of the department as they lined up to pay respects at the closed coffin; it would be he who would be responsible for seeing that the gold lieutenant's shield was removed from the top of the coffin when it was removed from the funeral home and would return the badge to the chief clerk's office; it would be he who would be assigned to see to the needs of the bereaved family.

When Harris walked into the Nine-three squad room shortly before 1500 he was wearing jeans and a blue work shirt. "The grapevine says that Joe was hit," Harris said to Scanlon after introducing himself.

Scanlon stared at Harris's manicured nails and black cowboy boots, and noticed the way the man tilted his lithe body to the right. His thumbs were tucked into the side pockets of his jeans.

"Where did you latch on to that information?" Scanlon said.

"That's the word that's going around the One-fourteen."

Scanlon was solemn. "Well, we don't want the word to leak out, especially to the press."

"So it is true."

"We're not sure. It might be."

Harris casually stretched out his boot and hooked the tip around the leg of a chair and dragged his seat over. He sat. "Not to worry, Lou. I'll see to it personally that every cop assigned to the One-fourteen puts a zipper on his mouth."

Leaning back in his seat, Scanlon locked his hands behind his head and said, "Answer a few questions?"

"You kiddin' or somethin'? Joe Gallagher wasn't only my boss, he was my friend. We were partners, worked the adjoining posts in the old Seven-seven. He brought me into the junk squad. You better believe I'll do anything to get the cocksuckers who wasted Joe."

"Did Joe ever discuss his gambling or his love life with you?"

Harris was annoyed. "Chasing pussy and gambling are a national pastime. Don't look to paint Joe bad just because he was human."

"I've spoken to a few of his lady friends. They tell me that his bedroom tastes ran the gamut from strange to kinky."

"Come on, Lou! What the hell is kinky today? Especially in this town. The damn city is being run by a clique of goddamn faggots. The Thirteenth just arrested two morgue attendants for screwing corpses. You got ten- and eleven-year-old boys peddling their asses along the Great White Way, and the movies' leading lady is into fucking German shepherds." Harris was agitated, shaking his fist. "And you talk to me about kinky sex? Joe Gallagher never forced any woman into bed. They went because they wanted to, and they did whatever they did because they wanted to."

A nod of the head, a flash of teeth. Scanlon recognized a good argument when he heard one. "Did his wife know that he was stepping out on her?"

"I don't know. But I don't think it would have mattered. Joe once told me Mary Ann was frigid."

"How is she taking it?"

"Pretty bad."

"I'm going to have to interview her, I'm afraid."

Harris thought it over in silence and then said, "I know. But can't it wait till after the funeral?"

"I guess so. When is it?"

"Monday morning."

"Did Joe ever talk to you about his gambling?"

Harris examined his boots. He buffed the right one on the back of his jeans. "He never discussed it with me, because he knew how I felt about it."

"And how did you feel about it, Sarge?"

"It's strictly for assholes. Only the bookmakers and the shys come away winners."

Scanlon changed the subject. "How do you like living on Staten Island?"

Harris shrugged and said, "It's okay. It beats driving in from the

Island. But it's no bargain having to drive over the guinea gang-plank every day, and it's expensive."

Scanlon felt his adrenaline rise at the sneering reference to the Verrazano Narrows Bridge. The complete urban cop, he thought bitterly. Jeans, cowboy boots, and a big mouth. "Did Joe change much after he became a boss?"

"Hah. Joe was always the public relations type. I remember when we worked in the Seven-seven, old Captain McCloskey called us into his office because our summonses were off. In those days the quota was ten parkers and five movers a month. We hadn't given out any in three months. McCloskey was really pissed off. He called us the worst cops in the precinct. Named us Useless and Lukewarm. Joe was Useless. McCloskey yelled at us, demanding to know why no summonses. Joe got his Irish up and yelled back. He told McCloskey that he didn't believe in hanging paper on working stiffs' cars, costing them a day's pay, while across the river the rich bastards are allowed to double- and triple-park all over the place and nobody does shit about it. He asked McCloskey if he'd ever driven through the theater district, or past the Waldorf, or down Fifth or Park Avenue, and seen the mounted cops who'd been assigned to help the rich triple-park their limousines. McCloskey had a shit fit and threw us out of his office. We were lucky he was transferred the following week, because he was getting ready to come down hard on us."

Summonses were a familiar sore spot for policemen. That was why precinct commanders were forced to have summons men. For doing this onerous duty summons men were taken out of the patrol chart and worked days, with weekends off. Statistics must be maintained.

"What was Joe like as a boss?" Scanlon asked.

Harris gave him a half-smile. "He was different, I'll say that much for him. And he'd gotten over the ambivalence of being a boss. He made it damn clear to everyone in the unit that he was the boss man. 'Don't do as I do, do as I say,' he'd tell them."

Scanlon leaned forward. "Herman the German told me that Joe wasn't much of a leader."

"Lou, you know as well as I do that there are a lot of ways to supervise people. Joe really hated the paper connected with the job. Herman the German is a paper pusher. That was the main reason why Joe had me brought into the unit, to take care of the paper while he played cops and robbers and partied. He was one of the greatest PR men I've ever known. But he was a tough cop when it came to things that he took seriously. And junk was number one on Joe's hit parade. Our unit led the entire Narcotics Division in buy-and-bust collars. There was no bullshit about him when it came to the Job. Every person in the unit was personally picked by Joe. And if a guy produced for him and needed a day, and had no time on the books, Joe'd give him the day and swallow the Twenty-eight."

"Where do you think he got his gambling money from?"

"I don't know. I never asked him."

"I've never been assigned to the junk squad, so I'm not too clear on how the buy money works. Tell me, will you?"

A hostile edge crept into Harris's voice. "Forget it. Every nickel has to be accounted for."

"I understand that, Sarge. But tell me anyway, please."

Harris shook his head. "We always have a few grand on hand to make buys. Our undercovers sign out the money, usually a few hundred at a time. They have to sign vouchers, and each time a buy goes down it has to be observed by a supervisor, or at least it's supposed to be. But naturally, sometimes a supervisor can't see what's going down because they're in a basement or on a roof. But anyway, buying junk is the same as buying chop meat at the supermarket. A pound of eye round cost so much and a bag of junk cost so much. An undercover can't say he paid forty dollars for nose candy when the going rate on the street is thirty. The humps in IAD who monitor our funds know what the price is as well as we do."

"Does your unit ever deal in kilo weight?"

"Depends on how many keys. We can deal up to thirty grand— after that we have to ask permission from the division to play. If it's a real heavy deal, we turn it over to the boys in Special Investigations. And sometimes the deal can be so big that we turn it over to the federal boys."

"How often is the fund audited?"

"Every quarter. And there are unannounced spot audits, too. There ain't no way anybody can play around with that money."

"There's always a way, Sarge. Some enterprising cop just has to think of it." Scanlon picked up a cigar packet, saw that it was empty, and rummaged around in the top drawer of his desk for his reserve supply. While doing this, he asked in a low voice, "Luise Bardwell your girlfriend?"

Harris's expression turned ugly. "Stay out of my private life, Scanlon."

"Lieutenant Scanlon, Sergeant. And by the way, my mother's name was Vitale." He found the green-and-white box behind an old *Rules and Procedures* manual.

"My private life is none of the department's business." A declarative statement that every cop knew to be false.

Scanlon took his time lighting up, studying the man in front of him. He got up and went over to the low metal library cabinet against the wall, pushed one of the sliding glass doors aside, and removed the *Patrol Guide* from the top shelf. He balanced the thick blue book on his palm, holding it in front of him. "Sergeant, I give you the Job's holy bible. In particular, I'd like to call your attention to procedure one-oh-four slash one, six pages of prohibited conduct printed single-space. Everything from engaging in unnecessary conversation while on patrol to incurring liabilities which cannot be paid as they become due. Now, I can't quote you chapter and verse, but I *can* guarantee that somewhere in these six pages is a phrase that goes something like this: 'If married, thou shall not lie with another.'" He returned the book to its place in the cabinet. He had enjoyed his little performance, particularly when he had addressed Harris as Sergeant. *Lieutenant* Scanlon, Sergeant. Perhaps lawyers did have the right idea; a little drama is good for the soul.

Harris caved in reluctantly. "The lady is married."

"Aren't they all, George." The plastic button on the telephone flashed. He slapped it down and brought the receiver up.

Deputy Chief MacAdoo McKenzie's strained voice informed him that the PC wanted to see both of them, together. Forthwith, he added ominously.

"Right," Scanlon said, hanging up. He stared intensely at Harris. "I know that Gallagher participated in a threesome with your girlfriend."

Harris made a dismissive gesture. "Luise is a strange lady. The threesome was her idea. She's into that kind of stuff. She never wanted any kids because they leave stretch marks."

"She goes both ways?"

"Yes. She's open about it, too."

"How did Joe get involved with her?"

"Luise first brought up the subject to me. Said she wanted to get it on with me and a woman who she had been having an affair with. I told her that that wasn't my bag and suggested Joe. She liked the idea a whole lot."

"Didn't it ever bother you that Joe and your lady friend were going to hop into the feathers together, not to mention the fact that she went both ways?"

Harris made a weary little gesture. "That thing she's got between her legs don't have an odometer on it, and it don't wear out. As long as the lady is available when I want to see her, I don't give a good shit what she does or with whom."

True love is wonderful, Scanlon thought. "What's the story with the lady's husband?"

"They have an open marriage. He's a psychoanalyst with a fancy Manhattan practice. Luise told me that he ain't above taking a little tap in the ass every now and then. She told me that they sit around the dinner table discussing their adventures with each other."

"Then the husband knew all about you and Joe and the three-some."

"I got to assume that he did."

"I'm going to have to talk to both of them," Scanlon said.

"Lou, do what you gotta do. I'm on your side." He began to run his nails over the blue denim, studying the white strain in the fabric. "I've asked the borough commander to assign me to the case. Any objections?"

"No. But if you really want to help, I'd prefer you to stay where you are. Mix with the people in your unit, with the cops in the precinct. I need some ears over there. I have to find out where Joe got his gambling money."

"I'll do what I can, but it won't be easy. Cops clam up whenever they think there might be a problem."

6

The anteroom of the PC's fourteenth-floor office at police headquarters was surrounded by a glass wall. Blue sofas, low white tables made of plastic, and chrome tubular sand-filled receptacles for cigarette butts filled the area. People waiting their turn to see the PC talked in hushed voices, or kept their faces buried in magazines, while they silently rehearsed the arguments that they would use on the police commissioner.

On the other side of the glass wall, to the left of the double door, sat the PC's aide. He was a tall, lean man with short hair and spit-shined shoes whose tailored uniform bore the gilt oak leaf of a deputy inspector. Occasionally he would glance up from the stack of Unusual Occurrence reports to check the lights over the door; the red one was still on.

Deputy Chief MacAdoo McKenzie was also watching the red light. He thought that the damn thing had been on for an interminable length of time when in fact it had only been three minutes. Scanlon was sitting next to him, browsing through the latest issue of *Police Magazine*. An article entitled "The Keys to K-9 Success" had caught his attention. He wondered if a canine corps might not be the answer that everyone was searching for. Enough properly trained dogs let loose in high-crime areas at night might reduce the two-legged-animal population who stalked the streets and subway stations. He liked that idea. He liked it a lot. When those doggies made a pinch, they *really* made a pinch!

The silver-haired pastor of the Harlem Tabernacle Baptist Church was there to ask the PC if he would be disposed to transfer the pastor's nephew, a God-fearing boy, from an active patrol precinct in the South Bronx to the Detective Division. The lad had confided to his uncle that he would really enjoy an assignment in the Pickpocket and Confidence Squad. The pastor intended to remind the commissioner of the help that he had given the department in defeating the move by some Harlem liberals to civilianize the Civilian Complaint Review Board.

The president and the recording secretary of the Gravesend Planning Board were huddled on one of the sofas rehearsing the argument they would use to persuade the PC to assign additional police to the Six-one.

E. Thornton Gray, the executive director of the American Civil Rights Union, was one of the people waiting. He passed the time reading the *Wall Street Journal.* He was a content man. And with good reason. Alza had closed yesterday at twenty-eight a share. He had bought five thousand shares at five in January of '81.

Gray was privy to a lot of inside information concerning future business trends and mergers. Captains of industry wanted him for their friend. They knew how to discreetly nurture a friendship: a chance remark over cocktails, a slip of the tongue after an apéritif. And a quick call to one's broker.

Gray wanted to see the PC because he had heard disquieting rumors that the department was testing a new heavyweight bullet. Gray had led the fight several years ago to force the police department to adopt a lighter load of ammunition, thereby reducing the bullet's stopping power. The police hierarchy had caved in under the political pressure. This abject surrender resulted in policemen being maimed and killed. When Abou 37X and a detective locked arms on a Harlem street corner and began shooting at each other, they were inches apart. Yet the detective's new bullets bounced harmlessly off 37X's field jacket. An FBI agent's bullet had brought the fugitive down, but not before the detective had been wounded. As police casualties mounted, the evidence grew overwhelming: the bullets that the police were using were not as effective as they should be in today's hostile environment. Police line organizations had waged an uphill fight for a new bullet. The department, stung by the increase in police injuries, had reluctantly agreed to start tests on a heavier cartridge. E. Thornton Gray intended to do everything in his power to prevent that from coming to pass.

Scanlon tossed the magazine onto the table and let his eyes roam around the room. They came to rest on a vaguely familiar face at the other end. The face had a dour expression and belonged to a broad-chested man with brownish-gray hair. He tried to remember where he knew that face from. A glimmer of remembrance. He nudged Deputy Chief MacAdoo McKenzie. "Isn't that Inspector Loyd?"

MacAdoo McKenzie whispered, "He's been assigned by the mayor to baby-sit the PC."

"Has it gotten that bad?"

"It has. Hardly a week goes by that Bobby Boy isn't stopped for driving his private car on one of the city's streets in an intoxicated condition. Up to now all the cops who have pulled him over have done the right thing. But it only takes one incident to be page one."

"That's too bad," Scanlon said, stealing a look at Inspector Loyd. He didn't care about the PC's little drinking problem but he felt sorry that Loyd was stuck with such a miserable job.

"That's only the half of it. He used to be in the closet with his lady friends, but lately he's taken to waltzing them around town. A few weeks ago he showed up in Part 3B of Criminal Court with one of his Carmelitas. Both of them had a load on. He started to throw his weight around the courtroom, disrupting the proceedings, and the judge came within inches of tossing him into the slammer for contempt. He was lucky that a lot of cops were there to hustle his ass out before the judge came down on him. So poor Loyd's been assigned to keep him out of trouble."

Bob Gomez paced the handsomely furnished office in front of the great desk that had once belonged to another police commissioner, Teddy Roosevelt. Sunlight filled the office. Gomez made a dashing figure: tall, erect, with a caramel-colored face that belied its fifty-three years. An extremely well-built man for his age, he was, as always, immaculately attired in a tailor-made sport jacket and slacks. His brown loafers had wide tassels.

Today's hangover was a particularly bad one. The belt of pain was like a vise on his forehead. They were getting progressively worse. He was just going to have to stop drinking. If he didn't, it was only a question of time until the mayor got rid of him. And he liked having cognizance and control over the largest police department in the country. But he knew the Job could only protect him so far. That was it, he resolved. No more booze.

Gomez was also annoyed at himself for having made a fool of himself in front of those goddamn television cameras at the scene of the Gallagher/Zimmerman homicide. He should have listened to the first dep's whispered message that there might be a problem, and his advice that Gomez play down the hero angle. If there was a scandal brewing over Gallagher's death he didn't want to be dragged into it. He'd been lucky so far in his relationship with the press and the rest of the power brokers. He had gone out of his way to maintain open lines of communications with the news media and the rest of them. And it had paid off. He did their favors for them, promoted their damn friends and relatives, spoke at their goddamn dinners, assigned motorcycle escorts to them whenever their inflated egos required it. And, in return, they praised him as the best police commissioner that the city had ever had.

He had been able, by manipulating crime statistics, to give the impression that crime had actually been reduced under his administration. We're winning the war; we've turned the corner. Bullshit. He had been surprised that no other PC had thought of the idea.

At his first Precinct Commanders' Conference he had told them, obliquely, to handle their Sixty-one forms "with discretion." Wise and wary men, tutored by years of experience in the subtle nuances of cop talk, understood. Soon grand larcenies were being classified petit larcenies; robberies were downgraded to simple assaults; burglaries were turned into malicious mischiefs. An outstanding PC, Gomez reflected sardonically and walked back to his desk. One of his major concerns now was the damn cops. They were forever pulling off outlandish stunts that ended up in the press. Yesterday he had read a report from IAD about a radio car team in the Tenth who not only abandoned their assigned sector, but abandoned the entire city. They drove out to Suffolk County to attend a lawn party the recorder's girlfriend was giving. In a police car, no less. He was going to have to start handing down stiffer penalties in the Trial Room. No more Mister Nice Guy. But right now his main concern was this Gallagher mess. He was terrified by the possibility that it might not sink into serene oblivion fast enough.

He stood in front of the large picture window peering out through the white vertical blinds. The rays of a dying sun felt strong as his eyes moved along the tops of the buildings of lower Manhattan. Far below he noticed a mounted cop checking the parked cars along Worth Street. A group of tourists were being shepherded through the vaulted underpass of the Municipal Building. A five-member band was playing ragtime for the tourists in Police Plaza Park. He thought about the next day. He was scheduled to pay a visit to Gallagher's widow and present her with five thousand dollars from the Police Welfare Fund. The press was sure to be in heavy attendance. He'd wear a dark suit and a grieved expression and pose with the widow and her fatherless child, or was it children? He couldn't remember, and what did it matter, anyway? What was important was that it would be good PR. Moving away from the window, he stepped up to the row of buttons on his desk.

Deputy Chief MacAdoo McKenzie shot upright in his seat and nudged Scanlon when he saw the green light flick on.

As the doors to his office began to open, Bob Gomez quickly grabbed the top report from the Urgent/In basket and began to read it. The report proved to be the translation of the Mexican police report on the arrest of José Torres, the escaped FALN terrorist who was known throughout the Job as No Hands because he had lost both his hands when he accidentally blew up his East Village bomb factory. "Damn Ricans could never handle that high-tech stuff," a Bomb Squad member had commented at the time.

Gomez read slowly and did not look up as his aide led the two police officials inside and quietly left the room.

They waited in front of the great desk, watching as the PC initialed the last page of the report and tossed it into the Urgent/Out basket.

With a sweep of his hand, Gomez motioned them to sit in the cushioned chairs arranged in front of his desk. "I'm glad that you both could manage to tear yourself away from your other pressing duties and come have a little chat with me," Gomez said.

Scanlon looked past the PC out the window to the glass-and-stone side of Pace University. Eager, wide-eyed students were in that building learning all there was to learn about the function of government in contemporary society. How little they'll learn, he thought, relaxing, ready for the civics lesson that he knew was about to begin.

Gomez said ominously, "I would like to know why I was not thoroughly briefed at the Gallagher crime scene." His glare fell on McKenzie, placing blame.

The deputy chief cleared his throat and squirmed. "It was my understanding that the first dep had been informed that there might be a problem."

"The first dep is *not* the PC. I am. And I should have been personally advised that Gallagher might be dirty."

Scanlon was looking down at his prosthesis; he had crossed the fake one over the real one. He looked up, his black eyes boring into the PC's angry face. "You were told," he said calmly.

Gomez sat ramrod-straight, his hostile stare fixed on Scanlon, his fingertips drumming on his desk. "Nobody told me *anything*, Lieutenant." His twisted face betrayed his lie. "But I do expect you to tell me now. I want to know exactly where the department stands on the Gallagher/Zimmerman homicide. And I want it all."

Unruffled, with professional nonchalance, Scanlon told the PC about the splash pad in Jackson Heights, the sexual aids to happiness, the girlfriends, the threesome, the gambling, the indebtedness to Walter Ticornelli, the shylock. When he'd finished, he leaned back in his seat and waited.

Gomez leaned his head back against the cushioned headrest of the high-backed chair and closed his eyes, sorting it all out.

A minute passed.

Gomez opened his eyes and spoke. "Yesterday in Federal Court, Detective Alfred Martin was convicted of kidnapping and robbing diamond dealers here and in PR. The *Daily News* ran five lines on page sixty-three, right next to an ad for Kal Kan dog food. The *Times* gave it ten lines on the obituary page. When Martin was arrested a year ago it was page one for three days and then died a natural death. But this Gallagher thing is different. It's the kind of story the press gets off on. It has page-one ingredients. Staying power. 'Sixty Minutes' would probably want to do a piece on the sex lives of American police." He was stern. "Gentlemen, this department, and *this* commissioner, does not want, or need, that kind of publicity." He shook his index finger at them. "No more rotten apples. What we want and need are heroes. John Waynes in blue. And I would be very appreciative if you two saw to it that Lt. Joseph P. Gallagher remained a hero, one of our honored dead." He raised his left eyebrow, sliding his gaze from one to the other. "Is my meaning perfectly clear, gentlemen?"

MacAdoo McKenzie pulled a filthy handkerchief from his rear pocket and wiped the sweat from his neck. "We understand, Commissioner. Whatever you want."

A smile appeared on Scanlon's lips. Every cop in the Job knows that every boss in the Job above the rank of captain has feet of clay. But when it goes up to their balls, it's hard to watch. "And what exactly do we do if the facts of the case do not warrant Gallagher's canonization?" Scanlon asked.

The PC checked the time. "Thank you for stopping by, gentlemen." Gomez pushed up out of his chair and went to the door. McKenzie followed. Scanlon remained seated. "Aren't you leaving, Lieutenant?" Gomez said.

"I'd like an answer to my question, Commissioner," Scanlon said, staring out the window at the distant clouds.

Gomez walked up behind him and whispered in his ear, "You do whatever you have to do, Lieutenant. But don't get me involved or it will be your ass."

Scanlon nodded his understanding and got up.

"I want a tight span of control on this," Gomez said. "You, Chief, will report directly to me. Lieutenant, you report to Chief McKenzie and to *no one else.*"

"And exactly what do I say to the chief of detectives when he calls and wants to know the status of the case?"

"You may tell that runty, Napoleonic psychopath to call me personally."

I guess they don't like each other very much, Scanlon thought, leaving the office.

It was after six that Friday when Scanlon arrived at Luise Bardwell's Battery Park penthouse. She was waiting as he stepped off the elevator. Five seven or so, he reckoned, trim body, capped teeth and a broad smile. She was barefooted and had on tight shorts and a white tank top that showed it all.

"Hi," she said cheerily.

"Luise Bardwell?" Scanlon asked, reaching for his shield.

"Yes."

He held up his identification for her inspection. "I'm Lieutenant Scanlon. I telephoned."

"Please come in, Lieutenant."

They were standing in a good-size entry hall of white marble. She led him into a glass-walled living room with a stone fireplace and Art Deco sculpture. "What a view," he said.

"Yes, it's quite nice." She moved ahead and slid open a glass door that led out onto a conservatory overlooking the Hudson River. The moist smell of heat and dirt came at Scanlon as he stepped into the rooftop greenhouse. It was warmer in there than it was outside. Tall plants stood between tables covered with potted greenery. In the corner, set against the glass wall, were two long pieces of furniture made of bleached planks. Patchwork pillows and cushions contrasted with the stark wood.

Luise Bardwell lowered herself onto the plank sofa and patted the space next to her. As Scanlon sat, she fluffed a cushion and pressed it to her chest. "Do you mind sitting out here?"

"Not at all. It's not often that I have the chance to take in such scenery," he said, looking out over the river.

"I find it very peaceful to sit here, with the smell of nature and the great view. Now. How may I be of assistance?"

"I would like you to tell me about your relationship with Joe Gallagher, George Harris, Valerie Clarkson, and Donna Hunt." He waved his hand and added, "And the rest of them."

She made a tut-tut sound, gave him a perplexed look, pressed the cushion close, and said, "My relationship with those people is not the concern of the police department."

"I'm investigating a homicide, Mrs. Bardwell. Not some college prank. I'd appreciate it if you'd answer my questions."

"Do I have to?"

"No, you don't. In that case, I'd have to get a subpoena and usher you in front of the grand jury. If you cooperate now I can guarantee you that there will be no mention of you or your husband to the press, no nasty publicity."

"My husband and I live in an open marriage."

"Hey? Whatever it takes, go with it."

She had a pretty face, a small nose, and a smile that was always there. She wore her yellowish-brown hair short, with bangs.

"I'm bisexual, and so is my husband. We both believe in enjoying the maximum pleasure that life has to offer."

"Will you talk to me about Gallagher and the other people you were involved with?"

"Yes, I will, if you promise that there will be no publicity about it."

"I promise."

"My husband is in his study—would you like to talk to him too?"

"I'd prefer to just speak to you, for now."

"Who shall I tell you about first?"

"Why not start with Harris?"

She ducked her head in a mock gesture of shyness, smiled, and for the next fifty minutes casually discussed her various and sundry relationships. When she'd finished, she rested her chin on the cushion and said, "Actually, I've got the best of both worlds."

"You have no children?"

"No. Max has three from a previous marriage. We have none together. I'm wise enough to know that I'd made a god-awful mother. Beside, I really believe that in this life, I was put on earth to give pleasure to men and to women. Do you believe in rein- carnation, Lieutenant?"

"I never really gave it much thought."

"In one of my previous lives I was an Egyptian princess. My name was Isis and I had a son, Horus. I know that just as sure as the two of us are sitting here."

Scanlon was aware of the ache in his stump. He rubbed his missing ankle. "Tell what kind of a person George Harris is."

"Self-centered, ambitious, with a need to be the man in charge."

"And Joe Gallagher?"

"A sweet man who needed to be in the spotlight. He was always on stage, even in bed."

"How's that?"

"Joe was always looking to do something kinky, or what he thought was kinky. But he didn't really enjoy sex. He had the need to perform."

"And on what basis did you reach that conclusion?"

"I majored in psychology and my husband is a psychiatrist, a rather good one, I might add."

"Did Harris or Gallagher ever discuss their work with you?"

"Not really. Now and then George would feel like letting off steam and talk about their unit. Especially whenever Joe would cancel some decision that George had made."

"Did that happen often?"

"No. But it did occur every now and then, and whenever it did, George got furious."

"How did they get along together otherwise, George and Joe?"

"Pretty good, I think." She raised her foot up off the floor and rested it on the seat of the couch, and began to slowly move her knee back and forth. Her tight shorts embraced the contours of her body, as if teasing Scanlon.

He struggled to keep his eyes topside. "Did Joe ever discuss money with you?"

"Money wasn't his thing."

"What about Harris—was it his thing?"

"Most definitely. Shortly after his divorce I remember George boasting about how he had concealed assets from his wife."

Scanlon hadn't known about Harris's divorce. But that was not unusual in today's Job. The divorce rate was so high that the subject of equitable distribution had long since become a bore to most cops. Still, Harris had not mentioned it. "How long has Harris been divorced?"

"I'm not sure. I guess about two years."

"Did he ever tell you what the assets were that he concealed from his wife?"

"He didn't, and I didn't ask. I deliberately avoid asking lovers questions about their personal lives."

What a sweetheart, he thought. "When you and Harris got together, did you use Gallagher's pad in Jackson Heights or did you use a motel?"

She looked at him queerly. "George would take me to his own apartment."

"On Staten Island?"

"No. He has an apartment on Ocean Parkway, in Brooklyn."

"Did you ever go to Gallagher's apartment in Jackson Heights?"

"Yes, when I went with him and the ladies to have our little threesomes."

"I understand that the threesome was your idea."

"Yes, it was. I don't usually go with blue-collar types, and I thought it might be interesting to see what they were like."

"Is that why you went out with Harris and Gallagher?"

"Yes."

Suddenly two of the biggest cats that Scanlon had ever seen slunk out from behind one of the plants and leaped up on his lap.

"Oh, my babies are here," she said. "I was wondering where you were hiding. This is Puss," she said, petting one of the purring cats. "And my other baby is Fellatio. Aren't they adorable?"

She's a fucking banana, Scanlon thought, taking one of the cats and putting it down. He then picked up the other cat and put it on the floor too.

"Don't you like my babies?"

"I love them, only not on me." He watched the two cats move off behind a plant. "What can you tell me about the women who participated in the threesome?"

"Rena Bedford is a young thing who is into just about anything that will give her a thrill. She was an active participant."

"And Donna Hunt?"

"A middle-aged housewife wanting to savor a bit of life before it's over. Bored with her marriage and her husband."

"Was she an active or passive participant in the threesome?"

She smiled, pressed the cushion close to her chest. "She was very active. I think that she was quite surprised to discover that she was bisexual. And more than a little afraid."

The door to the conservatory opened and a paunchy man with an elfin face and a pepper-and-salt beard appeared. He was wearing black cotton slacks and a wide-collared shirt that was open. A heavy gold chain with a gold figurine of Buddha was around his neck. "Hi, I'm Max Bardwell," he said. "You must be the policeman my wife told me was coming."

Scanlon got up, and the two men shook hands. "Would you like some coffee or a drink?" Max Bardwell asked.

"Coffee might be nice," Scanlon said.

"In that case, why don't we go into the kitchen and I'll make some," Luise Bardwell said, getting up.

Scanlon followed them into a gleaming white kitchen. The wife made coffee. The two men sat at a long white table that had white canvas chairs. "Continue with your questions, Lieutenant," Luise Bardwell said, pouring water into the pot.

"Max, did you know of your wife's involvement with Gallagher and Harris and these women?"

"Yes, I did," the husband said. "Luise and I have no secrets with each other. Most people, including yourself, I guess, would consider our marriage unorthodox. And in the ordinary sense, it is. But it works for us, and that's what counts."

"It doesn't bother you that your wife goes with other people?" Scanlon said, watching the wife lay out cups and saucers.

"No, it doesn't," the wife answered. "My husband knows that I love him and him alone."

"Luise is correct, Lieutenant. Our love for each other is the important thing."

"You're both lucky to have found each other," Scanlon said, looking at the wife. "Tell me about Valerie Clarkson."

She poured coffee and sat down next to her husband. "I brought Valerie out. She's gay. I think that she is much happier now that she knows who she is."

Max patted his wife's hand. "You're a regular little therapist, that's what you are."

Another banana heard from, Scanlon thought. "Do you still see George Harris?"

"No. I stopped seeing him and the rest of them about a month ago."

"Any reason you stopped seeing them?"

"I thought that it was time to move on. Broaden my horizons, so to speak."

"You're telling me, Mrs. Bardwell, that you do not see Harris or any of the women anymore?"

"Yes."

"Lieutenant, according to the newspapers and the radio reports, Gallagher and Mrs. Zimmerman died during an attempted robbery. I can't understand why you are checking into Gallagher's relationship with my wife, or Harris, or the rest of them."

"Whenever we have a double homicide we have to delve deeper into the case to make sure there is no connection that we've overlooked."

"What you are saying is that you are not convinced that it was a holdup murder," the doctor said.

"No, that is *not* what I'm saying," Scanlon said. "The facts of the case bear out that it was a robbery that went sour. But I still have to go through the motions and ask my questions, just to make sure that there is not something there that should be brought out into the light. The department likes everything tidy." He measured the husband. "Tell me, Doctor, by any chance do you know Dr. Stanley Zimmerman? He's the son of the woman who was killed."

An undercurrent of hostility seeped into Max Bardwell's answer. "No, I don't."

Scanlon got up. "May I use your telephone? I have to call my office."

"Of course," Luise Bardwell said. "There's one on the wall here, but why don't you use the one in the living room. You'll have privacy."

Scanlon stood looking into the fireplace, waiting for someone in the Squad to answer the damn phone, and wondering if people who lived in the fifteenth and sixteenth centuries were as screwed-up as people were today. An Egyptian princess, my ass.

He heard a quiet click on the line. Someone had picked up an extension.

"Nine-three Squad, Suckieluski."

Scanlon recognized Hector Colon's voice. "Suckieluski, anything doing?"

"*Nada.* Most of the team have called it a day."

"I'm going home from here," Scanlon said. "Sign me out."

"Right, Lou."

When Scanlon came back into the kitchen he was taken aback to see Luise Bardwell sitting at the kitchen table next to her husband reading the latest edition of *Screw* magazine.

"Would you like some candy?" she asked Scanlon. "They're quite good; solid milk chocolate."

He took a look at the box she held out to him and recoiled at the explicit shapes of the goodies. That one was a vagina. The others he wasn't so sure about. "I'm on a diet. But thanks anyway. Where does one buy such delights?" Scanlon asked, watching her select a piece for herself and stuff it into her greedy little mouth.

"Joe Gallagher gave me a box of them," she said.

"May I see it?" Scanlon asked.

She placed it on the table in front of Scanlon.

The lieutenant looked at the candies and shuddered slightly. He replaced the top and turned the box over. In the right-hand corner on the back there was a label: Luv-Joy Manufacturing Company, Brooklyn, New York.

7

———————————————

Great Jones Street is a continuation of East Third that runs for two short blocks between Bowery and Broadway. There is a wide stretch of undeveloped land on the west side of Engine Company 33's firehouse that is used as a commercial parking lot during the day and is empty at night, except for a few cars.

Tony Scanlon's second-floor loft could be reached by walking through the lot and using the fire escape zigzagging down the rear of the building. He enjoyed jogging up the metal steps. It helped him stay in shape. He also sometimes enjoyed shooting the bull with some of the firemen who hung out in front of the firehouse.

He parked his car in the rear of the near vacant lot and checked the time. Eight-sixteen P.M. He was tired of people and wanted to be alone. As he locked the car door he noticed a group of firemen ogling coeds rushing to a late Friday class at the nearby NYU campus. One of the firemen, a guy named Fred who lived out in Commack and had a large beer belly, spotted him and waved him over.

Approaching the group of firemen, Scanlon saw one of them make an obscene gesture at two passing coeds. "Did you catch the tits on them two?" the fireman said to Scanlon.

Scanlon wondered why firemen were always horny. "No, I didn't. What's up?"

"Whaddaya hear on the new contract? Think the mayor is goin' to go for eight and eight?" Fred asked.

"We'll probably end up with the same percentage increase spread over two years," Scanlon said, wanting to get away from the firemen, to walk. No matter how tired he was, a stroll through the streets of Greenwich Village always seemed to rejuvenate him. His phantom leg never hurt then; he was able to unwind and think.

The basketball games in the vest-pocket park on the Avenue of the Americas and West Third had attracted the usual throng of spectators and bettors. Sidewalk peddlers were selling batteries, pocket books, and gold jewelry along the curb. Artists were selling their horrible paintings.

Scanlon strolled, people-watched. Suddenly he saw an approaching couple. A big-boned black woman, outfitted in a black cowboy hat tilted rakishly to the side and tight red slacks and a tight red sweater into which she had poured two mammoth, unhaltered breasts, walked arm in arm with a white Greenwich Village Sikh with a beard down to his chest, a white turban rolled around his head, a white homespun that flowed down to his thonged sandals, and a ten-foot walking pole.

On Bleecker Street he passed a restaurant that had a hand-painted sign in the window that offered Szechuan and Thai food. He thought of the new wave of Asian immigrants that had taken over the city's produce industry and remembered how cops had had to learn to distinguish among these newcomers to our shores. The skinny black-haired killer extortionist from Hong Kong, the Korean stickup teams, and the Cambodian drug runners had all seen to that.

When he turned into West Fourth Street he noticed a group of giggling girls hurrying down the steps of the Pink Pussycat Erotic Boutique. He looked down into the display window and saw a collection of phalluses and edible panties. A big business, Gretta Polchinski had told him. He turned abruptly. There was homework to be done.

Tony Scanlon's loft had high ceilings and floor-to-ceiling windows. A teak polyurethaned floor had been laid diagonally. The galley kitchen had polished granite counters. The walls were natural brick, and there were two rows of iron structural pillars running through the middle of the loft. Rugs were scattered about, and there were groupings of natural wood furniture. In front of the kitchen was a dining area that consisted of four butcher blocks supporting a thick piece of glass. Nail barrels were used as seats. Off in the distance there was a sleeping area that consisted of a king-size platform bed with a heavy brass headboard. On the wall above the bed was a batik that depicted a sea god riding a dolphin through the depths.

Scanlon had bought the loft with money borrowed from his pension and a loan from the Municipal Credit Union. Jack Fineberg, who had owned the building and had converted it into co-op lofts, knew Scanlon and had offered him an insider's price. Fineberg was a retired bookmaker from Brooklyn who had invested his money in real estate. Fifteen years ago Fineberg's daughter had been raped while on her way home from Brooklyn College. Detective Tony Scanlon had caught the case. Three days after the date of occurrence Scanlon and another detective named Hawkins went to Bainbridge Street in the Seven-seven to arrest one Leslie Brown for the attack on Fineberg's daughter. Brown, a shaven-headed giant, resisted arrest. During the melee Detective Hawkins sustained a broken nose and a deep gash along his hairline. The Unusual Occurrence report stated how in his attempt to escape Brown had fled the apartment and gone out on the fire escape, where he had lost his footing and fallen three stories, impaling himself on the spiked fence in front of the brownstone.

Mr. Brown had been rushed to Brookdale Hospital, where a team of doctors had removed his testicles. Brown was later to claim before the Civilian Complaint Review Board and the American Civil Rights Union that Detective Scanlon, upon seeing his partner lying unconscious on the floor, had gone crazy and beaten him about the head and body with a blackjack. When Brown was semiconscious, he claimed, Scanlon had picked him up bodily and had thrown him off the fire escape.

Detective Scanlon had vehemently denied the accusation. The result of it all was that Leslie Brown now sang soprano and Tony Scanlon owned a loft.

Scanlon entered by the fire escape entrance and immediately went around the spacious loft rolling down the wooden matchstick blinds. When this was done he made sure that the doors were locked and then double-checked the blinds. Prying eyes were one of the annoyances of Manhattan living. Although Great Jones Street was a cheerless street of machine shops and factories, Scanlon still was on guard against the omnipresent danger of some creep with binoculars. What he was about to do was his secret, and he intended to keep it that way.

He walked into the sleeping area and undressed. Naked, he went over to the eighteen-drawer clothes chest, opened one of the middle drawers on the right side, and took out a fresh pair of heavy support pantyhose. Sitting on the edge of the bed, he worked the pantyhose up his legs, taking care not to run the fabric as he moved it up over his prosthesis. He stood and, with his legs apart, pulled the undergarment snug in the crotch. He then went back into the clothes chest and took out a gray sweatsuit and stepped into it. He bent at the waist and ran both hands over the prosthesis, ensuring that it was snug inside the pantyhose, which acted like an athletic supporter for his artificial leg.

He went over to the music system on the third shelf of the bookcase and switched on a Richard Simmons aerobics tape. For the next thirty minutes Tony Scanlon danced aerobics. No pilgrimage to Lourdes had rid him of his limp. His own personalized form of physical therapy had: solitary aerobics and long, hard walks around the city, pacing the borders of his loft thousands and thousands of times, but most of all, his tenacious determination to stay a cop.

After showering, he toweled himself, put the prosthesis back on, donned a blue terry-cloth bathrobe, settled in at the table with the glass top, and began to read Joe Gallagher's personnel records. The latest semiannual evaluation stated that Gallagher was an above-average supervisor who instilled a spirit of participation in his subordinates. Bullshit. That was not what Herman the German had told him. There were many letters of commendation from various religious and philanthropic organizations praising Gallagher for his good works. The UF 10a, Foreign Language and Special Qualification Card, showed that Gallagher had none. The UF 11, Time Record Card, stated that Gallagher was entitled to both July 4 and Memorial Day.

He began to read Gallagher's old memo books. A cop's memo

book is like a ship's log. Police regulations require that members of the force on patrol below the rank of captain maintain one. Before the beginning of each tour the date, tour, and assignment will be entered, and during the tour a full and accurate record of all duty performed and all police occurrences, including post changes and absences from post. If no police action was taken during a tour, "nothing to report" will be written and the entry signed. Gallagher's memo books were filled with nothing to reports. That did not surprise Scanlon. Streetwise cops put as little as possible in the serially numbered books. They know that once an entry is made it is etched in stone and subject to subpoena by the courts, the grand jury, the Trial Room, and the Civilian Complaint Review Board. No cop ever went to jail for an "I can't recall" answer under oath.

Time passed, and he became aware of the ache behind his right eyeball. He let the pencil fall from his hand and stretched in place. He pushed back from the table and got up. He walked into the kitchen, took down a bottle of scotch, and poured whiskey over ice. Clinking the cubes, he walked over the glossy floor to the bookcase, where he selected an Edith Piaf record and put it on the turntable. He went into the sleeping area, removed his robe and the prosthesis, and stretched out naked on the bed. There was a red halo around the tip of his stump. He put the glass down on the treasure chest that he had bought in a secondhand shop on Second Avenue and, leaning forward, massaged the stump with both his hands. It reminded him of a giant sausage. When the pain had subsided, he picked up the glass and lay back with his head resting against the brass rods. He strained the nerves in his stump, trying to wiggle his missing toes. He hated the way the stump looked next to his whole leg. A useless appendage. He looked down at his body. It was hard, lean, the stomach muscles clearly outlined. The tangled mass of black hair on his chest tapered into a line that led to his penis. His gaze followed the trail. He tweaked the organ and watched it jerk to life and fall back to rest on his body. In a sudden fit of anger he grabbed it, squeezing the head until it was blood-red. Man's lifelong fascination, his curse, his cross, he thought, pushing it aside.

He sipped scotch. Edith Piaf was singing "Mon Dieu." The haughty mournfulness of her voice and the relaxing effect of the scotch put him in a contemplative mood. That combination always did. Somewhere in the night a cat yowled. There was the sudden din of klaxon and horn. The men of Engine 33 were responding to a fire. He looked up at the skylight, peering out into the night, to some distant galaxy, permitting his thoughts to retreat into the past, to that awful day that had so inexorably changed his life.

It was the second week in February, a gloomy, dispiriting month. The pewter sky had dispensed three days of snow. The city was congealed in an eerie stillness. Plows had entombed cars, and only the foolhardy made unnecessary journeys. It was six P.M. and the detectives were responding to a location in an unmarked department auto. The wind howled, and Tony Scanlon had both his legs. Tire chains clanked; the window wipers appeared to be giving up the struggle. Detective Waldron had been driving. Keegan and Capucci relaxed in the rear. Detective Sgt. Tony Scanlon was in the passenger seat, gazing out at the falling flakes.

The Two-four Squad detectives had been on their way into Midtown Precinct North to arrest a suspect for an A&R that had gone down in their precinct. A female bird had dropped a dime. The son of a bitch was screwing her girlfriend, so sang the bird. Love's old sweet song.

Their destination had been a tenement on West Forty-seventh between Ninth and Tenth avenues. Driving was difficult. They had just passed Fifty-eighth and Eighth when the call came over the radio: "In Midtown North a report of a ten-thirty. Two male whites armed with guns. The Adler Hotel. 1438 Four-one Street. Units responding, K?"

The radio fell silent.

Central rebroadcast the alarm.

No response from the patrol force. The detectives were ten blocks away from the hotel. The *Patrol Guide* proscribed outside units from responding to crimes in progress that were more than five blocks away from their locations. Scanlon knew from experience that more than half of the patrol force scheduled for that tour had telephoned their commands and requested emergency excusals. They were snowbound in suburbia.

Central broadcast the alarm a third time.

The first response came: "David Edward George going."

"Any unit on a backup, K?"

Waldron glanced at Scanlon. The detective sergeant snatched up the radio handset from its cradle. "Two-four Squad detectives are five blocks away, Central. We'll back up."

"Ten-four, Two-four Squad."

The detectives were the first unit to arrive. They leaped from their car, leaving doors ajar and the roof light whirling flashes. They spread out, trudging through the packed snow, attempting to navigate their way up onto the sidewalk. The crust crunched under their feet. Scanlon and Capucci were the first to make it to the sidewalk. They arrived in time to confront two men fleeing the luxury hotel. Both suspects wore blue pea jackets and had ski masks over their faces. One of them carried a black valise. Capucci called out: "Stop! Police!" The two men stopped and whirled to face the policemen. Each of them was holding a Walther MP-K, a small machine pistol with a thirty-two-round magazine. Scanlon saw the weapons, and at first thought they were toys. His gaze was transfixed by the guns, each with its retractable tubular stock lashed to the side of the breech. He remembered that a small bird had lit on the hotel's gold awning. He crouched in a combat stance and fired. Explosions went off all around him. They hurt his ears. He was not wearing his goggles or his ear protectors. This was not the range; it was the street, and it was for real. He fired double-action. Snowflakes stuck to his nose. His gun was suddenly empty. Still crouching, he turned to one side and started to combat-reload. He had just closed the cylinder when he felt a sharp pain in his left leg. Suddenly he was upside down and the buildings were spinning all around him. He was on the ground, with his face in the snow. He struggled to raise himself up off the ground. Bracing himself on one hand, he leaned up and fired. Gunfire was all around him. He heard screams and wondered if it was he who had cried out. He managed to get off four rounds before he collapsed. His face was on fire. A warm sticky wetness gushed over his lower torso, and then blackness came.

He awoke scared and disoriented. He was in a bed with green sheets, and there was a gray curtain that hung from ceiling tracks. He heard muted gongs and a woman's voice over a loudspeaker, and a rattling trolley. Wires and tubes ran from his body to a monitor panel. His tongue was pasted to the roof of his mouth, and there was the sour taste of medicine. A blurred figure in a white winged cap hovered over him, saying incomprehensible things. Men in green tunics tended him. One of the men had bulging eyes and wore a stethoscope. A leaden numbness weighed down his left leg. He attempted to move it and couldn't. A dread made him suddenly feel cold all over. He moved his hand under the sheet and probed a mound of gauze, inching beyond, straining to get at the source of his discomfort. There was nothing beyond! His leg was not there. He screamed and sprang up from the bed, throwing off the covers. He had to see, to prove to himself that it was only a vivid nightmare.

Doctors gently forced him back down, trying to calm him. One of them told him he was lucky to be alive. A burst of machine-gun fire had partially severed the distal shaft below the knee. The surgical team had had no option. They had been forced to amputate. He would be as good as new, the doctor with the stethoscope told him with an uneasy grin. He had been measured for a prosthesis while he was still on the table. The new artificial legs were technological miracles, they told him; he would even be able to disco.

"But I can feel my leg," he insisted. "It's still there. See, I'm wiggling my toes." His desperate tone conveyed fading hope. One of the doctors explained to him that all sensation comes from the brain. And that his brain did not know that his left leg was no longer there. His brain was still sending nerve impulses to his missing leg and would continue to do so for the rest of his life. "Your missing limb will always be with you, a sort of phantom leg. It'll itch, fall asleep. There will be times when you will forget that it's not there and try to step on it."

Scanlon turned his face so that they might not see his tears. It was unseemly for a detective sergeant to cry.

No visitors were allowed until the next day.

It was late in the afternoon when Inspector Albert Buckholz, the CO of the Tenth Detective District, burst into his room full of false cheer. Buckholz was a grotesquely fat man with a small head, dainty hands, and a cheap black toupée that looked like a Cracker Jack prize. He was known throughout the Job as Fat Albert.

Buckholz went to great lengths to assure him that he was going to be okay. The PC wanted him to know that the Job was behind

104

him 110 percent, and that if he wanted to he could remain on the Job, and that his place on the lieutenant promotion list was secure. There were other handicapped men on the Job. Buckholz moved in close to confide, "The Job don't forget, Tony. We take care of our own."

Edith Piaf stopped singing. Scanlon abandoned his worn reverie and got up off the bed. He hopped one-legged over to the turntable and reversed the record.

Piaf returned. "C'est à Hambourg."

He hopped back into bed. Resting his glass on his stomach, he leaned his head back and again retreated into the past.

"Tell me what happened," Scanlon said to Fat Albert.

The right side of Fat Albert's face began to twitch. Capucci had been killed, Fat Albert related.

Scanlon looked away, watching the yellow beeps weave their way across the monitor screen.

". . . two perps were DOA at the scene," Fat Albert said with macabre glee as if their deaths evened the score for Capucci, for his leg. And then, in a sudden burst of exuberance, Fat Albert announced that there was an anxious lady waiting outside to see him.

Jane Stomer entered the hospital room with uncharacteristic timidity. She paused, her large black eyes darting between beds. When she saw him, she ran over and hurled herself across his chest in a relieved embrace. Her long brown hair fell in natural ringlets over his face. He breathed in her fragrance, relished her softness against his skin. His arms moved out from under the sheets and pressed her close to him.

At thirty-two, Jane Stomer was many things to many different people. To her male colleagues in the district attorney's office of New York County, she was the frighteningly intelligent, self-assured assistant DA who never walked into the courtroom unprepared; she was the lady who wore classic suits and sensible blouses that concealed an extraordinarily beautiful body. To her female colleagues she was the consummate professional. She was the girlfriend who warned against office romances with married men, but never chastised those women who did become involved. She was the acid-tongued feminist who championed women's rights within the male-dominated criminal justice system.

To Detective Sgt. Tony Scanlon she had been both lover and friend. They had met twenty-one months before he lost his leg. Scanlon and his detectives had arrested four men for the brazen daylight robbery of the U.S. Steel payroll. Jane Stomer had been assigned to prosecute. A week before the case was to be presented to the grand jury she summoned him to her office. They sat around her desk critiquing the original felony complaint and the supporting depositions, searching for legal flaws that might invalidate the accusatory instruments.

After the grand jury handed down the indictments, she scheduled more meetings with him to prepare for pretrial. During these meetings she quizzed him closely on the quality of the evidence supporting the state's case, and on the availability and reliability of the witnesses. Together they developed the People's strategy to defeat the inevitable defense challenges to the admissibility of the physical evidence.

He had known her by reputation and had expected her to be an antimale feminist. Instead, he discovered a pleasant, hardworking ADA who was skilled in the law and had an exceptional grasp of the real workings of the criminal justice system. He liked her crisp, businesslike manner and was impressed by her determination to win. Once during a brief lull he asked her if she had ever considered going into private practice. "You'd make a hell of an adversary."

She looked straight at him and said, "Someone has to get the licks in for the crime victims. Every one we put inside means one less to roam our streets murdering and stealing."

A week before the trial she summoned him to her office for a final conference. They began to work at exactly nine A.M. There were times during that final meeting that he found himself staring into her eyes searching for a message. He never found one. They broke for lunch at twelve-thirty and went their separate ways.

He walked out of the fortresslike Criminal Court building on Centre Street and sauntered down the wide steps, unsure where to eat. He passed the massive steel doors of the court's detention facility and crossed the street, heading toward Worth Street in search of a restaurant. He passed several, glanced inside, decided that they were greasy spoons, and moved on. Reaching Broadway, he moved north until he came to Duane Street, where he glanced to his right and saw a bright orange-and-yellow awning: Los Dos Rancheros. He didn't particularly care for Mexican food, but when he walked over to the window and looked inside and saw ADA Jane Stomer sitting alone at a table, he developed an overwhelming desire for guacamole and beans. He pretended to be surprised when he entered the crowded restaurant and saw her look up at him. She motioned him over to her table.

Conversation came easily, each agreeing on the screwed-up state of the criminal justice system and on the need for mandatory sentences. He liked her; they spoke the same language.

It was she who noticed the time. "We'd better get back. The distinguished district attorney does not countenance extended lunch hours for women," she said. They each paid their share of the bill and split the tip between them. During their hurried walk back he reached out and took hold of her arm. "Will you have dinner with me?" he asked. People passed them, intent on getting to other places. Some turned and stared at the two of them standing motionless, and unaware of what was happening around them.

She slowly freed her arm from his grip and pushed off ahead of him, saying over her shoulder, "I'd like that, Scanlon."

They decided that it would be wise to wait until after the trial before they went out together. Eight days later when the jury came in with a guilty verdict, they made a date for Saturday, two days off.

On their first date they went to Texas Roundup in Soho, where they ate barbecued ribs and chicken and rib-eye steak and home-made chili and bourbon baked beans. She had discarded her usual conservative clothes in favor of an oversize silk blouse and tailored jeans that were cinched with a narrow snakeskin belt. After dinner they went to Las Cuevas, where they discoed until dawn. The sun was up when he escorted her into the Art Deco lobby of her West End Avenue apartment and rode up with her to the fourth floor. She stopped in front of her door. "Thank you, Scanlon. I enjoyed myself."

He leaned forward and kissed her on the side of her lips. She smiled at him and turned to open her door. As she was inserting her key into the lock, he asked her if she was busy later that day.

They could drive out to the Island, eat lobster. She stepped into her apartment. "That would be nice. Why not make it around three."

It was a beautiful Sunday afternoon with thin motionless clouds bordering the horizon. The cool summer breezes were laced with ocean smells. Seagulls stalked the beach, glided aloft. Holding hands, they made their way along the rugged headlands of Montauk Point watching the whitecaps roll up onto the sand and rocks, each aware that they were on the threshold of intimacy.

Eventually they got around to talking about their jobs. "Sometimes I think our society is on self-destruct," he said, guiding her around a group of boulders.

Scuffing seaweed aside with her sneakers, she said, "But can you imagine what life would be like without our court system? We'd be at the mercy of revolutionary guards meting out their own system of justice."

"Sometimes I think we'd be better off."

She moved close, put her arm around his. "But you don't really believe that, do you, Scanlon?"

"I guess not," he admitted, conscious of her breasts pressing against his arm. Watching the retreating surf, he asked her to tell him how she had become involved with criminal law. She withdrew her arm and walked away from him. Going over to a cluster of boulders, she climbed up and sat, staring out at the ocean. He climbed up after her. Lowering himself next to her, he asked, "Did I say something to upset you?"

She looked at him, her expression clouded. She seemed unsure how much of herself she wanted to reveal. She touched his cheek, looked into his softening eyes. After long hesitation, she tugged her knees up to her chest and wrapped them in her arms. A breaker pounded their boulder, lightly spraying them.

"I've always been an overachiever, Tony. In law school I was the one who could always be counted on by the professors to rattle off the case law. Both my parents are lawyers. Dad's specialty is admiralty law, Mom's is blue-sky corporate stuff. My father went to Princeton. I went to Princeton. We have a house in Princeton. It has all the comforts: gardens, pool, pool house, tennis court. I'm the only child, and I guess I was fated to be my parents' legacy to corporate law." She frowned. Her eyes moistened. "You see,

Tony, I never knew my parents when I was growing up. I hardly know them now. They were too busy with their careers and their social obligations to spend time with a rambunctious little girl who peed in bed. I can hardly remember being hugged by my parents, or being kissed by them, or told that they loved me. At Christmas I would get toys from F.A.O. Schwarz and a firm hug. That was as much as they could manage.

"I was raised by a nanny. We lived in the south wing of the house, alone. Just the two of us, and Jasper, my cat. They're both gone now. Nanny's name was Helen McGovern. She was a warm, sweet old maid who showered me with her love and treated me as though I were her own child. I used to pretend that she *was* my mother, and that my parents were my cruel stepparents. She died last year, and I still miss her terribly." She unzipped the side flap of her white windbreaker and took out a package of tissues. She pulled one out and dabbed her eyes. "I was in my middle twenties before I realized that my parents probably loved me, but were undemonstrative, incapable of giving much of themselves." Jane looked at him, trying to decide whether to continue. She made a small dismissive shrug of her shoulders and leaned forward, resting her chin on her kneecaps. "I was a virgin until my senior year at Princeton. His name was David and he was the captain of the fencing team. We went together for seven months before David dropped me for a cutesy math major. I was devastated." She laughed self-mockingly. "Young girls are such romantic saps. They think love is forever. But I got over David. I'm a survivor, Scanlon. Anyway, after law school, Dad wangled me a position with one of the city's top firms. A very proper firm that accepts only top students from the best schools, people who have the proper family connections. And even then you needed what cops call a 'contract' to get a job with this firm."

He smiled. "Someone still has to make that old telephone call for you."

"Yes. It was while I was working there that I made the mistake of falling in love with one of the married partners. That little romance lasted a little over a year. And then one evening he announced that he could never leave his wife. And then he had the gall to add that I deserved more than a shabby little affair." She dabbed her eyes again with a tissue. "That bastard. He never did realize that I had never intended for him to leave his precious wife."

She took a deep breath, exhaled slowly. "I really hated working there. It was a dead, boring place full of assholes dressed in dark three-piece suits and fusty dresses and sensible shoes and high-collared blouses. I used to go home every night with a headache. It was only after eighteen months of paying a small fortune to a shrink that I realized I was living my life for the sole purpose of trying to gain my parents' love and approval. I decided it was time for me to grow up and start living my life for myself. My parents were disappointed, to say the least, when I informed them that I found corporate law a bore and had accepted a position on the DA's staff. 'But Jane, dear,' Mother said, 'criminal law is so *undignified*.'"

They both laughed.

"I don't know, Scanlon, perhaps I'm still trying to earn their approval. But I do know that I love my work and that I am damn good at it. And that, sir, is a very nice feeling."

He picked up a pebble, ran his thumb over its smoothness, and skimmed it out across the surf. "Are you seeing anyone now?"

"I haven't *seen* anyone in a long time. I need a strong man, Tony. A man who is not searching for a mother replacement. And, unfortunately, there just aren't too many of them around." She turned and looked at him. "Okay, Scanlon, it's your turn. What secrets are there in your life?"

Policemen find it difficult to talk about themselves, to let others peek into their world. The Job makes cops xenophobic. But slowly he overcame his reluctance and began to tell her of his life. He described the wise guys on Pleasant Avenue with their wide-brimmed pearl-gray hats, and pegged pants and pointy shoes, and how they used to hang out on corners with their hands clasped behind them, ready to drop the day's gambling action should any plainclothes cops appear. He described the rich, exotic smells inside Mr. DeVito's cheese store, and explained how they used to make pizza with pure olive oil.

They lived in a four-room apartment over a barbershop. He was the only child, and he had his own room next to his parents' bedroom. His father was a barrel-chested Irish drunk who also happened to be a sergeant in the NYPD. Haltingly he tried to tell her about his father's drunken tirades, and of the physical abuse that he and his mother suffered at his father's hands. His face expressionless, he recounted how he used to lie awake at night listening as his father staggered in after a four-to-twelve tour, of hearing his mother's whispered pleas, of trying to ignore the sounds of his parents' squawking bed, his father's hoarse grunts. He told about the times his father would pass out on top of his mother and of how he would have to get up and go and help his mother push the half-naked drunk off her slight body. He told of pretending to be asleep when his father would come home drunk and beat his mother. He spoke with bitterness of his father's hatred of Italians. "And my mother is Italian," he added balefully.

His mother had grown up on Center Market Place in Little Italy. She was short and had a strong peasant's face, olive skin, thick black hair, and luminous dark eyes. She was kind and generous and had a totally miserable life with his father. But still she maintained the pathetic and desperate illusions of a loyal wife: she told Tony not to judge his father too harshly.

He paused to light a De Nobili, his face flushed by emotions that he normally kept in the deepest part of himself.

Holidays spent with his father's side of the family were joyless. His Irish aunts and uncles shared his father's hostility toward Italians; in fact, he added with some dismay, they hated everyone who wasn't Irish Catholic. They were, as far as he was concerned, loathsome, miserable people. Days before a holiday, his mother would prepare. She cleaned the house, shopped for food, liquor, beer, spent hours in the kitchen making delicacies, baking. He could almost smell the big pots of simmering sauces, the strong aromas. When the relatives arrived in midafternoon they would trudge, many already drunk, into his home, ignoring his mother. They would treat her as though she were their servant. His mother's name was Mary. They'd address her as Maria. They would talk disparagingly of Eye-talians, in front of his mother, and tell awful ethnic jokes. With painful clarity he described the mounds of dirty holiday dishes in the sink, and him and his mother washing them while his aunts stayed in the parlor drinking cans of beer and smoking cigarettes. He told her about his childish fascination with the way his aunt's false teeth slid up and down when they talked. "Every one of them had store-bought choppers."

Jane Stomer stretched out her legs, crossing them at the ankles. She had a perplexed look on her face. "If your father felt that strongly about Italians, why in heaven's name did he marry your mother?"

A series of breakers rolled into their boulders. The spray felt good. He tasted salt on his lips. "I had trouble with that one too," he said, "until I took a few moments to compare my DOB with my parents' anniversary. It was off by four months."

Windsurfers offshore with brilliant orange and blue sails flew over the waves, while the people on them struggled to stay upright. His eyes followed them. "I grew up speaking Italian with my mother and her relatives. That was all we talked whenever my father wasn't around. The Italian side of my family was warm and wonderful. Kind, gentle people who went out of their way to make you feel at home in their houses. As a kid I dreamed of coming on the Job and of someday being my father's boss, and of making his life a living hell." He flicked ash into the ocean. "But he disappointed me in that too. Fourteen months after I came on the Job, he threw in his papers and ran off with his Irish girlfriend, another drunk."

"Where is he now?" she asked.

"Rotting in hell for all I know." He held up the De Nobili. "I began to smoke these when I came on the Job. I wanted the Irish Mafia to know that although my name is Scanlon, I'm a guinea through and through. It's my own personal affirmative action program."

"And what about Tony Scanlon's private life?" she said, staring out at the windsurfers.

That warm smile, that baring of teeth. "It's interesting."

"Come on, Scanlon, out with it. Don't try to palm off any of that laconic cop talk on me. I want specifics. Is there anyone important in your life?"

He became serious. "Not at the moment."

"Was there?"

"Sort of," he said with a sheepish grin.

"What do you mean, sort of?"

"Well, I was seeing two women at the same time." He added quickly, "But I liked both of them very much."

"And they, of course, did not know each other."

He became uncomfortable. "Well, not exactly."

His little-boy discomfort caused her to suppress a smile. "Out with it, Scanlon."

"As luck would have it they both went to the same place on the East Side to get their legs waxed. Anyway, they met there accidentally, and as women inevitably do, they got around to telling each other about their boyfriends. And it just so happened that they both were seeing a police lieutenant named Tony. You can guess the rest of it."

She pushed herself up and stood over him. Placing a friendly hand on his shoulder, she said, "Scanlon, you are a typical, lying, two-faced cop. You're the kind of man that women discuss in the powder room. Any woman who even considered becoming involved with you is a fool."

He made a weary gesture. "Guess I can't argue with that logic, Counselor."

The next night they went to Allen Street in the East Village to eat Indonesian food. They ate rijsttafel served by waiters wearing colorful headdresses, and folk garb over washed-out jeans. They had finished their dinner and their table was covered with many small dishes and rice crumbs. He caught her watching him and took note of her haunted expression. She lowered her eyes, brought her napkin to her lips. There was an awkward silence. She toyed with a skewer, avoiding his eyes. He became conscious of his own heartbeat. Reaching across the table, he took her hand in his. "Will you come home with me?" he said, an edge of uncertainty in his voice.

She squeezed his hand, scraped her chair back from the table, and got up.

They stood before his bed locked in a lingering kiss. His hand moved under her dress, and she stepped back, out of reach.

"Get undressed," she said, in a tone of mounting urgency. As he struggled out of his clothes, she came up to him, slid her arms around his neck, and kissed him.

Naked, he pressed into her, and again she pulled back from him, ordering, "Sit on the bed, Scanlon. I want you to watch me take my clothes off."

Standing a few feet away from him, her eyes locked on his, she removed her clothes, a garment at a time, carelessly letting each fall to the floor. Her slow, deliberate unveiling increased his desire for her. He sat motionless, breathing hard, his stare caressing her body.

She was now clad only in bra and panties.

He delighted in her long, smooth legs, her flat stomach, her breasts straining against her bra. His eyes swiveled down to the black mound that showed through her panties. They lingered there. His mouth dropped open, and he made a movement to go to her.

She thrust out a palm. "Patience, Scanlon. This is how I like it. Slow. Hard."

Her face was glowing with desire. She reached up to the front of her bra, paused, looked down at her cleavage, then to him, and unhooked her bra. Large breasts with protruding nipples rose and fell with each breath. She slipped her hand inside her panties and slid them down, stepping out of them.

"I want you," he gasped.

"Soon," she said, coming to him, lifting her leg over his, straddling him.

A searing sensation shot through his body as she lowered herself onto his penis, drawing him inside her body. She did not take him deep, but instead kept him at the entrance, slowly, methodically undulating her body over the head of his penis.

"Slow, Scanlon. Slow," she moaned.

Her exquisite torment caused him to catch his breath. His mouth was agape, dry. He made low grunts. He lunged his body up into her. She retreated. "Not yet, Scanlon. Soon."

Long deep guttural sounds came from her open mouth. Her eyes were closed in tight concentration. Beads of sweat dotted her brow. She was moving faster, faster, taking him deeper and deeper. He pulled her close, his mouth eagerly sucking on her nipple. She gasped. "Yes, Scanlon. Yes. Do it hard. Hard. Now. Now!" She plummeted onto his penis, wrapping her legs around his waist.

They lay in a naked embrace, gasping, their bodies exuding the sweaty scent of lovemaking. Time passed, and they dozed. He awoke first, his passion renewed. His lips moved along her neck, savoring the smell of her body. He pressed her close. His caresses stirred her out of her sleep. She began to respond. She pressed her body against his, and opened her mouth to his kisses. He slid down between her legs and sucked her up into his mouth, his tongue delicately caressing, and his finger probing deeper.

Her body was immersed in passion. Every touch, every tongue movement caused her to wrench, smear his face with her body. She was pulling her hair as her head thrashed on the pillows. She was making rough, grating sounds. Her body rose up off the bed at the waist, and she began to pound the mattress. Her nails clawed the sheets. "Yes! Yes!" she shouted. And then as orgasm ripped through her body, she grabbed a pillow to her face and screamed.

He moved up the bed on his knees, kissing her body as he went. When he was kneeling alongside her shoulder, he stopped and took her head into his hands and gently guided it toward his glistening penis.

Her face showed a momentary hesitation. She pulled back, vacillating, then looked up at him. "Please don't . . ."

"I won't," he interrupted softly, and then gasped and called out her name as her moist lips closed around him.

The needle scratched with annoying regularity. He came out of his reverie and put the glass down on the treasure chest. Pushing his hulk up off the bed, Scanlon hopped over to the turntable and changed the record. Then he hopped back, while Piaf sang "L'Accordéoniste."

A sip of scotch accompanied him on his now compulsive journey back into the past.

She appeared on his third day in the hospital: a tall, gangly woman in a hospital coat with an artificial leg under one arm and a shoe and several plastic envelopes in her hand. "Hi. I'm Alice Crowell. Are you ready to walk?"

He looked at her, and then down at his stump. "I wish the hell I could."

"I'm going to have you on your feet and walking in about five minutes. But first I'd like you to swing your legs over the side of the bed."

As he complied with her directions, she laid the prosthesis and the shoe on the bed. She stood in front of him and rolled the stump shrinker, which looked like an Ace bandage made into a sock, off his stump, and began to gently knead his stump. "There is a lot of swelling and edema, but that is to be expected."

Watching her hands work, he asked, "What's edema?"

"Body fluids that collect in the soft tissues. With your leg gone the normal body fluids that pass through your body can't make the return journey. Some of them collect in your stump and cause it to swell. Stump wrapping and elastic shrinker socks help reduce the edema." She lifted up his stump, examining it. "The surgeon did a great job beveling the bone into a cylindrical mass."

She carefully placed the stump down on the bed and picked up the plastic envelopes. She slid one envelope behind the other until she found the one she wanted and ripped it open. She put the remainder back down on the bed. "This is a stump sock, Tony." She dangled it in front of him. "From now on a good deal of your daily routine is going to be devoted to stump sock management."

He noticed that her teeth were slightly bucked.

"In the morning there is not much edema, so you might start off the day with a four- or five-ply stump sock. But as the day progresses and body fluids accumulate and swell your stump, you might have to change to a one-ply sock. You must wear a sock—otherwise there will be friction, which will cause abrasions, blisters, and denuded skin surfaces. And if you don't control the edema your stump might swell so much that it won't fit into the socket, and conversely, if it shrinks too much, the socket could become too loose." She smiled. "Got it?"

"Got it," he said, looking into the socket of the artificial leg.

She handed him the stump sock. "You put this on, and I'll put on your shoe."

She put a regular sock on his real foot, and then slipped a shoe on his foot. "You've probably noticed that the shoes and sock are yours. We got them from your mother." She tied the lace, then stood up. She picked up the prosthesis. Hefted it in front of him. The leg had the other shoe on.

"This is a temporary leg, Tony. The socket and the foot are adjustable. It'll take months until your stump has shrunk to its permanent size. At that time you'll be fitted for a prosthesis that will be made for the angulation changes for your best gait pattern."

He nodded at the prosthesis. "What's it made of?"

"Laminated polyester resin and fiberglass." She held the prosthesis up in front of him. "This is a PTB prosthesis. Which stands for 'patellar bearing tendon.' I want you to take both your hands and feel the little space under your right kneecap."

He cupped both hands over his right kneecap and pressed fore-fingers into the space.

"That is your patellar tendon," she said. "Your femur rests on top of it and the tibia below it. There are no pain receptors in that area, and the patella is therefore impervious to pain. It can bear somewhere in the neighborhood of fifteen hundred pounds of pressure per square inch. It's the patellar tendon that will bear the weight of your body."

"There are no straps. How does it stay on?"

She turned the prosthesis so that he might look inside the socket. "See this bar molded across the top of the socket?"

He looked inside to where her finger pointed. "Yes, I see it."

"That's the patella bar. Your tendon rests on that bar, supporting your body. It's as though your left leg were kneeling on top of the prosthesis."

"But what secures the stump inside the prosthesis?"

"Feel above the right kneecap. Feel that ridge on top?"

"Yes."

"Now raise and lower your leg. See how that ridge expands and then contracts?"

"Yeah. The ridge is there, and then when I lower my leg it's gone."

"That area of your leg is called the supracondylar. When you put your prosthesis on, you'll raise up your stump and slide the lip of the socket over the supracondylar. The lips of the prosthesis will cover the supracondylar, and when you lower your leg the bone will contract, locking the stump inside the socket." She lowered the prosthesis and held the socket a few inches away from his stump. "You ready to walk?"

"Alice Crowell, I'm good and ready."

She put the prosthesis onto his stump. "Slide off the bed, putting all your weight onto your right leg," she ordered, ready to catch him should he fall.

Gripping the mattress, he struggled off the bed onto his feet. He cried out from the pain and fell backward against the bed, gripping the frame.

She grabbed his shoulders. "I know. Your stump is swollen and very painful. But we have to get you walking today. So let's try again."

He took a deep breath and righted himself. His body felt as though it were balanced on an unsteady toothpick. Sweat rolled down his armpits. His stump felt raw and throbbed with pain. He watched her, waiting for her instructions.

"Just walk," she instructed him. "Right leg first. Heel, sole, heel, sole. Then bring your left leg through."

He had gone but a few steps when he lost his balance and crumpled to the floor. She hurried over to him and helped him up. Frustration gnawed at him. He was a cripple. On his feet once more, he pushed her away. He wanted to go it alone, to conquer this affliction. With his arms out at his side, he managed six exhausting steps before tumbling to the floor.

"That's enough for today," she said, bending to heft him up once more. Supporting him with her shoulders, she helped him back into the bed. He lay on his back, gasping for air.

She looked down at him with an expression of compassion and determination. "Listen, Sergeant, you're not the first guy to lose a leg, and you're certainly not going to be the last one. In fact, you are now a member of a very distinguished alumni association." She smiled at her stack of envelopes down on the bottom of his bed. "You'd be surprised who's in the club. We've got a federal judge who let his diabetes get out of control, a pilot who didn't exactly walk away from a bad landing. A lot of people who have one thing in common—and they call themselves the One Missing Club. When you feel ready, one of the volunteers is going to stop by and start working with you."

Scanlon looked up at her and asked bitterly, "And have you got any cops in your little club?"

For a moment she looked off balance, but she recovered very fast. "Well, we had a sergeant from your Bomb Squad a few years ago . . ." She blushed in confusion and came to a sudden halt.

"You mean Frank Lally?"

"I think that's the name. How did you know?"

"Because he didn't make it. He swallowed his gun."

Alice Crowell realized that she had a loner on her hands.

She pulled up his hospital gown and went to remove the prosthesis.

"No! Leave it. I'm going to wear it until it becomes a part of my body."

He was discharged from the hospital on Friday of the eighth week. Jane Stomer put in for a vacation day in order to drive him home. "I appreciate your visiting me every night, and, well, just being there."

She looked at him. Smiled. "You're a sweet man, Scanlon. But please don't go sentimental on me."

He reached across the passenger seat and touched her cheek. "I won't."

They entered his loft by the front entrance on East Fourth Street. There was an unwelcoming stillness about the loft that made him uneasy. It suddenly appeared to be too large, too dark, filled with too many inhibiting shadows. He limped over to the closest sofa and started to lower himself, then lost his balance and fell onto the cushions. She rushed to his aid.

"I'm a klutz," he said.

"You are not." She took him into her arms, comforting him. He pressed her close, needing the reassurance of her body. "Stay the night," he whispered.

She cupped his face in her hands, kissed him tenderly on the lips. "I thought you'd never ask."

She helped him off the sofa and over to the bed. She helped him undress. For the first time in his adult life he was dependent on someone else. He did not like the feeling; it scared him. Sitting on the edge of his great bed, he took off the prosthesis and handed it up to her. She took it and walked over to the clothes chest, examining it. She put it down on the chest and came back to him. Watching her, he felt a twinge of concern over the lack of sexual spontaneity.

Standing a few feet away from him, she began to undress, starting their foreplay. He gaped at her, anxious to see her step from her panties. When she was naked she came to him and slid onto the bed next to him. As she did, she took in his once-proud body, but looked quickly away lest her gaze linger on his stump. She began to kiss him. She saw that he was limp and ran her hand over his loins and took hold of him, stroking him gently. As he grew, she stroked harder. She had become the aggressor, he the passive partner. She was all over him, kissing, licking, saying arousing things.

Their foreplay proved arduous. His ungainly lopsidedness precluded the fluid, urgent movements of lovemaking. He could see her trying to avoid his stump's caress, because each time it brushed against her, gooseflesh came and she recoiled. She attempted to hide her revulsion behind a smokescreen of feigned passion.

When she had him hard she lay on her back and watched as he struggled to position his awkward body between her legs. She took hold of his frail erection and guided it into her dry body, rubbing it on the inside, hoping to lubricate. With his right knee bearing his weight, and with his torso balanced upright by the brace of his left hand on the mattress, and with his stump dangling weightily, he looked down and watched her efforts.

He felt himself going soft and thrust forward into her. She gasped from his tearing intrusion, and turned her face sideways so that he might not see her pained expression. Biting her lower lip, hoping that it would soon end, she moved her body to his thrusts. But it was no use. He became aware of her perfunctory movements, saw her expression, sensed her lack of passion. He lost his erection and withdrew from her body, falling dejectedly onto his back.

"I'm sorry if I hurt you."

"It wasn't your fault. I couldn't lubricate. It's been a long time since we made love."

"I guess I lost more than my leg."

She took hold of him and shook him violently. "Don't you dare do this to yourself. You've just undergone a great trauma. You can't expect to just pick up your life where you left off. It takes time for your body to adjust to the new situation. For us to adjust to each other."

A flash of teeth, a laugh laden with mocking sarcasm. "Sergeant pegleg limp dick at your service."

"Don't do this, Tony," she cried, suddenly overwhelmed with compassion for him. She felt a need to mother him, to make love to him, to make him a whole man again, to restore his self-confidence. She started to kiss his body, desperately wanting to reassure the man she loved. Her caressing palm massaged his genitals. Her tongue moved over his neck, down his body. He whimpered, closed his eyes, but did not grow hard. She shifted her body between his legs, pausing to gather the courage to finish the distasteful task that she had set herself. A task that she had done several times with her married lover; a task that when done to completion caused her to become sick.

He placed his hands on her head and nudged her down.

She felt his hot member on her cheek. She flicked the tip with her tongue, making wet little circles over the head. She leaned forward and ran her flattened tongue over the silky undershaft, glancing up at him, seeing that his eyes were half closed, his head writhing on the pillows. She moved her head up and closed her lips around him.

His body moved to the bobbing motion of her head. His cries encouraged her, and she drew him deeper into her mouth. Harsh sounds came from his throat, his grip on her head tightened, and he came in forceful spurts.

She froze, impaled upon his organ. And then, with one quick jerk of her head, she was free of him. A sour expression twisted her face. Her lips were pursed tightly together, and her eyes brimmed. She looked about, searching for some nearby place to unburden her load. She gagged and swallowed involuntarily. Slapping her hands across her mouth, she leaped from the bed and ran into the bathroom. With her hands gripping the cold rim, she leaned over the sink, her body racked by violent heaving. With her mouth wide, her tongue strained by dry retches, she lowered her face into the sink and vomited.

Scanlon lay on his back, listening to her. He wanted to rush from the bed to comfort her. But he could not. For in one frightful moment of insight he saw that he was now disgusting to women, and he knew that he never again would be able to make love to a normal woman. He buried his face in the mattress and cried.

They spent the night in his great bed with their backs to each other, staring out at the retreating darkness, falling in and out of restless periods of sleep.

The sense of emasculation affected his entire body, causing him to lie hunched over with his right leg blanketing his stump and his genitals tucked between his thighs, subconsciously trying to hide his shame. His manhood was gone, and Jane Stomer knew it. He would never be able to forget that look on her face every time his stump brushed against her. How could he forget her getting sick after doing that to him? He was a goddamn impotent freak.

And worst of all, she knew. It could never be just his dark secret.

Several times during that night he shivered, and she moved close to him, placing her warm back against his. And each time he inched away from her.

A disquieting silence separated them in the morning. They sat at the table with the glass top and ate a light breakfast of juice, coffee, and warm croissants.

The uneasy silence lengthened.

Suddenly she announced that she was leaving to buy the Sunday *Times*. She was gone a long time, and when she returned she had the heavy newspaper tucked under her right arm and was holding a book in her left. She was late, she explained, because she had taken a taxi to her home in order to get a book she wanted him to look at. She put the newspaper down on one of the nail barrels. Facing him, she opened the book to a page that had a sliver of paper protruding from it and began to read aloud. Erectile dysfunction was the most common sexual problem for men. Its most common cause was psychological, a common way for men to express anxiety. There was no need for embarrassment, she read.

He was sitting a few feet away from her, his hostile gaze riveted to the book in her hands. With astonishing agility, he lunged up and grabbed the book from her, throwing it across the loft. He lost his balance and stumbled backward onto the sofa.

"Scanlon!" she cried, rushing over to help him.

"Get away," he said, shoving away her helping hands, struggling by himself to sit upright in the seat. He squared his shoulders, brushed down his ruffled hair with his hands. His face was impassive. "Don't you worry yourself about me. I'm going to be just fine. And I really don't want to hear any more of that goddamn shrink bullshit."

She lowered herself onto the sofa next to him. "Yes, Scanlon. Whatever you say."

They spent the rest of that Sunday morning listening to Tchaikovsky's *Swan Lake* and reading the newspaper. They seldom talked. The one-o'clock movie was *Casablanca*. Jane cried at the end; she always did. When the movie was over she looked at him as though she were about to say something, but changed her mind, and instead leaned close and kissed him.

He was cold and unresponsive.

"Would you like to make love?" she asked softly.

An orange-juice commercial had his attention. He did not respond to her overture. She rested her head on his shoulder and in a reassuring voice assured him that his impotence was a temporary problem. If he was that concerned, he might want to get some professional help. He quickly became hostile.

"You should talk about it, Tony."

"There is nothing to discuss."

"But there is," she pressed.

"Don't you understand the English language? I said that there was nothing to talk about."

"Men! They can never talk about what's bothering them."

He got up and changed the channel.

The following week he did not return any of her many telephone calls. On the following Friday she called again. Listening to her talk, he realized how very much he missed her. But instead of telling her that, instead of asking to see her, he told her he had been too preoccupied with teaching himself how to walk to return her calls. He promised her he would call her in the morning. He didn't.

The specter of his impotence haunted him, filling his lonely nights with fitful periods of sleep. The nightmare was the same, night after night. He and Jane were in the great bed. He was unable to get it up. He knelt on one knee, balancing himself with his left arm while he masturbated with the right, desperately trying to become erect. She watched, said nothing. A strange man stood off in the shadows, watching. A funny smile would come to Jane's mouth. He'd remain limp, sweating. She would suddenly burst out laughing just as his father stepped out of the shadows.

He'd awake with a start, drenched in sweat and trembling.

A week later, on Saturday, there was a knock at his door. He opened it and found Jane Stomer standing there with both hands planted firmly on her hips, her beautiful mouth quivering with anger. She glared at him briefly and then pushed past him into the loft. He closed the door and leaned against it, waiting for the expected outburst.

She faced him. Her voice cracked. "I have a right to know just exactly what your plans are concerning our relationship. If it's over,

Scanlon, then damn it, be man enough to tell me so that I can get on with my own life."

Finding himself at a loss for the proper words, he looked at her pleading eyes and said nothing. How does a man tell the woman he loves that he will never see her again? How does a man sever from his life the only woman he has ever been completely happy with? "I'm sorry," he said feebly, his eyes falling to the floor.

She rushed at him, pushed him aside, threw open the door. "You're a fool, Tony Scanlon. A goddamn fool." She slammed the door and was gone.

The empty weeks soon became empty months. He became reclusive, spending his days in the solitary regimen of mastering his new leg. He'd jog in place, do aerobics, pace endless circles. Days sped by, nights lingered with loneliness.

He took to going to Roseland, always timing his arrival to coincide with the end of the evening's ballroom dancing and the beginning of the disco program. He would walk into the lobby and go up to the showcase and pretend to be looking at the collection of shoes worn by famous dancers, and look in the glass's reflection to see if there was anyone he knew. It would have been unseemly for a detective sergeant to be seen going dancing alone.

Once inside the ballroom he would walk onto the mammoth dance floor and lose himself among the twirling shadows, whirling himself under the glittering lights, clapping his hands to the booming beat. He had become a Roseland regular, one of the lonesome people harboring their own fears and their own secrets.

After eleven months on sick report Scanlon yearned to be returned to full duty. On his weekly visit to his district police surgeon he would ask the doctor to send him back to work. The doctor, a benign-looking man with a slight Scottish accent, would look askance at him and leave his request unanswered. On Monday of the first week of the twelfth month of sick report, Scanlon visited his district surgeon. When Scanlon entered the doctor's sixth-floor office in the Police Academy, the surgeon was writing in Scanlon's medical folder. "I'm sending you before the board, Sergeant. You're being surveyed."

"I don't want to go before the Medical Board. I want to stay in the Job," he protested. "I've been promised."

"I'm afraid you don't have any choice. The chief surgeon and I have decided that you're unfit for full duty." The doctor removed his glasses, assumed the expression of a maternal uncle. "Three-quarters tax-free isn't a bad pension, Sergeant."

"I don't want a goddamn pension."

"I'm sorry, you're out." He put his glasses back on and continued to write in the medical folder.

Scanlon rushed from the doctor's office. He telephoned Jim Gebler, the president of the Sergeants' Benevolent Association. He told the feisty SBA president what had happened, of Fat Albert's promise that he could stay on the Job and be promoted to lieutenant. "Can you get a contract in with the chief surgeon?"

"You get your ass over here now, I'll start making some calls."

When Scanlon arrived at the SBA office in lower Manhattan he went directly into Gebler's corner office. The SBA president's thickset face was flushed. "We got a problem, Tony," he said, going to shake Scanlon's hand. "I just got off the phone with the chief surgeon. He told me that the first deputy wants as many bosses as possible put off the Job during this fiscal year."

"But why?"

"They want your budget line so that they can promote friends. Things are getting rough. There ain't much money around for promotions. They gotta make vacancies."

"So I have to reach out to the first dep or the PC."

"Looks that way. And the first dep and I don't get along. I'll give the PC a shot for you." Gebler's face brightened. He snapped his fingers. "That's the way to go."

Scanlon quickened. "What? Tell me."

"Joe Gallagher. He and the first dep are asshole buddies. They go drinking and screwing together. If there is anyone in the Job who can put a contract in with the first dep it's Gallagher. Do you know Gallagher?"

"I was in the class behind him in the Academy. We still bump into each other in the Job."

Gebler went over to his cluttered desk. "The LBA is having their monthly meeting at Ricardo's this afternoon. Gallagher is sure to be there. You hustle your ass over to Astoria and I'll get on the phone and tell Gallagher to be expecting you."

The drive from Manhattan to Astoria, Queens, took Scanlon the better part of ninety minutes. He double-parked in front of the restaurant and hurried inside. The noontime meeting was long over, and most of the delegates and members were crowded into the large circular bar. Scanlon's eyes slid along the bar searching for Joe Gallagher. He picked out the largest group of men and pushed his way through, knowing that Gallagher would be in the center, holding court. "Joe," Scanlon called out, breaking through to the center.

"Tony Scanlon, luv. How the fuck are you?" Gallagher pushed away from the bar, draped his big arm around Scanlon's shoulders, and led him over to one of the cocktail tables on the raised part of the floor that circled the bar.

"Did Jim Gebler call you?"

"I spoke to him, luv. And you don't have a problem anymore." Gallagher's eyes held a gleeful glint.

"I don't have a problem?"

"Not anymore, luv. I got on the horn to the first dep. I told the lad of your difficulty, that you were one of the Job's true heroes, and that you were a personal friend of mine." Gallagher paused to sip the drink that he had brought with him from the bar. Good politicians always stop before they drive home their good deeds— it gives the supplicant time to ponder the magnitude of the favor that was just done him. "The first dep called the chief surgeon. He made an appointment for you to see your district surgeon in the morning. Nine o'clock. Okay, luv? Does Joe Gallagher do the right thing or doesn't he?"

Scanlon sagged with relief. "I owe you a big one, Joe," he said, taking Gallagher's hand, shaking it with enthusiasm.

"Nothing to it, luv. Maybe someday you'll be in a position to do the right thing for me. Right?"

That night Scanlon went to Roseland to celebrate. He'd never forget what Joe Gallagher had done for him, never. He thought that since he'd been returned to full duty, everything else might also have changed for the better, and perhaps now might be the time to try and make it with a woman. Perhaps being away from the Job had something to do with his problem. But how should he approach a woman, now? Every time he thought about it he was filled with anxiety and a tense ache gripped his chest. How does he tell a woman that he's an amputee? When does he tell her? What does he say to her? What if he does tell her and she rejects him, walks away? What does he do then? And worst of all, what if a woman does go with him and he can't perform, can't get it up? Hi. My name is Tony. I'm an amputee and I have erectile dysfunction. Why me? What did I do to deserve this cross?

He finally reasoned that he would be better off to try to make it with a hooker. He reasoned that they considered their bodies to be income-producing property, so there'd be no emotional involvement, no worry on his part about being able to perform, no embarrassment if he couldn't. It had to be different with hookers. They were used to servicing cripples. Hookers performed one of society's more useful functions.

He left Roseland around two in the morning and walked the four blocks to the Hotel Arnold. He stood at the green-cushioned bar studying the five ladies of the night who had staked out their territory with empty bar stools. The one on his far left looked hard and unsympathetic. The other one on his left, maybe. His hands were wet and he could feel the nervous twitch in his neck. The one closest on his right looked nice. She had short brown hair and hazel eyes and a lissome body. But most of all she reminded him of Jane. Perhaps it was her smile, or perhaps he just wanted her to be Jane. He really didn't know. But when she glanced in his direction, he smiled at her and she smiled back at him. Going over to her, one question plagued him: What will I do if she rejects me? He slid onto the stool next to her. "Hi. May I buy you a drink?"

"I only drink club soda," she said, hefting her glass at him.

"Oh, I see." He hesitated, aware of his heartbeat. Urging himself forward, he blurted, "My name is Tony Scanlon. I'm an amputee."

She put her glass down and put a cigarette to her lips. He picked up the white throwaway lighter from the bar and lit it. She held his shaking hands in hers and moved her head toward the flame. "I'm Sally De Nesto."

Scanlon put the empty glass down on the treasure chest and thought, No one ever promised you it would be easy. He picked up the receiver and dialed Sally De Nesto's number. When her machine answered he waited for the beep, and then told the machine to tell its mistress that he would like to see her tomorrow night. He knew that she liked him and that she would reschedule her appointments so that he would be her last date. He wondered how many tricks she turned in one day. But then, what did that matter? She was there for him whenever he wanted her. He still wished he could make it with a straight woman. If he could only get up the courage to keep trying. He turned on his side and beat his head into the pillow. Tomorrow he had an appointment to meet the Zimmerman family.

8

The streets were full of interesting people out for a Saturday-afternoon stroll. Scanlon decided to park his car several blocks from the Zimmermans' East Side town house and walk, people-watch.

He took the vehicle identification plate from behind the visor and tossed it onto the dashboard. It was one thing to work on your own time and quite another to feed a parking meter with your own money, especially at today's rates, twenty-five cents for twenty minutes. He slid out the ashtray and flipped the hidden toggle switch that cut off his car's ignition system, reached under the front seat and pulled out the Chatman mechanical brake-wheel lock, and secured it around the brake pedal and the steering column. Sliding from his car, he hoped that it would still be there when he returned.

Most of the houses on East Seventy-ninth Street had shield-shaped stickers glued in their windows—This House's Alarm System Is Connected Directly to the Police. There were other posted warnings: This Block Is Patrolled by the East Side Observer Corp. Arabesque grilles covered most of the first- and second-floor windows, designer bars to keep the burglars out.

Scanlon's concentration was fixed on house numbers when a woman jogger brushed past him. Her shorts were so brief that the cheeks of her behind jutted out like naked half-moons. He was reminded of the witness Thomas Tibbs: there had been something odd about the way the perp had fled the crime scene, the witness had stated. His thoughts about Tibbs ended when he noticed the chic woman with the blue rinse in her hair waiting patiently at the curb for her little fag dog with pink bows in both ears to finish its bowel movement. Secured in her hand was a yellow-and-brown pooper-scooper. Scanlon wondered if that was one of those designed by Mr. Henri of Paris, France. Shit shovels for the rich. Only in the Big Apple, he thought, pausing before a house to check the address written on the back of a matchbook.

Four strips of black Thermopane streaked vertically down the front of the antique orange brick facade. A brass nameplate by the door read: Stanley Zimmerman, M.D.

He rang the chimes and stepped back, glancing up at the scudding clouds. He breathed deep. Summer scents were in the air. No answer. He leaned forward and rang again. Peering through the square of glass in the center of the heavy door, he saw a narrow passage to the right of a mahogany staircase. Up against the left wall, next to the tall sliding doors that led into a room, was a table of carved, gilded wood with a top that was inlaid in ebony and pewter. He pressed the button again.

A man's voice came from the intercom set into the doorframe. "Who is it?"

He placed his mouth in front of the metal box. "Lieutenant Scanlon."

Zimmerman led the policeman into the room with the tall doors. Scanlon took in the delicate chairs with the bouffant cushions, the Queen Anne sofas. It was a stuffy room with a green-and-gold antique desk, a buffet, and a crowded bookshelf.

As Scanlon lowered himself onto one of the dainty chairs he noticed Stanley Zimmerman's hands. They were long and graceful, as though they had been sculpted.

"When we talked yesterday, I told you that our family would be sitting shivah today. I forgot that today was Saturday. We don't sit shivah on the Sabbath."

"I knew that," Scanlon said, hoping that the chair was sturdy enough to support him and his fake leg.

Zimmerman expressed surprise at Scanlon's knowledge of Jewish law. The policeman explained that as a rookie he had worked in the Six-four in Borough Park, a compressed Brooklyn neighborhood of over two hundred synagogues. Thirteenth Avenue had been his beat. It was there that he had learned to distinguish among the Lubavitcher and the Satmar sects, and it was there that he had learned the difference between kosher and glatt kosher, and it was there that he had learned about shivah, the seven days of mourning.

"I guess policemen learn a lot about other people's customs," Zimmerman said lamely.

"That we do."

Zimmerman's gaze fixed on some point behind Scanlon. "I miss her terribly."

Scanlon nodded sympathetically. He saw the anguish in the eyes, heard the sadness in the voice, and felt uncomfortable being there, as though he were an intruder among the bereaved.

"Tell me how my mother died," he said, looking down at the floor.

An attempted robbery that had gone awry, he told the doctor. He added that the entire resources of the department had been thrown into the hunt for his mother's killers, and that teams of detectives had been pulled off other cases to work exclusively on this one. Scanlon watched him closely as he talked. Everyone is a suspect, a truism among police adages. The doctor's face remained tense. Sunlight made a filigree design on the walls of the room. Scanlon finished his dismal narrative, leaned forward, waiting for the son's response.

"Why, Lieutenant?"

Thinking that he was referring to the heinous double homicide, Scanlon shook his head as though unable to comprehend the senselessness of the crime.

"Why would anyone, with an accomplice standing by, and with a van for a getaway, want to hold up a candy store? For what end? To steal some jelly beans and some small change?" Scanlon fell under his questioning gaze. "And why my mother's store?" The demand had sudden vigor.

Scanlon's phantom leg was distracting him. "Perhaps it was a target of opportunity for a couple of cokeheads."

"Really?" A mocking tone. "Has your investigation so far led you to any other conclusion?"

Scanlon shrugged. "There is, I guess, the possibility that it was a paid-for killing. Like the CBS murders, a contract on the life of one of the victims, the other unfortunate just happening to be in the wrong place at the wrong time."

"I suppose someone like Gallagher would make mortal enemies. Narcotics work must be a nasty business."

"That is true. And, of course, your mother might have been the intended victim."

Zimmerman leaped to his feet, his face ablaze with anger. "How dare you insinuate such a thing?"

Scanlon held up his palms in a gesture of appeasement. "I said a possibility, Doctor. That doesn't make it gospel."

"I don't want to hear any more of that talk. Do you understand that, Officer?"

"It's my job to examine every possible contingency, no matter how unpleasant or implausible it might seem to the victim's family."

"Not in my home, you won't. And for your information, my mother was a wonderful woman who didn't have an enemy in the world. She was a woman who did good for other people. She . . ." He began to sob.

Scanlon waited for him to regain his composure.

Wiping his eyes with a handkerchief, Zimmerman said, "I just don't know what we'll do without her. She was the rock that supported the entire family."

Scanlon thought of his own mother. "I understand that."

An air of uncertainty came between the two men.

Scanlon watched him twisting the handkerchief. "Do you know that your mother worked for organized crime?"

Zimmerman's eyes flashed at him. "You're crazy."

"She took gambling action for the local bookmaker. His name is Walter Ticornelli. Have you ever heard your mother mention that name?"

"No, I haven't. And I don't believe a word of what you've just said. Mother working for a bookmaker! It's ridiculous."

"No it isn't, Doctor. It goes with the franchise in that neighborhood. People didn't just flock to her store to see her, or to buy things. They came because they could lay ten cents or a quarter on a number, or bet the flats or the trotters. Your mother took that action. She might have accidentally stumbled onto something connected with the bookmakers' other business. Narcotics? A hit on someone? Something that made your mother a liability."

The air was heavy with unspoken anger. "I think you had better leave my home, Lieutenant."

"Our investigation to date leads us to believe that it was a hold-up, but, as I told you before, I have to look into every angle. If you don't want to help, there is nothing that I can do to force you. She was your mother, not mine." He started to rise up from his seat.

"Of course I want to help."

Scanlon lowered himself back down. The interview had become stressful; most cops agree that such interviews are counter-productive. "Do you live here alone, Doctor?"

"With my wife and daughter."

"Are they home?"

"My sister and my wife are shopping for shoes for my daughter. I persuaded them to go."

Scanlon saw the wrenching sense of loss in his eyes and felt sorry for him.

Examining his hands, Zimmerman said, "Andrea, my daughter, was nine years old yesterday. We were to have a birthday party. Mother bought a cake. Instead we sat shivah." His eyes filled again.

Scanlon recalled the crime scene: chunks of cake and whipped cream and raspberry filling mixed with body parts and gore. Walter Ticornelli had stated that he had observed Gallagher carrying a cake box into the store. "Tell me about your mother, Stanley."

Zimmerman's face molded into a disturbed expression. Slowly it turned contemplative and he began to scour memories. "Mother was born in Warsaw into an upper-middle-class family. When the war came she had a husband, and three small children, two girls and a boy. The Nazis rounded them up and shipped them to Auschwitz, where her family was killed in the crematoriums." Tears were streaming down his face as he talked. "Mother was spared because those savages needed people to translate the camp bulletins into several languages. Mother was fluent in German, Polish, Russian, and Hungarian. She met our father in Auschwitz. He too had lost his entire family. He survived because he was an accountant and they needed inventory writers to keep track of all the property they stole from the living and the dead. My parents worked in the same barracks. They were two human, breathing skeletons, working next to each other, day after day, who somehow sustained each other and fell in love.

"They were married shortly after they were liberated and came to this country as displaced persons. They had two children. My sister, Linda, is three years older than I." A painful remembrance made him look away. "Dad was killed by a drunk driver, crossing a Bensonhurst Street. The driver was convicted and given a suspended sentence. Mother opened the candy store to support us. She worked long hours, seven days a week. Linda had to come home directly from school to do the housework, the laundry, prepare dinner. On weekends my sister and I would help out in the store so Mother could get some sleep in the back."

He glared at Scanlon. "My mother work for organized crime? What nonsense. I'll tell you the kind of a woman my mother was. Look at me, Lieutenant. I'm not what you would call a handsome man. I'm short, I have a face like an owl, and my hair's like a monk's, but my mother made me feel nine feet tall and more handsome than Gregory Peck and Clark Gable. She was constantly telling me how wonderful I was, that I was going to grow up and be a great surgeon. That I was the one who was going to make up for our family that had been killed in the camps."

He held up his hands. "These hands held the power, Mother told me. It was my hands that made me handsome. My specialty is plastics, Lieutenant. My mother would send me neighborhood children who needed my special skills but could never afford to pay for them. Recently I did a cranial-facial reconstruction on a little girl who had a congenital birth defect. My mother sent her to me. And I should do it without a fee, Mother said. Because we have to give to those less fortunate than we are. To repay this great country for the good that it has done for us. And you tell me that my mother was a criminal. Does that sound like a criminal mind to you?"

Scanlon was determined not to become embroiled. His voice soft, he said, "How do you and Linda get along?"

134

"My sister and I are close. Growing up as we did made us protective of each other."

"How did your sister get along with your mother?"

"They were very close. Linda adored Mother."

There were sounds of people, the sudden babble of female voices. Scanlon craned his head in the direction of the door. Two women appeared. A girl followed behind them. A tentative silence filled the room. The doctor went to greet them. Moving a hand from one to the other, he introduced them. "This is my sister, Linda."

She smiled politely and moved over to one of the dainty chairs and sat in ladylike fashion.

Zimmerman introduced his wife. Rachel Zimmerman was an attractive woman with a curtain of banged brunette hair that fell to just above the eyebrows. She looked to be in her early thirties. She had on a plain cotton dress, Roman-style sandals, no hose, and was holding two shoe boxes. Standing beside her was a girl with chestnut hair, inquisitive brown eyes, and a shy little smile. She had on jeans and a baggy top with a big red-nosed Snoopy emblazoned on the front, and white sneakers with big blue tassels.

Rachel Zimmerman came over and shook Scanlon's hand. "Thank you for coming."

Andrea Zimmerman ran to her father, throwing her arms around his waist, hugging tight. "Mommy bought me a pair of penny loafers and Aunt Linda bought me sneakers."

"You really made out," said the father, hugging her close.

The girl turned and looked at Scanlon. "Are you a real policeman?"

"Yes."

"Are you as mean as Dirty Harry is in the movies?"

Scanlon grinned at her. "Meaner."

"Come on, young lady," the mother said. "Let's you and me go upstairs and try on those new shoes of yours. I'm sure that the lieutenant and your father have things they want to discuss."

Andrea Zimmerman looked up at her father. "Daddy, I miss Granny."

"So do I," Stanley Zimmerman said and cried. The room became silent.

"Why don't you go upstairs with them, Stanley? I'll talk to the lieutenant," Linda Zimmerman said.

Stanley Zimmerman took hold of his daughter's hand. "If you need me, I'll be upstairs," he told Scanlon, moving toward the door. When he came up to where his sister sat he stopped and whispered in her ear.

Scanlon could not hear what was said, but he did see Linda Zimmerman's eyes dart in his direction.

Linda Zimmerman pulled off her big-brimmed black straw hat and placed it on the walnut table next to her. She carefully tugged off one of her black lacy crochet gloves that matched her linen dress. She began to rake out her hair. Hair that flowed down to her shoulders and had a deep black sheen. She took her time removing the last glove, her face set in thought. She tugged it off and slapped it down on the hat's wide rim.

"Stanley tells me that you think there is a possibility that Mother's death was premeditated. He also said that you think that Mother was part of some criminal activity."

He made a dismissive gesture with his hands. "What I said was that I have to examine every possibility." He noticed that she wore no rings and wondered if she was married. He told her of her mother's gambling activities. Added, "All the evidence gathered so far indicates that it was a holdup."

"I see." She clasped her hands on her lap. "Would you mind telling me the details of the case?"

Scanlon related the official version of the case, taking care not to mention the Jackson Heights splash pad or Joe Gallagher's secret life.

"Those animals," she said, speaking with visible anger. "To snuff out two lives. Scum like that should not be permitted to live."

"It happens every day of the week. And most times it doesn't even rate two lines on the evening news."

An ugly expression of agreement came over her face. "Don't misunderstand what I'm going to say, Lieutenant. My brother and I want them caught and punished. What we don't want is unnecessary publicity."

"I can understand that, Miss Zimmerman."

"I don't think that you can, Lieutenant." She shifted slightly in her seat, tucked her dress under her thigh. "I am thirty-nine years old and I'm a vice-president of the trust department of Morgan Fidelity. My responsibilities at the bank include the maintenance of private investment portfolios for some of the wealthiest people in this country."

"I fail to see what that has to do with your mother's death."

"Banking, Lieutenant, is a stodgy world dominated by stodgy men who look down their stodgy noses at women. Scandal, no matter how far removed from me personally, could, and in fact would, hurt my career."

"Your mother's death could hardly be called scandal."

"In banking, it is indecorous to have one's name appear anywhere in a newspaper, except on the social page, the financial page, or the obituary page. It is one thing to have a close member of your family the unfortunate victim of a random killing, and quite another thing to have a member the victim of premeditated murder, or connected in any way to any illicit activities."

Scanlon went to answer her. "Miss Zimmerman..."

"Please, hear me out, Lieutenant. My family does not want to read any of your ridiculously absurd surmises about my mother being the victim of a contract killing or part of any crime family. Such stories would have an adverse affect on my and my brother's careers. If you want to look for reasons for the killings I suggest that you delve into your dead lieutenant's background, because there are no motives in my mother's. I hope you understand what I'm telling you."

He caught himself watching her with an intensity that surprised him. He looked down at his hands, politely hesitant to say what was on his mind. He leaned forward slightly and looked at her. "Miss Zimmerman, it is my job to arrest people who commit crimes. We are not talking here about a case of malicious mischief or Assault Three; we're talking about a double homicide in which a member of the force was one of the victims. We are going to break this case. And you and your family can be assured that the press will get nothing out of me or any of my men. You see, Miss Zimmerman, in the world of cops and robbers, newspeople rank several notches below whores and pimps. Do I make myself clear, Miss Zimmerman?"

A beginning smile caught her lips. "Perfectly. And my name is Linda, Lieutenant."

"And mine is Tony."

She put her fingertips to her lips and gave him a slow warming glance. "I'm glad that we understand each other, Tony."

He became aware of her fragrance. Evergreen and orange. She was more beautiful than he had first realized. "Did you and your mother speak often?"

"On the telephone, at least twice a day."

"Did she mention where she was getting your niece's birthday cake?"

"A cop friend of hers, she said. He was getting it for her wholesale."

Wholesale, a cop's way of doing business. "Was your mother a wealthy woman?"

Slight annoyance. "She was comfortable. And, before you ask, her estate will be divided between her children, equally."

"You and your brother appear to be successful people. Why was it necessary for your mother to work at her age?"

"It was necessary because she wanted to. My brother and I urged her to give up the store. She refused. Said that she would never become a burden to her children. You see, Lieu—Tony, my mother was a survivor of the Holocaust. Their minds never really recover. Mother would squirrel her money away, every cent that she didn't need to live on, preparing for the day when she would have to flee, to buy her freedom, her children's and grandchildren's freedom. It was only during the last few years that Stanley and I were able to persuade her to put her money in the bank and make prudent investments."

"Did you know that she took gambling action?"

"That was done as an accommodation for her friends in the neighborhood. I don't think she made fifty dollars a week taking those bets."

"How come your brother didn't know about the gambling?"

"Because mothers and daughters talk in more detail than sons and mothers. Women do generally."

"Did your mother ever mention Joe Gallagher to you?"

"She did mention the name once or twice. He was a friend from the neighborhood. That's all I know."

"What about Walter Ticornelli?"

"No, never."

"Gretta Polchinski?"

A frigid smile. "You mean the madam. Yes, Mother would talk

about her. We would laugh over Gretta and her whorehouse. The women used to come into the store in the mornings and tell Mother they were glad that their husbands bothered Gretta's girls and left them alone."

"Did your mother have any business dealings with Gretta?"

"Hardly. Gretta Polchinski was not the kind of woman my mother would associate with. In Poland my mother had women like that to clean her house, not to have dealings with."

He got up and walked over to the display of African shields and spears on the far wall. He felt a spear point and carefully examined the shields. She was next to him, explaining, "Stanley collects them. He has done a lot of work in Africa for the United Nations."

He loved her fragrance and was aware of a desire to sweep her into his arms, caress her body, consume her. He wondered if women ever had sudden urges like that, had blunt erotic images. Even if he made a move and she responded favorably, then what? He could never get it up with a straight woman. He felt antsy.

"Linda, can you think of anyone who might want to cause your mother harm?"

She fixed him with a penetrating look. "No, I can't."

"Thank you for your cooperation, and please accept my condolences."

She moved to where her hat and pocketbook were and took out a dark-colored card holder from her bag. She removed a card and handed him one. "I can be reached at that number during business hours."

"And if it should become necessary to contact you after business hours?"

Her cynical look became a small smile. She went back to her pocketbook and removed a silver pencil and wrote a number on the back of the card. "I can be reached at this number at night. But only if necessary, and never after eleven."

It was late afternoon when Scanlon walked into the Nine-three station house. A lone policeman manned the telephone switchboard, whiling away his tour by flipping through worn copies of *Screw* and *Hustler* magazines. The muster room was empty, save for the coffee containers and the waxed paper that was scattered over tables and sills. Nobody sat behind the raised desk. The sergeant had left his post and gone into the one-twenty-four room to aid a new female typist with an inviting smile. The old rules and procedures of the NYPD, rule 124, delineated the duties and responsibilities of the clerical patrolman assigned to each of the three platoons. Hence the cop assigned to clerical duties would forever be known as the one-twenty-four man and his workplace as the one-twenty-four room.

Scanlon was struck by the pervasive quiet inside the station house. It was the weekend, and the Palace Guard does not work weekends. The highway safety man, the summons men, the youth officer, the Community Relations people, the lead clerical man, his assistants, and the entire civilian clerical staff, save the few who work the clock, were all at home making like nine-to-fivers. A strange stillness becalms station houses on the weekends.

The TS operator looked up from his magazine and nodded to Scanlon, then returned his attention to the centerfold's delights.

After Scanlon had left the Zimmerman town house he had decided to pay an unannounced visit to the Squad to see if there had been any new developments on the case. Police management texts state that unannounced visits are a meaningful supervisory tool. Scanlon knew better. He knew that the moment he climbed the staircase out of sight, the cop on TS was going to dial upstairs to the Squad. "Your boss is on his way up," he would say, and turn to the next color photograph.

That was the problem with management texts: they never take into account the realities of the real world. Whenever the borough shoofly is spotted within a precinct, that precinct's emergency code is immediately transmitted over the radio. "Apache. Apache." Beware, a Judas is among us.

A realistic man, Scanlon knew that his unannounced supervisory visit was nothing more than a way of killing time before he went to pay his respects at Joe Gallagher's wake and keep his late-night appointment with Sally De Nesto. He had already cleaned his apartment and danced his aerobics, washed and hung out his pantyhose, and now there was nothing for him to do but play cops and robbers.

When he walked into the squad room he found one industrious detective at his typewriter. "Anything doing?" he said, moving to the line of clipboards that were hooked on the wall to the right of the detention cage.

The gray-haired detective, Steigman, who had a stomach that spilled over his wide western belt buckle, looked up from the machine. "They found the van. It was torched."

"Where did they find it?" Scanlon asked, unhooking the roll call.

"Laurel Hill Boulevard, right next to Calvary Cemetery."

Scanlon knew the area. It was a deserted section of real estate located under the Long Island Expressway and the Brooklyn-Queens Expressway. An artery that led into the major highways and avenues of both Brooklyn and Queens. A perfect place to abandon a getaway vehicle and torch it. "Was forensics called to the scene?"

"Yeah, they were there. The van was a charred hulk. There was nothing there to be found, but they went through the motions. The fire marshal said that the fire was started from inside the body of the van. The Five is on your desk," Steigman said.

Looking over the roll call, Scanlon asked, "Where is the rest of the team?"

"Biafra Baby and Colon are out doing a canvass where the van was found. There are a few factories around there. Somebody might have seen something. And Florio is available," Steigman said with a sly glance at the lieutenant.

"Available" in NYPD argot meant that Detective Angelo Florio's whereabouts were known to his partner, and that he could be reached quickly, if needed, and that there was a blank Twenty-eight with his signature affixed if something should go wrong. If that should happen, the UF 28, Request for Leave of Absence, would be filled out and filed, and Florio's name scratched off the duty roster for that tour. Double homicide or not, life within the NYPD goes on.

Scanlon moved over to the waist-high tray cabinet near the Dial-a-Brew machine and moved his finger over the index annotations on the front of each tray: Resident Known Criminal File, Known Gamblers File, Precinct Directory File, Parolee/Released Prisoner File, Vulva File. He pulled out the last tray. Detective Florio's "available" telephone number was listed along with the name and address of his girlfriend. In the back of the tray was a stack of blank Twenty-eights, all signed. It was each detective's responsibility to see that the Vulva File was kept current.

Walking into his office, Scanlon unhooked the remote from his belt. He sat on his desk and dialed his home number. The first voice that played back was that of his mother inviting him to Sunday dinner. She was going to have a few of her friends from the neighborhood, she said. He broke into a big smile, for he knew from long experience the meaning behind his mother's guileless tone. For sure, included among her friends would be a single woman who his mother and her cronies had decided would make him a perfect wife. The last one that she tried to fix him up with played the piano and spoke French, his mother had confided in the kitchen of her rent-controlled apartment. Her one great desire in life was to get him married.

Sally De Nesto's voice was next. She confirmed their date for later that night and asked that he not arrive at her place before ten. She offered no explanation; none was needed.

He read through the Gallagher/Zimmerman case folder, jotting reminders to himself. Had Maggie Higgins located the missing witness, Valerie Clarkson, the only one of Gallagher's girlfriends to pull a Mandrake? Call Thorsen woman to ascertain if she'll consent to being hypnotized. Interview Gallagher's wife. He wondered what it must have been like to be married to a living legend. He'd have to wait until after the funeral to find out. He had started to jot down something else when he caught a whiff of Linda Zimmerman's fragrance. He wondered what it would be like to hold her in his arms. At one time when he used to fantasize about women he'd feel a stirring in his stomach, sometimes a sudden hardness. And now . . . He tweaked his genitals. They felt useless. He snapped the pencil in half, threw the pieces down on his desk, got up, and hurried from his office.

The exercise room in the basement of the station house was empty. The heavy bag hung still; the speed bag glistened. Weights and barbells were neatly lined up in their cases. He stripped off his shirt, took his gun out of his holster, put it on the shelf, and began doing bench presses with ninety pounds of bells.

Limp dick, with the pegleg, he kept repeating to himself, as the sweat appeared on his body.

The E. G. McGuinness Funeral Home had a porte cochere of four stately white columns. Tara of Greenpoint. It was on Austin Boulevard between Baker and Furbish streets. Scanlon arrived a little before seven. Police cars were lined up on both sides of Austin and on the side streets. Policemen's private cars also clogged the streets. A detail of one sergeant and ten cops had been assigned by the borough command to ensure the free flow of vehicular and pedestrian traffic. Wakes of hero cops were public affairs. The precinct designations on the radio cars attested to the solidarity of the patrol force. Every precinct command in the city was represented.

Inside, the funeral home was thronged with mourners. Every cop wore his dress uniform; no savers here. Every shield bore a mourning band. The portable walls on the first floor of the home had been opened to form one enormous room to accommodate the overflow crowd. There were hundreds of floral pieces. Many stands were filled with mass cards. There were dozens of chasubles and chalices that would be donated to churches and priests. An honor guard of six lieutenants was formed around the closed, flag-draped coffin.

Mourners queued up to the prie-dieu to pay their respects. A grim-faced George Harris was there to greet each one, to lead them over to the cushioned prayer stand, and wait as they silently prayed. As each mourner stood, Harris would escort him over to the widow, who sat grieving in the first row. Harris would wait as condolences were mumbled and then usher the mourner away.

The widow's chair distinguished her as the primary mourner. It was a wing chair with walnut cabriole legs and was covered with floral needlework on a black background. The other mourners sat on metal folding chairs that had thin black cushions tied onto their seats.

Scanlon's eyes played over the crowd as he shouldered his way into the viewing room. He spied the familiar group of retired cops clustered together talking about the old days. There were no cops on the Job then with names like Abdul Illah Baihat or Kim Lee Song. In those days the Job was lily-white, Christian. Scanlon recognized a few of the old chiefs. Some of them had been powers in the Job when he was a rookie. Now they were shriveled old men with nothing to do but attend cop retirement parties and wakes in the vain hope that someone would recognize them and acknowledge their past glories with a "Howyadoin', Chief?"

Across the vast room, standing by themselves, was the PC, and the first dep and Deputy Chief MacAdoo McKenzie. Scanlon thought that the first dep had put on a few pounds. He grimaced inwardly when he saw what MacAdoo McKenzie was wearing: trousers with a purple-and-white tartan design, a maroon shirt with a black tie, and a black double-knit sport jacket with white saddle stitching over the lapels and pockets. A motley assortment of used parts indeed.

McKenzie looked in Scanlon's direction and quickly turned to the PC and said something.

Scanlon stepped into the crowd and began to edge his way forward toward the coffin. He reached the front of the room in time to see Harris lead an elderly woman over to the prayer stand. Scanlon thought that Harris's expression was a perfect blend of graciousness and solemnity. Perhaps a wee bit too perfect.

When Harris turned to lead the woman over to the widow, he saw Scanlon and motioned to a nearby cop to take over for him.

"Thanks for coming, Lou," Harris said, shaking his hand. "Come on, I'll introduce you to Joe's widow."

Mary Ann Gallagher had dark shadows under her eyes. Her long, light brown hair hung limp around her pallid face. She wore an unflattering rusty black dress and no jewelry, save her wedding band. She had a rosary clutched in her right hand, and she slowly beat her chest in dazed prayer.

Scanlon bent to express his condolences. Her lips were lined with a white pastelike substance. Despite her disheveled appearance, Scanlon could see an attractive woman in her late thirties, a woman who had exquisite blue eyes.

Mary Ann Gallagher gazed blankly into Scanlon's face as he whispered his sorrow at her loss. Duty done, he turned to leave, but Harris held him by the elbow and bent to say something in the widow's ear. Suddenly a cold clammy hand gripped Scanlon's wrist. He looked down and saw that her face had come alive in some strange frightening way. Her nostrils flared as though to breathe flames; her lips were curled into an ugly snarl.

Anchoring herself on his wrist, she hoisted herself up out of her seat. Her face was inches away from Scanlon's, her breath stale. "Get them!" she shrieked. "Those animals who took my husband from me. Those savages who destroyed our lives. Kill them!" She went limp and collapsed into the chair. Women rushed from their seats to console her.

For the first time Scanlon took note of the two frightened children sitting on either side of the widow. The girl was about ten and obviously suffered from Down's syndrome. She wore Mary Janes, white lace socks, and a blue dress.

The boy was about twelve or so and had brown hair. His thin black tie was askew and his serge suit too large.

"Let's go outside and grab a smoke," Harris said.

They made their way out to the veranda. A purple twilight filled the horizon. The outline of the Malcolm X Housing Project was stark against the backdrop. Scanlon glanced at the compact mass of azaleas in front of the home.

They made their way through the lingering policemen and down the wooden steps. The grass was freshly cut and had a clean smell to it. They made their way over to the weeping willow in the center of the manicured lawn. Scanlon noticed that Harris was wearing black cowboy boots with his uniform. The *Patrol Guide* mandated that uniform and equipment conform to Equipment Section samples: shoes—black, plain, smooth leather, lace-type with flat soles and raised rubber heels.

Sergeant George Harris liked to break the rules.

They leaned against the tree trunk; Harris took out a package of cigarettes and shook out a half-smoked butt. Scanlon watched him light it. "Are things that bad, Sarge?"

"Cigarettes are expensive. I don't toss nothing away. Waste not, want not."

Reaching up, Scanlon pulled down a branch and smelled the tassellike spike of flowers.

"A couple of your detectives were around looking for you."

Scanlon let go of the branch. It rustled upward. "Where are they?"

Harris nodded across Austin Boulevard to McJackoo's Bar and Grill.

"They said that they were going to stop for a taste."

Scanlon looked over at the line of policemen leaving the funeral home and making tracks to McJackoo's. "Were you able to find out anything at the One-fourteen?"

"With the wake and all I haven't had much time to nose around.

You gotta remember that Joe was a boss and didn't exactly socialize with too many cops. The few that I did rap with didn't know nothing about his private life."

Harris took a deep drag and then field-stripped the butt.

"You come up with anything?" he asked, with a side glance at the lieutenant.

"I interviewed the Zimmerman family. They're intelligent, affluent, and decent people. When I hinted that their mother might have been hit they were furious. Impossible, they said. The daughter said that if I don't believe it was a robbery then I should delve in Joe's life, because her mother's was as pure as the driven snow."

"Ain't we all," Harris said. "What makes you so sure that it was a hit and not a robbery?"

"Because we got witnesses that tell us that the perp just walked into that candy store, called out, 'Hey you,' and started blasting. We also know that the perp had a getaway van and an accomplice. There was no 'give me your money, get your hands up, open the till.' The guy who stepped through that door came to do murder."

"And you think that Joe was the mark?"

"He's the logical target. He was Mister Perfect in public, but we know what his private life was like. He wasn't exactly pure."

"Who the hell is?"

"I can't argue with that," Scanlon said. "Somewhere there is a motive, and I'm going to keep digging until I find it. And when I do, it'll be a blazing signpost that will point me in the direction of the perps."

"You got any ideas who or why?"

"All I got so far is suspects." Scanlon looked at him. "Joe ever talk to you about a woman named Valerie Clarkson?"

Harris's face hardened in concentration. "Not that I recall. Who is she?"

"One of his girlfriends. We asked her to come in for a chat and she agreed. Then she copped a mope. She was the only one of his lady friends to do that."

"You got people out on the streets looking for her?"

"Higgins," Scanlon said. "I didn't know that Joe had a child with Down's syndrome."

"Both them kids are adopted. Him and his wife made a home for two unadoptables. Gave them love, a family. The boy is slightly retarded. That's the kind of guy Joe Gallagher was. The fuck had a heart of gold. Never mind all that shit about his weaknesses. Look at those two kids. That will tell you the kind of man he was."

"How did you and Joe get along?"

"We were friends. On the job Joe was my boss. What he said went."

"You never had any disagreements over how to do things?"

"Of course we did," Harris said. "And Joe would listen to my side of the argument and then decide. Sometimes he saw it my way, and sometimes he didn't."

"I also interviewed Luise Bardwell and her husband." He watched for Harris's reaction at the mention of his girlfriend's name.

"What did you think of her?"

"A strange lady. And her husband certainly doesn't operate on all his cylinders either."

"Takes all kinds, Lou."

"Amen to that. You still seeing her?"

"Naw. I haven't seen her in a while. I'll tell you, with this AIDS thing I don't feature going with bisexual women. It's one thing if you don't know, but when you know it, and you still go with them, then you ain't operating with a full deck either."

"You going out with anyone else involved in the case?"

"No." Harris pushed away from the tree. "I gotta get back inside, Lou. I'll call you if I come up with anything."

A group of policemen left the funeral home and went down the stone path and across Austin Boulevard, heading for McJackoo's Bar and Grill.

More mourners arrived. Among them, dressed completely in black with a lace mantilla draped over her peroxide head, was Gretta Polchinski.

Scanlon caught up with her as she was about to go up the steps. He took hold of her shoulder, stopping her. Her face was heavily made up. "Black suits you, Gretta."

"I'm here to pay my respects to the dead. Not to get my balls busted by you."

He moved up close to her, said conspiratorially, "Got anything to tell me?"

She laughed and turned to leave. He stopped her. "I assumed

that a community leader like yourself would be able to pick up some tidbits for your friendly policeman on the beat."

She jerked her arm free of him. "I heard that your dead lieutenant and his sergeant were as close as a quarter to nine. Harris ran the show for Gallagher. And Gallagher never said thank you. But then, that's just like a cop."

"Anything else?"

"Don't you ever stop working? You oughta get yourself a wife. That way you'd have other things to fill your time with than just breaking my chops."

Scanlon's right eyebrow arched. "I have a friend who's been married three times. He always looks depressed." He watched her march up the stairs.

Denny McJackoo was a paunchy man with a round, thick-jowled face, a perpetual twinkle in his clever gray eyes, and the bogs of Ireland fogging his booming voice. As the proud owner of six bars, all of which were located within a three-block radius of the local funeral home, Denny McJackoo knew from experience that the wakes of cops and firemen were sudden bonanzas. "Aye, reposing the dead is a thirsty business, for the dear lads do truly love their whiskey," Denny McJackoo had confided on more than one occasion to his seven sons. When he found out that the Gallagher wake was to be held at E. G. McGuinness's he prudently gave his regular bartenders off and replaced them with his sons, with the following admonitions: buy back every fourth round, work from an open cash drawer, and ring up every sixth sale. "Aye, lads, there'll be undeclared cash that'll need burying."

A squeamish feeling made Tony Scanlon hesitate in front of the entrance to McJackoo's. Many sad experiences had taught every boss in the Job about the dangers inherent in St. Patrick's Day and cops' wakes. These were the occasions when drunken policemen shot other cops. Scanlon took a deep breath and reluctantly pushed his way inside. His apprehension grew as he took in the scene around him. Raucous policemen reeled through the crowd to greet friends. A heavy cloud of smoke hung under the ceiling. From somewhere a jukebox blared "Old Fenian Gun." A large dice game was in progress in the rear of the bar. The camp followers who go to all cop functions to gamble were out in force, from all parts of the city. The shuffleboard had been converted into a twenty-one table. Policemen crowded in around the long board, watching the dealer, a tall cop wearing the jodhpurs of a mounted cop and with a corncob pipe gripped between his teeth, toss out hole cards to the many players. As usual in such large games four decks of cards were being used simultaneously by the banker.

Uniform blouses, minus their shields, were stacked high atop the jukebox. The coatracks that extended upward from the green leatherette booths were bundled high with uniforms. Every cop had his shield clipped onto his gunbelt or tucked securely into his pocket. Drunk or sober, cops are a wary lot.

Scanlon stood among the crush searching for his men. "How-thefuckarya, Lou?" an unfamiliar voice shouted. Scanlon nodded in the direction of the voice. Taking in the scene around him, Scanlon decided that it was time to haul his ass out of there. Too many cops in too small an area, too many loaded guns mixing with too much booze. He had just started to go for the exit when he heard a familiar voice shout his name. He turned and saw two pairs of arms waving wildly over the tops of heads. "Shit," he mumbled, elbowing his way over to the arms.

Hector Colon and Simon Jones were squeezed in at the end of the bar. Lew Brodie sat on a stool, hunched over a shot of rye, glaring down into the whiskey glass. His harelip was pronounced and red, the result of the alcohol in his system.

"You wanted to see me," Scanlon said, pushing his way up to them.

Colon jerked a thumb at Simon Jones. "Me and Biafra Baby have come up with something."

"I'm listening."

Colon put down his glass of beer, wiped froth from his mustache. "We finished a canvass of where the van was found and came up with nothing, so we went into the house to bang out the Five. As we were coming out we ran into Stone and Trumwell coming in on a personal. They were the two cops first on the scene."

"I know who they are," Scanlon said, irritated because of where he was.

Colon continued, "Stone stopped us. He said that he remembered a case that went down five, six years ago that might have some connection to the Gallagher/Zimmerman caper." He took a gulp of beer. "An attempted homicide on a dude named Eddie Hamill. It seems that Hamill was a certified nut job, a burglar, and a heavy-duty-type gambler. According to Stone, Hamill was into Walter Ticornelli for some real bread. Around twelve large, Stone said. The story goes that Hamill unilaterally decided to cancel out his debt with Ticornelli. And when the shy demanded the vig from Hamill, Ticornelli done got knocked on his delicate ass." Colon drank more beer.

Lew Brodie threw down the shot, grimaced, and chased the whiskey down with beer.

The tumult had grown louder. A shouting and shoving match between two cops at the twenty-one table was quickly broken up.

Colon drained his glass, licked his mustache clean.

Scanlon grew more impatient. His phantom leg itched. He leaned sideways and scratched it. "Continue."

"Ticornelli was supposed to have sent three gorillas around to change Hamill's attitude toward paying his just debts," Colon said. "The word is that Hamill sent the three of them to the hospital with various parts of their anatomy in splints. People in the neighborhood started to say that Ticornelli didn't have the muscle to back up the money that he had out on the street. And that, *Teniente,* is bad advertisement for a shylock. Ticornelli was supposed to have made a pilgrimage to Mulberry Street to seek permission from the head goombah to have Hamill hit. Permission granted."

Colon caught the bartender's attention and swept his hand around the group to indicate that he was ordering another round of drinks. "One gray March evening our boy Eddie Hamill is about to enter his six-story walk-up when two Italo-American types reeking of Sicilian olive oil step from the shadows and proceed to peg nine-millimeters at ol' Eddie Boy. The story goes that Eddie, being the athletic type, does a header off the stoop and lands on top of some garbage cans and proceeds to take off like an Olympic sprinter. But he ain't fast enough, because he wakes up in intensive care minus one kneecap, a spleen, part of a lung, and three toes off his right foot.

"When Hamill gets out of the hospital, the first thing he does is to telephone Ticornelli and tell him that he intends to return the fucking favor in spades."

A fight broke out in the dice game. Two cops were rolling on the floor, trying to punch each other. Several policemen attempted to pry them apart. Scanlon was reminded of the cop who shot his best friend while they were driving home after three days of St. Patrick's Day partying.

The fight was broken up, the game resumed.

Scanlon was determined to cut it short and get the hell out of there. He had no desire to be dragged before the grand jury or the Firearms Review Board as a witness to one cop shooting another. "So where the hell is the connection with Gallagher?" Scanlon asked, glancing in the direction of the dice game.

Biafra Baby took up the story. "Stone told us that Ticornelli was in the habit of showing up at Yetta's candy store around the same time every day to pick up the day's action. Fourteen hundred. Gallagher and Ticornelli are the same size and have the same build. And they both drive Fords. It could have been a case of mistaken identity. Hamill, or someone he hired to waste Ticornelli, might have mistaken Gallagher for Ticornelli. And they hit the old lady because she was a witness."

"So were the kids in the back of the store witnesses," Scanlon said.

"Yeah, but they were in the back of the store. And it's one thing to take out adults and another to take out a couple of kids," Colon said.

Scanlon was skeptical. "Why would Hamill wait so long to take Ticornelli out?"

"That's just it," Biafra Baby said. "Hamill didn't wait to get his revenge. The word is that there have been several botched attempts on Ticornelli's life over the past five years. And the word is that Eddie Hamill was behind every one."

"Stone also told us that Ticornelli has people scouring Greenpoint for Hamill and can't find him. Eddie Boy has become the Phantom of Greenpoint," Colon said.

Scanlon shook his head. "I'm conversant with every open case that the Squad is carrying. And I can't recall any attempted murder on Walter Ticornelli."

"Stone said that the first attempt came shortly after Hamill was released from the hospital. Stone and his partner responded to the ten-ten—Shots Fired. Trumwell took the original Sixty-one. And this all happened before any of us were assigned to the Nine-three Squad," Biafra Baby said. "And as for the other attempts on Ticornelli, he ain't exactly the type to file complaint reports with the police."

Scanlon leaned his back against the bar, digesting what he had just been told. Like it or not, he had just been tossed another suspect.

A heavy-set detective named Jerry Allowman from the Eight-three Squad tottered over and flopped an arm around Lew Brodie's shoulder. "You guys got a hump of a homicide on your hands."

Brodie scowled up at him. "No shit, Dick Tracy." He shoved Allowman away.

The Eight-three detective started to complain about the gross indignity that he had just suffered at the hands of a brother detective, then saw the ferocious look in Brodie's eyes, thought better of it, and stumbled backward into the crowd.

"Did you go back and check the Sixty sheets and the Sixty-ones for the original complaint on Ticornelli's life?" Scanlon asked Biafra Baby.

"We checked back three years," Biafra Baby said. "We couldn't go beyond that period because those files are locked up in the old record room."

"So? Why didn't you get the key from the desk officer and check them out?" Scanlon said, annoyed.

Lew Brodie's head shot up. "We couldn't get the key because the desk officer didn't have the key. The only people in the Nine-three who do have the key to the old record room are the lead clerical man and his gofer. And neither of them scumbags work weekends." He gulped down his whiskey and slammed the glass on the zinc bar counter.

Scanlon sighed frustration. "First thing Monday, dig out those files."

9

Sally De Nesto raised her head off the pillow and kissed the cleft in his chin, then sank comfortably into the crook of his arm. She liked Tony Scanlon; she liked him a lot. With the regular ones it was just business, but not with the sad ones. It was different with them. Her passion was real. She counted among her sad ones a paraplegic, two blind ones, and a cute nineteen-year-old who had been born without arms. Sally De Nesto considered herself to be a sort of social worker. A Sister Theresa of the hookers. And why not? Didn't she help emotional and physical cripples? Without women like her, where would those poor souls go? Most people never think about things like that. What does a man without arms and legs do for sex? She had a feeling of drowsy contentment. She moved in close to him and closed her eyes.

Scanlon half-turned his head and planted a light kiss on her cheek, content to let himself drift into a peaceful sleep. He had that warm exhausted feeling of a man who has just gotten laid, and he was damned if he was going to permit himself to wallow in self-pity by spending half the night staring into the darkness wondering why he could only get it up with hookers, and realizing how very much he missed Jane Stomer. Not tonight. Tonight he felt whole, and whole men sleep after they make love.

Not too far from Sally De Nesto's one-bedroom Yorkville apartment, Stanley Zimmerman lounged on a comfortable couch in his fifth-floor sitting room, his outstretched legs supported on an ottoman, a brandy snifter held loosely in his hand. He glanced at his wife, Rachel, sitting next to him with her knees tucked under her supple body, her head at rest on his shoulder.

It had been a long three days since Thursday. First the appearance of those two somber policemen in his office to tell him that there had been an accident. Then the shock of being told the truth, and the horrible experience of having to identify his mother's body at Kings County Morgue. And then notifying the relatives, the insincere platitudes, the cremation. What was he going to do with all those baskets of fruit that people had sent? He'd more than likely end up donating them to the hospital. He was going to miss his mother. There'd be no one to make him kasha varnishkas or give him chocolate-covered matzoh every Passover, as his mother had done. A practice which he automatically continued with his daughter. Funny, his mother was very Jewish, yet she wasn't a bit religious. He'd been surprised when the rabbi asked him to say the Kaddish. There are just some things that you never forget. They're in your subconscious, ready, waiting for recall.

He felt his wife's body pressing close to him. He kissed the top of her head. "Bed?"

She smiled. "Sounds good to me."

Holding hands, they walked down the corridor until they reached their daughter's bedroom. They tiptoed inside. A large room decorated with pink ruffles and frills. Rachel walked over to the bed and kissed the sleeping child. Tucking the soft summer blanket into the mattress, she beamed at her husband. "She's so precious."

He nodded his smiling assent.

He lay in bed patiently awaiting his wife, who was in the bathroom. No matter how difficult the loss, he and the rest of the family had to get on with their lives. He'd been impressed with the policeman. There was something strong about him that he liked.

Rachel came out of the bathroom in a black nightgown. As was her habit, she went over to the window and opened it a few inches from the bottom. She turned back in time to see her husband struggling out of his underpants. Walking to the bed, she felt a familiar tingling come to her stomach.

She stood next to the bed and slipped the lace straps of her gown off her shoulder. She pulled it off and dropped it at her feet. She remained motionless, permitting her husband's gaze to take in her body.

He tossed the covers back and she slid into bed next to him.

The Kingsley Arms, a six-story building with an Art Deco facade, had gone co-op three years ago. It was directly across the street from the Zimmerman town house.

It was after midnight, and a few scattered lights were on in the Kingsley Arms. The door leading onto the roof was ajar, the hasp hanging precariously by one screw. More screws lay on the stairwell along with long slivers of wood and chips of green paint.

A figure moved cautiously among the shadows. It was the outline of a man, bending low, taking his time, making sure of his footing. He made his way over to the ledge and knelt, carefully placing the case down beside him. Crouching, he snapped open the case slowly so that the clicking of the clamps was not carried in the quiet night.

He removed the rifle stock from its padded recess inside the case and unscrewed the indented screws in the butt of the stock. Removing the covering plate, he shook out an eighteen-inch barrel. He raised himself up and peered out over the ledge, his gaze going to the open bedroom window. Ducking down, he inserted the barrel into the opening at the front of the stock and turned clockwise until the barrel locked in place. Next he removed the trigger housing and slid it into place, sliding the side latch, securing the mechanism. He removed a piece of black felt and unwrapped a magazine containing six hollow-tip 5.56 caliber bullets. He slid the magazine into the housing. The night scope was removed from its protective cover and its flanges inserted into the grooves atop the barrel. He tightened the screws with a small screwdriver, fixing the scope in place.

A long bulbous sound suppressor was removed from the case and screwed onto the end of the barrel. With his right hand he slid back the bolt and guided it forward, sliding the first round into the chamber.

Kneeling with the heel of his right foot secured under his buttocks and his shoulder leaning firmly into the stock, he firmed the weapon on the roof's ledge and aimed downward. Peering through the scope, adjusting the magnification knob, he saw Stanley Zimmerman's head come into the gray-white light of the cross hairs. A head full of sweet dreams and good deeds.

He took a breath, held it, and began his squeeze.

When the bullet plowed into Stanley Zimmerman's head his body stiffened, jerked up, and sank back onto the bed.

Rachel Zimmerman awoke with a start, conscious that something was wrong. The hand that was between her legs was unnaturally limp. "Stanley?" She could feel something oozing over her shoulders and into her hair. There was the strange smell of oxidized iron in the air. She reached her hand behind her, into a pool of blood, and sprang up, causing the bullet that was meant for her head to plow into the headboard.

In horror, she gaped at her dripping hand. She screamed. Paralyzed with fear, she gnawed on the knuckle of her hand.

The third bullet exploded into her face just below her left eye, tearing a passage through the head and leaving in its wake a bloody path of torn muscles and ruptured tissues.

"Mommy, Mommy," cried the little girl, expecting her mother to come rushing into her room to comfort her. In the past her mother had always come. Andrea would be reassured that everything was all right and kissed affectionately, and then tucked back into bed with a loving hug. The hug was the best part. She had been dreaming of wearing her new sneakers to her best friend's birthday party when a shriek scared her out of her dream. Her head shot up from the pillow; her eyes darted around the darkened room. She began to cry.

Where was Mommy? She cried louder. Her throat was getting hoarse. Gradually her sobs subsided. Her feet slid off the bed and she padded her way out of the bedroom. A nightlight was on in the hallway. Strange black shapes dived out of the shadows at her, trying to capture her, to eat her. She panicked and ran for the safety of her parents' room. She rushed inside and froze.

At 0115 that night the team of a cruising radio car spotted a dazed little girl wandering down Lexington Avenue in a pink nightshirt with a giant lollipop on the front.

10

The bloodstained bodies lay cold and waxen. Several hours had passed since they ceased to live. It was early Sunday morning, the city's after-hours joints were closing. Throughout the city priests were preparing to offer mass. On East Seventy-ninth Street grim detectives stalked over a new crime scene with the impersonal demeanor of men used to working in the disquieting presence of death.

Detectives from the Nineteenth's night watch had made the connection with the Nine-three's double homicide. A police lieutenant and a candy store lady named Zimmerman had been murdered.

A telephone message had been transmitted to the Nine-three Squad. When Scanlon did not answer his phone at home, the Vulva File was consulted and Sally De Nesto's number dialed.

Scanlon leaped up in the bed, listening to the terse notification: Nineteenth Squad detectives report that Dr. Stanley Zimmerman and his wife, Rachel, were the subjects of a homicide at their residence on or about 0100 hours this date.

"Call everyone in," Scanlon had said, slamming down the phone and throwing off the sheet, wondering what it was that he had overlooked.

Detectives clustered in small groups inside the bedroom, comparing notes. A photographer took pictures.

The ME had come and gone; he had issued a preliminary finding of death by gunshot.

Scanlon stood at the foot of the bed staring down at the bodies; his face was a mask of unbearable sadness. An awful sense of guilt welled up inside him, his head ached, his stump throbbed. Were they dead because of some failure on his part, some omission? Had his personal problems made him neglect his duty as a cop?

Higgins and Colon came up behind him. Glancing at the bodies, Higgins read from her steno pad: the who, what, when, how, and why of death.

Scanlon listened, unable to take his eyes away from the bodies. Higgins finished her report, said softly, "That's it, Lou. It's not very much."

"Where's the daughter?" Scanlon asked in a whisper.

"In Doctors Hospital being treated for shock. Her aunt is with her," Colon said.

Scanlon nodded. He would have to face Linda Zimmerman. What could he say to her? "I'm sorry"? That just didn't seem to cut it, not now. He turned from the bed and saw Frank Abruzzi, the ballistics detective, looking through a surveyor's transit. "There seems to be a big black cloud over your head when you work, Frank."

"Ain't that the truth, Lou."

"What can you tell me?" Scanlon asked the ballistics man.

Abruzzi led Scanlon over to the window. "Let's start with the glass fractures," Abruzzi said, pointing to the three holes in the window. "You'll notice that the radial lines are longer on the bottom of the cones. That means that there was downward pressure, which means that the perp fired from some point above this window." He took a pencil from his breast pocket and pointed to the center bullet hole. "This one was the first shot. See how the radial lines go all the way to the bottom of the glass, and see this small fracture that comes out of the other two's concentric fractures and connects to this hole's concentric fractures. That shows us that this one was the first shot." A thin stick had been stuck through one of the holes and pulled up against the outside of the window. A string was wound around the stick and ran through the hole and across the bedroom, and was fastened to the bullet hole in the headboard. Abruzzi pointed along the line of the string. "Your perp missed one, and it lodged in the headboard. With two impact points we can fix the trajectory of the bullets. Using the surveyor's transit we set one end on one impact point and the other end on the other and we have the trajectory."

Scanlon peered into the surveyor's transit. One end was aligned with the roof of the Kingsley Arms. He saw men huddled on the roof, pointing to the bedroom. He looked at the detective. "Thanks, Frank."

"Anytime, Lou."

Scanlon's eyes wandered the room. Most of the detectives were from the Nineteenth of Manhattan South Detective Area. The Nine-three Squad had been brought in as a courtesy, to compare notes. This one was a Manhattan caper.

Scanlon turned abruptly and left the bedroom.

Higgins and Colon followed close behind.

Hurrying down the staircase, Scanlon reached the second level, where he heard a burst of raucous laughter that had come from one of the rooms off the hall. He followed the sounds into a large room that had a bizarre display of scythes and antique pistols on the wall and, next to the French window, a maple bar with four wicker stools. Three unfamiliar detectives with their shields pinned to their jackets were at the bar. One, a big black man with thick glasses, was acting as the bartender. Another, a younger man with brown forelocks, was slouched in a chair with his right leg draped over the arm, talking into the telephone. His silly expression told Scanlon that the call wasn't official business. The third detective was older, heavyset. He was perched atop a stool. Rémy Martin and Chivas Regal bottles were on the bar. Scanlon glared at the three glasses in the three hands and couldn't keep the image of the two gory bodies in a single upstairs bed from overwhelming his mind. Police texts talk of unity of command: one man in command of each situation and only one man in direct command of each officer. Outside supervisors aren't supposed to order around cops who are not under their personal supervision unless there is an emergency situation that demands it. According to the books, Scanlon was supposed to report these three beauties to their own boss. "What the hell is going on here?" Scanlon demanded.

Higgins and Colon hurried down the staircase to the first level.

The three outside detectives took in the lieutenant's shield pinned to Scanlon's sport jacket.

"We stopped for a taste, Lou," said the bartender.

"A taste?" Scanlon said, glaring at the detective with the telephone glued to his ear. "And I guess that's official business."

The detective said quickly into the mouthpiece, "I'll get back to you," and hung up.

The detective who was on the stool put down his glass and slid off.

"Unless you three super-sleuths have an overwhelming desire to be flopped back into the bag, I'd strongly suggest that you haul ass out of here and do whatever it was you were supposed to be doing."

"Right, Lou," said the bartender, leading the other two detectives from the room.

Scanlon took in the open liquor bottles. Who the hell wrote those damn supervision texts? he thought. They were never on the Job, that was for sure.

"A crowbar was used to pry this door open," explained the forensics man to the group of detectives atop the co-op's roof. He pointed his bony finger at the gouges in the doorframe. "The claws made characteristic impressions in the molding. We're going to remove the molding and make casts of the striations." He looked slyly at the detectives. "If any of you aces come up with the right crowbar I'll be able to make a positive ID for you." He moved away and walked up to the first of a file of upturned garbage cans that ran from the door to the edge of the roof. He righted the can and squatted next to a cluster of plaster of Paris that was set into the tar roof. "The warm weather softened up the tar. So when the perp knelt to fire, his toe and part of his sole pressed into the tar." He pointed. "Here is the heel of his left foot. We added salt to hasten hardening."

The detectives gathered in close around the forensics man.

"This moulage is going to give us the perp's approximate size and weight. From the position of his foot when he knelt to fire,

I can already tell you that the guy you're looking for is probably right-handed." He stood, carefully replaced the can over the impression, moved to the next can in line, righted it, bent. "More footprints. We're going to develop a 'walking picture' of this guy."

A fat detective who was busy sucking on a toothpick said, "Exactly what is that?"

The forensics man waved his hand in front of him as he explained. "A lotta things make up the walking picture. The direction line tells us the angle at which this guy put his foot down. The step line, which is the centers of two successive heelprints, is gonna tell us his size and whether he limps." A hint of humor came into his beady eyes. "All you aces gotta do is bring the hump and his shoes to me and I'll cement them both onto this roof."

"I was wondering why all that garbage was dumped in front of the building," commented the fat detective with the toothpick, looking down the line of upturned cans that had been brought up to the roof.

Scanlon stood at the edge of the roof listening to the forensics detective and looking down at the green, windowless ambulance: Department of Hospitals, Mortuary Division. Police vehicles were parked helter-skelter. A line of unmarked vehicles stretched to the corner. Two TV camera trucks were on the scene. Reporters pressed against the cordon, shouting questions at detectives.

Scanlon strained his calf muscles in an attempt to shoo away the gray numbness that had taken hold of his body. The painful, nagging feeling that he had missed something or had overlooked something he shouldn't have, that he could have prevented the murders, just would not leave him. A soul-wrenching thought kept going over and over in his mind: he'd fucked-up because his thoughts were concentrated on his personal problems, his limp dick.

A policeman came out of the town house and fastened open the door. Morgue attendants appeared wheeling collapsible gurneys that had black body bags buckled to them. Policemen helped the attendants get the gurneys down the steps. There was a sudden surge of people against the police lines. Death seems to fascinate civilians; but then they can deal with it from afar.

The bags were unbuckled and hefted off. The remains of Stanley and Rachel Zimmerman were slid into the body of the ambulance.

The meat wagon drove off, its siren wailing.

What's with the siren? Scanlon thought. There's no rush, not now.

"Don't lay a guilt trip on yourself, Lou," Biafra Baby said, attempting to flatten inky spikes of hair. "Ain't no way we could have prevented this."

"We missed something," Scanlon said.

"That's a crock of shit," Lew Brodie responded.

"We're only human, Lou," Higgins said.

Scanlon walked away, heading for the group of Nineteenth Squad detectives standing around the air vents in the middle of the roof.

Lieutenant Jack Fable, the Whip of the Nineteenth Squad, saw him coming and went to greet him. "Howya doin', guy?"

Scanlon cringed inwardly at Fable's salutation. "Guy" was the common greeting in the Job when the speaker knew the face but not the name. "Scanlon, Jack. Tony Scanlon, Nine-three Squad."

Belated recognition brightened Fable's face. "Oh, yeah. How are ya?"

Jack Fable wasn't the lanky, baby-faced kid Scanlon remembered as the class standard bearer. The years of drinking and eating on the arm in the city's top-drawer hotels and restaurants had taken their toll. A pelican chin sagged beneath Fable's heavy jaw, and his beefy neck overhung his collar.

"We were in the Academy at the same time," Fable said, patting Scanlon's shoulder. "Too bad you got so old-looking."

Scanlon wasn't in the mood for jokes. "Got anything on this caper?"

"We don't have shit," Fable said, rubbing his chin. "A radio car team discovered the daughter wandering the streets. They managed to get her name and address out of her. The rest is history. All the preliminary canvasses have proved negative so far. Nobody saw or heard nothing. The goddamn doorman was inside the package room making Zs. The perp pranced in and out without anyone seeing him."

The lieutenants strolled to the rear of the roof and looked out over a jumble of fire terraces and grilled windows.

"There's gotta be a connection someplace with your Brooklyn caper," Fable said tonelessly.

Scanlon shrugged, holding out his hands palms upward. "But where?" He glanced around the roof. "Where's all the brass?"

"It's a little early for them. But they'll all get here eventually. All except the PC. Command and Control can't locate him. His wife told the sergeant on the Situations Desk that she didn't know her husband's whereabouts."

Scanlon grimaced. "One of these days he's going to trip over his own cock." Scanlon watched a woman in a far-off apartment cupping her breasts and running in place.

Fable looked at Scanlon. "Wanna tell me what went down in Brooklyn?"

Scanlon gave a rundown on the Gallagher/Zimmerman case to Fable. When Scanlon was finished, Fable said, "I can't figure which end is up with this caper."

"Welcome to the club. When it first went down I thought that Joe Gallagher was probably the mark. Now? I just don't know."

"What about this Eddie Hamill guy?"

"Who knows? I guess it could have been a case of mistaken identity. Hamill or someone he hired to hit Ticornelli mistaking Gallagher for the shylock. It's certainly something that we're going to have to take a close look at."

Fable's eyes narrowed. "What's your gut reaction?"

Scanlon exhaled. "Gallagher."

"Tell me why."

"Shortly before the time of occurrence we put the perp inside McGoldrick Park. We have him leaving the park about the same time as Gallagher is parking his car."

"And you figure that an accomplice signaled the perp that Gallagher had arrived on the scene."

"Something like that."

"The same accomplice who drove the getaway van," Fable said.

"Probably. But who knows? There could have been a third person involved," Scanlon said, making a mental note of how many times the woman in the apartment had run in place.

"Why not Yetta Zimmerman as the mark?"

"Then why wait for Gallagher to come upon the scene? She could have been taken out anytime."

"Maybe because someone wanted them taken out together?" Fable said. "An object lesson to others."

"I thought of that," Scanlon said. "And I have to admit that that theory does hold water."

Fable scratched his chin. "If Gallagher is the mark, why take out the doctor and his wife?"

"It doesn't make sense," Scanlon said. "Unless..."

"Unless what?"

"Unless we can tie Gallagher and Yetta Zimmerman into some heavy-duty money transactions that somehow spilled over into her family."

Reaching down the front of his trousers to scratch his scrotum, Fable nodded and said, "We got a real fucking mystery on our hands here."

"It do appear that way," Scanlon said, wondering where he was going to get the manpower to search for Eddie Hamill, do the other things that needed doing, and still have detectives available to cover the chart. He was going to have to get a couple of precinct anticrime cops on a "steal" for a day or two, he decided.

"We might get lucky," Fable said, leading Scanlon away from the edge of the roof, over to the upended garbage cans. He righted one, and the two lieutenants squatted around the rough piece of drying plaster.

Higgins came over and hunkered down beside Scanlon.

"When the lab boys lift this impression and clean it off, we're going to have a pretty good *portrait parlé* of the perp," Fable said.

Hector Colon wandered over to the three squatting figures. His eyes fell to Higgins's opened knees, and his lustful gaze darted under her dress.

"There's something funny about this footprint," Higgins noted, suddenly conscious of an intrusive presence. Her eyes flicked up and she brought her legs together and replaced the garbage can over the plaster.

Colon came up to her. "Señorita Higgins, you are indeed a very beautiful woman."

"Why thank you, Hector. Did you like what you saw?"

He moved in close to confide, "Very much. Latin men are turned on by hairy women." He looked around to make sure no one was listening, and said, "If you ever have the urge to change your luck, call me. I'd love to come inside you."

She patted his cheek. "How thoughtful of you, Hector. But to tell you the truth, I don't think you could come if I called you."

The lieutenants moved off by themselves. "Do you think we should form a task force to work both cases?" Fable asked.

Taking in the chiseled outline of Manhattan, Scanlon replied, "Off the top of my head, no. Task forces are cumbersome. Too many chiefs pushing their weight around, and too many Indians looking to get lost."

"I couldn't agree more," Fable said. "We'll work together, co-ordinate over landline. You and me are a couple of old hairbags who ain't goin' nowhere in the Job. There shouldn't be any ego problems with us."

"You're right. I'll send you copies of my Fives and you send me yours. If anything heavy goes down, I'll get on the horn to you."

"And I'll do the same."

Deputy Chief McKenzie arrived on the scene a little after 0800 hours. He went directly to the edge of the roof and stared down into the Zimmermans' bedroom window. After a few minutes he turned, scanned the crowd, and called out to Scanlon.

Scanlon heard him and came over to him.

McKenzie was solemn. "Thank God we're off the hook with Gallagher." He wiped the back of his neck with his handkerchief. "It's obvious that Gallagher was just a poor slob who happened to be in the wrong place at the wrong time."

"That's not so obvious to me."

"Whaddaya wanna make problems for, Scanlon? Let it go, for Chrissake."

Scanlon's voice was full of barely controlled anger. "We got four DOAs. One of whom was a police lieutenant. We have a little girl who has been orphaned. And you got the balls to tell me to let go of it?"

"Scanlon, the Nineteenth caught this one. The solution to both cases is across the street in that bedroom. Be reasonable, bang out a Five, and transfer your Sixty-one to the Nineteenth. They'll combine both cases. We'll be off the hook and you'll be able to take an exceptional clearance on your case."

"The answer is no. I'm one of those old-fashioned detectives who still believes in clearing homicides by arrests, not by statistical flim-flam." He stormed off.

McKenzie went after him. "I've been approved by the promotion board. This Gallagher thing is a Roman spear that can turn on all of us. Drop it!"

"No."

"You're an obstinate wop, you know that, Scanlon?"

With his right forefinger and middle finger pressed into his thumb, Scanlon shook his hand in McKenzie's face in an Italian gesture of contempt and said, *"Va'ffa'n'culo."*

"Whaddaya say?"

"I said that I'd love some capicola. That's an Italian cold cut that's made out of salami and mortadella. You people usually eat it on white bread with mayonnaise." He walked away leaving the deputy chief pounding fists against the sides of his legs.

Chief of Detectives Alfred Goldberg appeared, half an hour after MacAdoo McKenzie, accompanied by his usual retinue of Palace Guard flunkies.

Fable and the rest of the Manhattan South brass rushed up to the CofD to fill him in on the preliminary investigation.

Scanlon motioned to his detectives to make themselves scarce.

Nine-three Squad detectives began to drift toward the stairwell. Scanlon noticed Colon lean into Higgins and whisper something. Higgins's elbow smashed into Colon's ribs.

MacAdoo McKenzie ambled over to Scanlon. "Why don't you make yourself scarce before Goldberg spots you? He's bound to ask you questions about Gallagher. Questions that the PC don't want you to answer."

"What a way to run a police department," Scanlon said, moving off toward the stairwell.

"Hey, Scanlon, I wanna talk to you," Goldberg shouted from inside a circle of detectives.

Scanlon sighed and started to go to the CofD.

"Wait there. I'll come to you," Goldberg yelled, dismissing the others with a mere flick of his finger.

Scanlon rested his fake leg on the rim of a skylight and waited.

Goldberg stopped several times to ask questions of forensics technicians. Scanlon noticed that the CofD talked out of the side of his mouth. The CofD worked hard trying to enhance his public image as a tough guy. But within the Job he was known as a guy with short arms and deep pockets who got his fashionable clothes on the arm from his friends in the garment district.

He was shorter than most of his contemporaries and tried to compensate with platform shoes and by smoking big cigars. He was in his middle fifties and wore his hair stretched across his head like a starched rug. He only patronized the city's best hair stylists, and he always went to great pains to tell the owners of the salons to send their bills to his office at police headquarters. The bills never came, and Goldberg never inquired why.

Goldberg shifted the oversize cigar over his thick, protruding lips. "I don't see your friend Bobby Gomez," he said threateningly to MacAdoo McKenzie.

"I guess the PC got stuck someplace else," McKenzie said. "There's a triple homicide in the Bronx—he's probably there."

"Bullsheeit. He's probably in El Barrio sucking on some cuchifrita's cunt," Goldberg said.

"That don't make him a bad person," Scanlon said. "Besides, I'm sure there's a good reason for him not being here."

Goldberg looked at McKenzie. "You're a long way from Brooklyn, Chief."

"Command and Control notified me what went down here. I thought I might be able to help," McKenzie said, wiping his brow.

"That shows a high degree of professionalism, Chief. But I really don't think we're going to be needing your expertise on this one. But thanks anyway."

"Right," McKenzie said and left.

Scanlon took a deep breath of the cool morning air, looked up to the soft blue sky, and thought of Jane Stomer. He wondered if she ever thought about him, and hoped that she had not been with another man. He wondered, not for the first time, what life must be like for men with normal jobs and families. He suddenly felt terribly sad and very old. He came back to the present and saw Goldberg looking at him strangely.

"McKenzie thinks this double homicide washes out yours. But we know better, don't we?"

"Do we?"

Goldberg pulled the cigar from his mouth and pointed the wet end at Scanlon. "You, McKenzie, and Bobby Boy are trying to keep the lid on the Gallagher case. Bobby Boy's escapades are beginning to leak into print. He can't afford any more scandals. A little shove and El Spico is out."

Scanlon made a noncommittal shrug. "I don't know where you get your information from, but—"

"Cut the shit, Scanlon. Gallagher's rep for broads was well known in the Job. He used to score pussy on city time." He pumped the cigar back into his mouth. "I'd like you to tell me exactly what you've come up with on Gallagher."

Scanlon made a gesture of helplessness. He was trapped in a private war between the PC and the CofD. It was not because the PC had told him not to tell Goldberg the details of the case that Scanlon decided not to say anything. It was because he did not want to drop the match that would start a wildfire of rumor about Joe Gallagher. Gallagher was no straight arrow, but he was a cop, and he was the cop who was responsible for Scanlon's being able to stay in the Job after he lost his leg. He owed Gallagher. And Italians don't forget. It's all a matter of honor. "It's all in my Fives, Chief."

A nasty smile was his reward. "I've read every Five you've sent in on the Gallagher/Zimmerman case." His voice stretched thin in anger. "They all read like *Alice in Wonderland.* I've spent most of my life reading Fives. All I have to do is glance at one to know if a score has been made on a case, or whether some sharp-ass detective or squad commander is not putting everything he knows down on paper." He moved in close, said, "Why dontcha tell me about Gallagher?"

"Because there's nothing to tell."

Goldberg pointed his stubby finger at Scanlon's chest. "I'm going to be the next PC. So be advised that I've got a long fucking memory." He turned away and stamped off.

Scanlon stepped out into the street and immediately picked up on Lew Brodie's warning look. Brodie's stare led to a group of reporters trying to talk their way past the police line. Scanlon spotted Daniel J. Buckman, an investigative reporter from the *New York Times,* standing apart from his peers. Buckman, an avowed cop hater, was described by most of the cops in the Job as the Cocksucker with Lockjaw.

Scanlon and Buckman's eyes met.

Scanlon made for the double-parked department car. Higgins

was behind the wheel and Colon was in the passenger seat, pressing his knee against hers. Biafra Baby was squeezed in next to Colon. Christopher sat in the rear, eating sunflower seeds and carefully placing the shells in the door's ashtray. Lew Brodie was standing in the roadway, holding open the door.

Scanlon was just about to reach into the car when Buckman rushed over to him. "Don't you have a good word to say to the press, Lieutenant?"

"Long live the First Amendment."

Undaunted, Buckman said, "A little bird told me that there is a cover-up in the Gallagher case."

"Did your little bird happen to be wearing platform shoes and was he smoking a big cigar?"

"He might be your next PC."

Scanlon wrinkled his face. "PCs come, PCs go." He went to get into the car.

Buckman stopped him. "I'm not a bad guy, Scanlon. And I could help you in the Job. Might even arrange a transfer back into Midtown."

"From your lips to God's ears, Sweet Lips."

"The public has the right to know about its public officials, Scanlon."

"Do they now?" Scanlon said, leading the reporter away from the car. "In that case, I'll give you the inside scope. Gallagher died in the performance of duty, trying to prevent a holdup. Period. End of case."

"I've been in this business too long not to know where there is smoke there is fire. Your own CofD has been shut out of the case. No one in the Detective Division with the exception of you and McKenzie knows anything about the case. That tells me that there is something afoot. And now Dr. Zimmerman, son of one of the victims, and his wife have been murdered. No. There's a story here, Lieutenant, and you're trying to sit on it."

"I have no idea why the doctor and his wife were murdered. The only thing I can tell you for sure is that Joe Gallagher's death was LOD."

"Line of duty?" the reporter scoffed. "That's bullshit and you know it. I'm going to keep digging, and while I do, I'm going to show you just how much pressure I can bring to bear to get at the truth."

"You do that, Buckman. I'm a strong believer in freedom of the press and all the rest of that shit." He slid into the car and slammed the door.

Higgins looked at him in the rearview mirror. "Where to?"

"Doctors Hospital."

The unmarked department auto drove into the emergency cul-de-sac and parked.

"Wait here," Scanlon said, pushing open the door. He moved past the two receptionists and scanned the crowded benches in the waiting room of the emergency room. No Linda Zimmerman. He spotted a square-badge standing next to a corn plant in the corner. He went up to him and identified himself, and inquired about Andrea Zimmerman.

The square-badge was in his late sixties and had thin gray hair. "I retired from the Job in '66. Used to work out of the old Fourteenth."

"Who was the captain when you were there?" Scanlon asked, trying to humor the old-timer.

"Fitzpatrick."

"Ol' Blood and Guts Fitz. I worked with him during the Harlem riots."

A forlorn expression came over the older man's face. "I guess the Job's changed a lot since my days."

"The Job never changes, only the cast of characters changes."

"Yeah, I guess you're right," the square-badge said. "Wait here, I'll check on those two names for you."

Scanlon watched him go over to the reception desk and shuffle through forms. He yanked one from the pile, read it, and motioned Scanlon to follow him.

They passed through two large doors that were edged in thick rubber and entered a tiled passage lined on both sides with examining cubicles. "Room nine, around the corner, to your right," the square-badge said, shaking Scanlon's hand.

"Thanks," Scanlon said, watching the retired cop walk away and wondering what it must be like to be out of the Job.

Linda Zimmerman was slouched against the wall outside examining room nine, her composure and elegance gone. Her clothes did not match and her hair was in disarray. She appeared to be in a state of disbelieving shock.

"How is Andrea?" he asked gently, his concern genuine.

Her tone was feeble, her gaze fixed downward on the gleaming tile floor. "My niece is in shock."

"I wish there was something I could say to lessen your pain. I'm so very, very sorry."

She started to rock back and forth on her heels, tapping her head against the wall. "First my mother, then my brother and Rachel. My entire family is gone. I'm alone with a little girl to raise." She stared at him with anguished eyes. "You were supposed to protect us. Why didn't you do your job? Why?" she screamed, and began to slam the back of her head repeatedly against the wall.

"Linda!" He grabbed her.

She fought to free herself from him, screaming, continuing to fling her head back. "Why? Why?"

He pulled her to him, trying to calm her. The back of her head was bloody.

"You murdered my family!" she cried, pounding him with her fists. "Murderer! Murderer!" She collapsed into his arms.

He caught her.

Several nurses rushed over to them. One of them pulled up a gurney. He lifted her onto the medical trolley.

"Are you the husband?" asked one of the nurses.

"A friend."

"Please wait outside in the waiting room."

Scanlon sat in the pew with the other anxious people. An hour passed. The square-badge offered him the privacy of the doctors' lounge. He declined; he wanted to wait with the others. He kept telling himself over and over that logically there was nothing he could have done to prevent what had happened to the doctor and his wife. But that nagging kernel of doubt would not leave his mind.

"Zimmerman?" the intern said, pushing through the double doors.

"How are they?" Scanlon asked, going up to the intern.

"Both sedated."

"Are they going to be all right?"

The doctor looked into his concerned face. "When the girl comes around we'll have a child psychiatrist take a look at her. As for the aunt, we're going to keep her here a little while to check her out. She did a number on her head. We want to make sure there's no fracture." He took a deep breath. "I knew Stanley Zimmerman by reputation. He did good work. It's a real loss."

11

he detectives filed into the Nine-three station house and went upstairs to the squad room to telephone their families that they would not be home until late Sunday night, if then. Scanlon moved behind the Desk and took the key to the property room out of the key drawer. He walked into the room and switched on the lights. He saw the animal lasso and the bolt cutters leaning against the side of the money safe. Two vandalized parking meters were next to them. Property envelopes with their vouchers stapled to the front of them were scattered about the shelves. A stack of old license plates, each wrapped in its letter of transmittal ready for their weekly delivery to the Motor Vehicle Bureau, was piled on the bottom shelf. There was a bicycle with one wheel.

The file that he was looking for was on top of the narcotics safe, a one-drawer metal card file with a notice stenciled in orange on the top: CONFIDENTIAL—UF 10, FORCE RECORD FILE.

He slid out the file and fingered the tabs to the Gs. He pulled out Officer Horace Goodman's Ten Card and left the room. Standing behind the Desk, Scanlon checked the home telephone number as he dialed. He turned to the cop on telephone switchboard duty and asked him what the other cops called Goodman.

"Hank," the TS cop said, turning the centerfold upside down.

Policemen do not answer their home telephones. Their wives and children have been trained to do that for them. My husband is upstate hunting, or my dad is fishing, and thus unavailable. Unavailable, until his next scheduled tour.

A cheerful female voice answered. "Hello?"

An equally cheerful voice replied. "Hi. Is Hank around? This is Tony."

"Hank," she sang out, "it's for you. Tony."

A pleasant male voice. "Hello, Tony."

"Hank, this is Lieutenant Scanlon from the Squad."

Goodman had been snared. Scanlon visualized the lead clerical man making ugly faces at his wife. "Yeah, Lou?"

"We have to get into the old record room, and the keys aren't at the Desk."

"Can't it wait until the morning? This is Sunday."

"No, it can't wait until the morning," Scanlon said, annoyed. "And if the keys aren't here soon I'm going to give the order to kick in the door. And in that case I'll have to make a blotter entry. And someone from the borough is going to want to know why the keys weren't at the Desk as the *Patrol Guide* prescribes they should be. And then it'll be somebody's ass."

"I'll drop them off in a few minutes."

The detectives sat around Scanlon's desk studying the old records.

The original complaint report was dated August 5, 1978. The Sixty-one detailed how at 1957 hours Walter Ticornelli went to get his car, which was parked on the S/E corner of Engert Avenue between Diamond and Newel streets, and discovered that the left rear tire was flat.

Ticornelli was in the process of jacking up his car when several shots rang out. The reluctant complainant stated that he fell to the ground and rolled under the car that was parked behind his.

The investigating officer, Detective Jack Weinberg, reported under details of the case on the original complaint report that the preliminary canvass failed to produce any witnesses to the shooting including the anonymous neighbors who had phoned in the report of shots fired. A search of the immediate vicinity by the patrol sergeant revealed four bullet holes in the complainant's car. Emergency Service responded and conducted a search of the surrounding area for victims of stray bullets. NR. An examination of the flattened tire revealed four punctures, each in close proximity to the others.

When questioned, the complainant could offer no explanation for the attempt on his life other than to state that it was probably the result of some kids fooling around. The attached Fives reported on the result of additional canvasses and on the result of checking the recovered slugs against the Ballistics File. Both proved negative.

Scanlon let the heavy report fall from his hands and looked up at his detectives. He had divided six years' worth of Sixty sheets among them and told them to check the chronological record of cases by complainants and crimes: Walter Ticornelli—Attempted Murder or Assault 1.

It took the detectives a little over one hour to complete this task. NR.

"Looks as though there was only one attempt on Ticornelli's life," Higgins said.

"If there were other attempts," Christopher said, "they probably went unreported, or went down somewhere else."

"Or there were no other attempts," Scanlon said. "This thing between Ticornelli and Eddie Hamill might be nothing more than neighborhood gossip." He looked at Lew Brodie. "What have you come up with on Hamill?"

Brodie consulted his steno pad. "I called the Identification Section and had them read me Hamill's sheet over the phone. His B number is 435897–2. A male, white, forty-three. His yellow sheet starts out in '60. Grand Larceny, Auto. He was adjudicated a youthful offender on that one." Brodie went on to enumerate Hamill's eleven other arrests. "Our boy Eddie has been naughty," Brodie said.

"This is true," Scanlon said. "Lew, I'd like you to go to the big building and pull Hamill's yellow sheet and copy it. Then take out each Nineteen, note the accomplices on each arrest, and—"

"I got the idea, Lou," Brodie said, slowly getting out of his chair.

"And Lew, we're in a hurry, so no stopping off," Scanlon said.

"Ten-four, Lou," Brodie said, leaving.

Scanlon turned his attention to Higgins. "What have you done about our missing witness, Valerie Clarkson?"

"She works as a waitress in the Santorini Diner on Linden Boulevard in Brooklyn. I spoke with her boss, Kostos Kalyviotis. He told me that she's worked for him for ten years, she's always on time, and is seldom out sick. She called in last Friday and told him that she needed a few days' vacation because of a personal problem."

Scanlon leaned back in his seat and put his legs up on the desk. "What else?"

"I got a list of her toll calls from the telephone company. There were two numbers that showed up consistently. Both in Suffolk County. One was in Deer Park, and the other in Huntington. I—"

"Goddamnit!" Hector Colon shrieked, leaping up off his seat and scampering around the office after a cockroach. He caught up with the creature near the corner steam pipe and crushed it with his foot. "I hate them! The son of a bitch tried to crawl up my leg."

"Is macho man afraid of a tiny cockarochee?" Higgins said, aping baby talk.

"Knock it off," Scanlon said.

Smiling at Colon, Higgins continued her report. "I ran Clarkson's name through the precinct computer. She owns a '78 Volvo, which, according to one of her neighbors, is suffering from terminal dents. I had the Suffolk PD check both addresses. Her car is parked in the driveway of her sister's house in Deer Park. Do you want me to take a drive out there and see if she's there?"

"Get me the *Patrol Guide*," Scanlon said to Higgins.

She reached out and took the thick blue book from the library cabinet and handed it to him.

Scanlon checked the rear index, then flipped pages until he came to procedure 116–18, Leaving the City on Police Business. He read the pages, then put the thick book down. "This has to be done right. A request to leave the city requires a Forty-nine through channels to the borough commander, and that takes time."

"Lou," Higgins said, "I'll take a drive out to Suffolk County on my own. No big deal."

"No good, Maggie. If you got into a fender-bender with a department auto there'd be hell to pay. And if you used your own car and had an accident, and your insurance company ever found out that you were on police business, they'd cancel your policy."

"Why not have the Suffolk PD pick Clarkson up as a material witness?" Biafra Baby asked.

"That takes too long. I want her in here today."

"But, *Teniente*, Señora Clarkson don't know that, does she? We can lure her back into the city," Colon suggested.

Scanlon looked at Higgins. "Maggie, contact Suffolk and ask them to lay a phony material witness collar on Clarkson. Have them tell her that she can avoid the collar by making a phone call to us."

Scanlon telephoned the Nineteenth's temporary headquarters. When Jack Fable came on the line he asked him if anything had developed on his double homicide.

"Nothing," Fable said, adding that the CofD had hung around the scene for two hours, breaking everyone's balls.

Scanlon hung up and dialed Doctors Hospital. Linda and Andrea Zimmerman were in stable condition.

"Lou, what was Hamill's B number?" Colon asked, checking over his notes.

Scanlon told him.

"You ever wonder where the term 'B number' comes from?" Colon said, jotting down the number in his notes.

Scanlon leaned forward to massage his stump. "It comes from Alphonse Bertillon. He was a Frenchman who originated the method of classifying perps by their body measurements." He pulled up his trouser leg and leaned back. "Years ago it was known in the Job as the Bertillon number. But like everything else it was shortened, to B number." He took off his prosthesis and stood it on top of his desk.

"Lou? That's fucking disgusting," Colon said queasily.

"What is, Hector?" Scanlon said, feigning innocence.

Colon pointed to the prosthesis. "That is."

"It's only a leg," Scanlon said, pulling off his stump sock and balling it up and tossing it into the bottom drawer. He took out a clean one and stretched it over his stump. "Ahhh. That feels much better."

Colon left the office shaking his head.

* * *

An air of casual expectation had taken over the squad room. Christopher had flipped channels until he found *Back Street* on eleven. Maggie Higgins had gotten her period. She quietly left the squad room and went to the female locker room and got what she needed, and knowing that the precinct CO was on his RDO, she went downstairs to avail herself of the privacy of the captain's bathroom.

Scanlon had finished the Sunday papers. On impulse he snatched up the phone and dialed Jane Stomer's home number. He felt like an adolescent as he sat listening to her recorded voice. He hung up before the beep. Then he dialed his mother and spoke to her in Italian, telling her that he would be unable to come for dinner and that he loved her. When, to his surprise, Sally De Nesto answered her phone, he said, "I'm sorry I had to rush out on you last night."

"I understand."

He was aware of a sudden hollowness in the pit of his stomach. "What about tonight?"

She hummed a few bars of "Never on Sunday." "A working girl needs one day of rest."

His hands were wet. He forced an edge of confidence into his voice. "Dinner. Nothing else."

She hesitated, making up her mind. "Dinner, nothing else?"

"Right."

"Pick me up at eight."

He checked his watch. "Make it nine."

After he had hung up he thought, Why the anxiety attack? Certainly he couldn't be falling for a hooker. Every cop who ever did that ended up swallowing his own gun. Crazy thoughts. It's just that he didn't want to be alone tonight, that was all there was to it. He was better off with the Sally De Nestos of the world. He picked up his prosthesis, leaned back in his chair, lifted up his stump, and fitted the beveled end into the socket.

The lazy quiet was broken ten minutes later when Biafra Baby answered the telephone. "It's for Higgins. Where is she?"

"Probably taking a piss," Colon said.

Higgins strolled back into the squad room. Biafra Baby held out the receiver. "Valerie Clarkson on three."

"Lou," Higgins called out, "our missing witness is on three."

"Now," Scanlon said, and he and Higgins pushed down the blinking buttons.

"Hi, Valerie, this is Maggie Higgins."

A scared voice. "I'm no material witness."

"Valerie, we have reason to believe that you are in possession of information that is vital to our investigation. You were given the opportunity to come in and talk to us, but you elected to run instead."

"I've never been involved with the police. I was scared."

"I can understand that, Valerie. You're no criminal. You're a working woman, like me. Look, why don't you come in of your own volition? That way there would be no publicity, no one would ever know that you talked to us, and I promise you that whatever you tell us will be held in strict confidence."

Biafra Baby mimed playing a violin. Colon wiggled his tongue at Higgins and undulated in his seat. Higgins turned her back to them.

"My parents mustn't find out about my private life. Dad has had two heart attacks. It would kill him."

"No one will ever know, I promise."

The reluctant witness said, "Okay, I'll come in."

"How long will it take you to get here?"

Lew Brodie walked into the squad room forty minutes later carrying three bulging folders. Moments later a nervous Valerie Clarkson appeared. Higgins went up to the railing, opened the gate, and ushered the witness into Scanlon's office. Scanlon motioned to Brodie to wait, and followed Higgins and the witness into his office, closing the door behind him. Higgins moved behind the Whip's desk and sat down in his department-issue swivel chair.

Valerie Clarkson glanced around at Scanlon, who had positioned himself in front of the door.

"Do you mind if he stays?" Higgins said. "It's regulations."

"I don't mind."

Higgins began by asking the witness how her trip into the city had been. Clarkson told her that there had been hardly any traffic so she had made good time. Higgins leaned across the desk to admire the witness's pearls. "They're beautiful."

"Cultured. I bought them on sale in Fortunoff's."

"I love pearls," Higgins said, fingering the strand. "I have a string of opera-length pearls that I just love."

Within a short time the two women were chatting as though they had been lifelong friends. The witness's brother-in-law had been laid off from his job at Republic, and Valerie had helped her sister to pay the mortgage. Higgins lied and said that she had just gone to contract on a co-op and confided that she was sweating out mortgage approval. She was a little afraid of the new adjustable mortgage rates.

Scanlon edged along the wall in order to get a better look at the witness. She wore her chestnut hair short and had on a white pleated skirt and violet-colored blouse. Her figure was trim, her face pretty, and with the exception of a little mascara she wore no makeup. When the witness was completely at ease, Higgins gently guided the conversation around to the dead lieutenant.

Joe Gallagher had not employed his favorite traffic ploy to meet this witness. Nine months ago, the witness said, Gallagher began showing up at the Santorini Diner around lunchtime. He always took a booth at her station. He was a big tipper, and never told off-color jokes, or came on to her, like most of her male customers did. Higgins nodded her understanding.

The remainder of Valerie Clarkson's story paralleled those of Gallagher's other girlfriends. Higgins let the witness finish her story before asking her first question. "The Santorini Diner is on Linden Boulevard near Conduit Avenue, right?"

"Yes."

"Do you happen to know what he was doing in that neighborhood?"

"No, I never thought to ask him."

"But you knew that he was a police lieutenant."

"Yes, but we never discussed his job."

"When he came to the diner was he alone?"

"Sometimes, and sometimes he came with a friend. And once he met some man there and they ate and then left."

"Who was the man he used to come into the diner with?"

"I don't know. I think he was a cop, but I'm not sure."

"And the third man that he met there, who was he?"

"I don't know."

"Was Luise Bardwell the other woman in the threesome?" Higgins asked casually.

The witness shifted uncomfortably in her chair and glanced around at Scanlon. She moved her head close to Higgins's and whispered, "It's hard for me to discuss that with him here."

Higgins motioned to Scanlon to leave the room. When Scanlon walked out into the squad room and closed the door, he asked, "Where is the *Coles?*"

"There in the bottom of the supply cabinet," Colon said.

Christopher moved to the cabinet and said, "What borough do you want?"

"Brooklyn," Scanlon said. The *Coles Directory* is a reference source that lists the telephone numbers and the names of subscribers in every building in the city. The directory is cross-referenced by address and telephone exchanges. Christopher put the thick book on a desk. "What's up?"

"For the past nine months Gallagher has been dropping around a diner in Brooklyn," Scanlon said. "That's a long way from where he worked and lived. I want to know what the hell he was doing around there. The name of the diner is the Santorini. I want you to look up the phone number of the diner, and then pull out Gallagher's address book and check to see if there are any telephone listings around the diner for anyone connected to this case."

"You got it, Lieutenant," Christopher said.

Scanlon moved across the squad room to where Lew Brodie had arranged the criminal record into neat stacks.

"Now, what do we have on Mr. Eddie Hamill?" Scanlon asked Brodie.

"He did a stretch in Attica and is on parole until '89," Brodie said.

"And the Nineteens?" Scanlon said, picking up a handful of DD 19s, Prisoner Modus Operandi and Pedigree Forms. He turned them over to the back where the associates on that arrest were listed.

"Hamill was busted with associates on eight of his eleven collars. A dude named Oscar Mela took the fall with him six times. Mela's folder is here, along with the folders of Hamill's other associates," Brodie said.

"Anyone know this Oscar Mela?" Scanlon called out.

"I know him, Lieutenant," Christopher answered, looking up

from the *Coles*. "He's an empty suit who hangs out in Astoria. In the pool halls along Steinway Street."

"I guess Mela is our best shot to find Hamill," Scanlon said. "What was his last known address?"

Brodie checked Mela's package. "Thirtieth Avenue, in the One-ten."

"Call the One-ten Squad and ask them to check their Resident Known Criminal File and their Released Prisoner File. Get Mela's current address. And if he has moved out of the One-ten, call that Squad."

"Right," Brodie responded.

Higgins and Valerie Clarkson walked out from the office together, chatting like old friends. Higgins moved ahead of the witness and unlatched the gate. Clarkson stopped and smiled at Higgins.

"Thank you," Clarkson said.

"I'll call you," Higgins said, pushing open the gate.

"Don't forget," Clarkson said, leaving the squad room.

When the witness had gone, Higgins perched on the edge of a desk across from the lieutenant. "The material-witness bit scared her. She was petrified that the newspapers would pick up on her involvement with Gallagher. Especially the threesome. She told me that after the trio finished playing their game together she stopped seeing Gallagher." Higgins took hold of the sides of the desk and leaned forward. "But she continued to see Luise Bardwell."

"Bardwell told me that she isn't seeing Clarkson," Scanlon said.

"She isn't, according to Clarkson. They only saw each other four or five times after the threesome, and then Clarkson stopped seeing Bardwell too."

"Did she say why she stopped seeing Bardwell?" Scanlon asked.

"She didn't want that kind of a relationship, she told me," Higgins said. "She thought she was gay and then realized that she wasn't."

"Lieutenant, what was the name of the woman who came to see us first?" Christopher asked.

"You mean the first of Gallagher's girlfriends?"

"Yes."

"Donna Hunt," Scanlon said.

"What was her husband's name?"

"Harold."

"Want to take a look?" Christopher said, stabbing a line in the directory with his finger.

Scanlon looked over Christopher's shoulder. Harold Hunt, CPA, had offices on Pennsylvania Avenue. His telephone exchange was 739, the same as the Santorini Diner's.

Jack Fable telephoned Scanlon to tell him that he had decided to assign men to guard Linda and Andrea Zimmerman.

Scanlon told him that he thought that was a good move.

"Oscar Mela still resides on Thirtieth Avenue. I have the address," Brodie said, hanging up the receiver.

A telephone rang. Colon answered. "Nine-three Squad, Suckieluski." He shoved the receiver at Higgins. "For you."

Higgins took the phone, and her voice became strained. She turned her back to the others, arguing in whispers. She slammed down the receiver and stormed into the Whip's office, banging the door closed.

Scanlon said to Brodie, "I want you, Hector, and Christopher to hit Mela's flat. Get him in here *now.* I don't want to waste any time on this Eddie Hamill thing if it's going nowhere." He rummaged through Mela's criminal record and took out several 4x4 mug shots of Mela. "Take these with you. It might help if you know what he looks like."

"We have nothing to hold this guy on—want us to flake him?" Brodie said.

"No. Put on a little performance for him."

When the detectives had left, Scanlon slipped into his office and gently closed the door behind him. Higgins was standing by the window, looking down into the street.

"Anything I can do?" he asked.

She dabbed her eyes with a tissue. "Gloria can't get used to me being on the Job. We were supposed to go shopping on the East Side for sheets today. She's pissed off that I had to come into work on a Sunday that was my RDO." She turned and looked at him. "Civilians will never understand this Job."

"That's what makes us special, Maggie."

She blew her nose.

"Why don't you call it a day? We can handle it."

"No way. But thanks anyway."

"In that case, why don't you make yourself useful and take your cute little behind out of my office and go into the prop room and get a baseball bat and a few collapsible chairs and set them up around the squad room in anticipation of the drama that is about to unfold."

She sniffled, kissed him on the cheek, and said, "My backside isn't cute. It's too big."

When she had left his office, Scanlon wrote a note to himself: "Luise Bardwell and Valerie Clarkson?? Donna Hunt's husband, ck."

"Take your motherfucking hands off me!" screamed Oscar Mela as Lew Brodie heaved him over the squad room's railing. Brodie threw open the gate and stormed in after the frightened man.

Colon and Christopher restrained Brodie. "Take it easy," Colon said to the seething detective.

Biafra Baby went to help Oscar Mela up off the floor and onto one of the wooden chairs that Higgins had placed around the room.

Scanlon rushed from his office. "What the hell is going on out here?"

Lew Brodie pointed at Mela. His eyes were wide with frenzy. "While on patrol," he began, "we observed this man drive past a red light on the intersection of Morgan and Nassau avenues."

"You're a fucking liar!" Mela shouted. "I wasn't anywhere near there. You kidnapped me from in front of my house. What's his name? I want his name."

"His name is Detective Suckieluski," Biafra Baby whispered to the suspect.

"You got the balls to call me a liar!" Brodie screamed, breaking free of the detectives and rushing at the suspect.

Biafra Baby stationed himself between Brodie and Mela. Colon and Christopher grabbed Brodie and pulled him away from Mela. Scanlon placed a calming hand on Mela's shoulder. He noticed the thin man's gaunt face and weak mouth. He had on a dirty pair of jeans and a grimy white T-shirt. Tattoos covered both his arms. Scanlon took note of two of them. A dripping dagger piercing a skull...Death Before Dishonor. A dagger piercing a heart... Mother. "Let the officer tell his side of it, and then you'll get to tell your side. Okay?"

Mela rapidly nodded.

Brodie leaned against the railing, his right hand inches away from the baseball bat that Higgins had strategically placed there. He continued with his complaint. "I observed that the suspect was driving a '79 Bonneville that had the vent window broken on the driver's side—"

"You broke that window with a blackjack," Mela shouted.

"Please, sir," Scanlon said, gently squeezing the suspect's shoulder. "Let Detective Suckieluski finish."

Brodie continued, "Having reasonable cause to believe that the offending vehicle was stolen, we identified ourselves to the driver as police officers and directed him to pull into the curb.

"While Detective McCann was inspecting the suspect's license and registration, I noticed that the vehicle identification number on the dashboard was altered. I observed that the Car Make Serial Symbol and the Body Style Symbol had been changed. 'N' is the symbol for a '79 Bonneville. The VIN number on this car was 'W,' which is the style symbol for a Firebird Trans Am." He inched his fingers closer to the bat. "I advised the suspect that he was under arrest for forgery of a vehicle identification number as an E Felony, and for Offering a False Instrument as an E Felony. I thereupon advised the prisoner of his rights. It was at this point that the prisoner lunged at me and began to beat me about the head and body with his clenched fists. Necessary force was required to subdue the prisoner."

An exasperated Oscar Mela screamed, "You lying cocksucker!" Brodie grabbed the bat and swung it at Mela, striking the rickety chair's left leg, causing it to shatter, and tumbling Mela onto the floor. Screaming for help, Mela scrambled over the floor in a desperate flight to escape the crashing bat. Holding the bat high above his head, Brodie rushed after Mela.

Every detective in the squad room rushed to subdue Brodie. They dragged him screaming into Scanlon's office, where he continued to vent his rage by shouting and hitting the cabinets with his bat.

"I wanna lawyer!" Mela shouted as he scrambled up off the floor.

"Now calm down," Scanlon said, lifting the receiver. "I'll call Legal Aid and ask them to send someone." He dialed his home number and had a brief conversation with his machine. Inside the Whip's office, Brodie, Christopher, and Colon settled down into a fast game of stud poker. Brodie would intermittently halt the game to emit an angry howl and bang the bat against the side of the desk.

Biafra Baby tried to calm Oscar Mela.

Fifteen minutes later Maggie Higgins walked into the squad room and announced, "I'm Linda Wade. I would like to see my client, Oscar Mela."

Biafra Baby motioned to Mela. "He's all yours."

Higgins dragged a chair over to where Mela was sitting and positioned herself in front of the prisoner so that she blocked his face with her body and whispered, "Tell me what happened."

Scanlon left the squad room and hurried downstairs. He crossed the muster room and went behind the Desk. Pete Doyle, an old-time lieutenant with a brogue, was doing desk duty.

"How are you, Anthony?" the desk officer asked, looking up from *U.S. News and World Report.*

"Okay, Pete. Anything doing?"

"It's quiet. It's always quiet when I work. The lads know better than to bring any bullshit into the house when I have the Desk."

"Anticrime working today?"

"I have two units out there."

"They busy?"

"Anthony? In the Nine-three on a Sunday. You can't be serious?"

"Mind if I borrow one of your teams for a while?"

"The lads are yours." He spun around on the swivel chair to face the TS operator. "Give Anticrime a ten-two." The TS operator picked up the radio and transmitted: "Nine-three Anticrime, ten-two."

No response. The operator waited a few minutes and rebroadcast the message. Still no response. The desk officer glanced with paternal annoyance at the squad commander, as the message was broadcast for a third time. There was still no response from the field.

"It's not like the old days, Anthony, when a desk officer told a cop to shit, and the cop asked how much would you like, sir. The new breed is young, most have never been in the service, and only a few of them have heard terms like 'military discipline' and 'military courtesy.' So every now and then I have to put on my tight pants and give the lads a little in-service training." He angrily spun around to the TS operator. "Get on that radio and let them know that I am good and pissed off at them."

"Right, Lou." The operator transmitted: "Nine-three Crime! Ten-two! Forthwith! Acknowledge! K!"

The response was immediate: "Crime, Zone A, ten-four." "Crime, Zone B, ten-four."

A self-satisfied grin crossed the desk lieutenant's face. "The lads will be right in." He turned serious. "Have you come up with anything on poor Joe Gallagher?"

"Nothing solid. We're working on a few things."

"Any connection with that double homicide in the Nineteenth this morning?"

"We don't think so." Scanlon leaned against the Desk. "How long you been on the Job, Pete?"

"Thirty-two years."

"You thinking of making it a career?"

They laughed.

"Ever think of getting out, living a normal life?" Scanlon asked.

"Himself invented this Job for poor lads like myself. They'll have to drag me kicking and screaming from the Job."

The doors of the station house swung open and four bearded anticrime cops in old clothes came in and lined up in front of the Desk. The desk lieutenant winked at Scanlon, got up out of his seat to lean across the Desk so that he was staring down at the four cops. "Are your radios working, lads?"

"We didn't hear your transmission, Lou," the oldest of the quartet explained. He looked to be about twenty-four.

The desk officer picked up the roll call and studied it. "You didn't hear my transmissions? In other words you remained on patrol with defective radios." He let the roll call drop from his hands. "I have four more tours to do before I swing out. I come back in on late tours. And I see that you four lads are going to be doing late ones with me. I think that I'm going to have to motivate you lads to pay more attention to radio calls. As dear, departed Sergeant Flynn used to say, ten thousand miles I come to be your boss and be your boss I'll be. Now. Frazier and Walsh, you both have a post change. Frazier, you have traffic post six; Walsh, you have traffic post two. Go upstairs and get into the bag and take your posts, and be quick about it. And you had better be out there, because I'm going to send the sergeant around to give you 'sees,' at infrequent intervals, of course."

The two cops who had just received the post change started to protest, but when they looked up into the restrained fury in the desk lieutenant's face, they just shrugged and moved off up the staircase.

The two remaining cops waited apprehensively for their turn. The desk lieutenant said, "Tomorrow you lads will be assigned to a traffic post along with your two friends. But for now, the good detective lieutenant has a little job that he wants you to do for him. And after you're done doing what he wants, I'd like you to do a little something for me. Stop by Tony's and get me a large pizza with extra cheese and sausage. And also pick me up a cold one. Day tours make me thirsty."

Scanlon walked with the two cops out of the muster room and into the sitting room. He handed them the mug shots of Eddie Hamill that he had taken from Hamill's criminal folder. "In a few minutes a weasel with an armful of tattoos is going to come barrel-assing down the stairs. I want you to follow him and let me know where he goes. I'm particularly interested in knowing if he runs to see this man," he said, tapping the photo of Eddie Hamill.

"Do you want us to lean on this guy, Lou?" one of the cops asked.

Scanlon looked into the babyface playing the tough guy and had to struggle to keep a serious countenance. "Just follow and report, nothing else."

When Scanlon walked back into the squad room he found Oscar Mela and his "attorney" waiting for him.

"You have nothing to hold my client on," Higgins protested, straight-faced. "My client informs me that he was accosted by detectives in front of his residence. He wasn't even in his car."

"That's not the story my detectives tell, Counselor."

Higgins went back into conference with her client.

Scanlon said aloud, "We might be able to work something out."

"For instance?" Higgins said.

"It's my understanding that your client comes from around this neighborhood. There are a few people from around here that we're interested in talking to. Perhaps we can play, make a deal."

A sullen Oscar Mela called out, "What are their names?"

Scanlon walked over to him. "Tony Russo, Tommy Edmonds, Eddie Hamill, and Frankie Boy Siracusa."

"Whaddaya want 'em for?" Mela said, openly hostile.

"That's my business," Scanlon said.

"I never heard of any of them guys," Mela said, folding his arms across his chest. "Any more questions you got, ask my lawyer."

Scanlon scowled at Higgins and then turned on Mela. "You're on parole. You might be able to walk away from some of the charges, but I can promise you that enough will stick to put you back inside." He glanced at Higgins, back to Mela. "Go on, get out of here. You're lucky that you caught me in a good mood and that you got a good lawyer. Go, before I change my mind."

Mela looked for approval from his attorney. "It's okay. Go home," Higgins said.

Mela leaped up from the chair and took Higgins's hand. "Thanks, Miss Wade." He rushed out of the squad room.

Higgins looked at Scanlon and smiled. "Want me to make out a Two-fifty?"

"A Stop and Frisk won't cover it. Make out an arrest report and then void the arrest. Under details, put that further investigation revealed that a speck of dust had covered the 'N' of the VIN number causing it to look as though it was a 'W.' Add that the arrest was voided and the prisoner released under Section 140.20 of the CPL."

The anticrime cops didn't report back to Scanlon until 1800 hours. They had followed Mela back to his Thirtieth Avenue tenement and waited down the block. An hour and fifteen minutes had passed before Mela reappeared. He got into his car and drove to Manhattan, into the Seventh Precinct to a six-story walk-up on Chrystie Street. A man was waiting for Mela in front of the building. The two men shook hands and talked for a few minutes, and then Mela got back into his car and drove off. The man whom he had met was Eddie Hamill. After Mela had driven off, Hamill hailed a taxi and left. The anticrime cops decided to check out the building where Mela had met Hamill. A check of doorbells revealed that an Eddie Hamilton lived on the fifth floor. Bad guys feel comfortable with aliases that are similar to their real names. When the anticrime cops telephoned Scanlon and asked what to do, they were told to return to base.

"Do you want to hit his flat now?" Brodie asked Scanlon.

"He's not there now. I want to hit it when we're sure he's going to be there."

12

Vincent's dining room was crowded with loyal patrons. A violinist strolled among the garish banquettes. A waiter rolled a menu blackboard over to Scanlon and Sally De Nesto. She smiled at the waiter and ordered Scampi in Graticola. Scanlon ordered Red Snapper al Ferri. They decided that they would share an appetizer: Crostini. "Shall I order a bottle of wine?"

"I don't drink, remember?"

"I'm sorry, I forgot." He ordered a half carafe of house wine.

As they talked, he noticed how her freckles spread down her nose, and the way her lips parted into a crooked line whenever she smiled. She wore white slacks and a turquoise voile blouse and white sandals and had gold bangle bracelets on her thin wrists and gold studs in her ears.

Taking in her shapely body, he said, "Did you ever think of modeling?"

"I toyed with the idea when I first came to New York."

"What made you give it up?"

"I got fat."

"Fat? There isn't an ounce of flab on your entire body."

She patted her thighs. "Everything that I eat goes right here."

He shook his head and an incredulous smile lit up his face. "Where did you grow up?"

"I was born in Piscataway. That's in New Jersey. I went to school in Piscataway. And my family still lives in Piscataway. Any more questions?"

"Yes. Were you ever married?"

He had touched a sore spot. Her eyes fell to her water glass, her long fingers stroking the rim. "What do you want from me?"

He became uncomfortable. "To be friends."

She studied him, her gaze settling on his lips. "You have never shown anything but a professional interest in me. Now you ask me to dinner, you want to know about my personal life. It makes a girl in my line of work wary when a john tries to get chummy."

"Perhaps I'm falling for you."

Her look turned hostile. "Please don't make fun of me. I do have feelings."

He felt his ears burn from embarrassment. "I'm sorry. I guess the truth is that I just wanted to see you. To be with you. I don't know why." His sudden candor surprised him.

Her tone softened. "I have other handicapped clients. And I can relate to their loneliness, and to their special needs. But you, I can't figure you out. Your problem is not all that terrible." She leaned forward and asked softly, "So why me? Why not a steady girlfriend, or even a wife?"

He looked away from her. "Because I can only perform with hookers." He shook his head. "I can't believe that I just told you that."

She lowered her voice. "You would be surprised at what people tell me." She brought the water glass up to her lips, gazed down the stem. "Do you want to talk about it? I'm a very good listener."

His eyes drifted around the room. Somebody banged down a pot in the kitchen. They could hear the sounds of a party in one of the private dining rooms at the rear of the restaurant. A cork popped. A waiter stood nearby tossing salad in a wooden bowl.

She brushed a strand of hair from her face, waited for him to speak. The waiter came and served them their appetizer, poured wine, and backed away.

The silence between them lingered.

He picked up his fork and speared a piece of butter. "It began when I lost my leg. . . ."

They picked at their food as he talked. His words came easily. When the waiter returned with their entrees, Scanlon was still talking. He stopped and watched the waiter set down the plates and leave.

He sipped wine. "That's it. The whole mess."

"Did you ever see Jane Stomer again?"

"No. A man doesn't continue to see a woman he can't satisfy."

"I am constantly amazed at the depths of men's ignorance about women," she said, cutting her food. "Women want to be loved and to love in return. Sex to women is secondary."

Scanlon nodded and picked up his knife and fork. He cut his fish, hesitated, put the utensils down on the side of his plate, looked at her, and said, "I wonder why I had this need to lay all this on you?"

She reached out and caressed his cheek. "Because I mean nothing to you. Psychiatrists and hookers have one thing in common. There can be no personal involvements, so clients can confide in them. My johns tell me things and do things in bed with me that they would never say or do with another human being."

"Makes sense," he said, picking up his utensils.

"Did you ever realize that you never address me by name? Whenever you telephone and leave a message on my machine, you never say your name. You assume that I will recognize your voice." She looked into his eyes. "And I seldom use your name, Tony. Or do you prefer Anthony?"

"Tony is fine."

She asked earnestly, "Do you know why you are able to get it on with me and not with Jane Stomer?"

He squirmed, shook his head.

"The shallowness of our relationship makes erection possible for you. I expect nothing from you, want nothing. Love is a complicated game, Tony. People expect things from their partners, they make demands. Hookers and shrinks don't. We only want our money."

"Where does a girl from Piscataway pick up on all this insight into people?"

She laughed. "One of my johns is a blind shrink. We talk a lot.

And I'm into daytime talk shows. You would be amazed at how much women learn from watching those programs."

"I didn't mean to unload my problems on you. I'm sorry."

"Don't be. I like to help people when I can. It helps my self-image, which ain't exactly great."

"You're a nice lady, Sally De Nesto."

"Why thank you, kind sir. Are you ready for me to lay a 'Good Morning America' word on you?"

"Go ahead."

"Premorbid personality."

"Which means what?"

"A person who has a tendency to overreact to things. Say a man loses his pinky in a car accident and as a result he can't talk or he becomes paralyzed. His premorbid personality caused him to over-react emotionally to a minor injury."

Scanlon picked up his glass and swirled the wine around. "And what caused him to overreact?"

"Something in his past, his childhood. Talk shows only cover so much ground, Tony." She placed her hand on top of his. "My practice is limited to the bedroom."

The next morning Scanlon awoke fresh and revitalized. He sat on the edge of the bed staring at the rays of morning sun coming through the blinds. He looked around at Sally's sleeping form and smiled. A nice lady. He looked down at his flaccid member. You are most definitely a bothersome son of a bitch.

He saw his underpants on the floor. Last night when they arrived back at her apartment he had asked her if he might spend the night. She said yes and he assumed that she had changed her mind about making love. While she was in the bathroom, he telephoned the Squad to let them know that he was at his Vulva File location and to ascertain if there were any new developments on the case. There weren't, so he hung up, and thought about Eddie Hamill. The whole thing with Hamill didn't make sense to him. He wished that there were some way that he could forget Hamill, but there wasn't. He was going to have to check the lead out.

When Sally came out of the bathroom in a white nightgown, he hurriedly worked off his underpants. To his profound disappointment, she crawled into the bed, kissed him lightly on his head, turned her back to him, and went to sleep.

Watching the golden rays, he began to run over in his mind all the things that needed doing that day. Joe Gallagher was to be buried this morning, and there were still people to be interviewed. It was going to be a long day, and he'd better get started. He stepped off the bed on his missing leg and tumbled onto the floor. "Goddamnit!"

Startled, Sally sprang up in bed, saw him on the floor, threw off the sheet, and rushed over to him. "What happened?" she asked, kneeling down on the floor beside him.

Vexed, he snapped at her, "I stepped off on my missing leg."

"Does that happen often?"

"Sometimes I forget." A sour smile. "Would you say that was the result of my premorbid personality?"

"I'd say that was the result of your being a klutz." She passed her hand over his prostrate body. "Big tough cop flat on his ass dressed in the altogether." She kissed his nose. "You're cute."

His hand slipped inside her nightgown.

She closed her eyes. "Hmm. That feels good." She reached behind and glided her nails over his naked stump. "Are you sensitive here?"

"Very," he said, aware of the tightness in his chest. He felt his member springing to life. His fingers gently kneaded her nipple.

Arching forward, she lifted up her nightgown and sat astride his stump. Moving to and fro, she humped him.

His nerve endings bristled and his stump brimmed with strange, wonderful sensations. Pleasure surged through his body. His breathing became hard, and he made little yelps as his head lolled over the carpet.

She slid down the stump and rubbed the beveled tip hard against her body.

He groaned.

She gagged from the pleasurable torment and cupped her fingers over the head of his turgid member, kneading the swollen rim, sliding her butterfly fingers up and over the throbbing head.

His moans were deeper, louder. He felt like a boiling caldron ready to erupt. Their bodies moved in harmony. She squeezed hard, milking him, increasing his exquisite torture.

She was humping him faster and faster. Beads of sweat dotted her brow. Her mouth was agape, her tongue out. "I want to watch you come. Come!"

His gagged mumblings had become a loud yell, and then he came, and she continued to hump his stump. She took hold of it with both her hands and pressed it hard into her body, rubbing it against her clitoris. Suddenly, she went into a spasm of humping. She let out a long wail and then collapsed on top of him.

13

A gentle wind blew from the southeast. The sky was clear.

Three police helicopters overflew the crowd gathered outside St. Mary's Church on Provost Street in Greenpoint. Rows of grim-faced policemen stood at attention, tendering the final salute. A bugler sounded taps. Police pallbearers paused with the flag-draped casket at the top of the stone steps. Bystanders bowed their heads. Tearful women leaned out windows, watching the unfurling panoply of an inspector's funeral.

Taps ended. The coffin was carried down the steps to the waiting hearse. The grieving widow, dressed in black and supported on one side by Sgt. George Harris and the other by the Catholic chaplain, followed behind the coffin.

Tony Scanlon stood on the sidelines a block and a half away, lighting a De Nobili. He saw the widow's knees sag, and he was overwhelmed by the pathos of the moment. A lump rose in his throat, and a burning stung his eyes. He swallowed, champed down on his cigar. He thought of the two worlds in which he lived. His cop world of ambiguous loyalties and oversized egos that bore lifetime grudges. He thought of the world of the rookie cop, a pristine place where everything was reduced to its simplest terms: the good guys against the bad guys. Innocents in blue, they were quickly hardened and made cynical by the realities of the Job. He thought about his private life, his days of uncertainty and loneliness, of hookers, and stump-sock maintenance. How easy it had become for him to step between the parts of his life. This morning he had put forty dollars on Sally De Nesto's night table, said goodbye, and stepped into his police world.

The cortege crept away from the curb.

Scanlon said a silent farewell to Joe Gallagher, the man who had helped him stay a cop.

"They gave him some sendoff."

Walter Ticornelli's black ringlets looked as though they had been soaked overnight in a vat of grease. The shylock's reeking aftershave caused Scanlon's nose to wrinkle.

"Do you take a bath in that stuff?" Scanlon said, moving downwind.

"Whaddaya mean? That's Musk for Men by Le Claude."

"It smells like panther piss for schmucks."

"Whadda cops know about fancy things?"

"I guess nothing. But I am glad to see you here, because I want to ask you a few questions."

"About what?"

"Eddie Hamill. I hear stories."

Ticornelli's face darkened with anger. "I hear them too. They're old wives' tales. Don't believe them."

"Someone pegged those shots at you."

Ticornelli made a gesture of frustration. He spoke in Italian. "Hamill never shot at me. Believe me, there was nothing between Hamill and me, nothing." He shook his finger at Scanlon and his pinky ring sparkled. "Besides, what would that have to do with Gallagher and Yetta?"

Scanlon answered in English. "Mistaken identity. You might have been looking to take Hamill out and the guy you hired to do the job mistook Gallagher for Hamill."

Ticornelli slapped his forehead, said in Italian, "And I suppose that I also had the old lady's son and wife killed?"

"I have to follow up on every lead, every rumor." Scanlon was aware of the unconvincing sound of his response. He was also aware that he did not have the manpower to squander on leads that made no sense, rules or no rules. Still, he probably could put the Hamill thing on the back burner for a while. He knew where Hamill had burrowed. If he wanted him, he could always reach out for him.

Ticornelli glanced around to make sure that no one was within earshot, moved up closer to Scanlon, and confided in Italian, "This Gallagher thing is hurting a lot of good people. Your Irish cop friends got their strawberry noses stuck up everyone's ass. We'd like for things to get back to normal. This is a quiet neighborhood, and we like to help it stay that way." He held up one finger and switched to English. "Whatever you heard about Eddie Hamill and me is nothing but pure, unadulterated bullshit. Forget it. Don't waste your time."

Scanlon grabbed Ticornelli's finger. "And you wouldn't bullshit a cop, would you, old friend?"

The shylock worked his jaw muscles. "Of course I would. But I ain't. And you fucking well know it."

He's telling the truth, Scanlon thought. "Will you work with one of our artists and prepare a composite sketch of the driver of the getaway van?"

Ticornelli was surprised. "Are you going soft in the head? I work the other side of the street, remember? You and me, we talk. Now and then I whisper something to you in Italian. But that's between us. I help you make a sketch, and the world knows."

Scanlon spoke softly in Italian. "A few seconds ago you told me you wanted to help, get things back to the way they were. You help me, no one is ever going to know. I promise."

"A cop's promise is about as good as a barroom promise."

Scanlon's unflinching glare held the shylock's eyes. He said in Italian, "I keep my word, Ticornelli."

A sullen silence came between them and lingered.

Minutes passed. Scanlon said, "I'd owe you one, one that you could call in anytime."

"No one would ever know? They'd be no grand jury, no court, no testimony?"

Scanlon nodded.

"Okay. I'll meet with your artist."

Scanlon left him and moved through the thinning crowd. Rented buses lined up to take out-of-command policemen back to their borough's marshaling points. Several pipers from the Emerald Society band headed for the Dunnygall Bar and Grill. Another group of policemen followed behind the pipers. Scanlon thought, They'll get their loads on, some cop will pull up a piper's kilt, the piper will cold-cock the cop, and the donnybrook will have begun.

Maggie Higgins came out of the church and walked over to Scanlon. "I stayed behind to light a candle for Lieutenant Gallagher."

Scanlon nodded approvingly. "How's everything going at home?"

"It sucks. We never should have moved in together. My car is parked a few blocks from here. I'll meet you back at the Squad."

Watching her shove her way through the crowd, he thought, We all got our problems.

Biafra Baby, Colon, and Lew Brodie were standing beside the department auto, talking. Christopher was leaning against the car reading a book on nutrition. Scanlon walked over to them and told Biafra Baby and Christopher that he wanted them to check out Harold Hunt, the accountant husband of Donna Hunt. As they talked, Scanlon noticed the shopping bag filled with boxes that Hector Colon held in his hand. "What's with them?"

Colon reached into the bag, took out one of the black boxes, and held it up. "Roach motels," he announced proudly. "The *cucarachas* crawl inside and get stuck in the glue. They die a slow, miserable death. I'm going to put them around the squad room."

The long entrance hall of the Gallagher apartment had rooms on both sides. Green linoleum covered the floor. People were arriving bearing platters and trays covered with aluminum foil.

Scanlon made his way around a group of beer-drinking policemen who were standing just outside the entrance and moved into the apartment. He turned to his left and entered the first room. Cigarette smoke tainted the air, and intermittent bursts of laughter punctuated the hum of conversation. A long table had been set up against one of the walls. It was covered with food: bowls of potato salad, macaroni salad, tuna casseroles, platters of American and Swiss cheeses, and baloney, liverwurst, and ham. There were bowls of baked beans and beets. A dozen or so bags of potato chips and pretzels were piled along the back of the table, and there were long loaves of white bread, and large jars of mayonnaise and pickles.

A second, smaller table contained a large electric coffee urn, stacks of white cups, and homemade pies and cakes. A third table was covered with bottles of booze and mixes. Two cops acted as bartenders for the thirsty crowd.

Scanlon looked around and pushed his way out of the room. The parlor was down the hall on his right. It had a Colonial-style sofa with a wooden frame. On the wall above the sofa was a painting of Galway Bay. A cross made of palm fronds was stuck into the right-hand corner of the frame. A large color television and stereo were on a portable stand. A St. Patrick's Day hat was perched on top of the television set.

Scanlon moved through the parlor. When he did not see George Harris or the widow, he left the room. The kitchen was at the end of the passage; it too was mobbed with people. Scanlon glanced in and noticed the old-fashioned gas stove with the heavy doors and black legs, and was reminded of his Italian grandmother and of all the wonderful meals she had cooked for him on a similar stove.

He moved through the apartment. A drunken woman pushed her way past him, babbling, "Where's Mary? Mary Gallagher, you poor soul, where are you?"

Scanlon came to a closed door in the middle of the hallway and paused to listen. He heard voices inside, so he knocked and went in. Mary Ann Gallagher was sitting up on a queen-size bed that had a blue chenille bedspread. Her head was back, resting against a headboard covered with tufted burgundy fabric. A dressing table in the room had mirrors on its sides and top. It was covered with jars and tubes. There was a large television, and a dark blue rug, and two overstuffed chairs.

Mary Ann Gallagher was holding a cup and saucer on her lap. Three other women were in the room along with a tired George Harris, who had a mourning band stretched over his shield and a spitshine on his black cowboy boots.

Harris moved to greet Scanlon. "Glad you could make it, Lou." He placed his hand flat on Scanlon's back and guided him over to the bed. "Mary, this is Lieutenant Scanlon. You met him at Joe's wake."

She offered a limp hand, and Scanlon took hold of it. "I'm so very sorry, Mrs. Gallagher."

"You were at the wake," she said.

"Yes, I was."

"Wasn't it grand? Did you see all the flowers? They certainly did Gallagher proud."

"Yes, they did," Scanlon said, looking at Harris and whispering, "I want to be alone with her."

"Can't it wait? She just got back from the cemetery," Harris whispered back.

"No, it can't," Scanlon said.

Shaking his head in disbelief, Harris motioned the other women to leave the room. One of them, a skinny thing with a flat backside and a head of blond hair that was black at the roots, came over and kissed Mary Gallagher on the head. "We'll be right outside the door if you should need us, Mary dear," she said, in a squeaky voice as she cast a hostile look at the Italian interloper.

You frigid, shanty-Irish bitch, Scanlon thought, watching Harris usher the women from the bedroom. When they had all gone, Scanlon dragged over one of the chairs and sat down beside the bed. "We have to talk, Mrs. Gallagher."

"About Gallagher?"

"Yes."

Her striking blue eyes moved slowly over his face, taking his measure. The dark circles that he had seen at the wake were no longer there. And her skin was no longer pallid and sickly. Color had returned to her cheeks, and she wore a light shade of lipstick.

Scanlon saw something in those eyes, deep down. It wasn't sadness. It was a wariness and a hint of her determination to have her way. He wished he had brought Maggie with him. Women are better at questioning other women. They speak the same language, understand the unspoken questions.

"Mrs. Gallagher," he began, "there are certain questions concerning your married life with Joe that I—"

"Why?" she snapped. "Why is it necessary for you to pry into my married life?" She turned and stared at the wall. "Our life together is nobody's business."

He watched her sip tea. Maggie should be here, he thought. She'd probably have started by complimenting her on her nails or something.

Mary Ann Gallagher had long, graceful hands with nails that

were beautifully cared for and painted a deep red. They were pampered nails, out of place in Greenpoint, Brooklyn, and out of character for a new widow. He found himself looking at her and thinking that she didn't seem quite right in the part she was playing. Her black chemise dress draped her body, outlining an attractive figure. Her ears were pierced, but she wore no earrings.

"Gallagher died a hero. I really don't have to answer any of your questions, Lieutenant."

His left ankle itched. He tilted down to scratch it, and when he felt the fiberglass he cursed himself for forgetting. He did not want to waste time with the widow. "Mrs. Gallagher, your husband isn't a hero until I say he's a hero."

She looked at him, her thoughts blazoned across her face: You guinea bastard. "What do you mean by that?"

"My Squad caught your husband's case. And I make the final determination on how he died."

"But it was in the line of duty," she protested.

"Not until I say it was." He toyed with the tightly knit balls of the chenille bedspread. "What was your married life like?"

She raised the cup to her lips. Sipping tea, she contemplated the gray hexagon design of the wallpaper. She lowered the cup into the saucer. "My married life with my husband was unsatisfactory."

"In what way?"

She looked into the cup, straining to read tea leaves. "When we were first married, Gallagher wanted me to do certain unnatural acts, things that I could never bring myself to do. I really never enjoyed that part of married life. In time Joe came to understand that and we got along fine. We grew to respect each other."

"How often did he..." Damn, he thought. "How often did he make love with you?"

"Once every six months or so," she said casually.

Scanlon felt as though he were one of those creepy, nose-picking detectives with stained ties who get off on asking female complainants for unnecessary details of sex-related crimes. How did you react when the perp came, my dear?

He watched her finish her tea and lean over the side of the bed to put the cup and saucer on the floor. As she moved, her dress clung to her body, outlining bikini underpants.

Scanlon decided that Mary Ann Gallagher was indeed an incongruous woman: pampered nails, sexy underpants, a magnificent ass, and an avowed distaste for sex. "How did Joe spend most of his off-duty time?"

"Gallagher expended most of his time and energy on being a police department celebrity. He belonged to over a half-dozen police-related organizations. And he was active in every one of them."

"Then it's safe to say that he was out most nights of the week."

"He was always at one meeting or another."

"Do you think that there might have been other women in his life?"

Her lips narrowed and tightened. "There was never another woman in Gallagher's life. My husband was a Catholic! A Fourth-Degree Knight."

His thoughtful expression gave way to a question. "Is George Harris a good friend?"

Her slanting eyebrows arched in the center, an involuntary expression of distress. "Yes he is, a dear friend. I don't know what I would have done these past days without him."

"Did you and your husband socialize with Harris and his wife?"

"Occasionally we would attend department functions together. Once we went to the Lieutenants' Benevolent Association's Winter Carnival at the Nevele Country Club."

"Did you or your husband have any contact with Stanley Zimmerman or his wife, Rachel?"

"No we didn't. Really, you certainly don't think that their deaths were in any way connected to Gallagher's? It was nothing more than a horrible coincidence."

"Maybe. Do you work, Mrs. Gallagher."

"No."

"How did you and Joe manage financially?"

"Just fine. Everything is so expensive today, but we managed. We don't owe a soul."

"Did Joe ever gamble?"

"Of course not."

"Did he moonlight or have any other business dealings outside the Job?"

"The department was Gallagher's life; he gave it his all."

Scanlon's mind raced, trying to find new questions. He noticed that she had mentioned going out with Harris and his wife, but not that Harris was divorced. He wondered if she knew, and decided not to ask. Never put your cards on the table, any cop worth his salt will tell you that. An image of a scared little girl in Mary Janes with the wide, lolling tongue of a Down's syndrome victim and the uncomfortable face of a twelve-year-old boy came to mind. "How are the children taking all of this?"

"The poor darlings really don't understand. They only know that their daddy is gone, and that they will never see him again." She choked up, began to sniffle. Reaching into the Kleenex box on the night table, she pulled out one and dabbed her eyes. "I have to give the darlings back now."

"Give them back? I don't understand."

"They are foster children. We've had them for four years. And now that I'll have to go to work, I'll be unable to care for them."

"I thought they were adopted."

"No, they're not adopted. We couldn't have any of our own so Joe decided to take in some foster children."

When Scanlon left the bedroom he noticed clusters of people standing around in the hallway. He found George Harris standing outside the kitchen, drinking a can of beer. "How'd it go?" Harris asked.

"Okay," Scanlon said, watching a woman inside the kitchen drain a can of beer. He saw her bend the can in half, arch it into a plastic garbage bag, reach down into a metal garbage can that was filled with ice, and pull out another can. She was talking to a man in a bus driver's uniform.

"What did you think of Mary Ann?" Harris asked.

"There was something about her that made me uncomfortable." The muscles on the right side of Harris's face made a lopsided smile. "She's a good woman, Lou," he said, shaking out one of his clipped butts.

"I'm sure that's true, George."

Gales of laughter came from the beer-drinking woman in the kitchen. "Let's get out of here," Scanlon said, and led the way through the crowd.

The fresh air felt good. Scanlon leaned back against the wrought-iron gate and glanced up. He began to admire the Greek Revival houses on the block. He liked the three-sided projecting bay windows. There were two Italianate brownstones in the middle of the block with delicate ironwork and detailing over the doors and windows. A stream of people bearing food threaded their way up the steps of the Gallagher house.

"Have you come up with anything on the case?" Harris asked.

"A lot of stone walls. What happened in the Nineteenth really threw us for a loop," Scanlon said. "I don't know which end is up anymore. Who the hell would want to murder the Zimmermans?"

"Beats the hell out of me, Lou. But you know, both sets of homicides don't necessarily have to be related."

"That's what I keep telling myself. Have you found out anything?"

"I spoke to every cop in our unit and to most of the cops in the One-fourteen. Not one of them knew a thing about Joe's love life or about his gambling."

"That's bullshit. Cops were with him when he stopped women for phony traffic violations. I'm going to have to speak to them myself."

"Lou, they'd speak to me a lot faster than they would to you."

Scanlon looked at Harris. "Do you think Joe could have been getting it off with one of the policewomen in your unit?"

"Anything is possible, but I don't think so. Joe liked the conquest. If he ever made it with a subordinate, he'd never know if he'd scored because he was her boss or because he turned her on."

Higgins was drafting the supplementary Unusual on the double homicide in the Nineteenth when Scanlon walked back into the squad room. "If you had a couple of foster kids, would you be able to just up and give them back?" he asked Higgins.

She looked up from the typewriter. "No way. I love children." She looked down at the keys. "That's my one big regret, not having children."

Scanlon went into his office and telephoned the Nineteenth. Jack Fable had nothing to report. Patient Information at Doctors Hospital informed him that Linda Zimmerman and Andrea Zimmerman had been discharged. He took out the card that Linda Zimmerman had given him and dialed her home. There was no answer. There was also no answer at the Stanley Zimmerman residence. He plucked a pencil out of the coffee can on his desk and jotted in block letters on the pad in front of the can: "WHY? WHERE THE HELL IS THE DAMN MOTIVE?" Staring out into the squad room, he thought, There has to be a connection between Gallagher and the Zimmermans, someplace. He wondered what Jane Stomer would say if he called her. Knock it off, he thought with disgust. You have a homicide on your hands.

Brodie stuck his head into the office. "Lou, we got shots fired on Kent and Franklin streets."

Scanlon broke out of his trance and rushed out into the squad room. The detectives had all gathered around the radio set, heads bowed in concentration. Tension was high. Scanlon lowered himself to the edge of the desk, folded his arms across his chest, and listened to the transmissions.

"We have numerous reports of shots fired at Kent and Franklin. Subject a male, white, heavyset, wearing maroon slacks with a white belt, white loafers, and a long-sleeved brown shirt. Units responding use caution."

"Nine-three sergeant to Central. Advise units, no sirens."

"Ten-four, Sarge. Units responding to Kent and Franklin, do not use your sirens. Authority, Nine-three sergeant."

An excited voice burst over the wavelength. "George Henry, Central. We have 'im in view, walking east on Kent."

The radio fell silent.

Radio cars on patrol in Brooklyn North pulled into curbs, double-parked, their crews refraining from giving back the dispositions on jobs, anxiously awaiting the next transmission. Inside station houses clerical men hurried from offices and gathered around precinct radio sets. The Nine-three detectives fidgeted uneasily and glanced impatiently at one another. The absence of traffic on the radio was ominous.

"Nine-three units on the scene Kent and Franklin advise Central of the condition at that location, K."

No response from the field.

"Nine-three sergeant advise Central of the condition Kent and Franklin. Is further assistance required? Acknowledge, K."

A nonchalant, self-assured voice crackled over the wavelength.

"Er, Central, this is the Nine-three sergeant. No further, Central. Call it off."

"What is the condition, Sarge?"

"We're investigating at this time, Central. Will advise by land-line."

"Ten-four, Sarge."

Scanlon kicked the side of the desk in anger. "Sheee-it! Just what we need." He hopped off the desk and stormed back into his office. That last transmission from the patrol sergeant had told it all: they'd be dragging trouble in off the street. He figured that he had about ten minutes before it arrived. He made another quick call to Linda Zimmerman, with negative results. He dialed Sally De Nesto's number, and reminding himself to use her name and to mention his, he told her machine that he would like to see its mistress that evening, and hung up. Staring at the phone, he thought, We've become a society of automatons. Machines dial and talk to each other, machines add and subtract for us, pay bills for us. Someday soon we'll be able to stick our dicks into the mouthpiece of telephones and get blow jobs. I'd better hurry out and buy some telephone stock.

Nine minutes later he heard the expected commotion outside in the squad room. Loud, gruff voices, and shuffling, stumbling feet. A boisterous drunken voice shouted, "Get your hands off me. I'm on the fucking Job."

Scanlon pushed himself up out of the chair and calmly walked out into the squad room. A sergeant and five cops were tugging and pulling a drunk through the gate. Scanlon leaned against the doorframe, watching the all-too-familiar sight. The detectives had all found something to do; nary a head was not bent over a type-writer. What you don't see, you don't know, and can't be expected to testify to.

Sergeant McNamara had a ruddy complexion and thinning gray hair. He left the drunk and came over to Scanlon. He shrugged helplessly. "His name is McMahon, Lou. He works in the Four-nine. He went to Lieutenant Gallagher's funeral and afterward him and his buddies stopped in the Dunnygall for a taste." The sergeant moved in close and whispered, "His uncle is Chief McMahon, the Bronx borough commander."

Scanlon eyed the thrashing drunk attempting to straddle a chair. "How many did he let go?"

The sergeant scratched the back of his ear. "Six." He shrugged one shoulder. "Can we say it was a car backfiring?"

"Backfire? Have you canvassed the area to see if his *backfire* resulted in any dead or injured?"

"Emergency Service is on the scene now. They're checking."

Scanlon nodded toward the drunk. "Keep him quiet." He walked back into his office and found Higgins waiting with a smile on her face.

"Seeing you in action reminds me of Baryshnikov making great leaps across the stage, graceful, smooth, always in command."

"And what is that supposed to mean, Detective Higgins?"

"That means, Lieutenant Scanlon, sir, that before you are finished with that caper outside, you are going to be holding a lot of IOUs."

"Why, Maggie chile, whatever do you mean?"

Sergeant McNamara stuck his head in. "Chief McMahon is on the line for you."

"My, the word do travel fast in the Job," Scanlon said, pushing down the blinking button. "Hello, Chief."

The authoritarian voice on the other end was full of concern. "I understand you're holding my nephew."

"He's here."

"What's the story?"

"He might have to take a fall for Reckless Endangerment. He got his load on and let six go." As he talked, Scanlon reached into the top drawer of his desk and took out the Department Directory. He quickly flipped the pages to the M's. Assistant Chief Joseph McMahon was born February 11, 1927, and came on the Job June 1, 1946. That would make him fifty-nine. With the mandatory retirement age set at sixty-three, Scanlon would have four years to call in any markers. Plenty of time.

"Can anything be done?" Chief McMahon said. There was that familiar undercurrent, that slight modulation of tone.

"I'm not sure. Depends on whether or not he hit anyone. If he did, then nothing can be done, and he'll have to take a collar. If not . . ." He did not finish the sentence. The next move was McMahon's.

"I'd be very grateful for anything you could do, Lou."

"I'll get back to you, Chief."

The next call came from Frankie Lungo, the PBA's borough trustee. He too wanted to know if anything could be done, and he too would be grateful. The third call came from the duty captain. He was anxious to dance away from the entire matter, and asked Scanlon to call him with the results of his investigation.

Scanlon got on the horn to the desk officer in the Four-nine. He asked the desk lieutenant one of the Job's most-asked questions: What kind of guy is this McMahon?

"When he's sober, a gentleman. When he's got his load on, he's trouble."

It was almost one hour before the sergeant in charge of the Emergency Service truck telephoned Scanlon and told him that the canvass failed to reveal any casualties or property damage from PO McMahon's unauthorized discharge of six rounds. Scanlon thanked the sergeant and went out into the squad room. The off-duty cop was slumped in a chair, still babbling, "I'm on the fucking Job."

Scanlon went over to him and stared into his blurry eyes.

"Whatharfuck you looking at?" McMahon said truculently.

"I'm looking at you. I've never seen an asshole up close before."

"I know who you are," babbled the drunk. "You're that pegleg lieutenant, ol' shit on a stick himself."

Scanlon kicked the chair out from under the drunk. With arms thrashing upward, McMahon tumbled backward onto the floor.

"I'm the pegleg lieutenant who is going to hand you a collar for Reckless Endangerment."

McMahon sat up, shook his head trying to clear the drunkeness away. "I didn't do nothing. I wanna PBA lawyer," he demanded.

Bending, cupping his palms over his kneecaps, Scanlon said into the drunk's face, "You didn't do anything, huh? I'll tell you exactly what you did. You fired six rounds from your off-duty under circumstances evincing a depraved indifference to human life thereby recklessly engaging in conduct that created a grave risk to human life. And that, asshole, is a D Felony."

McMahon tottered up onto his feet. His cheeks were crimson and his nose a patchwork of broken capillaries. Bracing himself on the edge of the desk, he shook his head, trying to clear the craziness from his mind. He was suddenly scared. "I've got fourteen years on the Job. I've got a family."

"You should have thought of that when you drew your gun." Scanlon looked over at Lew Brodie. "Read him his rights and book him." Scanlon went back into his office and slammed the door.

Higgins was sitting down, applying polish to her nails. "Beautiful, Lou," she said, carefully gliding the brush over a nail. "I just love your lighthearted leaps, your angular foldings and unfoldings."

The door burst open. McMahon teetered over to the desk, gripping it for support. Higgins got up from the chair and with her fingers fanned limply out in front of her moved out into the squad room.

"Please, Lou," McMahon pleaded, trying to hold his swaying body upright. "I'll do anything. My family. Please."

Scanlon glared at him. How many tragedies involving cops had he seen? Too many to remember. Scanlon always thought of the wife and children. How they are made to suffer punishment too. He wondered how many times his drunken father had gotten jammed up and had been cut loose. "You're a police officer. You're supposed to protect lives, not endanger them."

"I can't stop once I start. I lose control. I . . ." He hung his head and cried.

"I'm going to let you slide," Scanlon said, "but I'm dropping the net over you. You're going into the Program."

"Oh, God, thank you, Lou, thank you."

"It means going away to the Farm to dry out and then attending the AA meetings. One slip, and it's your job. Understand?"

McMahon nodded.

Scanlon dialed the Counseling Unit of the Health Service Bureau and told the cop who answered that he had a live one for him.

A harried desk officer was fending off a barrage of reporters' questions. He grabbed the telephone, dialed the Whip's extension, and when Scanlon answered, turned his back to the reporters and said, "I've got a million fucking reporters down here breaking my balls about the Gallagher/Zimmerman connection. Better come down and speak to them."

When Scanlon appeared on the staircase, someone shouted,

"There's Scanlon," and the herd turned and stampeded over to the staircase.

"What's the connection between Gallagher and the Zimmermans?"

"Why were the doctor and his wife murdered?"

"What leads have been developed?"

"Do you have any suspects?"

Scanlon moved down to the bottom step and held out the palms of his hands, signaling to the reporters to quiet down. "Gentlemen, our investigations have failed to reveal any connection between the homicides that occurred within this command and the ones in the Nineteenth. At this point in the investigation, we believe it was nothing more than a sad coincidence."

This only triggered a new burst of questions. The desk officer shook his head, signed out in the blotter on a personal, and stepped into the lieutenants' locker room to the right of the Desk.

Scanlon shook his head in frustration.

"Look, guys. I'd be more than happy to give you whatever I had. But the simple truth is, I have nothing for you that you don't already know."

A disbelieving murmur came from the crowd.

"Look. The Nineteenth caught the Dr. Zimmerman case. Maybe they have something to give you."

"That's the same bullshit that Fable fed us," a reporter shouted up at Scanlon.

"Are you and your superiors convinced that Lieutenant Gallagher was killed while preventing a holdup?" a woman reporter shouted.

"Absolutely."

Her raven-black hair was pulled back into a bun, and she wore oversize, tinted aviator glasses. "Would you not agree, Lieutenant, that there is always the remote possibility that you and your superiors are wrong, and that Gallagher was murdered, and that there is, in fact, a direct connection with the homicide in the Nineteenth?"

Scanlon looked directly down at her. "I'm sorry. Would you mind repeating the question?"

She scowled, took a few seconds to gather her thoughts, and then repeated the question in a different form.

"No, I don't see any connection," Scanlon answered, and immediately answered another question. "Ladies and gentlemen, I'm really not conversant with what happened in the Nineteenth. Captain Suckieluski of Press Information has been designated to act as press coordinator for both cases. He's the man you should be talking to, not me."

"And where do we find this Captain Suckieluski?"

"I believe he has an office at One Police Plaza. Room 1010, I think."

The reporters wheeled and headed for the station-house door. Daniel J. Buckman, an investigative reporter from the *Times*, aka the Cocksucker with Lockjaw, was leaning against the Desk's brass railing, smiling broadly and clapping his hands slowly in mocking applause.

Scanlon walked over to him.

"Suckieluski shows originality. Most cops are only capable of a McCann or a Smith, but Suckieluski, I like it." He sucked air through his uneven teeth. "And I do believe that Room 1010 is the Pension Bureau."

"What's on your mind, Buckman?"

The reporter looked around at the cop on the switchboard and moved away from the railing, going over to the staircase.

Scanlon went with him.

"Your cover-up on Gallagher's death and the link with the double homicide in the Nineteenth is on my mind. I can't help but wonder what the connection is and what Gallagher was into that caused everyone to get gray hair."

"You're playing with yourself, you know that?"

"I can smell it." He put one foot on the bottom step and gripped the banister. "You know, my job is a lot like yours. I make a pest of myself asking questions, suborning, making promises that I know won't be kept. I keep at it until I find that one person who will talk to me. Tell the truth."

"If you want to waste your time, that's your business." He started to go back upstairs.

"Wait."

Scanlon stopped.

"The public does have a right to know the truth."

"What the public has is the right to expect its public officials who are charged with the enforcement of criminal law to do everything possible to protect the integrity of their investigations. And that is done, Mr. Buckman, by not revealing information that will end up as blaring headlines. So you see, what we have is a conflict of rights."

"They need not be mutually exclusive."

"That is true. But, sadly, they are."

"I've always admired you, Scanlon. Losing your leg, electing to remain a cop. I'm sure that it wasn't easy for you."

"See ya around," Scanlon said, lifting his fake leg up onto the first step.

"A deal?"

Scanlon froze. "I'm listening."

"I'll lay off. I'll even suggest to my colleagues that there is no cover-up, no connection."

"And the bottom line?"

"When it's all over you sit down with me and give it to me chapter and verse."

"You're a whore, you know that?"

"Even a whore has to make a living."

Deputy Chief MacAdoo McKenzie's white shirt had sweat stains around the collar. Pacing Scanlon's office, he growled, "I've just come from the PC. He's a little more than just concerned. The fucking press has been all over him regarding this Dr. Zimmerman case. Even the mayor is taking heat."

"Chief, it's just another homicide."

"That's bullshit. Anytime the rich and famous get blown away it ain't just another fucking homicide. All we need now is for Gallagher's love life to leak out." He wiped his palms with his handkerchief. "What about this Eddie Hamill thing? Anything to it?"

"Hamill's not involved," Scanlon said. "I talked with Walter Ticornelli at the funeral this morning and he assured me that the vendetta story is nonsense."

McKenzie threw up his hands. "And you believe him?"

"Yes, I do."

"Do you think you should at least go and have a talk with Hamill?"

"Probably. But I haven't had the time. As soon as I do I'll go and have a sit-down with Hamill."

Higgins came into the office, nodded to the Chief, and said to Scanlon, "Sigrid Thorsen, our witness with the baby in the park, called. She's agreed to be hypnotized. I've arranged an appointment for her on Wednesday. A policewoman from the Six-oh will be assigned to baby-sit."

"Anything else?" Scanlon asked.

"The spectrographic report from the lab on those peanut shells Christopher sent in was in the morning mail. The shells contained traces of mineral oil, water, propylene glycol, glyceryl stearate, lanolin oil, and other assorted goodies."

"Which all adds up to what?" Scanlon said.

"A hand cream or some kind of skin moisturizer," she said, perplexed. "A woman, you think?"

"Too many people say a man. Besides, men use hand creams. Especially older men with dry skin."

"I suppose so," Higgins said.

When Deputy Chief McKenzie left the Squad thirty minutes later, Scanlon got on the horn to Jack Fable at the Nineteenth Squad and told him about the deal he had made with Buckman. Fable told him that his detectives had come up with a witness, a man who had had a fight with his lover and could not sleep. They lived two houses down from the Zimmerman residence. The witness was looking out the window and saw a man enter and then leave the Kingsley Arms around the time of occurrence. The man was carrying an attaché case and had a mustache. The witness stated that the man appeared to be in his late thirties. The witness was working with the department artist. Fable would send Scanlon a copy of the Five.

The afternoon department mail arrived late.

Scanlon opened the multi-use envelope addressed to CO 93 Sqd. It contained a mimeographed letter from the Lieutenants' Benevolent Association authorizing precinct delegates to solicit donations for the Joseph P. Gallagher Memorial Fund. There were similar mimeographed letters from the Patrolmen's Benevolent Association, the Sergeants' Benevolent Association, and the Detectives' Endowment Association. They were all signed Fraternally Yours.

Scanlon took the letters out into the squad room and pinned

them on the bulletin board. "Hector, did you put in a request for the exterminator?" Scanlon asked, seeing Colon looking into a roach motel.

"Sí, *Teniente*, I sent a Telephone Message to Building Maintenance. One'll be here on Monday." Peering into the motel, he added, "Look at all them son of a bitches squirm." He put the motel back on the floor and resumed typing.

Detective Christopher telephoned and told Scanlon that he and Biafra Baby had located the accountant husband of Donna Hunt. They had tailed the husband from his Pennsylvania Avenue office. Taking turns, the detectives had entered buildings with the accountant as he visited clients. The detectives had noted the names and addresses of several of the clients. Hunt was back in his office now, Christopher reported. Did the lieutenant want them to stay on the accountant?

Scanlon checked the time. 1905 hours. "Call it a day."

"Biafra Baby and I swing out tonight. We're not scheduled back till Wednesday. Do you want us to take our swing or be on deck in the ayem?"

"Come in, I'll owe you the time."

"You got it, Lieutenant," Christopher said.

At nine o'clock that Monday night Scanlon was at his desk with his prosthesis standing in the wastebasket. He felt tired and grubby. He had reread all the reports, looking for something, and found nothing. He had signed a stack of Fives and had made three different attempts to contact Linda Zimmerman, with negative results. He had touched base with Jack Fable twice more and on the last occasion had asked him if he knew the whereabouts of Linda Zimmerman. Fable told him that he didn't. He went on to inform Scanlon that she had adamantly refused his offer of police protection.

Scanlon rubbed his tired eyelids. He took the talc out of the drawer and rolled up his left trouser leg. He powdered his stump, dumped some into the socket, and took out a clean stump sock. He rolled it up over his stump, picked up the prosthesis, leaned back, and slid his stump into the socket.

Taking the bag of dirty socks out of the bottom drawer, he got up, went out into the squad room, and signed out in the Log: "Lieutenant Scanlon left, end of tour."

14

The sky was overcast. The humidity was rising.

The approach to the Williamsburg Bridge was clogged with Tuesday-morning traffic. Scanlon slowed his car to a stop. A swarm of derelicts ran out from the curb, threading their way among the cars, cleaning windows. He waved two of them off. He had spent a lousy night and was not in a charitable mood. Last night when he arrived home he found Sally De Nesto's message on his answering machine changing their date from Monday night to Tuesday night. At loose ends and not feeling much like being alone, he had gone to Roseland and had danced alone among the swirling shadows. Later in the night he had stopped for a drink at Du Soir, Columbus Avenue's latest in spot. He had stood among the crush, sipping his drink, trying to summon the courage to speak to one of the many attractive women in the bar. His problem would not go away. What does he say, when does he say it, and how does he say, I'm an amputee?

A woman in her late thirties pushed her way through the crowd and stood next to him, cuddling her glass in a napkin as her eyes slowly roamed over the crowd. She was tall, thin, and a trendy dresser. She had short two-tone hair, the bottom blond, the top

218

brown. Her look fell on Scanlon. He smiled. She smiled back. Her name was Sid. They began to talk to each other and it was wonderful. He was relaxed, almost confident. Their conversation veered back and forth across many subjects. He searched for an opening to tell her that he was an amputee. Perhaps the terror was behind him, perhaps he had conquered the fear. At one point she reached into her bag to get her cigarettes when another woman bumped into her, causing Sid to stumble. Her keys tumbled from her pocketbook to the floor, and she made a grab for them. In so doing her hand collided with his prosthesis. "What's that you got there?" she asked, straightening, a questioning look spreading across her face.

His heart sank. Trying to force a confident edge into his voice, he said, "I'm an amputee."

"Oh?" She smiled at him. "I really don't think I could handle that." She excused herself, and was quickly swallowed up in the crowd. Scanlon gulped down his drink. He shoved his way out of Du Soir and drove directly to Gretta Polchinski's place.

When Scanlon arrived at the Nine-three on Tuesday morning he parked in the space reserved for the squad CO and went to the corner candy store to buy his daily ration of De Nobilis. Leaving the store, he paused to look at the skyline across the river, glad to be back on his own turf.

He went into the station house and followed his usual routine of going through the latest orders and reports. Two arrests had been made last night by the patrol force. The Gallagher/Zimmerman Unusual was the last one in the folder.

Nearing the top of the staircase he was cheered by the smell of freshly made coffee.

"Anything doing?" he asked, unlatching the gate.

Lew Brodie was sitting with his legs up on a desk, sipping coffee. "Eric Crawford went sick. I put him out in the Sick Log and notified the borough."

Scanlon pulled the handle on the spigot back, filling his mug. He walked over to the row of clipboards hooked onto the wall and took down the weekly roll call. Studying the official form, he said, "Nagel and Lucas are scheduled to do the evening duty with Crawford. They can cover two-handed." He returned the clipboard to its place. "Did Crawford say what was wrong with him?"

"The flu," Brodie answered.

Higgins looked up from the *Times* crossword. "I hope Fatso keeps his tiny weenie warm."

Detectives smiled, remembering Crawford's macho act with Higgins, and her dare to Crawford to break it out.

Grinning, Scanlon went into his office. He had just settled in behind his desk and had begun to look through his messages when someone out in the squad room barked, "Attention!"

The *Patrol Guide* mandates that attention be called whenever a member of the force above the rank of captain enters a room. This procedure is routinely complied with in the Patrol Force. But not in the Detective Division. There are two exceptions: the PC and the CofD.

Scanlon had almost made it to the door when Police Commissioner Robert Gomez propelled himself into the office and slammed a newspaper down on the Whip's desk. "We made the front page of every goddamn paper in this city. Chrissake, we're even nationwide."

"Coffee?"

"Black, no sugar," Gomez said, picking up the newspaper, looking at the front page.

Scanlon returned in a few minutes and closed the door. He put the PC's cup down in front of him.

"Did you see this?" Gomez said, stabbing a finger on a story in the paper. "See? A radio car killed a man crossing the street and the driver of the car fled the scene. In my day whenever you got your load on you went out and got laid. No more! The new breed wants to play at being Attila the Hun." He closed his eyes and rubbed his hands hard into his temples. He inhaled deeply through his mouth and let the air out slowly.

"They're coming at me from all sides, Scanlon. The Job seems to be falling to pieces. I need time so that these scandals can die from natural causes. Gallagher is the only hero that the Job has at the moment. And now with what has happened in the Nineteenth it appears that even Gallagher might end up going down the tubes." He gulped coffee. "I've been the PC for fifty-five months. Five more months and I'm entitled to a PC's pension. I need time, time to get the press off my ass, off our ass."

Scanlon told him about his deal with Buckman.

"There are a dozen other reporters to take his place. What I need is an arrest in the Gallagher caper. That way the press would believe that there was no connection with the Zimmerman homicides in Manhattan." He looked sternly at the Whip. "There is a connection, isn't there?"

"Yes, I believe that there is."

"Is Lieutenant Fable of the same opinion?"

"Yes, he is."

"Have you come up with anything in Gallagher's background that connects him to the Zimmermans?"

"No. Nor have I come up with any *official* improprieties on Gallagher's part that could hurt the Job."

"His personal life is enough to wreak havoc with the department." He thought a moment, staring into his mug. "Lou, I don't want to be boxed into making stupid moves by all this negative publicity." He slammed his fist on the desk. "But I want you to buy us some time so that we can get on with the investigation without the pressures of the press and television cameras."

"Jack Fable has come up with a witness who might have seen the perp enter and leave the Kingsley Arms."

"Eyewitnesses are about as useful as tits on a bull," Gomez said, swirling the contents of his cup. He put the mug down, got up, and moved to the grated window, where, looking into the dirty glass, he straightened his tie.

Always the fashion plate, Scanlon thought.

"If I didn't know better I'd think that that psychopathic midget I inherited as my CofD killed the doctor and his wife just to get my job." He turned. "Let's you and me go over the whole thing from the top."

For the next thirty minutes Scanlon walked the PC through the details of the Gallagher/Zimmerman homicide. Gomez listened without comment. When Scanlon finished, the PC's expression was grave. "Tell me about this Eddie Hamill again."

Scanlon did.

"You've found out where Hamill lives?"

"Yes."

"I think we should pick Mr. Hamill up, go through the motions of an arrest. It would relieve some pressure, give us breathing time.

An arrest is the best way to make the press lose interest in a case."

Scanlon sighed. "Commissioner, Eddie Hamill is not the type of guy to come the easy way." He rubbed the side of his face. "Anyway, if we should pick him up, what do we charge him with, barratry?"

"Mopery, impersonating a human being, whatever you want. As long as you buy me some breathing room."

"Commissioner, you just got done telling me that you didn't want to be forced into making a dumb move. Going after Hamill, in my judgment, would be a dumb move."

"Maybe. But it's straw-grabbing time, Lieutenant." He pointed a finger at the Whip's prosthesis. "You owe the Job. It did the right thing for you, now it expects you to do the right thing for it. And besides, you could be wrong about Hamill. Haven't you ever made a wrong move on an investigation? Your friend Walter Ticornelli could be lying to you. There could be a hundred answers. Hamill just might be your hit man."

"I still think it's a bad move."

"Make the PC happy, Lieutenant. Bring Hamill in for questioning. Who knows, you might hit the jackpot."

Scanlon was about to utter another mild protest when the door burst open and a sweating MacAdoo McKenzie plunged into the room. "Commissioner," he said, nodding.

The PC looked at Scanlon and smiled. The Job's unofficial communication system had acted with its usual efficiency. As soon as the PC had climbed the staircase out of sight, the Nine-three desk officer had telephoned upstairs to warn the Squad. Hector Colon had dashed out into the hallway, seen the PC trudging the steps, and run back into the squad room and called attention. Meanwhile, the desk officer had gotten on the horn to Brooklyn North. The sergeant manning the operations desk received the notification, and he immediately got on the horn to Brooklyn North Uniform Command and Brooklyn North Detective Command. Within ten minutes every patrol precinct and detective command within the city of New York knew that Bobby Gomez was out of the big building and in the Nine-three Squad.

"Chief," Gomez said, his smile lighting up his handsome Latin face. The PC had Scanlon fill McKenzie in on the Hamill matter. When Scanlon had finished, Gomez asked McKenzie what he thought of Hamill as a suspect in the Gallagher/Zimmerman caper. "I'm inclined to go along with the lieutenant. I don't think that Hamill is involved."

Scanlon was surprised at McKenzie's support.

Gomez pulled his lips together. "You two might be right. Then again, you might be wrong. I let the chief of operations talk me into letting the cops wear those stupid-looking baseball caps. That was a bad mistake on my part. They look like goddamn truck drivers instead of police officers. Anyway, my gut reaction tells me to pick up Hamill."

Twelve minutes later MacAdoo McKenzie accompanied the PC down the staircase into the muster room of the station house. The PC's female chauffeur was standing at the side of the desk talking to the cop on the switchboard. When she heard the PC coming down the steps she ended the conversation and rushed over to open the door for the PC.

Gomez went behind the desk and signed himself out in the blotter. As he walked out from behind the Desk, his chauffeur called out, "Where to, Commissioner?"

"Let's take a drive over to the Two-four. I'm in the mood to visit a few houses. I don't get out in the field enough," he said in an equally loud voice.

As the PC was walking out of the station house, the desk officer's hand slid over the Desk toward the red department telephone.

The detectives cautiously climbed the tenement's staircase. Music blared from some apartments; canned TV laughter came from behind multilocked doors.

Scanlon had made the proper notifications: Communications had been notified that Nine-three Squad detectives were going into the Seventh to hit a flat; the Seventh's desk officer and the Seventh Squad had also been apprised. The Seventh's desk officer had assigned a marked RMP with two uniform cops to assist the Nine-three detectives—and avert the tragedy of uniform cops shooting at unfamiliar detectives.

The tenement had a weathered brick facade with white trim and black fire escapes winding down the front of the building. Many windows showed chartreuse, electric-blue, and bright orange shades and curtains. Where do they get them? Scanlon thought, studying the tenement's front.

Hamill's fifth-floor apartment was the first one off the staircase, to the right. When the detectives reached the second landing, Scanlon motioned to Brodie to turn off the radio so that Hamill wouldn't be tipped off by the police transmissions. The detectives stopped at the top of the fifth landing. Scanlon and Brodie dashed to the other side of Hamill's door, flattening themselves against the wall.

Higgins and Colon lay back on the staircase. A baby wailed. The detectives drew revolvers.

Scanlon had a nagging feeling in his gut that told him to get the hell out of there. Against his better judgment, he nodded to Higgins.

She stretched out her gun hand and rapped the barrel lightly against the door. The music inside the apartment suddenly ceased. Higgins rapped again. Muffled footfalls came up to the door.

"Yeah?" The voice was gruff, mean.

"Maggie Suckieluski," she said softly. "Oscar Mela sent me. He thought you might be in the mood for a little relaxation."

"Good ol' Oscar."

The detectives heard the loud clicking of tumblers and the rattle of safety chains. Colon nudged Higgins to get behind him. She stuck her tongue out at him. The door jerked open. Displaying her shield, Higgins stepped in front of the door. "Hi, Eddie," she said. Scanlon and Colon stepped into view, their shields held high. Hamill's eyes widened with anger. His left hand was concealed behind the door, gripping the steel bar of a Fox lock.

"We want to talk to you, Eddie," Higgins said, pushing her way into the apartment.

"What do you have in your hand, Eddie?" Scanlon said, noticing the floor plate that the bar wedged into.

"Nothing," Hamill said, pivoting and smashing the bar across Higgins's chest.

She doubled over and crumpled to the floor. Scanlon and Colon jumped over her body and went after him. Hamill made a springing leap toward a room on the left side of the apartment. As he did this, he thrust his hand under his polo shirt and came out with a .38 Colt.

"He's got a piece!" Scanlon warned.

Scanlon and Colon dove for cover behind the furniture. Lew Brodie wheeled and threw himself over Higgins's prostrate body. Hamill ran with a slight limp into the other room and slammed the door.

Lew Brodie dragged Higgins out of the apartment. Colon knelt behind a chair with his revolver trained on the door.

Scanlon rushed outside to see how Higgins was. She was clutching her chest, gagging for breath. Brodie unbuttoned her jacket and the top of her blouse. He and Scanlon propped her up against the wall. Inside the apartment Hector Colon called to Hamill to come out of the room with his hands over his head. Two shots rang out. The bullets smashed through the door and impacted into the wall behind Colon.

Hector Colon did not return the fire.

Scanlon ran back into the room and knelt beside Colon. "You all right?" Scanlon asked.

"Yeah," Colon said.

"Eddie, don't get stupid," Scanlon called out. "Toss out your gun and come out."

Another shot smashed through the door.

Scanlon dashed back out into the hallway and took the radio from Brodie and switched it on. Before he could say anything, the transmission he heard caused him to curse: "All units in the Seventh. We have a confirmed report of detectives engaged in a gun fight. A ten-thirteen at 132 Chrystie Street. Use caution. Units responding acknowledge, K." A spate of hurried acknowledgments flooded the airwaves.

Detectives prefer to operate by stealth, away from the harmful glare of the limelight. In and out quickly, quietly. Scanlon knew that at that very moment mobile press crews had picked up the police transmissions on their car radios and were speeding toward Chrystie Street. He pressed the transmit button. "Nine-three lieutenant to Central, K."

"Go, Lou. What's the condition? Do you require heavy weapons on the scene?"

"Negative, Central. Call it off. Everything is under control. There's no thirteen."

"Were shots fired at that location, K?"

"Negative, Central. Some kids must have set off firecrackers."

"Ten-four, Lou. All units responding to the thirteen on Chrystie Street resume patrol. Authority, Nine-three lieutenant on the scene. Mark that run ten-ninety Y, Unnecessary Call."

Scanlon looked up and down the hallway. The doors were closed, the apartments silent. He checked Higgins once more and rushed back inside, cursing the PC.

The furniture was cheap leatherette and veneer. A velvet painting of the Brooklyn Bridge hung on the wall. The bridge's towers and cables were illuminated with little yellow lights. Scanlon moved the radio to his mouth. "Biafra?"

Biafra Baby and Christopher had been assigned by Scanlon to stay with the two uniform cops from the Ninth and watch the front of the house, the side with the fire escapes.

Biafra Baby's voice came over the airway. "Yeah, Lou?"

"Three."

"Right."

Scanlon switched the wavelength to the third setting, the seldom-used detective channel licensed by the FCC for person-to-person communication.

"Anyone hurt?" Biafra Baby asked.

"Maggie had the wind knocked out of her," Scanlon said. "Who put over that thirteen?"

"The boys in blue," Biafra Baby radioed. "They did it before we could stop them."

"Can you make out the apartment?"

"Yeah. Do you want us to give it a shot?"

"Yeah. He's holed up in what I think is the bedroom. The fire escape cuts across both rooms," Scanlon said. "And for Chrissake, be careful."

In the hallway, Lew Brodie hovered over Higgins. Color had returned to her face and her gasping had stopped.

"You gonna be okay?"

She looked up into his massive face and smiled. "You threw your body over mine to protect me. Thanks, Lew."

He squirmed. "Hey, anything for a free feel. You know how horny us cops get."

"Yeah, I know. Get inside, you big lummox. I'll be all right."

Brodie kissed her on the top of her head. "You're an okay kid,

226

Higgins. I'm goin' inside and get a chunk of that guy's ass for you."

A snarling, avenging bull rushed into the apartment. Before Scanlon could react, Brodie had hurled his massive hulk against the closed door and let out a blood-curdling yell.

The sound of splintering wood filled the dingy apartment. The door flew off its hinges.

Scanlon and Colon rushed into the bedroom behind Brodie. Eddie Hamill had been hastily unscrewing the window lock when the door caved in. He wheeled with his gun pointing at Brodie. Scanlon and Colon spread out, stalking Hamill. Colon was low, in a combat stance, his revolver pointed at Hamill's chest. Scanlon's revolver was aimed at the belly.

Hamill's nervous eyes darted from detective to detective as they spread out.

"I'm getting out of here," Hamill said. "I'll blast anyone who tries to stop me."

Brodie stopped a few feet from Hamill. He aimed his weapon at Hamill's face and cocked the hammer. "You're gonna die, motherfucker."

Hamill's gun hand trembled as the fear spread across his face.

Biafra Baby and Christopher appeared on the fire escape.

"I'm counting to five," Brodie announced, "and if that piece ain't on the floor, and your hands reaching for sky, I'm gonna send you to hell. One . . . two . . . three . . ."

Biafra Baby smashed the window with his revolver.

Instinctively, Eddie Hamill whirled to the sound of the breaking glass. Brodie and Colon leaped on Hamill. Colon's hand gripped the cylinder of Hamill's gun, preventing its discharge. Lew Brodie grabbed Hamill by the balls. Hamill screamed and his knees sagged. Keeping a relentless grip on the cylinder, Colon forced the gun upward, exerting pressure against Hamill's wrist.

Brodie twisted Hamill's testicles, crushing them together. Hamill squealed and his body bent in half. Retching, Hamill toppled to the floor. Colon, with his hand still around the gun, knelt beside the downed man and prized the weapon from the resisting hand. Brodie raised his foot to stomp Hamill's face.

Scanlon grabbed Brodie's shoulder. "Enough. We have the gun." Scanlon yanked Hamill up off the floor and slammed him against the wall, pulling his hands behind his back, handcuffing him.

Colon opened the cylinder of Hamill's gun. "He let three go at us."

"Check them out," Scanlon ordered Colon.

Biafra Baby and Christopher opened the window and climbed inside.

Eddie Hamill cringed up against the wall. "Ahhhh, my balls. My balls. Why'd ya have to grab my balls?"

Scanlon turned the prisoner around and rammed his elbow across Hamill's throat, pinioning him to the wall. "This ain't Sesame Street, pal. We get annoyed when people peg shots at us."

"I thought you were burglars," Hamill grunted.

"With police shields stuck into your ugly face?" Scanlon said. "Save your bullshit for Legal Aid."

"Whaddaya want with me?" Hamill said. "I didn't do nothing."

Eddie Hamill had a cloud in his right iris that spread outward into the pupil. Scanlon recalled the description of Hamill that Colon had given him in McJackoo's Bar and Grill. He remembered the clumsy way Hamill had run into the bedroom. "You're missing three toes off your left foot, right?" Scanlon asked.

"Yeah," Hamill snarled.

Hamill was a muscular man with bushy eyebrows and a crooked nose that looked as though it had been broken on several occasions. There were large gaps between his front teeth.

Colon came up behind Scanlon and whispered that the slugs had lodged in the wall without causing injuries.

"Good," Scanlon said.

"Take a look," Biafra Baby called out, holding up a plastic bag containing white powder and the silencer that he had found on top of the battered chest of drawers.

"You can't introduce any of that shit in court," Hamill shouted. "You got no fucking search warrant."

Biafra Baby came over to Hamill, dangling the evidence. "It's gonna be used, m'man. It's gonna be used because we were legally present inside your stinking dom-i-cile, and because the discovery was inadvertent, and because the incriminating nature of the objects were immediately apparent to us police-type professionals." Biafra Baby did a fast shuffle. "And that, m'man, bees known as the Plain View Doctrine, cha, cha, cha."

Scanlon looked at Christopher. "Get him out of here."

Christopher and Biafra Baby hustled the prisoner from the apartment. Hector Colon went outside in the hallway to see how Higgins was, and to help her downstairs.

Brodie was on his knees rummaging through the bottom of the closet. Scanlon glanced around the room, made sure that they were alone, and went over to him. "Lew?"

"Yeah?" Brodie said, looking up at the Whip's angry face.

"Don't ever pull a stunt like that again."

Brodie raised his palms in a gesture of surrender. "That hump pegged shots at us and dumped on Maggie."

"Your Charge of the Light Brigade could have gotten yourself and us dead. You had no way of knowing what kind of artillery was on the other side of that door."

"Aw. You're right. It won't happen again."

"And don't ever cock your hammer unless you damn well intend to shoot."

"Not to worry on that score, boss. I'm one of those cops who leave the first chamber empty. I've seen too many accidental discharges in my day."

"Did you find anything in the closet?"

"Nothing."

"Then let's get the hell out of here."

15

The Seventh Precinct is located on Pitt Street, a dilapidated block of boarded-up buildings and ruined foundations amid weed-filled lots in Manhattan's Lower East Side.

Scanlon had used the direct line to notify the PC of what had happened at the Chrystie Street address. How did the PC want him to proceed? Scanlon had asked.

"Make your notifications, Lieutenant."

Scanlon notified Manhattan South Detective Command and Brooklyn North Detective Command of the arrest of Eddie Hamill. Both commands in turn notified the chief of detectives. CofD Goldberg upon hearing of the arrest got on the horn to the press.

News briefs interrupted regular programs to announce that the NYPD was questioning a suspect in the Gallagher/Zimmerman homicides. The Seventh was soon besieged by reporters.

Scanlon would have preferred to question Hamill back at the Nine-three, but department regulations required that prisoners be processed at the precinct of arrest, in this case the Seventh. Hamill was closeted in the Seventh Squad's interview room, a cell-like place of cinder-block walls and two-way mirrors.

Scanlon felt the tug of frustration gnawing at his gut. He knew damn well that Hamill was a dead end and that valuable time was being squandered, the case's momentum lost. He walked into the interview room and sat across the table from Hamill. Shaking his head from side to side, he looked into the subject's face.

A faint smile came to Hamill's lips. "You ain't got shit and you know it."

Scanlon leaned forward. "Eddie, I'm going to be a nice guy and tell you exactly what we got. For openers, Assault Two on Detective Higgins. And the silencer that we found on your dresser, criminal possession of a weapon, a D Felony. The junk was felony-weight and carries with it a presumption of intent to sell, a C Felony. And then there is that matter of your gun and the shots you fired at us. Attempted Murder of Police Officers, a B Felony."

Hamill folded his arms across his chest and leaned back onto two legs. "Bullshit, and you fucking-A well know it."

"Eddie, I've been lying guys like you behind the wall for years."

Hamill nervously stretched his neck.

"It's time to play 'Let's Make a Deal,'" Scanlon said.

"Fuck off."

"A wise man would at least listen."

Hamill's gaze wandered, stopping at the two-way mirror set into the gray cinder block. "I'm listening."

"I want to know what went down between you and Walter Ticornelli. I also want to know your whereabouts when Lieutenant Gallagher and Yetta Zimmerman were taken out."

Hamill's expression brightened. "That's what this is all about?"

"That's what it's about, Eddie."

"And suppose I tell you, then what?"

"Then I'll be a nice guy and see to it that when the complaint is drawn up no mention is made of Clear View. The evidence will have been discovered in a closet in your apartment. You'll be held for the grand jury and they'll indict. But at the first Huntley hearing to suppress the evidence your Legal Aid lawyer will be able to get the evidence suppressed and the case will go bye-bye."

"And the gun and the shots I took at you?"

"What shots?"

Hamill grinned. "I'm on parole. I owe eight on a seven and a half to fifteen for burglary. I'd have to go back inside."

"I'll square things with your parole officer. You won't have to go back inside, I promise," Scanlon lied.

"In that case . . ." Hamill flipped his palms. "I was into Walter and couldn't make the payments. We had a sort of falling out."

"All of it, Eddie."

As Hamill told it, when he missed two vig payments, Ticornelli dispatched three of his Mulberry Street gorillas to have a talk with him. The Greenpoint burglar took a bad beating and was forced to redouble his efforts to steal enough money to get Ticornelli off his back. It took him three weeks to raise the money.

"I had the hospital records checked, Eddie. You were confined to St. John's with gunshot wounds. Was that Ticornelli's handiwork?"

"He had nothing to do with that," Hamill said, annoyed. "That's them Greenpoint biddies and their rumors. It just so happened that about the same time I was having a problem with Ticornelli I was also seeing this Cuban chick. Her old man found out about us and sent some of his relatives around to see me. I almost didn't get away that time. I'll tell ya, them damn Cubans still live in the stone age. I hadda go out and rob more money to lay on the head spic in order to square myself with them. Tell ya, that was one expensive pussy."

"Someone tried to take Ticornelli out about the same time. Was that you?"

Hamill placed his elbows on the table and held out his hands, palms out. "Look at my sheet, man. I'm a burglar and a lover. Not a strongarm guy. I never tried to hit Ticornelli or anyone else." He held up a finger. "If you'd bothered to check back you'd have seen that the paisanos were having one of their pizza wars at the time Ticornelli got shot at. It was his own people who tried to take him out."

"Where were you when Lieutenant Gallagher and the old lady were hit?"

Hamill suppressed a smile. "I got the best alibi in the world. I was with Mr. Greenspan, my parole officer. Check it out."

"Your stomping grounds are Greenpoint, Eddie. Why are you living in Manhattan under an alias?"

"Guys in my line of work don't advertise, Lieutenant."

Scanlon scraped his chair back and got up.

"We got a deal, ain't we?"

"Yeah, Eddie, we got a deal."

The Seventh's squad room was a very busy place. Detectives manned telephones, answering the queries of overhead commands who wanted the who, what, when, where, why, and how of the Eddie Hamill arrest. The Seventh's Second Whip was out in the muster room keeping the reporters at bay. Nine-three Squad detectives were at typewriters banging out the considerable paperwork connected with Hamill's arrest.

Scanlon was anxious to leave the Seventh and get on with the investigation. He knew that they'd all be stuck in the Seventh until all the paper was done and all the notifications made. Tradition dictated that detectives who made out-of-command arrests process their own prisoners.

Scanlon went into the Whip's office and telephoned the PC. He told him of his interview with Eddie Hamill and restated his belief that Hamill was nothing but a waste of time and effort. The PC agreed, but still wanted Scanlon to buy him some time.

Scanlon walked out into the squad room. He went up to Higgins, who was sitting at a desk scratching out the property voucher. "How do you feel?"

"All right, Lou."

"I want you to do an LOD request."

She let the pencil fall from her hand and looked up at him. "I really don't want to go through the hassle of a line-of-duty-injury request, Lou. I'd have to have the guys prepare witness statements, go to the hospital and get a doctor's diagnosis, wait around to be interviewed by the duty captain, call the sick desk and get a serial number. All that paperwork, and I feel fine."

Leaning forward, Scanlon placed a hand on the back of her chair and another flat on the typewriter. "Maggie, if you start to hemorrhage tonight at home, it'll be too late to put in for LOD, so do me a favor, and do it now."

"But Lou . . ."

"Now, Maggie," he whispered into her ear.

Covering the mouthpiece of the phone with his hand, Colon hollered, "Lou, you got a call. Some broad."

"What's her name?" Lew Brodie hollered back.

"Not you, the lieutenant," Colon said.

Linda Zimmerman's voice was strained and very low. "A news bulletin just announced that you have taken a suspect into custody in the Seventh Precinct. Is that true?"

"I can't discuss that over the telephone. Where are you?"

A maid led Scanlon into the sitting room of the Sutton Place apartment. The furniture was wicker and the room overlooked the river and the East Side Highway.

Linda Zimmerman was slumped in a sofa with her left arm hanging limply over the woven arm. Her hair was carelessly pinned up and her face was without makeup, save for some caked-on mascara on her long eyelashes. She was dressed in jeans, an oversize cotton shirt, and Docksiders. Her grim stare followed Scanlon as he crossed the sun-drenched room.

"Are you okay?" he asked, lowering himself down next to her.

"The man that you have in custody, is he the one who slaughtered my family?"

"No, Linda, he isn't. We're holding him on another matter. The press somehow got hold of it and got their wires crossed."

She clutched her arms and shivered. Her body began to shake.

Scanlon was saddened by the sight. "Please believe that we are doing everything possible to catch them."

"Sure you are," she said with a heavy dose of sarcasm.

"I've been trying to contact you. Whose apartment is this?"

"My Aunt Rae's. She's my father's sister, and you can't interview her because she is not here. She's out making the arrangements for the cremation of my brother and his wife."

Scanlon caught a faint whiff of her evergreen-and-orange fragrance. He recalled their first meeting in the drawing room of her brother's home. Then she had been wearing a wide-brimmed hat and black crocheted gloves, and sat on a fragile Queen Anne chair with her long legs crossed at the knees. It seemed as though it was an eon ago, in some far-off place. "How is your niece?"

"Oh, Andrea is just wonderful. Would you like to see her?" She got up, held out a hand to him. "Come, I'll bring you to her."

The exuberance of her tone put him on his guard. She led him through the luxury duplex to a curving white staircase. There was a large window in the wall that overlooked the East River. She hurried up the stairs ahead of him and opened a door at the head of the staircase. Pointing into the room, she said, "Here is my niece, Lieutenant. Andrea, dear, this nice policeman would like to ask you a few questions. When..." She wheeled and placed her forehead against the doorjamb and cried.

Scanlon came up behind her and looked into the room.

Andrea Zimmerman, the birthday girl with the shy smile and inquisitive eyes, lay in a big bed expressionless, her blank eyes fixed on some black hole in time. Scanlon clenched his fists, digging his nails into the skin of his palms. His eyes began to fill and his chin quivered. He leaned quietly into the room and pulled the door closed. He put his arm around the crying woman and led her downstairs.

Throwing herself onto the sofa, she said, "I didn't think that I had any tears left."

"What do the doctors say?" he asked softly, sitting down next to her.

"Their glowing prognosis is that time will tell. The truth is, they just don't know. They hedge and say that she'll probably come out of it. She has periods when she focuses her eyes and seems to recognize me."

"Have you made any plans?"

"I've taken a leave of absence from the bank. Andrea and I are going to live here for a while. If Andrea should come around I want her to have a sense of family."

"Will you allow me to look through your mother's and your brother's personal papers?"

"Lieutenant Fable asked me the same question. I'll tell you what I told him. No. I have had enough policemen in my life these last few days to last me a lifetime. I don't want policemen poking around my family's history. And I especially do not want police protection."

Stone walls everywhere. "Now that you have had time to think, can you recall any connection that Gallagher might have had to your family?"

"No, I can't. Your lieutenant was getting Andrea's birthday cake as a favor to Mother."

"Nothing else?"

"Gallagher was not one of Mother's priorities." She glowered at him. "What will happen to them if you catch them? Will they die in the electric chair?"

"No, Linda, they won't. This state does not have the death penalty. If they are convicted, and if they don't plea-bargain, the most that they could get is twenty-five to life on each homicide." He grimaced. "And the sentences more than likely would be made to run concurrent instead of consecutive, which means twelve, fifteen years inside and then parole."

"Parole!" she shouted at him. "And you call that justice?"

"I don't call it anything, Linda. I don't make the law, I enforce it."

On the seat of an armchair in front of the sofa where she sat was a massive glass ashtray overflowing with cigarettes from which, in most cases, only a few puffs had been taken before they'd been stubbed out. There was a box of cigarettes and a Zippo lighter on the chair next to the ashtray. She picked up the lighter and toyed with the cover, clicking it open and closed. She lit a cigarette.

"I wish you would consider allowing us to look through those papers."

She took successive drags on the cigarette and crushed it out in the ashtray. "No."

"Don't you want to help us find the killer?"

She glared at him. "I've already helped your investigation. I've supplied the bodies. People I loved." Crying, she added, "It just isn't fair. Parole after a few years. No. No. That isn't fair." She toppled over and lay on the sofa, crying.

"Let it out, Linda. Let it come," he said, soothing the side of her head with his hand.

Her sobs subsided after several minutes. He continued to soothe her, murmuring calming words.

She abruptly pushed his hand away and sat on the sofa. "I guess you're my only hope of getting justice."

Scanlon made a plea for her total cooperation and said, "You can't hold anything back, because you don't know what is important and I do."

Again she picked up her lighter and clicked the Zippo's top open and closed, then she lit another cigarette, took several nervous drags, and crushed it out in the ashtray.

"I've given Mother's clothes and furniture to the Salvation Army. Her papers are in the dining room. If you want to, go ahead and look."

"When did you gather up your mother's belongings?"

"The day after she was murdered. There were personal things that I wanted to get out of there before the neighborhood burglars had a picnic at my family's expense."

"The day after she died?" he said. "You were composed enough to go to her apartment and clean it out?"

"I told you, there were personal things that I wanted."

"What sort of things?"

"Lieutenant, I'm not one of your suspects. So don't press me to tell you very personal things that I don't want to tell you."

"I'm sorry. Sometimes I can be a little overzealous."

She got up and led him into a formal room with a long mahogany table and a brass chandelier. Three cartons were on the table. She stood by his side, watching, as he sifted through the first of the cartons. He moved slowly, carefully, removing the contents an item at a time, examining them, searching for a reason for murder.

Scrutinized, each item was laid down on the table beside the carton it came out of. He found old letters bound together with rubber bands. There was an old pocket-size address book with odd telephone exchanges: Buckminster, Esplanade, Ingersoll. There was a music box that did not chime, some old photographs, an antique ring, and some long-paid bills.

He put the items back into the carton and went on to the next one.

In the last carton he found a novel: *Rebecca and the Jewess* by Mrs. Madeline Leslie. The copyright date was 1879. He turned the brittle pages.

"A friend of Mother's gave that to me when I was nine years old. I'd forgotten all about it."

He nodded thoughtfully and put the book down.

She reached into the carton and pulled out a slender leather-bound book. "My God. My yearbook from junior high. Mother must have saved it," she said, looking through the book.

Scanlon reached into the last carton and scoured through the debris of a life. To his disappointment, he found nothing significant.

"My brother used his basement as his office. His secretary is there now. I'll telephone her to tell her to expect you."

She walked with him out into the entrance foyer, where he rang for the elevator and turned to face her. "Why did you change your mind about permitting me to look through her papers?"

She looked away from him. "Because you're all I've got. And, God knows why—I trust you."

1853 hours. Scanlon arrived back at the Nine-three Squad. He had wasted five hours sifting through Stanley Zimmerman's personal and medical records. It had been a hot, muggy day and the city's grime clung to his skin.

Scanlon unlatched the squad-room gate and went into his office. He threw himself into his chair, pulled up his trouser leg, removed the prosthesis, and stood it in the wastebasket. He yanked off the smelly stump sock and threw it into the bottom drawer of his desk. He took out the talc, sprinkled it over the stump, and sighed, relishing the soothing effect of the white powder and his massaging hands.

One by one the detectives filtered in and hovered around, watching the Whip tend to his stump. Lew Brodie was the first to speak. He told the Whip that Eddie Hamill had been processed and was lodged in Central Booking for the night. The prisoner was scheduled for arraignment in the morning in Part 1A of Manhattan Criminal Court. The PC had telephoned to say that he wanted Scanlon to attend the arraignment.

Christopher stopped eating his yogurt to tell Scanlon that after he and Biafra Baby had finished in the Seventh they drove to Brooklyn and continued their surveillance of Harold Hunt, the accountant. They tailed Hunt from his office to the Santorini Diner. The accountant had a hamburger and a cup of tea and left. Valerie Clarkson waited on him. The detectives followed him from the diner to a factory on Dumont Avenue. They discovered that it was one of those urban slave plantations that employ Haitian and Hispanic illegals for below the minimum wage.

Christopher paused, watching the Whip kneading his stump, checking the edema. "Are you ready for this one, Lieutenant?" Christopher asked.

"I'm ready," Scanlon said, pulling on a clean stump sock.

"The name of the company was the Luv-Joy Manufacturing Company. Harold Hunt, Donna Hunt's husband, is the accountant for the company that made all those things that you found in Gallagher's splash pad."

Scanlon looked up at Christopher. "Harold Hunt?"

"You got it," Biafra Baby said. "I took off my coat and tie and moseyed into the factory and applied for a job. As I was filling out the application I looked into the adjoining room and saw Harold poring over ledgers."

"Do you think he made you?" Scanlon asked.

"Naw. He has no idea that we've been on him," Biafra Baby said.

"What about Valerie Clarkson—did she see you in the restaurant?" Scanlon asked.

"We didn't go inside," Christopher said. "Biafra Baby waited in the car and I sat in the diner's vestibule watching Harold eat."

"Did Harold and Valerie Clarkson seem to know each other? Were they friendly?"

"Not really," Christopher said. "They seemed to have a casual acquaintance, nothing more than that."

"Find out who owns that company," Scanlon said to Christopher and Biafra Baby.

Higgins said, "Lieutenant Fable telephoned a couple of times. Nothing important, just touching base with you. He said to tell you that he sent you some stuff in the department mail."

Scanlon rummaged through the pile of reports cluttering his desk. He found two multi-use envelopes from the Nineteenth. There was also an envelope from the department artist addressed to CO 93 Sqd. *Personal.*

He pulled the three envelopes from the pile.

"*Teniente,* did you get a chance to read the latest department bulletin?"

"Not yet," Scanlon said, leaning back and affixing his prosthesis.

"Listen to this shit," Colon said, reading. "'The Gay Officers Action League will hold its annual Stonewall memorial service and breakfast on June 29, 1986, at 0830 hours. Upon completion of the breakfast, members of GOAL will assemble at GOAL Hall in preparation for the Christopher Street Liberation Day March and Rally of 1986. Uniformed and civilian members of the service

who are members of GOAL and wish to participate in these functions . . .'" He looked up from the bulletin, troubled. "You know
the rest, they throw in a Twenty-eight and take the tour off. You
know, *Teniente*, when I came in the Job the precinct whore was
always a female and a civilian. And now?" He wafted the green
bulletin down onto the desk. "This job has really gone down the
tubes."

Higgins glared at Colon, the rebuke on her lips. Instead, she
shook her head with disgust and walked from the office without
saying anything.

Scanlon checked the time: 1910 hours. "Go home," he told the
detectives. "I'll see you on deck in the ayem."

"Sure you ain't going to need us?" Colon asked.

"I'm sure," Scanlon said, scanning a Five, signing it.

"Anyone wanna stop for a taste?" Lew Brodie asked.

"Sounds good to me," Biafra Baby said. "I'm in no rush to get
home. My wife took the kids to the Monet exhibit."

Hector Colon stopped at the water cooler for a drink. He gulped
the water. From the corner of his eye he saw a cockroach flow into
his mouth. He dropped the cup and gagged. He clutched his throat,
retching.

Higgins rushed over to him. "Hector, what's the matter?"

His handsome Latin face was pale gray. "I swallowed a cocka-
roach," he gasped.

"Is that all?" Higgins said, walking away. "There is absolutely
nothing to worry about, Hector. Roaches are extremely clean crea-
tures."

Clutching his throat in horror, Colon gasped. "You sure?"

"Of course I'm sure." She turned and hurled a concerned look
at him.

"What? Tell me!" Colon said.

"Well, it's nothing. But I just realized that the roach that you
ingested might be a female cockroach, a pregnant female cockroach." She let her words hang.

Shrinking away from her, Colon asked feebly, "So?"

Higgins grimaced. "Well, cockroaches lay seven, eight hundred
eggs at a time. And your stomach is a dark, wet, warm place. It
would be a perfect nesting place for baby roaches. It is conceivable
that you could end up with thousands of cockroaches nesting in

your stomach lining, a whole darn colony of them. I mean, you could actually have dozens of them crawling in and out of your penis."

"Aaaaaaaahhhhhhhh!" Colon ran screaming from the squad room.

"I guess he's rushing to the Stonewall Parade," Higgins said, taking a lipstick from her pocketbook. Scanlon sat at his desk, listening, suppressing a grin. Higgins strolled deadpan into the office. "I guess Hector doesn't like roaches."

"Guess not," Scanlon said, unable to keep from smiling. "You heading home?"

"I want to work on my term paper," she answered. "I'll hang around here and do it. Somehow I work better in the squad room."

The first envelope Scanlon opened contained the composite sketch of a man with a walrus mustache and an accompanying Five of the interview of the witness who had seen the mustached man enter and leave the Kingsley Arms apartment building.

He read the Five. He leaned the composite up against the gray department desk lamp, scrutinizing the face. There was something about that face that was familiar. He tried to imagine the face without the mustache. But who was it? Scanlon opened the Gallagher/Zimmerman case folder. He searched through the folder for the composite of the perp the two female witnesses had seen. An old man running from a candy store. He found it near the bottom of the pile. He leaned it against the lamp with the other composite. The pigeon feeder's face was old, while the composite of the mustached man depicted a young man, a man in his late thirties or early forties.

The envelope from the department artist contained the composite of the driver of the getaway van that he had talked Walter Ticornelli into working on with the artist. The sketch showed the side view of a young face with sunglasses and a hat pulled down over the brow. Scanlon recalled that the shylock had only caught the driver's profile.

With the three composites arrayed in front of him, he compared one to the other. He reached out and picked up the sketch of the pigeon feeder. The more he studied the remaining two, the more convinced he was that the man with the walrus mustache and the man in the sunglasses were the same man. He leaned back and rubbed his tired eyes. The phone rang. He snapped it up.

"Lieutenant Scanlon."

"Lou, this is Sergeant Vitali. You know me from the Columbians."

"How are you, Vic?" Vic Vitali had run for recording secretary of the Italian-American police organization two years ago and lost by twelve votes.

"Lou, I just responded to a call from the emergency room of St. John's. They're holding one of your detectives under restraints. He's ranting about colonies of cockroaches nesting in his stomach and crawling in and out of his cock. We had to take his gun for safekeeping."

A broad grin spread across Scanlon's face. I wonder where he got that idea? he thought, looking out into the squad room at Higgins talking on the telephone.

"What do you want me to do about this guy?" Vitali asked.

"It's fate getting back at him for being a wise-ass with one of his partners. He had a practical joke played on him. Where is he now?"

"Strapped onto a trolley outside the examining room."

"Keep him there for a while. I'm sending one of my detectives over to get him. Her name is Higgins."

"I'll take care of it, Lou. See ya at the next meeting."

Scanlon went out into the squad room and told Higgins what had happened to Colon and asked her if she would go to the hospital and get him released.

"It would be a pleasure, Lieutenant," she said, taking her pocketbook and getting up.

Scanlon went back into his office and opened the remaining multi-use envelope. It contained the copies of the forensics reports on the Stanley and Rachel Zimmerman homicides. Included with the reports were photographs of the striations on the roof door of the Kingsley Arms. Each individual characteristic was noted and numbered. There were also photographs of rusty screws that showed fresh screwdriver marks on the heads, and photographic enlargements of screws with small pieces of wood wedged between their threads. The perp lost his patience and tore off the hasp with a crowbar, he thought, examining the photographs. The last batch of photographs in the envelope were of the plaster casts made of the footprints found on the roof of the Kingsley Arms.

Etched sharply into the tarred roof were the deep impressions of a heel. Black lines and numbers noted each characteristic: nail marks, chips in the rubber, wear striations, an imbedded pebble. It was a narrow heel. Scanlon looked down at his own heel. His was much wider. The photographs of the toe showed a triangular impression with a narrow convex tip.

Scanlon read the accompanying Five. The perp's walking picture put him at five-eleven and approximately 185 pounds. The Five detailed each characteristic that made up the walking picture. He had read down to the last paragraph of the report when a phrase leaped up at him: "The sum of these configurations leads the undersigned to conclude that the perpetrator in this case wore cowboy boots."

Scanlon's eyes darted to the array of composite sketches, back to the phrase on the bottom of the Five, back to the composites. He heaved himself up out of the chair and rushed from the squad room.

A string of firecrackers exploded as Scanlon drove into the One-fourteen's walled-in parking area. It was 2110. He rushed up the echoing iron staircase and entered the offices of the Seventeenth Narcotics District. Undercovers and their backups were going over the strategy for the night's buys. Everything seemed to be back to normal at the Seventeenth District. Scanlon moved to a bearded round-faced man who was logging a telephone message. "Is Inspector Schmidt around?"

The bearded man lined off the message and looked up. "He's gone for the day. I'm Sergeant Quigley. Can I help you?"

Scanlon identified himself to the sergeant. "There are a few matters concerning Joe Gallagher that need tidying up. I'd like to take a look at your personnel files."

Quigley looked down at the message he had just logged. "Gallagher's replacement has just been assigned. Frank Devine from the Eleventh District. Know him?"

"I know Frank from around the Job. What about those records?"

Quigley showed Scanlon into the Whip's office. "Yell if you need anything," the sergeant said, backing out the door.

The files were alphabetical, by rank. Scanlon fingered the tabs to the sergeants' section of the file. His fingertips danced over the folders until he came to Harris, George.

Sitting with the folder on his lap, Scanlon stared at the pin maps on the wall, silently admonishing himself. Harris wasn't the only man in this town who wore cowboy boots. So what if there was a resemblance between Harris and two of the composites? That didn't mean that Harris was the perp. Still, Harris was the only person connected with the case who did wear that damn kind of footwear. But Harris involved in Gallagher's death? That couldn't be. He opened the folder.

Harris had submitted two Chief Clerk 30s, Change of Residence or Social Condition. One had notified the department of a change of residence: Long Island to Staten Island. The other form informed the Job of a change in social status: married to separated.

Both forms were dated February 5, 1984.

Scanlon read through years of evaluation reports that attested to Harris's above-average performance. He read letters of commendation from satisfied citizens, and he read requests for departmental recognition that certified to Harris's exemplary performance of duty, his bravery. He came across an old Ten Card, and noted that Harris was forty-two years old.

The off-duty employment requests were pinned together, in chronological order. Permission had been given for Harris to engage in off-duty employment at the Stevens Manufacturing Company. In the space on the form captioned "Describe specific duties and responsibilities," Harris had written, "Administrative." The first request was dated March 10, 1980. It was pinned to four annual renewal applications, each one dated ten days prior to the expiration of the current approved request, as required by Section 120-14 of the *Patrol Guide*.

Scanlon pinned the off-duty employment applications back together and flicked past them through the remainder of the file. Finding nothing else of interest, he began to shape the uneven edges back into a neat pile. Something nudged his memory. He shuffled back through the stack of forms to the off-duty requests. The Stevens Manufacturing Company and the Luv-Joy Manufacturing Company were both on Dumont Avenue, Brooklyn.

All the shadows had triangular shapes.

Scanlon lay in Sally De Nesto's bed staring up at them, vaguely aware of her efforts to make him erect, his thoughts filled with Harris and those damn cowboy boots. He raced mentally over the recent police scandals, and wondered if they presaged a new breed of cop, a breed unable to distinguish between the good guys and the bad guys, a breed that considered themselves a law unto themselves, a breed willing to go to any length to see that their concept of justice prevailed. What if his growing suspicion was correct? What if Harris was the perp? What would that scandal do to the Job? But it couldn't be. Why would Harris be involved in Gallagher's death? For what motive? And what about the doctor and his wife? There was no connection between Gallagher and Harris. It was all wrong.

"I'm tired," Sally De Nesto said, resting her face on his groin.

He pressed her head to his body. "I've got things on my mind."

She crawled up the bed and lay next to him, staring up at the ceiling. "You're not upset, are you?"

"There's a lot on my mind. I'm just not in the mood."

"Would you be upset if I were Jane Stomer?"

He found himself openly measuring her. "Of course I'd be upset," he said tersely.

"Then I think that you should ask yourself why."

"Because I can relax with you and not have to worry about satisfying you."

"That should tell you something about your problem."

"It tells me that I can't relax with a straight woman, especially if I care for her."

She turned on her side, facing him. "But why?"

"Because I'm afraid of failure," he blurted.

A satisfied smile spread across her face.

He pulled her to him. "What am I, your psychological profile of the month?"

She shook her head. "I've discussed your problem with my shrink friend."

"What shrink?"

"My blind psychiatrist trick. I've mentioned him to you."

"Yeah, I remember."

"He said that your problem was more than likely the result of a premorbid disposition caused by some childhood relationship. A fear of being unable to satisfy someone you loved."

In a brief flash of recall he saw his drunken Irish father standing in the shadows, laughing at him. "If you keep up with the psychoanalysis I just might not need you anymore."

"I know," she said, flopping off her side onto her back and turning her face from him.

"I'm really drained. May I stay the night?"

"You can, but it will cost you extra."

"What the hell is it with you? One minute you're soft and caring, and the next you're all business."

"I *am* in business, Tony. And I can't let myself forget that I am." She reached out and turned off the soft light on her night table.

Staring into the darkness, Scanlon thought about his parents and Jane Stomer, unaware of Sally De Nesto's silent tears.

16

The pews in the Manhattan Criminal Court complaint room were filled with dozing policemen waiting to be interviewed by an ADA. Coffee containers and blackened cigarette butts littered the floor. Scattered sheets of newspaper added to the mess. Morning rays fought a losing battle to penetrate the filthy windows.

Five court clerks were assigned to the complaint room to assist arresting officers in drawing up the complaints against prisoners, listing the specific crimes charged, detailing the elements of each crime, spelling out a *prima facie* case against each prisoner. The law required that a legally sufficient case be established at the prisoner's arraignment; bail would then be set.

It was 1015 hours and one of the clerks still had not arrived for work. The four who had showed up were sitting behind a long counter that was covered with legal forms and about a dozen manual typewriters. One of the clerks was discussing his margin account over the telephone, one was reading yesterday's *New York Post* and sucking jelly from a sugared doughnut, and the two remaining clerks were typing affidavits by the court's renowned hunt-and-peck method.

A line of waiting policemen stretched out into the hallway.

Scanlon and Brodie entered the courthouse and went directly into the police sign-in room. After they signed in, they went to the complaint room. When the Whip saw the line he told Brodie to draw up the complaint against Hamill. He was going down to the lobby and make some telephone calls, and he would meet Brodie in the courtroom. Scanlon was anxious to put the Hamill caper behind them.

Scanlon crossed the cavernous lobby, taking in the ornate construction, rich in marble. It had been some time since he had been in Manhattan Criminal Court. Jane had been an important part of his life then; now she was nothing but an aching memory. He saw many familiar faces, lawyers holding morning court, doing what they do best, fleecing the unwary, the uninitiated. He spotted Sammy Gold, the court's resident bookmaker, taking down the day's action. His footsteps echoed off the marble floor. Nothing much ever changes around here, he thought, stopping at the building's newsstand to take in the morning headlines.

The NYPD had finally made if off the front page. The PC had been right—there was nothing like an arrest to end public interest in a case. He wondered if Buckman, the Cocksucker with Lockjaw, had anything to do with the sudden loss of interest.

He went over to the telephone bank and slid into a booth. He telephoned the Squad, and when Detective Suckieluski answered, he told Biafra Baby that he wanted him and Christopher to find out if the Luv-Joy Manufacturing Company on Dumont Avenue had once been named the Stevens Manufacturing Company. And if the owners of both companies were the same people.

When Scanlon left the phone booth he spotted Higgins and Colon in the lobby. He called to them. Approaching the two, he noticed a shamefaced Hector Colon looking up at the rococo molding.

"How you feeling today, Hector?" Scanlon asked.

"I don't know what to say, Lou. I mean, thanks for what you did for me. I mean, I guess them fucking cockaroaches just got to me. Where's Brodie?" he asked, obviously anxious to change the subject and get away from Higgins.

"He's in the complaint room," Scanlon said. "Why don't you go and help him draw up the complaint."

"Right, Lou," Colon said, and hurried off.

248

"What happened last night at the hospital?" Scanlon asked Higgins.

She gave vent to a partly suppressed laugh. "Macho man was tied to a hospital gurney. He'd calmed down, but he'd had the starch taken out of his sails."

Scanlon and Higgins pushed through the padded doors into the courtroom. He gazed at the burnished wood paneling. They never scrimp, he thought, sliding into a rear bench. Higgins slid in next to him.

Policemen lounged around the courtroom, waiting for court to be called into session. A lone court clerk sat in front of the bench arranging the day's arraignment calendar. Lawyers ambled into the courtroom. Some went up to the court clerk; a whispered conversation would ensue, after which a fast handshake would take place, after which the court clerk would move an affidavit from the bottom of the pile to the top of the pile.

The criminal justice system in action, Scanlon thought, slapping another fold into his newspaper. Time passed. Scanlon worked the crossword. Higgins read a Harlequin Romance. A man in a seersucker suit and conservative tie carrying a stack of folders under his arm entered the courtroom and called out Scanlon's name.

"Over here, Counselor," Scanlon said.

"I'm ADA Rabinowitz," he said, sliding into the pew next to Higgins. "I've been assigned the Hamill arraignment." He opened one of the folders on his lap and read off the details of the arrest. "Is there anything else I should be aware of?"

Scanlon looked at Higgins. They both concentrated on the ADA's question, and shrugged. "You got it all, Counselor," Scanlon said.

"As I read this case, Hamill is not a suspect in the Gallagher/ Zimmerman homicides," said ADA Rabinowitz.

"Not at this time," Scanlon said. "The investigation is continuing."

"What the hell does that mean, Lieutenant?" the ADA said.

"That means, Counselor," Scanlon said, "that the investigation is continuing."

"You brought me a red herring, didn't you?" Rabinowitz said.

"We're just doing our job, sir," Higgins said.

"I'll go see if I can rush this thing along," the ADA said. "I want to get rid of this case as fast as I can."

At 1120 hours, Scanlon, the ADA, Eddie Hamill, and a Legal Aid lawyer all stood before the bench listening to the court clerk read the complaint.

The prisoner's head was bowed.

The clerk intoned, ". . . all the physical evidence in the case be admitted into evidence under the Clear View Doctrine."

Hamill's head shot up. He looked at Scanlon with a stunned expression.

Scanlon shrugged innocently and whispered, "So I lied a little."

The judge set bail at two hundred thousand dollars. The sullen prisoner was led away by two court officers.

The detectives walked out of the courtroom. Colon and Higgins were waiting. Scanlon noticed Colon sneaking glances at him. Higgins was smiling.

"Hello, Scanlon."

He heard her voice and froze, excitement ripping at his chest. "I'll catch up with you guys later," he told the detectives, watching them cross the lobby.

Jane Stomer was standing to the right of the courtroom's padded doors. She was wearing a paisley skirt and a matching paisley blouse and white shoes. She had a deep tan and her lips sparkled. She wore no hose and her legs were smooth; he recalled how she used to open her legs to him, and he felt the beating of his own heart.

"Hello, Jane," he said feebly.

A wistful smile was on her lips. "You look fit, Scanlon."

"So do you."

"I heard all about your big arrest," she said. "The word is that it's a throw-out."

"How have you been?"

She looked at him strangely, as though checking to see if he was the same man. "I've been good. How is your mother?"

"Very good, thanks. And your parents?"

"The same."

"I've missed you a lot."

"Obviously not enough to call."

He looked down at the floor. "I've still got that problem."

"That *problem* could have been worked out. And I suppose you still haven't sought professional help."

He sighed. "Not yet."

A forlorn look came over her face. "It was good to see you again, Scanlon." She nodded at him and walked away.

A terrible sense of loss possessed him as he watched her thread her way through the swelling crowd. Suddenly he heard his voice calling out her name, and he saw her stop. He rushed through the crowd, shouldering people from his path. He grabbed her by the wrist and led her away, searching for some place where they might be alone. Finding no privacy, he led her out of the building by the Baxter Street exit.

"I have to be in court in five minutes," she protested, tugging her wrist free.

"One minute, please."

The compact street was clogged with double-parked police cars. Department of Correction vans were queued up outside the massive steel doors of the court's detention facility, waiting their turn to discharge their cargo. Scanlon looked up and down the street. Gripping her by the hand, he pulled her along, angling around cars and between bumpers, and led her to a bench inside small Baxter Street Park.

Camera-laden Japanese tourists were milling around the park taking photographs of Chinatown.

"Well?" she demanded, sitting next to him.

Unrehearsed words spilled from his lips. Knowing that he was fighting the clock, he talked fast and convincingly.

Her stern countenance and her unrelenting stare did not deter him; he plodded on. He told her that he realized how badly he had handled his dysfunction. He told her that he had been unable to cope with losing his leg and his manhood at the same time. He told her of the nightmare that he had had in the hospital: naked, she would go to straddle his legs, see that one was missing, and back away, laughing. He told her how much he had missed her in his life, how empty his life had been without her. "I know that I made a mess of things," he said, taking her hand in his.

"Yes, you certainly did." She pulled her hand free and checked the time. "What is the purpose of this exercise, Scanlon?"

"I'm in love with you, Jane, and I want you back in my life."

She sighed. Her voice softened. "I can't, Tony. There is another man in my life now." She got up. "Goodbye."

The Mohawk hairstyle accentuated her high cheekbones. Detective Alice Guerrero was a shapely woman in her middle thirties. She had clever catlike eyes and a narrow chin. She stood in front of Sigrid Thorsen with her forefinger held parallel to the witness's eyebrows. "Sigrid, I'd like you to keep your eyes on my finger and lower your lids, but be sure to keep your eyes fixed on my finger."

Detective Guerrero moved away when she was finished and sat alongside the desk in the soundproof interview room of the Scientific Research Unit on the eleventh floor of the big building.

"What was that for?" Sigrid Thorsen asked, brushing a tendril of blond hair from her shoulder.

"That was a test that helps me to determine if you are a good subject for hypnosis."

"And am I?"

"Yes."

"How can you tell?"

"You were able to keep your eyes fixed on my finger while you lowered your lids. A bad subject is not able to keep his eyes up." She crossed her legs and leaned forward, facing the witness. "Sigrid, we use the relaxation technique of hypnosis. I'm going to relax you, and help you bring down your conscious and bring up your subconscious. Then I am going to take you back in time to that Thursday afternoon in McGoldrick Park. But before we start, I want you to tell me everything you can remember about what you saw in the park that afternoon."

Sigrid Thorsen told her tale to the department hypnotist. When the witness finished her story, the detective said, "I want you to know that when you are under hypnosis you will not say or do anything that you do not want to. We all have skeletons that we want to remain in the proverbial closet. So if I ask you a question you do not want to answer, just say so. Okay?"

"Fine."

"Do you have any questions before we start?"

The witness turned in her seat and motioned to the large mirror that was set into the wall. "Is that a two-way mirror?"

"Yes, it is."

"Are there people watching us?"

"Yes. Lieutenant Scanlon and detectives Higgins and Colon are in the adjoining room, watching. They can also hear everything we say. Do you have any problems with that?"

Sigrid Thorsen smiled into the mirror. "No, I have no problem with that."

"Shall we begin?" the hypnotist said, sweeping her hand toward the recliner that was set up in front of the mirror.

The witness took a deep breath, looked into the mirror, and got up. She lowered herself onto the recliner, paused, then swung her long legs around and stretched her body out over the chair.

"Comfortable?" the detective asked.

"Very."

"I want you to close your eyes and relax." Her soothing voice went lower, taking on a soft, hypnotic resonance. "Relax your body. Feel how comfortable it feels. Feel the relaxation spread, relaxing your mind and your body. Feel it as it travels down your forehead, into your cheeks, into your lips, and your mouth. I want you to find a comfortable place in your mouth for your tongue. Feel your tongue as it relaxes. Feel your neck relax, feel the relaxation spreading down into your body, into your chest, feel it as it moves down your arms, down into your fingers. Feel your stomach area, feel all the organs of your body as they relax, let them go, relax, relax..."

On the other side of the mirror, Colon nudged Scanlon. "She's making my balls numb."

"That's because she's putting all your cockroaches to sleep," Higgins said.

Colon gave her a dirty look, mumbled, "Dyke," and looked back at the witness.

"Feel the concentration coming up into your head. Feel the relaxation as it travels down. Let it roll through your mind, your body. I want you to imagine a clock. See the hands moving backward in time, bringing you back in time, back to that Thursday afternoon in McGoldrick Park. See yourself in the park. Tell me what you are doing."

"I'm playing with Jennifer. Beautiful little baby. Mommy loves you, yes, she does. Look at those chubby cheeks. Yes, they're so pretty."

"An old man sits down on the next bench," the detective said. "Tell me about this man. Focus in on him and tell me everything that you can about him."

"He's wearing baggy black pants that have paint stains on the legs. He has on a dirty white pullover and some kind of an army jacket. He must be warm in all those clothes. His hair is gray and shaggy. His face is wrinkled. I smile at him. He glares back at me. The hell with him. He has a shopping bag on his lap. It's filled with rags and old newspapers. He reaches inside and pulls out a bag of peanuts. He's wearing a lady's wristwatch with a gold link bracelet. He's tossing peanuts onto the ground. A doddering pigeon snaps one up. Other pigeons are coming."

Detective Guerrero looked hard into the mirror. "What else can you tell me about *him?*"

"Her legs are together, ladylike, not spread apart as a man would sit. She has an old face, but her eyes are young, alive. They keep darting around the park as though searching for someone."

Scanlon's color deepened with anger. He punched the sound-proof wall. "A woman!"

"It's sure beginning to look that way," Higgins said. "Remember the peanut shells with the hand cream?"

"What else can you tell me about this woman?"

"She just got up from the bench. She is walking away. Where is Tom? He sure is taking his time parking the car. Jennifer! You're drooling on Mommy."

17

I t was late afternoon when Scanlon returned from the Scientific
Research Section. He immediately set about reading the Fives
on each of the women connected to the case. If the pigeon
feeder had in fact been a woman, then there was a good chance
she was one of these witnesses.

The walking picture of the perp who took out Dr. Zimmerman
and his wife showed that their killer was about five-eleven and
weighed around 185 pounds. None of the women involved in the
case was that tall or weighed that much. There must have been
two killers, Scanlon reasoned. And in that case, how could the
cases be connected? It was beginning to look as though there were
no link between the two double homicides.

Scanlon set aside the interview reports of the two women who
had been on their way to the A&P supermarket when the perp
fled the candy store and ran to the van. He was sure that they
were in no way involved in the murder.

Donna Hunt's report was next. It bothered Scanlon that Donna
Hunt had not asked him to return the nude photograph of herself
that Gallagher had taken. Could this demure Queens housewife
be involved in murder? He glanced over the notes that he had

stapled to the Five: "Witness nervous, cried, went to john with Maggie. Colon gave her glass of water."

The next report was of his interview with Mary Ann Gallagher, the dead lieutenant's widow. He read it, pondered its contents, decided that the widow was a dead end, and pushed the report aside along with the statements of the two shoppers.

He had begun reading the next interview report when Lew Brodie ambled in and announced, "It just came over the radio, someone planted a bomb in the PBA's office."

"Anyone hurt?" Scanlon asked, concerned.

"Not so far. The reports are still coming in."

"Fun City," Scanlon said, and went back to reading.

Rena Bedford, the college girl who drove a Porsche and was experimenting with life, and who had come to the Squad with her shyster uncle, was next. He recalled staring into her virginal face and listening to her boldly describe her sexual encounters. He wondered if such a woman would have the nerve to do murder.

Mary Posner, the knock-around lady who had married Sy Posner, the factor, and who had refused to participate in any of Gallagher's parlor games, came next. Sy Posner had been her last shot, she had told Scanlon. What if Gallagher had tried to extort money from her? Greenbacks in return for the nude photograph of herself. Gallagher needed money to pay off Walter Ticornelli. Twenty-one hundred and fifty dollars. And that exact amount had been discovered hidden in the wheel well of Gallagher's car. Had Gallagher become a threat to her?

The Zimmermans. He always returned to them. Although it did appear that two separate killers were involved, he always came back to the Zimmermans. He knew down deep that there *was* a connection. It was there someplace. He knew it, he just knew it. He thought about Linda Zimmerman, the banker who had had her life shattered by the murder of her family. The banker who managed investment portfolios for some of the wealthiest people in the country. Maybe she was involved in some hanky-panky at the bank. Needed money bad enough to kill her family. She had the presence of mind to go and clean out her mother's apartment the day after the woman was murdered. She had wanted to get something from the apartment, she had told Scanlon, something personal. If Scanlon's mother was murdered he wouldn't think of getting property, he'd only think of getting even. He realized that he had never checked out the investment bank where Linda Zimmerman worked. Indecorous or not, he was going to have to check out the bank. Then he caught himself thinking about what he would do if his mother had been murdered, and realized that he hadn't spoken to her in days. He picked up the telephone and called her. When she answered he spoke in Italian and told her that he loved her. Would he come to dinner this Sunday? "I'll try, Mom."

Valerie Clarkson, the waitress who worked in the Santorini Diner, and who had chestnut hair, and who wore pearls, was the next interview report he read. Had he overlooked some connection between her and Gallagher?

Luise Bardwell's Five was the last. Luise Bardwell, Sgt. George Harris's girlfriend. Luise Bardwell, the married bisexual who had been the third participant with Gallagher and Donna Hunt and Gallagher and Valerie Clarkson and Gallagher and Rena Bedford. Luise Bardwell, who bragged to Scanlon that she had brought Valerie Clarkson out of the closet. Why couldn't this have been a simple mob hit where the facts are known, but unproven, and nobody, but nobody, gives a shit? Detectives don't like real mysteries, they give you gas.

He pushed the Fives aside and reached for the pad that was at the top of the heap in the out basket. He wrote "Sgt. George Harris" in the left margin and underneath wrote: "Face similar to composite sketch of driver of van and similar to composite of mustached man seen running from Kingsley Arms. Mustache = makeup. Pigeon feeder a woman = makeup. Impression cowboy boots found on roof. Harris/cowboy boots."

To the right of Harris's name he wrote: "Physical evidence— Sweet Sixteen shotgun, tools used to force roof door, rifle used to kill Zimmermans. Makeup, where purchased?"

He listed the female witnesses on the right side of the page. He boldly underlined Luise Bardwell's name. She was the woman who was connected to more of the people involved in the case than anyone else.

Luise Bardwell offered him a drink, and when he declined, she lowered herself down next to him on the thick, soft cushions of the sofa. She was wearing a loose wine-colored top and tight white slacks. She smiled. "It's nice to see you again, Lieutenant."

"Nice to see you too," he said, watching her arm slide over the back of the sofa.

She leaned in close to him. "I could never refuse to talk to a handsome man."

"That's good to know."

"What are the few questions that you wanted to ask me?"

"How did you first meet George Harris?"

"Two years ago, during the summer. I was driving downtown to go shopping. I stopped for a red light. My car's air conditioner was on the fritz, so I had the window open. Some boys ran up to my car and snatched my pocketbook off the front seat. I dialed nine-one-one. A police car came and escorted me into the station house so the detectives could interview me. And that's how I met George."

"Did he come on to you?"

"No, actually he was very professional. But he was interested, I could tell."

"How could you tell?"

"By the way he kept looking at me and by the questions he asked. He wanted to know if I was married and what my husband did for a living. I mean, it was only a purse snatch and George was making it into a major crime spree."

It was SOP for uniform officers to bring attractive female complainants into the detective squad to be interviewed.

"When did he make a move on you?"

"He telephoned me the next day."

"And you went out with him?"

"I found his arrogance exciting. I thought he might be a man worth getting to know."

"And was he?"

She leaned forward and winked at him. "No," she whispered. "Your sergeant was a passive lover."

"George must have been transferred into narcotics shortly after he met you," he said, remembering Herman the German telling him that Harris had been transferred into the junk squad two years ago.

"Yes, that's right. And George was really annoyed by the transfer.

It seems that Joe Gallagher had him transferred without consulting him."

"How did you know that?"

"I was with George one night shortly after his transfer. He bitched most of the night about how he was sick and tired of baby-sitting for Gallagher and having to pull his fat out of the fire while Gallagher spent all his time playing the police department's fair-haired boy."

"What else did he tell you about his relationship with Gallagher?"

"Nothing much, except that he would get very upset every time Gallagher countermanded one of his orders."

"Tell me again how you became involved in Gallagher's parlor games."

She rubbed her breasts against his arm. "Are you sure you wouldn't like to take a break?"

"Later," he said, moving back.

She made an annoyed *tut* sound with her tongue. "I'd become bored with George and thought that it might be exciting if George and one of my lady friends got together. When I suggested it to George he said that he didn't go in for that sort of thing, and he suggested Gallagher."

"And who provided the women?"

"Joe Gallagher."

"I thought you said that you wanted to use your lady friends."

"Originally I did. But when Gallagher said he'd supply the women I saw an opportunity to broaden my horizons."

"Was Linda Zimmerman ever a friend of yours?"

"No, she wasn't," she snapped. "I never met the lady. This is beginning to sound like an interrogation."

"It is."

"Are you serious?" she asked, open-mouthed.

"Your name keeps popping up at every stage of the investigation."

"What investigation?" she demanded. "Gallagher and Yetta Zimmerman were killed in a holdup. You don't seriously think that I took part in a robbery?"

"When the doctor and his wife were murdered we were forced to take a closer look at Joe Gallagher's death. And do you know what we found?"

She scowled and slapped her hands onto her knees. "No, tell me."

"We found you." He held up his hand and ticked off fingers. "You knew Gallagher, Harris, Donna Hunt, Rena Bedford, Valerie Clarkson. Almost everyone connected to this case is known by you."

"You really think I could kill those people?" she said with genuine concern in her voice.

"I think it's possible that you conspired with someone else to have it done."

She got up and moved across the room to the glass wall of her Battery Park penthouse and gazed out at the river. He went and stood alongside her. Yellow fingers of light shimmered across the water.

"Why would I do such a thing?" she asked, her eyes following the wake of a sightseeing boat.

"Love? Jealousy? Revenge? Greed? Take your pick."

"When was Gallagher killed?"

"June 19, 1986. A Thursday, about two-fifteen in the afternoon."

"I think that the time has come for me to put you out of your misery, Lieutenant. From June 8 to June 19, my husband and I were attending a convention in San Francisco. We stayed at the Palm Hotel. I paid the bill with my American Express Card, and I can give you the names and addresses of at least a dozen people who can attest to our being there. We flew home on the red-eye." She turned from the glass wall and left the room.

Scanlon remained staring at the distant shoreline. When she returned she went over to the sofa and sat down. He abandoned the view and sat next to her.

"Here are the names and phone numbers of people we were with in San Francisco," she said, handing him a slip of paper.

"Why didn't you mention this to me the last time?"

"Because the last time you didn't tell me that I was a suspect."

He picked up her wrist and admired her watch. It had a gold link bracelet. "Nice watch."

"Thank you. It's kind of exciting being a murder suspect," she said, leaning in close.

"Really?" he said, checking the time.

She kissed him, plunging her tongue into his mouth and sliding her hand up his leg.

He pushed her away. "I have to get back to the office."

"Don't I excite you?" she said softly, rubbing his groin.

"I couldn't relax. Your husband might come home."

"Then we could have a threesome," she said, starting to work down his zipper.

He lifted her hand away from him.

"Would you like me to suck you?" she said, brushing her lips over his.

"I'd love it," he said, "but I just couldn't relax. Another time."

"Would you like to go down on me?"

"I'm on duty. I can't."

She pushed back. "You're what?"

"On duty. It's a violation of the *Patrol Guide* to do that while you're working."

"Cops! They're all duds."

The door was ajar. Scanlon pushed it open with his foot and stepped inside. A thin coat of dust was collecting on the furniture. He sensed another presence, heard the steady beat of a slight sharp noise. He moved down the foyer to the patients' waiting room on his right.

Linda Zimmerman was slumped on a leather couch, clinking the top of her Zippo lighter open and shut, open and shut. She looked gaunt and tired. Her hair was unkempt, tangled, and there were black rings under her eyes. She was wearing a loose brown dress, the folds of which were draped between her legs. An antique lapel watch was pinned over her left breast. He saw the anguish in her eyes and went and knelt down beside her. "Are you all right?"

"I have a sense of devastation that I can't shake. My body is numb. Why did you want to meet me in my brother's office?"

"There are some questions. And I wanted to have another look through his records. I might have missed something the last time."

"Andrea opened her eyes yesterday and recognized me. The doctors say that's a good sign."

"I'm glad."

She looked at him. "Why are you wasting so much of your time prying into my family's past?"

He met her stare. "Why, Linda? Because it's my job."

A resigned smile came to her lips. "Do you want to check his records first?"

"That'll be fine. We can talk as I go through them." He pointed his finger at her lapel watch. "Do you always wear that? Don't you have a wristwatch?"

"I can't stand anything on my wrist," she said, and got up and led him into her brother's office. The record room door was open, the telephone console silent. She reached into the room and switched on the lights. Fluorescent fixtures fluttered to life.

"There are a lot of folders to go through," she said, motioning to the rotating file racks on both sides of the room.

"Did your brother have a safe in his office?"

She squeezed past him into the room. The plastered walls were painted pink. The center wall between the file racks had an oil painting of a ballerina with her foot on a stool tying on her ballet slipper. She took the painting off the wall and leaned it against the rack. A combination safe was built into the wall. She reached into the file tray and read off the numbers that were written on the wall behind a file of folders. She twirled the black-faced dial several times and pulled the door open. She reached into the safe, removed the contents, and passed them to Scanlon.

There were some business records, stock certificates in a company that Scanlon had never heard of, ten one-hundred-dollar bills, and a packet of love letters that had been written by Stanley Zimmerman's future wife, Rachel.

He looked through the material and passed it back to her. "Nothing of importance here," he said.

She took the contents from him and put them back into the safe, all but the letters. She read one letter. "Oh, Rachel," she said, putting the letter back into the envelope and clutching the packet to her chest.

Scanlon spent the better part of the next two hours going through the files. She stood in the doorway watching him, leaving once to call her aunt to inquire about Andrea. Scanlon finally turned off the light and left the record room. Was there anything he'd missed the last time he was here, he wondered, looking around the doctor's modern office.

"What happened to your brother's secretary?"

"I let her go. The practice is on the market. I have no need for a secretary."

He realized that he had not looked inside the closet the last time he was there. He opened the door and jumped back as a cluster of African spears fell out of the crowded space and came crashing out onto the floor.

She knelt down beside him and helped gather them up.

"Stanley did work in Africa for the UN. They were always giving him these things as presents."

A short time later she stood inside the bedroom and watched him search her brother's dresser. The blood-soaked bed had been removed; in its place was an unfaded square of carpet.

"Do you have any idea what you're looking for?" she said, leaning against the bedroom wall.

"Not really." When he finished his search he went and leaned against the wall next to her. "Do you know a woman named Luise Bardwell?"

"No, I don't believe I do."

"Donna Hunt?"

"No."

"Rena Bedford?"

"No."

"Valerie Clarkson?"

"No."

"Mary Posner?"

"No! Why are you asking me about these people?"

"They are people I interviewed in connection with the case, and I just wondered if you knew any of them."

"Well, I don't. Why all these questions?"

"Just fishing around for some answers." He pushed away from the wall. "What about George Harris? Do you know him?"

"No, I don't," she said, losing patience.

"Did your brother happen to own any rifles or shotguns?"

She waved him off. "No more questions. I have to get back to my niece."

Scanlon drove Linda Zimmerman back to her aunt's Sutton Place apartment and returned to the Squad.

He entered the squad room and went directly into his office, where he took out the Fives on Linda Zimmerman and sat studying them. Why did she rush to her mother's apartment to clean it out? he thought. What was there that she wanted so badly that she couldn't wait? He called Lew Brodie in. "I want you to sit on Linda Zimmerman." He wrote the aunt's address on a slip of paper and handed it to the detective. "You know what she looks like?"

"Yeah, I know," Brodie said. "You want her covered day and night?"

"We don't have the manpower for that. Sit on her till eighteen hundred each day."

"We got nothing on that broad, Lou," Brodie said, putting the slip of paper in his shirt pocket.

"I know that. Sit on her anyway."

"You're the boss."

Scanlon went out into the squad room and called to Higgins. "Grab your pocketbook, Maggie. We're going for a ride."

Donna Hunt was framed in the doorway of her Bayside, Queens, home, staring with wide-eyed dismay at the photograph Scanlon held up in front of her. It was the same one that Joe Gallagher had taken of her in his Jackson Heights splash pad. She was naked on a bed with her legs apart and a dildo in her hand.

Her frightened eyes swiveled to Higgins, who was standing at Scanlon's side, and then to the gray sedan that was parked at the curb. Without a word, she stepped back into her home and watched the policemen enter.

Donna Hunt lived in an attached brick bungalow that had dormered windows and a tiny lawn. She was dressed in jeans and a blue work shirt with the tails hanging out. A feather duster was clutched in her hand.

Higgins smiled at her as she slipped past. The witness managed a weak smile in return.

Scanlon looked around the house. Traditional furniture swathed in plastic, a gold rug, a room divider that contained a collection of Hummels.

"I didn't expect to see you again," the witness stammered. "Is there anything wrong?"

The diminutive woman's face was chalk-white and her lower lip was quivering. Scanlon felt sorry for her. She was a woman on the edge, in danger of losing everything. Yet she was also a murder suspect, and he had come to tighten the mental thumbscrews. He did not like that part of the job.

"Mrs. Hunt," he began, "something has come up that we think you might be able to help us with." He moved to the breakfront and looked over the collection of Hummel figurines.

"I collect them," Donna Hunt said, glancing at Higgins for understanding, perhaps salvation.

Scanlon carefully picked up one of the figurines: a rosy-cheeked girl dressed in the traditional dirndl, with a yellow kerchief around her blond hair. She was drawing water from a white brick well. Scanlon studied the figurine and then returned it to its place on the shelf. As he did, he took in the family photographs on top of the shoulder-high divider.

"What do you want?" the witness pleaded.

Scanlon looked at Higgins. She was dressed in a black cotton dress and a print oversize vest. She always dresses to the nines, he thought, no bib overalls for her. He looked at Donna Hunt. "Why didn't you ask me to return this photograph to you when you were in my office?"

An uneasy laugh. "I was afraid to." Her stare fixed on the photograph in his hands. "Please put that disgusting thing away. Please!"

He slid it into his breast pocket. "Would you like me to return it to you?"

"God, yes. If Harold ever found out, or my children..." She began to cry softly.

Tough cop, browbeating a frightened housewife who never as much as received a traffic summons. Sometimes the Job really sucks, he thought, saying, "You can have the photograph, but in return, I want something from you."

She grew wary. "What?"

"Your husband is the accountant for the Luv-Joy Manufacturing Company. I need to know who owns that company, and I don't want your husband to know that I know."

Donna Hunt clutched her chest. "My Harold isn't involved in any of this, is he?"

"No," Scanlon reassured her, "he's a bystander, nothing more."

Relieved, the witness said, "Harold never discusses his work with me. I have no way of knowing who owns that company. And if I asked Harold, he'd want to know how I even knew the name of the firm and I'd have to explain the sudden interest in his practice."

"Does your husband keep any business records at home?" Higgins asked.

"He has an office in the basement that he uses around tax time," Donna Hunt said, "but I don't know what he has there."

The office turned out to be a green file cabinet and a painted desk that were set between a damp cinder-block wall and a flight of squeaky wooden steps. A washer and dryer were next to the file cabinet, and on the floor was a plastic basket full of clothes. Donna Hunt sat on the cellar steps looking down as the two detectives searched through her husband's business records.

Scanlon had taken the file cabinet, Higgins the desk. They were professional scavengers, working methodically, going quickly through each record, ever mindful of the detective maxim: Do it fast and quiet and get the hell out. The tops of the desk and the file cabinet were soon both covered with old records: accordion folders stuffed with out-of-date balance sheets and old bank statements, outdated tax returns, and long-paid bills.

After a half hour, Scanlon complained, "Nothing here."

"Zilch here too," Higgins said.

Scanlon looked up at the cellar steps. Donna Hunt had green eyes and wore a Timex watch with a pink band. "Are there any more records?" he asked the witness.

Donna Hunt lifted her small shoulders. "Not that I know of. Everything that Harold keeps at home from his business is there. Look, please, it's almost six. Harold's going to be home any second."

The policemen took several minutes to tidy up. Leave it exactly the way you found it, another maxim born from cop lore. With the witness in the lead, they climbed the staircase into the house's spotless kitchen. The witness moved across the tiled floor and leaned against the dishwasher, looking apprehensively at Scanlon.

Higgins glanced at him, her brow knitted with curiosity.

Scanlon took in both their expressions, read their questioning eyes: Would he give back the photo as he'd said he would? The photograph was evidence in a homicide case, evidence he had intentionally failed to voucher, evidence that at some point might prove crucial to the case.

Looking into Donna Hunt's brimming eyes, he thought, She's no killer, and she's paid a high enough price for her romp in the hay with Joe Gallagher. He went to her and took hold of her hand. He slid the photograph out of his breast pocket and slapped it down into the palm of her hand. "Goodbye, Mrs. Hunt."

The band played "Moonlight Serenade."

Scanlon sat in a chair behind the brass railing watching the dancers glide around Roseland's dance floor. The disco program would be starting shortly. That was when he would slip out onto the floor and lose himself among the swirling people. He wanted to put some distance between himself and the case, to relax and be with civilians in a noisy place. He looked around at the women and wondered if he was destined to spend the rest of his life going with hookers. He began to run over in his mind all the things that Sally De Nesto and he had talked about concerning his dysfunction. How wonderful it would be to be a normal man again, to be close to Jane Stomer, to live his life out of the sexual underground.

The disco beat boomed. He got up and moved toward the dance floor. A woman in her late thirties who had uneven teeth was standing a few feet in front of him. She looked in his direction. He smiled at her. She looked away. He slipped past her and edged his way out onto the dance floor.

Jane Stomer stood naked before him, caressing her breasts. He was sitting on a strange bed, in a strange room, his manhood in full bloom. There was a soft smile on her face and a tinge in her cheeks. He went to lunge up at her, but she shot out a restraining palm. "Stay there, Scanlon. I'll come to you." It was so wonderful to hear her say his name again, to be with her, to see her body, to gaze with desire at her triangle of tightly knit ringlets. But wait. Where were they? When did they get back together? He couldn't remember them getting back together. All of a sudden they were in a bedroom together. Was he dreaming? No, that was not possible. Everything was too real. She came toward him, sliding her hands around his neck, straddling his legs, lowering herself onto him.

"Jane, I've missed you so. I love you. I love you."

"Yes, Scanlon. Yes. Now. I want it to happen together. Now."

He did not want the exquisite moment to end. He wanted to hold back, to relish the pleasure, but he could not. As his love burst forth he saw his father standing in the shadows laughing at him.

Scanlon sprang up in his bed. A dream? It had been so real. He would have sworn that it was happening. He felt the discomfort and yanked off the sheet. "Son of a bitch!" he shouted across the empty loft. He rolled off the bed, balled up the sheets, and angrily threw them out into his loft, and hopped on one leg into the shower.

18

S canlon paced the Nine-three squad room, his hands thrust deep into his pockets, aware of the brooding silence around him. He glanced up at the clock: 0346 hours. The new day was two hundred and twenty-six minutes old. The sounds of the night filtered in through open windows: firecrackers exploded, tires screeched off in the distance, and somewhere a woman screamed at someone. The night team was sacked out in the dormitory, catching forty winks. A telephone rang and a lazy arm reached out of a bunk and snatched up the extension. Muted words came from behind the dormitory's frosted-glass door. Scanlon lit a De Nobili as he paced the floor of his office. He had gone back to bed after his shower and tried to sleep. But he had not been able to. A wet dream at forty-three. It sounded like a song title. He was upset and disgusted with his private life, so he got dressed and retreated into the Job.

His brain felt leaden and dull. The list of people that Luise Bardwell had given him to prove her alibi had checked out. They had substantiated her presence in San Francisco with her husband when Gallagher had been killed. Donna Hunt was probably too small to be the pigeon feeder. He reminded himself to check out

Linda Zimmerman's place of employment. George Harris? Could he somehow be involved? Where was the damn motive? He paced. The De Nobili had gone out. It was cold and soggy and had a foul taste. He grabbed it from his mouth and plunged it into a nearby wastebasket. From the corner of his eye he caught sight of the announcement-crammed bulletin board. He stopped, took some tentative steps toward the board, his stare locked on the LBA flyer authorizing the solicitation of funds for the Joseph P. Gallagher Memorial Fund. I wonder, he thought. I just wonder.

At 0900 hours that same morning, Tony Scanlon hurried into the ornate lobby of 250 Broadway in lower Manhattan. Stepping off the elevator on the twenty-first floor, he immediately saw the bomb damage: the scorched walls, a boarded-up elevator bank, bent fire doors hanging from hinges. He walked down the wide corridor toward the uniformed guard on duty outside the offices of the Patrolmen's Benevolent Association of the City of New York, Inc.

"ID," said the thickset guard.

Scanlon produced his credentials. The guard compared the official photograph on the laminated card with the face of the man standing in front of him. Handing the leather shield case back, the guard said, "Sign into the Visitors Log, Lou."

The reception area was small and sparsely furnished with a few leatherette chairs and two drooping plants. A gum-chewing receptionist with oversize pink-tinged eyeglasses slid open one side of the alcove's glass partition and said in Brooklynese, "Can I be of some help to you, sir?"

"I'm Lieutenant Scanlon. Louie Pots and Pans is expecting me."

The receptionist typist buzzed open the door leading into the PBA's executive offices.

Patrolman Louie Mastri, the PBA trustee for Patrol Borough Brooklyn South, had been a tough street cop, and a vociferous defender of the Police Officer's Bill of Rights. But Louie Mastri's reputation in the Job had no relationship to his union activities or his arrest record. His reputation had been built upon his lifelong avocation, cooking. Wherever he had been assigned in the Job his reputation as a cook soon caught up with him, causing him to spend most of his patrol time in the basement of station houses cooking for the platoon.

Louie Mastri had been out of the Academy for about two years when an old salt of an Irish desk officer in the Six-two Precinct turned to the cop on the switchboard during a four-to-twelve tour and said, "Call that kid, what's his name, Louie Pots and Pans, in off post. I'm in the mood for that spaghetti he cooks." Henceforth, in the eternal lore of the Job, Louie Mastri would forever be known as Louie Pots and Pans.

"Lou, how the hell are you?" barked Louie Pots and Pans, from across his large corner office. The trustee was standing over three gas barbecue grills that had been set up in front of the window air conditioner. He was wearing a blue apron with the word "Chef" emblazoned across the front.

"I'm fine, Louie. How's the family?" Scanlon asked, taking in the police memorabilia scattered around the office.

"Everything is great. Louie Junior is a sophomore at Albany State, and Maria is a freshman at St. John's. And the little lady is as beautiful as ever."

"Time marches on," Scanlon said, moving over to the grills.

"I'm preparing the sauces for lunch. You gonna stay and eat with us. I'm making Scampi alla Romana."

"I'd love to, but I can't. I've got a lot of things on the agenda today." He moved across the room to the display of police hats on the windowsill and picked up one from London. He put the helmet on his head. "How do I look?"

Louie Pots and Pans glanced over his shoulder. "You look fuckin' adorable." He returned his attention to his sauces. "Can you imagine us wearing a hat like that on patrol in this city? The fucking mutts would use it for target practice."

"You're right," Scanlon agreed, taking off the hat and replacing it. He picked up another, examined the white embossed emblem on the front. "Where's this one from?" he asked, holding it up.

Louie Pots and Pans turned to look. "That's from the Tokyo PD." He adjusted the flame on the grills and went over to his desk and sat.

Scanlon returned the hat to the windowsill, walked up to a chair in front of the trustee's desk, and looked sternly at the trustee. "I love the ambience of your hallway."

"That's known as Ghetto Blight. Some mutt sashayed into the ladies' room and planted a bomb inside one of the commodes. We were lucky no one was inside when it blew."

Scanlon studied the face in front of him, the gray eyes, the dark hair with a silver tinge. "I'm here to pick your brains, Louie."

"Go ahead, pick." Louie Pots and Pans snapped his fingers and scuttled out from behind his desk over to the barbecue grills. He picked up a jar and shook something into the simmering sauces. "I almost forgot to add the oregano," he said, going back to his desk.

"I want our conversation to remain between us, Louie."

Louie Pots and Pans turned wary. "I haven't seen you at the last couple of Columbian meetings."

Scanlon answered in Italian: *"Ho avuto un cacco di problemi personali."*

"We all got personal problems," Louie said, his stern eyes holding the lieutenant's. "This thing that you want to remain just between us, could it be used in any way to hurt cops?"

Scanlon put on a pained expression. "Louie!"

"What do you wanna know, paisan?"

"You sit on the Board of Trustees for the Police Pension Fund, right?"

"Don't tell me you're looking to get out with three-quarters?"

"No, Louie, I could have had that when I lost my leg. I'm in the Job for the full count." He leaned forward, looking directly into the trustee's eyes. "You must be conversant with line-of-duty death benefits."

"Yeah, I am. Why?"

"A lieutenant, twenty-two years on the Job, age forty-four, LOD death, how much?"

Louie Pots and Pans closed his eyes and groaned. "I heard whispers that there might be a problem."

"How much, Louie?"

The trustee said in Italian, "Tony, you can't be thinking what I think you're thinking?"

"I'm not thinking anything. How much, paisan?"

Louie Pots and Pans picked up a pencil from his desk and began to jot numbers onto a police department scratch pad. "I happen to know that your *fictionalized* lieutenant was a member of both the PBA and the LBA and therefore entitled to both organizations' group life insurance. The PBA pays seventy-five thousand and the LBA pays a hundred. In addition, on all LOD deaths the city contributes one year salary to the family—that would be, roughly, another fifty thousand. So for openers, we got two hundred and twenty-five."

The two men looked solemnly at each other.

Louie Pots and Pans got up to check on his sauces. He added more seasoning to one of the pots and returned to his seat. "The widow would have the option of taking an LOD pension or taking the death gamble. In almost every case we strongly recommend that they take the death gamble."

"Why?"

"Because LOD pensions are paid out in monthly installments over the course of the widow's lifetime and would stop when she dies or if she should remarry. Whereas the death gamble is paid up front, in one lump sum."

"What about taxes?"

"Hardly any. A few grand in state and local taxes, that's all."

"Like most guys in the Job, I know the death gamble exists, but I'm ignorant of its provisions. Explain it to me, will you?"

"The death-gamble bill was passed several years ago by the state legislature to protect the pension rights of guys who die in the Job after putting in their twenty. Under it, your lieutenant would have been deemed to have retired the day before his death. With his time in the Job, he'd have been entitled to an annual pension of about twenty-seven thousand.

"The Pension Bureau woulda looked at their actuarial tables and seen that he had a life expectancy of about sixteen years. Then they'd multiply his annual pension by his life expectancy." Louie Pots and Pans did the arithmetic on the scratch pad. "Four hundred and thirty-two thousand dollars. That would be in addition to the group life insurance policies and the city's contribution of a year's salary. The total would be six hundred and fifty-seven thousand. And then you'd have to throw in any private insurance he might have had."

Scanlon sank down into his seat and slapped his forehead. "LOD widows are wealthy ladies."

"That money don't give them their husbands back. And if they got young kids to raise and see through college, all that money don't go too far."

Scanlon's mind raced ahead. "What about the donations that are made within and without the Job?"

"They can add up to a nice piece of change. If the case gets a lot of publicity it can mean a lot of public sympathy. Especially if there're children involved, and especially if one of the kids got Down's syndrome and the other was slightly retarded. Sometimes those donations can run into six figures."

"Thanks, Louie," Scanlon said, pushing himself up from the chair and going over to the grills. He picked up a wooden stirring spoon, scooped up some sauce, sipped it, and said, "Not bad, Louie, not bad. But it could use just a touch more garlic."

Police Commissioner Roberto Gomez's drawn face reflected his deepening concern as he listened to Scanlon recount the latest developments in the Gallagher/Zimmerman homicide.

Also present in the fourteenth-floor office were Scanlon's immediate boss, Deputy Chief McKenzie, and Inspector Herman the German Schmidt.

"Goddamnit, Scanlon," the PC shouted, angrily slamming his palm down on the desk. "You don't have one ounce of evidence to support this new theory of yours. Nothing that will stand up in court. And you know as well as I do that evidence obtained under hypnosis is inadmissible."

"Commissioner," Scanlon countered, "the death-gamble motive is a lead worth following. It might come to something and it might not. And as far as the hypnosis is concerned, the courts have ruled that it can be used as an investigative tool. That is how we used it, as a tool to find out that the perp was a woman."

"But suppose the perp wasn't a woman?" McKenzie said. "Then what? The entire thrust of your investigation will have been misdirected."

"I'm following up on every lead that we developed. Even if they end in a dead end, like Eddie Hamill."

"Let me understand this new hypothesis of yours," the PC said to Scanlon. "You think that there is a possibility that Gallagher was murdered for his death-gamble money, and that Sgt. George

Harris and Mrs. Gallagher conspired to kill her husband. Is that the basic plot?"

"Yes."

"Then tell me, Lieutenant," the PC said, "who killed Dr. Zimmerman and his wife, and why were they killed?"

"I don't know," Scanlon said tightly.

"Assuming for a moment that I buy your new theory, which, I hasten to add, I don't, how would you proceed with the investigation?" Gomez said.

"If the perp who took out Gallagher and Yetta Zimmerman was in fact a woman, and if that woman was Mrs. Gallagher, and if George Harris was her accomplice, then we know who has the evidence that we need to obtain a conviction."

"That's a lot of ifs," Gomez said.

"And would you please tell me what evidence you're talking about?" MacAdoo McKenzie said to Scanlon.

"The shotgun that was used to kill Gallagher and Yetta Zimmerman, the cowboy boots that were worn on the roof of the Kingsley Arms, the rifle that took out the doctor and his wife, and the makeup that was used to turn a woman into a man," Scanlon said.

"Good God, man, do you think that they'd still have that evidence in their possession? They'd have gotten rid of it immediately after the killings," McKenzie said.

"I don't think they had the time to dispose of it, at least not all of it," Scanlon countered. "They've both been in the spotlight from the beginning of this case so I don't think that they would have taken a chance of being seen dumping the stuff. Besides, Harris is cocky, the type of guy who thinks he's smarter than everyone else. People like him can't conceive of getting caught. They're too smart."

Unconvinced, the PC said, "Would someone go to such lengths as to wear a disguise and then forget to remove a wristwatch that could blow her cover?"

"Absolutely," Scanlon said with conviction. "It happens all the time. No matter how clever they are, or how much they plan, there is always some minor point that they manage to overlook. Mrs. Gallagher wore long sleeves, and she probably forgot all about her watch."

"Why kill Yetta Zimmerman?" MacAdoo McKenzie said.

"To make it look as though it were a holdup and to throw us off the scent," Scanlon said. "Gallagher had his time in the Job, so Mrs. Gallagher would have collected on the death gamble in any event. But it's hard to fake an accidental death. The best way to murder a cop is to make it look as though he died in the line of duty. This way you would also collect money through donations. But more important, anything that resembled an LOD death would throw us off, make us look for phantom perps."

Silence fell over the four men as they sat contemplating the monstrous implications of Scanlon's words. For a police sergeant to have engaged in the premeditated murder of a brother officer, for profit, was to their minds the ultimate act of betrayal.

Herman the German shifted in his chair. "I keep coming back to the doctor and his wife. Why them?"

"As I said before, I just don't know," Scanlon responded. "But off the top of my head, I can think of two possibilities."

"I'm listening," PC Gomez said.

"First off, there is a chance that Harris and Mrs. Gallagher might not have had their facts straight regarding the death gamble. They might have thought that in order to collect under it, Gallagher's death had to be designated LOD. And when they saw that it might not be, they decided to ensure that it was by killing the doctor and his wife."

"How the hell would that ensure an LOD designation for Gallagher?" a skeptical MacAdoo McKenzie asked.

"Their deaths gave credence to Yetta Zimmerman being the intended victim of the original hit, thereby setting up the scenario whereby Gallagher died protecting Yetta, guaranteeing an LOD designation."

"And the second reason?" demanded the PC.

"To keep us off balance until nature took its course and the case died a natural death," Scanlon said.

McKenzie stamped his foot. "Do you realize what the hell you are saying? Really realize?"

"Yes, I do," Scanlon said.

Disheartened, the PC got up and walked over to the window. He pushed aside the white vertical blinds and looked out. "Old Steve Kennedy was the PC when I came on the Job. I remember his terminating a rookie in my class because the investigating unit missed three speeding tickets on the original character investigation. And look at the Job today," he lamented. "We're forced to appoint functional illiterates, female dwarfs, and people with criminal records." He kicked the wall. "No wonder the Job is in the state it's in." He went back and flung himself into his chair. "You intend to follow up on this new lead of yours, I gather," Gomez said to Scanlon.

"I think that I should, yes," Scanlon said.

"Then you listen to me, Lieutenant. I don't want you to go near Harris or Mrs. Gallagher until you come up with some corroborating evidence besides hypnosis, composite sketches, and footprints left on a roof. I want something to hang our hats on, something we can go into court with. Mrs. Gallagher is the widow of a dead hero, and Harris is a decorated member of the force. Do I make myself clear, perfectly clear?"

"Yes," Scanlon said.

"In that case, tell me what your next move is," PC Gomez said to Scanlon.

"I've made a list from the Yellow Pages of every theatrical makeup store in the city. I have two detectives checking them out now. I saw to it that they brought along photographs of Harris and Mrs. Gallagher to show the store owners."

"Where did you get their photographs?" PC Gomez asked.

"Harris's is from the department's Force Record File and Mrs. Gallagher's is from a newspaper clipping."

"Why theatrical makeup?" McKenzie asked.

"Because if our perp was a woman, the stuff she used to look like a man sure as hell wasn't bought in the five-and-ten."

Leaning his head back against his headrest, the PC closed his eyes and massaged his forehead. "What else have you done?"

"I have people out checking on the owners of the Luv-Joy Manufacturing Company."

"Why?" the PC asked, rubbing the bridge of his nose.

"We have Gallagher visiting the Santorini Diner on a regular basis for a couple of weeks. The diner is located near the Luv-Joy plant. Gallagher visited the diner during his tour of duty. He had access to a lot of the company's products. There is a connection, and I want to find out what it is. It might prove to be nothing, and then again, it could be important," Scanlon said.

"What else?" the PC asked, his eyes still closed, the deceptive calmness of his voice causing a knowing glance to pass between Scanlon and Herman the German.

"I took it upon myself to ask Inspector Schmidt to come here today because Harris is assigned to his command. I'd like Inspector Schmidt to keep Harris busy, fly him on details. I'm going to start snooping, and I'd prefer it if he wasn't around."

"Do you think that Harris and Mrs. Gallagher were making it together?" the PC asked.

"I don't know," Scanlon said, "but if they were, and she didn't know about his thing with Luise Bardwell, then we just might have a wedge to drive between them."

"Before you use any wedges, you come to me with some solid evidence linking them to the crime," Gomez said.

"Are you thinking of using wires?" McKenzie asked.

"I've decided against using them," Scanlon said.

Surprised, the PC asked, "Why?"

"Because of Section 700.50 of the Criminal Procedure Law," Scanlon explained. "After the eavesdropping warrant expires, you're required to notify the subscriber that you had a wire on his telephone. This case could run longer than sixty days, and I don't want them to know that we're on to them."

"You're going to need extra men on this one," the PC said. "I'm going to assign some people from the Internal Affairs Division to help you out."

"If you don't mind, Commissioner, I'd rather not use anyone from IAD. I believe their involvement in this case would be counterproductive."

Bewildered, the PC asked, "Why?"

Scanlon said, "Because the people in IAD are all mealy-mouthed scumbags who consider street cops to be the enemy. And because all of my detectives are fallen angels, and none of them would be able to work with anyone from IAD."

Scowling, the PC appeared on the edge of rebuking him when Herman the German jumped into the fray: "Commissioner, it might not be prudent to bring IAD into this case, at the present time."

"And why the hell not?" the PC asked.

"Because if we are able to bring this case to a successful conclusion, you will be able to take the credit for personally directing the internal investigation that resulted in arrests, thereby blunting the harmful publicity that the case is bound to generate. And that can only be done if you maintain control of the case."

In an annoyed tone, the PC said, "The CO of IAD reports directly to me."

"I realize that, sir," the inspector said, "but I also know that the special prosecutor has his own spies in IAD who report directly to *him*. And under the special prosecutor's mandate from the governor, he has the legal authority to take over the Gallagher/Zimmerman matter once there is any hint of police corruption." A glint came into his deep-set eyes. "So why let him know? If he ever got wind of this case he'd snap it up in a second. It's tailor-made for his journey to the Governor's Mansion. And then we'd be on the outside, unable to see what the hell was happening on the inside, and more important, unable to protect our own asses."

"You can always notify the special prosecutor later," Scanlon added with a crafty smile. "Especially if the case goes nowhere. Just pass him the ball and step back."

The PC stared down at the black onyx desk set that was embossed with miniature replicas of police shields from patrolman to police commissioner. The set had been presented to him at the Hispanic Association's Man of the Year Award dinner in 1983.

Scanlon noticed the PC's forlorn stare and guessed what he was thinking. It had been a long, hard haul from walking a foot post to sitting behind Teddy Roosevelt's desk on the fourteenth floor of One Police Plaza. He had stayed on the Job too long, a common mistake. He wanted to get out, but he wanted to leave with his three-quarter PC's pension intact. Another major scandal and the mayor might be forced to ask for his resignation. Only five months to go before he was eligible for that pension, five long, precarious months.

Gomez looked up at Scanlon, held his eyes, sensing that he had read his thoughts. "Where would you get the extra men that you need, Lieutenant?"

"I would use some of Lieutenant Fable's detectives from the Nineteenth Squad. It'd be a joint investigation directed and co-ordinated personally by the PC," Scanlon said.

A perverse smile lit on the PC's handsome face. "You got some line of shit, Lou."

"It's hard surviving in the real world, boss," Scanlon said.

"Tell me about it," Gomez countered. "And while you're at it, someone tell me how we're going to keep this from the CofD."

"I don't see how you can, now," Scanlon said.

"Goldberg is going to have to be brought in on the case," the PC said, "but that's my problem."

Scanlon and Herman the German walked out into the bright sunlight and moved along the tree-lined arcade that connected police headquarters with the open square of Police Plaza.

Scanlon veered off to the right and sat down on one of the concrete cubes. Herman the German followed and sat next to him. "Wonder why the PC wanted McKenzie to remain behind?" the inspector said.

"My guess is that he wanted to discuss how to gracefully bring the CofD into the case," Scanlon said.

"Ain't no graceful way, not now. Too much time has gone by."

"Bobby Boy will think of something. He always does." Scanlon looked upward at the budding maple tree.

Herman the German glanced at him. "Thanks for bringing me into the case the way you did. You've probably saved my career."

"When you allowed me to remove Gallagher's records I told you I'd do the right thing if I could."

The inspector smiled bitterly and said, "A lot of people in this Job threaten to do the right thing, but they seldom do."

They sat in silence, watching the passing crowd; policemen hurrying in and out of police headquarters, civilian employees on extended coffee breaks. Music wafted through the air from a string quartet playing in Police Plaza. Both of them saw familiar faces from the Job and acknowledged faces with mouthed how-are-yous and quick handwaves. The inspector leaned forward, his beefy hands clasped between his legs. "McKenzie was right, you know— you just might be wrong on this one. All you have is motive, and the similarities of a few composite sketches, some peanut shells, and some inadmissible evidence garnered under hypnosis."

"I'm painfully aware of all that, Inspector," Scanlon said, waving at a familiar face. He took out a De Nobili and lit it. "But it's a lead that deserves to be followed up, I think."

"You're probably right."

"Harris told me that he had interviewed everyone in Gallagher's unit. I'm going to have to speak to each of them myself, now."

"You start talking to those cops and Harris is bound to find out."

"I know that. But I can't think of any other way."

"Maybe you don't have to speak to them all. Maybe there are one or two guys in the unit that Gallagher was close to besides Harris. Maybe..." He snapped his fingers. "His chauffeur!"

"Damn. Why didn't I think of him? Of course. Gallagher used to go to the Santorini Diner with the same man most of the time. That was probably his driver."

Bosses in the NYPD are assigned cops to drive them during their regular tours of duty. In practice every boss selects his own driver. There are two qualifications to be a boss's driver: a short memory and a zippered mouth.

"Gallagher always used Bert Nocarski as his driver," Herman the German said. "If Gallagher was into anything, Nocarski would certainly know about it."

"What tour is Nocarski working?" Scanlon asked, admiring the backsides of passing policewomen.

"He's working days. I've assigned him to drive Gallagher's replacement until the lieutenant gets to know his people and selects his own driver."

"I'd like to talk to him as soon as possible."

"This is Thursday. The Queens Narcotics Squad's social club holds its monthly meeting tonight. Nocarski is working days, so he's sure to be there."

"Does Harris usually attend the meeting?"

"I'll arrange it so he's too busy to attend."

"Will I have any problem getting in?"

"Naw. You'll be with me. Past and present members and their guests are welcome." He looked at Scanlon. "You know, they usually have *entertainment* at these meetings."

Scanlon drew on his cigar. "That don't bother me."

Lt. Jack Fable's pelican neck was crimson with anger as he listened to Scanlon reveal his suspicions concerning Harris and Mrs. Gallagher. The Whip of the Nineteenth Detective Squad sat shaking his head from side to side. "What the fuck has happened to this Job? Even with a scorecard, you can't tell the players."

"I'm afraid you're right, Jack," Scanlon said, adding, "I've just come from the PC. He wants it to be a joint investigation from now on."

Fable threw up his arms, exasperated. "That's fucking wonderful. I've got some goddamn necrophile using the Nineteenth as his playpen. This weirdo goes to posh hotels with his ax and makes himself dead sex partners. He did one last night in the Hotel Astor. I've been up most of the night." He leaned back and rubbed his tired eyes. "My problem with a joint investigation is that I don't have any warm bodies to assign. I've got five men off the chart on the ax murders, and one off the chart on the Zimmermans. With days off, and court appearances, I don't have enough people to cover the chart."

"Why not ask the borough for some extra bodies?"

"A waste of time, you know that. Every squad in Manhattan North is knee-deep in homicides. And we can't treat them like aided and accident cases like you guys in Brooklyn do."

Scanlon was used to the refrain. There were never enough men and never enough time to do it all. He wondered many times if that was the way the Job always had been. Maybe that was why the first twenty flew by you. You're too busy playing cop to notice the years melting away. He pondered his own manpower problem. "I'll get by using my own people, Jack. If I get stuck, I'll give a holler. And if and when a collar goes down, I'll call you so that you can be in on it."

"I appreciate that, Tony. I really do."

The obligatory phone call had been made. How is your nephew, Chief? Scanlon had asked Assistant Chief Joseph McMahon, the CO of Patrol Borough Bronx. The chief told Scanlon that his nephew was still in detox in St. Vincent's and that he should be leaving for the Farm in a few days. Scanlon was going to be in the Bronx later in the day and would like to drop in and say hello, if that would be convenient.

Driving through the endless rows of shells of buildings that formed the urban devastation that was the South Bronx, Scanlon thought about how the Job really ran; it was the favors that greased the wheels of justice and made them turn.

Scanlon parked in front of the Four-eight station house on Bathgate Avenue. He identified himself to the two uniform cops assigned to station house security and entered the house. Assistant Chief McMahon rose up from his chair to greet Scanlon. The two men sat in the office exchanging gossip about the Job. No mention was made of the favor that Scanlon had done the Chief in not arresting his nephew for discharging his off-duty when he had his load on. That would have been . . . unseemly. Both men knew the drill, the protocol. During a lull in the conversation, Scanlon looked searchingly at McMahon and said, "Chief, I need a favor. . . ."

When Scanlon left Patrol Borough Bronx twenty-five minutes later he had the names of four Bronx anticrime cops that he had been given by the Chief on a one-week steal.

The four-to-twelve platoon was filing out of the station house when Biafra Baby and Christopher returned.

"Nothing, Lou," Biafra Baby complained, slumping into a chair in the Whip's office. "We checked the tax records and came up with no owner of the Luv-Joy Company. One goddamn corporation blends into another. You can't tell who owns what. And we checked out every theatrical makeup store in Manhattan and Brooklyn and came up dry."

"What about the other boroughs? That makeup had to have been bought somewhere," Scanlon said.

Munching on a carrot stick, Christopher said, "We're going to hit the other boroughs now, Lieutenant."

"Then why are you here?" Scanlon said, looking disapprovingly at the two detectives.

"We came in for gas," Christopher said.

It was an old detective ploy to kill a few hours in the house by coming in off the street for gas. Scanlon felt his anger rise. "The Nine-three isn't the only gas-dispensing precinct in the city. Get your gas and get back out. I want to know where that makeup was purchased."

"Right, Lieutenant," Christopher said.

"Detective Jones, Mrs. Jones is on three," Lew Brodie sang out from the squad room.

Scanlon looked at the two detectives, momentarily forgetting that Biafra Baby's real name was Simon Jones. Biafra Baby snatched up the phone on the Whip's desk. Listening, then nodding his head, he said, "Yes, right. I won't. Right. A half gallon of low-fat milk and whole-grain bread, right." Hanging up the receiver, he arched his brow and said to Scanlon, "That woman is *always* on my case."

Using a department scratch pad, Scanlon began to make a list of the physical evidence that he hoped was still in the possession of Harris or Mary Ann Gallagher. No one does murder and walks away without the fear of getting caught. That raw edge of fear was what he was going to use to break the case. He fumbled around in the case folder until he found Gallagher's Ten Card. He noted the telephone number and dialed.

The dead lieutenant's wife came on the line. "Hello? Hello?" Silence. His hand clamped the mouthpiece. He imagined her standing by the phone straining to hear who was on the other end of the open line. He replaced the receiver and sat back. So it begins, he thought.

Twenty minutes later Higgins and a subdued Hector Colon entered the squad room and went into the Whip's office.

"How did you make out?" Scanlon asked.

"We didn't find any cockroaches, Lou," Higgins said gleefully.

Colon squirmed, embarrassed. *"Teniente,"* he said, trying to ignore Higgins, going on to tell Scanlon that they had canvassed the area where Harris lived on Staten Island, and had discovered that the sergeant's official residence was a frame dwelling at the end of a rutted dirt road. Discreet inquiries by Higgins had revealed that Harris did own the house, but was seldom there. Colon went on to say that the Ocean Avenue splash pad of Harris, the one Luise Bardwell had told them about, was in an eight-story building that was in the process of going co-op.

Scanlon was about to ask Colon a question when they heard Lew Brodie's tense, anxious voice call: "Attention!"

Chief of Detectives Alfred Goldberg bounded into the office followed close behind by a tense deputy chief, MacAdoo McKenzie.

The CofD paused just inside the office and coldly regarded

Higgins. He rolled his cigar to the other side of his mouth, looked at Colon, and said, "Excuse us, will ya, Hector?"

Hector Colon and Higgins left the office.

CofD Goldberg closed the door, looked at Scanlon. "The PC filled me in on the Gallagher case."

Scanlon's right hand brushed at his hair as his gaze shifted to MacAdoo McKenzie.

The deputy chief nodded confirmation.

"Whatsamatta, Lou? Don't you trust me?"

"Of course I trust you, Chief," Scanlon said.

Goldberg braced his hands on the desk and leaned across. "You ain't supposed to keep things from the chief of detectives." His dour expression broadened into a smile. "But under the circumstances I forgive you. I happen to be a very forgiving man. Ain't that so, Chief?" he said, looking at MacAdoo McKenzie.

"Absolutely, boss. Very forgiving," McKenzie said, rubbing his palms down his trousers.

"We gotta see to it that the PC is protected on this one," Goldberg said, pointing the chewed-up end of his cigar at the lieutenant's face. "We also gotta see to it that if Harris and the widow are the perps, it's us who make the collars and hand out the press releases—very carefully worded press releases." Shoving the cigar back into his mouth, he asked, "How do you intend to proceed?"

Scanlon told him that his main concern was that Harris and Mrs. Gallagher not be given the opportunity to dispose of any of the evidence that he believed was still in the possession of one of them. When Goldberg asked him why he thought that, Scanlon repeated what he had told the PC. "That evidence is someplace. All we have to do is find it," Scanlon finished.

"Maybe," Goldberg said. An expression of doubt clouded his face. He flicked a thick chunk of ash onto the floor. "You got enough manpower to do the job?"

"Jack Fable is sending a few of his detectives over to help, and I've scrounged up a few anticrime cops for a week," Scanlon said.

"Howzat? Fable is up to his ass in homicides and he's sending you men?" There was humor in Goldberg's questioning stare.

Scanlon shrugged off his doubtful look. "We all have to pull together on this one, boss."

Goldberg gave Scanlon a friendly punch on the shoulder. "It

really gratifies me to see two of my squad commanders exemplifying such leadership. That's what command is all about. Right, Lou?"

"Right, Chief," Scanlon agreed.

"You know, of course, that I know that you're full of shit. But that's between you and Fable. Just make sure to keep me informed this time around. Got that? The PC and I are operating on the same wavelength on this one." He turned to McKenzie. "Let's go."

MacAdoo McKenzie moved ahead and opened the door for the CofD. Scanlon scuttled out from behind his desk and hurried over to McKenzie. "What brought about *that* change?" he whispered.

McKenzie looked at the CofD's retreating back, whispered, "The PC told him that he was getting out in five months, and if Goldberg played ball with him on the Gallagher thing, the PC would recommend Goldberg as his successor. Goldberg figures that with Bobby Boy's endorsement he'll be a shoo-in for the job."

"That's if the PC really throws his papers in."

"McKenzie?" Goldberg shouted over his shoulder.

"Right behind you, boss," McKenzie shouted back.

Scanlon looked anxiously into the stern face of Herman the German. They were parked on Carroll Street, in the Park Slope section of Brooklyn. The Carroll Street Bridge, a tiny span that arches over a black stream of polluted water, was down the block from where they were parked. A trucking company was on their right. It was a street of one- and two-story frame houses. Men in undershirts lounged around the sidewalk on lawn chairs. Boys sped by on skateboards. It was 1915 hours. They had been parked there for over fifteen minutes watching off-duty policemen double-park their cars and hurry into the Vito Longoni Hall of the Veterans of Foreign Wars. The hall was across the street, to their left, set back off the street. It was a long one-story frame building that had two wooden steps with a blue-and-white portico.

A Seven-eight Precinct radio car cruised by, slowing to check on the policemen's private cars, to make sure they remained unmolested. The Seven-eight roll call man had received a call earlier in the day from the club's sergeant-at-arms informing him that a meeting was scheduled for that evening. The cops who were assigned to the sector where the hall was located, and the patrol

sergeant, had been notified to give the hall "special attention."
Cops take care of their own.

Scanlon watched three laughing cops bound up the steps into
the Hall. He nudged the inspector. "You ready?"

"As ready as I'll ever be," Herman the German said, opening
the car door.

Three cops sat around a bridge table just inside the entrance
checking membership cards. The recording secretary, a chunky man
with a small head, stood up when the inspector walked into the
Hall.

"Glad you could make it, Inspector," he said, extending his hand
across the bridge table.

Motioning at Scanlon, the inspector said, "I brought a friend
along."

"No problem, boss," the recording secretary said, nodding to
Scanlon.

Scanlon made his way into the hall. It consisted of one enormous
room with a large open kitchen in the rear that was set off from
the rest of the hall by a long counter. Swirling blue clouds were
painted across the ceiling. Three kegs of beer were set up in front
of the counter; many bottles of liquor were on top of the counter
along with gallon jugs of wine. A cop was standing over the big
pots on top of the gas range. An aluminum folding table had been
set up across one side of the room to act as the dais, and there
were five rows of metal folding chairs arranged in front of it. An
American flag stood behind the aluminum table. Six card tables
were scattered about the hall, each one filled with cardplayers.
Each table had two pitchers of beer on it.

"Do you see Nocarski?" Scanlon asked Herman the German.

"No," the inspector said, making his way over to the large dice
game that was in progress in one corner of the hall. Scanlon moved
along behind him. They watched the dice game for a few minutes,
the inspector taking in the faces of the players. Herman the German
shook his head. "He's not here." They made their way through to
the staircase that led downstairs to the cloakroom.

The horseshoe basement bar was mobbed with policemen. There
were round tables with flickering candles inside white lanterns. A
crap game was in progress in the middle of the room. Herman the
German examined each face in turn. Narcs came over to say hello

to their boss. Scanlon had never noticed before just how many different kinds of faces made up today's Job. There were oriental faces, and Latin faces, and Mediterranean faces, and black faces, and bearded faces. There were cops in shabby clothes and Italian-cut suits. Cops dressed as Hell's Angels. There were women dressed to look like housewives and business executives. They all had a common denominator, their shields, NYPD Queens Narcotics.

Herman the German moved about greeting his men, listening to their jokes, roaring with laughter, enduring their slurred conversations. Watching the inspector maneuvering among his men, Scanlon thought, A lot of things go into being a boss in the Job. You really have got to know your people, their strengths, their weaknesses. You have got to get them to produce for you, yet, you have to remain aloof from them, not become part of the car pool.

"Nocarski isn't here," Herman the German said. "Let's go back upstairs."

The dice game up in the hall was in full swing. A female undercover was on her knees talking to the dice. "Come a seven, come eleven. Baby, talk to your mama!" She rolled the dice.

"Eight's her point," a male voice said. "Twenty says she don't six or eight in two."

Music blared from a tape deck under the long counter.

The cook shouted, "Chow down!"

Policemen began to drift up to the counter.

"Let's eat," Herman the German said.

Holding a paper plate overflowing with frankfurters, sauerkraut, baked beans, salad, and white bread, Scanlon eased himself down onto one of the metal folding chairs and gingerly balanced the plate on his knees. Using a flimsy plastic knife and a fork, he began to cut into the steaming frankfurter. "It takes a certain kind of dexterity to eat at one of these meetings."

Champing on a mouthful of food, Herman the German grunted something that Scanlon took for agreement. They finished eating. Nocarski still had not arrived. The policemen inside the hall had divided themselves into three groups. The boozers congregated around the bar, slopping down drinks; the cardplayers and the crapshooters were intent on their games; the rookies had collected around the dais, exchanging youthful war stories.

"Yoho, m'man," came a harsh voice from the middle of the dice game. "You don't gate in this motherfuckin' game. This ain't no motherfuckin' schoolyard."

Deep lines creased the inspector's brow. "It might be a good time to get out of here."

Scanlon's stump ached. "A little while longer. I gotta speak with Gallagher's driver."

A bearded black man wearing cut-off jeans, sandals, and a T-shirt walked up behind the dais and began rapping a blackjack on the aluminum table, calling the meeting to order. "All stand for the Pledge," he ordered.

Activity stopped as everyone in the hall stood and faced the flag. After the Pledge of Allegiance was over the club's president asked for a moment of silent prayer for the deceased members of the force. All bowed their heads. Prayer over, all activities resumed in muffled tones as the president announced the calendar of coming events: a boat ride in July leaving from the Captree Boat Basin; a family picnic in August; the annual promotion and retirement dinner dance in September.

Scanlon saw two cops moving about the hall, tacking green garbage bags over all the windows. "Looks like the *entertainment* is about to start," he said to the inspector.

The club's treasurer read the financial report.

The club's president rose from his seat. "I'll take a motion to ajoin."

The motion to adjourn was shouted up from the floor and seconded. The din grew. Willie Nelson sang "Till I Gain Control Again." A loud pounding came at the door. The sergeant-at-arms moved up to the door and peeked out from the side of the refuse bag. Nodding in recognition, he unlocked the door.

A stocky blond man with short hair ambled into the hall. Two women followed him inside. One of the women had jet-black hair that was teased up into the shape of a beehive. Her thin body was squeezed into iridescent pink toreador pants. She had on a black pullover with a wide patent-leather belt with a large white buckle. A heavy dose of black eyeshadow gave her small face a chalky hue.

The other woman had a long, angular black face. Her head had been shaven save for a clump of hair on the top that had been styled into a large pompom. She wore a green pullover and Kelly-green toreador pants with a white belt.

Both of the women had on four-inch spike heels.

Scanlon and the inspector had been watching one of the poker games when the women sauntered into the hall. "The guy with them is Bert Nocarski, Gallagher's driver. He must have gone to pick up the hookers," Herman the German told Scanlon.

"Shit, now we're stuck here," Scanlon said.

The cardplayers and the crapshooters ignored the new arrivals. With hoots and howls the rookies rushed to greet the hookers, quickly surrounding them. The two women strutted their wares among the circle, cooing sexual promises, laughingly tickling scrotums. Most of the policewomen who had been in the hall when the hookers entered made their way downstairs to the basement bar. Three remained, trying to ignore the hookers, but every now and then casting side glances at them.

Bert Nocarski shoved his way through the crowd up to the bar and poured himself a shot of whiskey. He held up the tumbler, studying it for a long moment, before he downed the drink in one quick gulp. He poured another and turned to the cop next to him, and Scanlon heard him say, "Did you hear about the fag who walked into the bar with a parrot on his shoulder..."

Scanlon made a move to go up to the bar. Herman the German stopped him. "Wait."

Nocarski drank, poured another. Herman knows his men, Scanlon thought, turning his attention back to the poker game. The music was loud. The card and crap games continued unabated. The hookers had taken off all their clothes, except for the spike heels, and were dancing around the hall, swirling and swaying to the beat of the music. Three rookies rushed out onto the floor and began to dance with the hookers.

The white hooker with the teased hair shimmied her body over to one of the card tables and began to hump on one of the player's arms. The annoyed player shoved her away. She danced off. The recording secretary opened the front door for the Seven-eight patrol sergeant and his driver. The hookers danced over to the two uniformed policemen, circling them, rubbing their bodies against them. The hookers began to jostle the sergeant's boyish driver. The black hooker threw her arms around his neck and kissed him, grinding her body against him. The white hooker began to work the zipper of his fly down. The sergeant laughed and walked back toward the bar.

The three remaining policewomen made their way through the crowd to the staircase and hurried downstairs. The sergeant's driver struggled to escape from the hookers' amorous clutches.

Several rookies rushed out from the sidelines to restrain the driver. The white hooker had worked down the driver's fly and was fishing out his penis. To the delight of the rookies, the black hooker went down on her knees and began to suck the driver. The sergeant's driver was turned on. He stood with his head all the way back, his eyes closed, his hands guiding the hooker's head.

The cardplayers anted.

The club's president made six straight passes.

Scanlon threw a quick glance at the raucous policemen and thought, This scene would make one helluva recruitment poster. The white hooker danced her way over to the card game that Scanlon and Herman the German were watching. She dragged a chair from the sidelines and sat with her legs spread up in the air. She smiled at Scanlon. "Wanna taste, handsome?"

Scanlon looked down at her. "No thanks, honey. I'm on a fat-free diet."

One of the rookies rushed over to the white hooker, fell to his knees, and buried his face in her muff. Rookies ran over and circled the kneeling policeman, shouting encouraging advice.

A paper plate sailed through the air. Someone shouted that the Martians were coming. The dice game and the card games continued, undaunted by the ear-piercing din. A fight broke out at one of the card tables. "Let's get this over with and get the hell out of here," Scanlon said to the inspector.

They began to shove their way over to the bar. The sergeant's driver pushed past them, zipping up his fly. The black hooker was spread-eagled on the dais with the sergeant-at-arm's face buried between her legs. Cops were three-deep around the counter. Scanlon shoved his way up to Nocarski. He waited for the inspector, who had been stopped by a drunken cop. Herman the German had just made his way over to Scanlon when silence descended over the big hall. The dice stopped rolling. No pots were anted. No glasses were hoisted. The rookies fell silent.

Scanlon knew what that meant and winced. He turned to look.

The hookers were out in the middle of the floor, grinding their bodies into each other, their flailing tongues touching, their hands probing the other body, caressing. The black hooker slithered down onto her back. Her partner knelt down alongside her, kissing her body, her tongue slowly working its way downward.

Scanlon took in the cops' wide-eyed expression, their unconscious gnawing of lips, their heaving chests and flared nostrils and crimson ears. Nothing, but nothing, turns a man on like watching women getting it off together, Scanlon thought, tapping Bert Nocarski on the shoulder.

They went downstairs and sat at a table in the bar, the flickering candle throwing fingers of light onto their faces. Bert Nocarski was fidgety. He looked with suspicion at Scanlon. "Ain't you the Whip of the Nine-three Squad?"

Before Scanlon could answer, Herman the German said, "Bert, I'd like you to continue driving the new lieutenant until he gets his feet wet."

"Whatever you want, boss," Nocarski said, relaxing.

"Bert, how long did you chauffeur Lieutenant Gallagher around?" Scanlon asked, picking at the netting around the lantern.

Nocarski looked at Herman the German.

"Bert, this is a friend of mine," the inspector said, not mentioning Scanlon by name. "He's here to do me a favor, and we need your help."

"Around eleven months," Nocarski said.

Herman the German leaned across the table to confide, "Someone dropped a letter on Joe Gallagher. One of the allegations is that Joe had a girlfriend that he used to visit on city time."

"That's bullshit," Nocarski said. "The boss was a happily married man who never fucked around."

"Hey, everybody knows that, Bert," Scanlon said.

"Anyway, what difference does that make now? He's dead," Nocarski said.

"It makes a big difference to his family and to his reputation on the Job," Herman the German said. "Those humps in IAD would love to be able to smear the reputation of a solid street cop like Joe Gallagher."

"They'd get their rocks off all right," Scanlon said.

"Fucking-A right," Nocarski said, angrily scraping back his chair and walking over to the bar. "Anyone wanna taste?"

Scanlon and Herman the German declined.

Lowering himself back onto the bentwood chair, Nocarski said, "The letter writers in this Job should have their balls cut off."

Assuming a conspiratorial air, Scanlon hunched forward and said, "We know that Joe used to visit the Santorini Diner from time to time."

"He was entitled to a meal period," Nocarski protested.

"Absolutely," Scanlon agreed.

"We want to reach out to whoever Joe used to meet in that diner and tell them that if anyone from IAD comes snooping around asking questions about Joe, they never heard of him," Herman the German said. Stiffening his back in drunken pride, Nocarski said, "I'll take care of it, boss."

"No," Herman the German said. "I don't want you involved. My friend here will take care of that. There is no way anyone can tie him into Gallagher."

"But I am involved," Nocarski insisted. "I was with him every time that he went to that diner, and I even met his pal a coupla times."

"You're not involved," Scanlon countered. "Department regulations prevent supervisor's drivers from being used as witnesses against their bosses for violations of department rules and regulations. You more or less have department immunity. But if you go to that diner now and attempt to head off anyone from talking to IAD, then you'd be sticking your head into a noose."

"I never thought of that," Nocarski said.

He was a small man with a pitted complexion. He sat behind a rather large desk, in a rather big chair, adjusting his rather fluffy orange bow tie. His name was Milton Tablin, and he was a factor, an old competitor of Sy Posner—and an "intimate" friend of Posner's adventurous wife, Mary, who had enjoyed herself with Tablin before Gallagher came into her life. And thus Joe Gallagher knew *all* about Tablin and his work. Tablin was an entrepreneur who lent money to other entrepreneurs, and he was the man Scanlon had rushed to see early the morning after Nocarski gave him the name.

A shapely brunette led Scanlon into the eleventh-floor office at

1380 Broadway, in the teeming heart of the garment district. Walking into the comfortable office, Scanlon took in the photographs and plaques that covered the walls of the rather large office.

Milton Tablin was in every one of the photographs, outfitted in the uniform of a ranking police officer and posing with other uniformed men, most of whom Scanlon recognized as bosses in the Job. The plaques were from different police line organizations, given in grateful recognition to a financial benefactor, Milton Tablin, a cop's friend.

Scanlon was quick to conclude that the factor whom he had come to see was a dyed-in-the-wool cop buff.

"What can I do for you, Lieutenant?" Tablin asked, centering his tie as he watched his secretary's retreating rump.

"I'd like to speak to you about your lunchtime meetings with Joe Gallagher."

On guard, Tablin asked, "Who told you about them?"

"Joe's driver, Bert Nocarski."

"Joe asked me never to mention those meetings to anyone." The factor cast a thoughtful glance at Scanlon. "Where do you work, Lieutenant?"

Scanlon made a quick decision to charm the cop buff by using cop language. "I'm the Whip of the Nine-three Squad."

Milton Tablin grabbed over the telephone console that was on his desk and made a call. "Who got the Nine-three Squad?" he asked into the mouthpiece, his questioning eyes fixed on his visitor. He listened. Thrusting his chin at Scanlon, he said, "You got an artificial leg?"

Scanlon lifted up his prosthesis, rapped knuckles on fiberglass.

"Thanks," Tablin said, hanging up. "That was a friend of mine in the CofD's office. I had to make sure that you weren't one of those snooping humps from Internal Affairs."

A silent smile, a gesture of understanding. Cop buffs think, talk, and try to act like the genuine article.

"Joe is dead," Tablin said. "Why the interest in our meetings?"

"My Squad caught the squeal on Joe's death," Scanlon said. "A few things popped up during the course of the investigation."

"Anything heavy?"

"Minor stuff, but it has got to be answered out."

"Coffee and . . . ?" Tablin asked with a friendly smile.

"Love it. Haven't had my first cup yet."

Tablin pushed a button on the intercom and asked his secretary to get them some coffee and danish. He settled back in his seat and with great delight began to tell Scanlon about all his friends in the Job. Scanlon did not want to alienate Tablin, so he listened attentively, his brow knotted with interest.

Milton Tablin was a captain in the Auxiliary Police. Scanlon was forced to endure an insufferable litany of Auxiliary Police complaints: regular cops consider the auxiliaries psychos and labor scabs; auxiliaries are not permitted to make arrests or carry firearms; the auxiliaries' only function is to give a police presence and to report suspected violations of law. Scanlon swallowed a yawn, smiled, and listened with all the sympathy and understanding he could force himself to muster.

Tablin, with great glee, went on to tell Scanlon the latest scuttlebutt in the Job: who was scheduled for promotion, who was being greased for the slide downward, and who was sleeping with whom. Suddenly Tablin was on his feet, throwing back his suit jacket to reveal his Smith and Wesson automatic pistol in a quick-draw holster secured on his hip. "It's a double-action nine millimeter," he said, caressing the automatic. "I had battle sights put on."

Another psycho heard from, Scanlon thought, saying, "How many rounds does it hold?"

"Ten in the clip," Tablin said smugly, letting his jacket fall back over the weapon and sitting down. Dejectedly, he said, "I'm a captain in the Auxiliary Police and I had to get a carry permit to have a concealed weapon. I mean, I ask you, Lou, is that right? How do they expect us to uphold the law without being armed?"

"I think that sucks, Milton. You guys are an integral part of the Job," Scanlon said, relieved when a soft knock came and Tablin's secretary entered. While Tablin was taking the goodies from the bag, Scanlon said, "Why don't you tell me about Joe Gallagher?"

Handing him a container of hot coffee, Tablin began to talk about the dead police lieutenant. When Tablin had first joined the auxiliaries in '71, Gallagher had been a sergeant assigned to the Auxiliary Forces Section. Gallagher used to lecture Tablin's class on the Penal Law and the Law of Arrest. Tablin liked Gallagher immediately. Gallagher seemed to go out of his way to be nice to the auxiliaries. The both of them hit it off together, almost an instant friendship. One evening after Gallagher had finished giving his lecture he came up to Tablin and asked him if he would like to go to a precinct club meeting. "I think you might enjoy yourself, Milton," Gallagher had said with a mischievous twinkle.

"That was really something," Tablin said, fondly recalling his first witnessing of an act of public sodomy as he bit into his prune danish.

Sipping coffee, Scanlon thought about how the wheelers and dealers on the Job were always on the lookout for businessmen to ingratiate themselves with. One of the best ways of doing that was to invite the entrepreneur to a precinct racket or a precinct club meeting that was going to have *entertainment*. A small segment of the cop world was thus revealed, causing the civilian to feel as though he were now one of the boys, as though he were on the Job, almost.

Scanlon was sure that Tablin's name had been added to Gallagher's list of people who were good—people to whom he could go for a favor. He was just as sure that his own name had been on Gallagher's list. "I've taken care of it, luv. You owe me one," Gallagher had said to Scanlon that long-ago day in Riccardo's restaurant, alluding to the contract that Gallagher had put in with the first deputy commissioner that allowed Scanlon to remain on the Job after he had lost his leg. Scanlon never imagined that the payback would be to a dead Irishman.

"Did you and Joe remain friends after your training ended?" he asked.

"We'd have lunch every couple of months." And Gallagher never once picked up a tab, Scanlon thought. "And we'd run into each other at rackets," Tablin said.

The smart ones always maintain the friendship, Scanlon thought, asking, "Why were you meeting Joe at the Santorini Diner?"

Looking down his coffee container, Tablin said, "Joe made me promise that I would never tell anyone about that. Joe's gone now, but a promise to a buddy is a promise kept."

Scanlon nibbled on his danish, thinking about what to say next. Tell no one, extract the promise, a cop's way. He looked up at Tablin. "I wouldn't ask you to tell me if it weren't important, really important. We really need your help on this one, Cap," Scanlon said, using the diminutive of captain.

Milton Tablin's face glowed. "Well, I don't know, Lou."

"Cap, I assure you, one cop to another, that if Joe was in this room with us now, he would tell you to tell me. In fact, he'd insist."

Tablin relented. "Well, since we're both on the Job, I guess it'd be okay." He took a gulp of coffee. "Do you know what a factor does?"

"He lends money to businessmen," Scanlon said, breaking off a piece of danish.

"It's more complicated than that," said the factor. "We lend money to our clients on the strength of their commercial paper for ten over prime." The factor saw the puzzled expression on Scanlon's countenance and explained, "Ten over prime means that we take a commission of ten percent over the prime rate. And commercial paper is those instruments that are used in business in place of money." He was no longer the police buff; he had made the transition back into his other world; he was now Milton Tablin, factor. Waving a hand for emphasis, he explained, "Commercial paper can be almost anything—short-term notes, checks, acceptances, bills of lading, orders for the delivery of merchandise."

Unconsciously scratching his left knee, Scanlon asked, "How does it work?"

"Take the rag business, which by the way is where ninety-eight percent of my business comes from. It's a business with a desperate need for ready cash. Manufacturers need money to buy materials for the next season. They don't want to have to wait thirty or sixty days to get their money from a department store. So they come to me with their invoice and I buy it from them, less ten percent. They assign the invoice to me and the department store pays the money to me. This way a dress manufacturer can have cash in his hand in one day and not have to wait a month or two to get paid."

"Joe wanted you to lend him money?"

"No, a friend of his who had this cockamamie company that made dildos and other dreck. His friend wanted to expand the business but didn't have the capital."

"Did you lend the money?"

"No. That wasn't the kind of company that I could get involved with. That business was basically a mail-order house. They had some orders from retail outlets, but not enough for us to get involved. I told Joe this, and I offered some suggestions on how his friend might raise the money."

An anxious feeling welled up in Scanlon's chest. "Who was Joe's friend?"

19

The blinds were drawn in Tony Scanlon's apartment. His dark hair flopped about his head as his body moved in fluid movements to the beat of aerobics music. His support hose felt tight in the crotch, and his body glistened with sweat. He had been at it now for almost one hour, and the gamy smell of his body told him it was almost time to quit.

One, two, three, four, scissor your legs and clap your hands, one, two, three, four. Yesterday he had thought that there was a good chance he had figured the whole thing out. But his morning visit to Milton Tablin had showed him that he hadn't. One, two, three, four, stretch your arms over your head.

With hands on hips and head bowed slightly, he stood catching his breath, aware of the trickle under his armpits. Peeling off his support hose and casting them aside, he moved into the bathroom. He opened the shower door, picked up the slatted folding chair he kept inside, slapped it open, and set it down inside the stall. He took off his prosthesis and placed it over the toilet seat, hopped into the shower, and sat down on the chair. He adjusted the faucets, quickly turning on more cold because he had almost scalded himself with too much hot.

He turned his face upward so that he might better enjoy the stinging spray of water. He had made a ten P.M. date to see Sally De Nesto. Her sex and therapy sessions had begun to intrigue him. In some strange way, everything she had told him about himself made sense to him. The last time they were together he had told her about his childhood, and how his drunken father used to beat up on his mother. When he saw her eyes grow wide and a knowing glimmer lit up her face, he had demanded, "What?"

"You really don't see it, do you, Tony?" she had said, firming herself up on pillows.

Three fingertips touching in an Italian gesture, he shook his hand at her face. "See what?"

"It's so clear," she insisted. "Your drunken father abuses your mother, and you do nothing to stop it, and then you feel lousy about yourself for doing nothing to protect your mother, for not rushing to her aid. Then years later you meet Jane Stomer, and just like your mom, she gave you her love. And then when you lost your leg and had your problem, you saw yourself as unable to return her love, to protect her, just as if you had let your mother down. So what did you do? You began to seethe inside yourself, and to punish yourself by only being able to get off with people like me."

"Where did you pick up on all that psychological shit?" he had ranted. "I know. I know. From your trick, the blind shrink."

He turned his lathered face up to rinse off. Why the hell did Sally spend so much time trying to help him solve his problems? She must have a mound of her own stashed somewhere.

It was after seven P.M. when Scanlon walked from his apartment by the front entrance. He wasn't much in the mood to climb down the fire escape. The flow of people had spilled over into the roadway. Traffic crept along; swarms of people dodged between cars. The sidewalk cafés and the coffeehouses were jammed with people. Greenwich Village was alive, vibrant.

Thirty-six minutes later when Scanlon drove his car through the sleepy Greenpoint streets he saw a lone woman walking her collie.

He plunged his car up onto the curb cut and honked his car's horn. Rheumy eyes peered out the peephole, and in a matter of seconds the door leading into Gretta Polchinski's garage was churning open. He saw Walter Ticornelli's Ford parked in the first row of cars. Scanlon got out of his car, handed the attendant a two-dollar tip, and moved quickly along the cinder-block passage that led into Gretta Polchinski's brothel.

Men milled about the knotty-pine bar, talking to heavily made-up women in revealing clothes. The jukebox blared. Couples shuffled around the dance floor. Scanlon moved through the crowd, taking his time, checking out faces. One of the bartenders, a short man with big spaces between his teeth, spied Scanlon and mouthed, "Do ya wanna drink, Lieutenant?"

Scanlon shook his head and mouthed back, "Where's Gretta?"

The bartender's thumb jerked in the direction of the dance floor.

She was sitting alone in a shadow, studying the dancers, a teacup in her hands and a silver tea egg on the table next to the saucer.

Uninvited, Scanlon went over to her and sat across from her. She looked at him, lowered her cup into the circle, and asked, "You here for pleasure or for business?"

"I saw Walter's car in the garage," he said, motioning away the waitress.

"He's upstairs comforting his lover. You want to see him?"

"Actually, it's you I've come to see."

Toying with her necklaces, she said, "Don't tell me you've decided you want to throw a hump into me." Overlapping rows of gold chains glistened around her withered neck.

Scanlon grew stern. "I'm here to discuss the Luv-Joy Manufacturing Company with you, since you're the sole stockholder."

"My business interests are none of your goddamn business." She made a move to get up and leave.

He anchored her wrist to the table. "Be advised that I'm not in the mood for any of your parlor games."

"Fuck you!" she yelled, attempting to tug her hand free.

Several of the dancers turned to look in the direction of the disturbance. He continued to pin her hand to the table. "You talk, I listen. If you don't, I not only close down this place, I also sic the IRS on your ass. Think of all those secret business interests of yours, all that undeclared cash stashed in safe deposit boxes. The IRS boys would have a field day with you." He released her wrist.

"Why you pissing on my parade, Scanlon? I didn't kill anyone. You should spend your time busting murderers and dope dealers, not breaking my chops."

"You cause me a lot of extra work, lady. You should have told me about your connection with Gallagher."

"You're making something out of nothing. I needed money for capital improvements. Joe tried to help me arrange financing with a guy. It didn't work out. I gave Joe one large for his troubles. That's it, end of story."

"Not quite. You also lent him an extra fifteen hundred so that he could get Walter Ticornelli off his back. That was your money that we found in the trunk of Gallagher's car."

"And what the hell makes you so sure it was me who lent him money?"

"Street smarts. You're the only one around with a lot of extra cash who would lend a cop money without a vig."

She reached out and patted his face. "You know that I've always been a sucker for a cop."

"What connection did Gallagher have with your company?"

"None. He'd come around every now and then to grab some dildos and things. You know how much cops love to grab things that they get for nothing."

"Does George Harris still work for you?"

"No, he doesn't," she snapped. "He used to work for old man Stevens, the guy I bought the company from. When I took over I decided to reduce my overhead. I put in my own man as manager and got rid of all the moonlighting cops and firemen. I wanted people working for me who were dependent on me for their living, not people with a city paycheck coming in every week."

"Did you ever raise the money you were looking for?"

"After Milton Tablin turned me down, I decided to forget expanding until I had the money."

"Why not try the banks?"

"And use what for collateral—hookers? Banks don't lend money to madams. Them chauvinistic bastards only launder money for drug dealers."

"What about Walter? His vig is probably the same as the banks'."

"Any businessman who borrows money from them ends up with them not only owning his *kishkas*, but also his soul."

"Do you know Mrs. Gallagher?"

"Never met the lady. All I know about her is that she used to work as a teachers' aide in one of the local junior high schools.

That was how she met Gallagher. He went there one day to address the school assembly on the evils of narcotics."

"You must have known Gallagher and Harris pretty well."

"What civilian really knows a cop? Gallagher would drop by every now and then. Sometimes he'd take a fancy to one of the girls." She scowled. "He didn't pay either. Harris? He only came in with Gallagher, never by himself. He was a quiet guy, he always seemed preoccupied. Whenever they were here, Gallagher did all the talking. Once I asked Harris if he had a tongue. Gallagher chimed in that he did the talking for both of them. 'But not the thinking,' Harris barked back. Gallagher got real pissed off at Harris over that remark. And I'll tell you something else—Harris was a cheap bastard. The few times he was in here with Gallagher they'd have drinks at the bar. Once Harris actually paid for their drinks and he consulted a tipping chart to see how much of a tip to leave."

"How come Harold Hunt is your accountant?"

"You know about Harold?" she said, surprised. "I'll tell ya, Joe Gallagher recommended him. Said he owed him a favor, and that he was a right guy and a good accountant. And he was right, Harold is a good accountant. I let him come by every now and then for a free screw. I'll tell you, Scanlon, with all this goodwill I pass out, I don't know how I'm able to make a living."

Scanlon heaved a weary sigh. He had wasted a lot of time and manpower on following Eddie Hamill and Luv-Joy leads. That was one of the painful realities of the Job. You can never tell where an investigative lead is going to take you. Most of them end up dead ends. And then there are those that will break a case wide open. The time had come for him to make amends with Gretta. Hookers are one of a cop's best sources of information. No cop wants to lose that source. A warm smile, a flash of teeth. "Can I buy you a drink?"

She shook her fist at his face. "Sometimes you make me so mad that I want to ram this down that beautiful throat of yours."

He guffawed. "Like I told you before, I have that effect on some people."

"What about the money you found in Gallagher's car? My money?"

"I'll see to it that you get it back."

"And you're going to buy me a drink? Here and now?"

"It'll be my pleasure."

"This I gotta see. A cop putting his hands into his own pockets for a change." She motioned wildly for the black waitress. "Siobbhan, a bottle of champagne. And give the bill to my friend here."

Yorkville had changed. The Von Westernvogen Brau Hall no longer existed. The slinking German spies of the forties had been relegated to the pages of pulp fiction. It was a little before ten P.M. when Scanlon drove his car into East Eighty-sixth Street. Human hulks slept on cardboard mattresses along the building sides and in doorways. Pimps lurked in the shadows, watching their women prowl their curbside turfs. A drunk was urinating between parked cars. Café Geiger and Kleine Konditorei were open, well-dressed people inside, savoring German beer and other delicacies.

Sally De Nesto lived in a building with small terraces, a condominium on Eighty-sixth between First and East End Avenue. Scanlon parked on Eighty-sixth Street, off First. He looked at the traffic sign. No Stopping No Standing No Parking 8 A.M. to 6 P.M. No Standing No Stopping 7 P.M. to Midnight. Towaway Zone.

He spent several moments deciphering the sign and decided that it was all right to park. He switched on the car's alarm system, bolted the steering wheel in place, clicked out the radio and tape deck and stashed them under the passenger seat.

A junkie sat in a shoe store's doorway smiling at his precautions. Scanlon saw him and pantomimed a pistol with his fingers and pegged three harmless shots at him. The junkie shrugged his hands slowly and nodded off. Scanlon felt like Charles Bronson. Death Wish One, Two, and Three. Whadda town!

Sally De Nesto greeted him at the door with cheerful enthusiasm, throwing her arms around him, bending her legs up off the floor.

"What got into you?" he exclaimed, bearing her into the apartment, kicking the door shut.

"I'm in a wonderful, upbeat mood, and I'm glad to see you. I like a quiet Saturday night. But not *too* quiet." She slid her hands from around his neck. "May I get you something to drink?"

"No thank you."

"Then in that case, let's you and me get right down to business." She untied the blue terry-cloth robe she was wearing.

A yelping siren pierced the night. The soft hum of an air conditioner added a sense of permanence to the darkened room. They lay on rumpled sheets, she with her head on pillows, her ankles crossed. Both of them were naked, both spent and relaxed, both coming down from a lovemaking high.

"Have you given any thoughts to what we discussed the last time?" she asked softly.

"Jane Stomer and me?"

"Yes."

"Sally, I told you, it's over. There is someone else in her life now."

"Like the man said, Tony, it's not over until it's over."

He glanced sideways at her. "And exactly what the hell does that mean?"

"It means that sometimes scorned women say untruths that they know will hurt, that are intended to hurt."

He flushed. "Jane Stomer isn't that kind of woman."

The darkness hid her smile.

He twisted his torso toward her. "Now I have a question for you."

"What?" she said, measuring the ceiling.

"Why the interest in my personal problems?"

"I'm interested in all my clients," she said defensively.

"But why? Tell me why, Sally."

She turned her head away from him, lapsed into a thoughtful silence. At length, she asked, "Have you ever wondered why I never drink?"

"I never really gave it any thought."

"I'm not allowed to drink because I take phenobarbital. I have epilepsy."

"Oh?" he said, at a loss.

"And did you know that I was once engaged to be married?"

"No, I didn't," he said, sensing a delicate moment.

"I was twenty-two and in love. His name was Carlo. We were going to live in Parsippany and have four children. Two boys and two girls. It was to have been a June wedding. Carlo had his best man deliver his Dear John letter to me three days before the wedding. I still have it. I read it over every now and then. It serves to remind me what the real world is like, if I'm ever tempted to forget."

Scanlon pulled her into his arms. "I'm sorry."

"I had my first seizure three months later. And one year after that I found myself living in Manhattan, alone and very lonely. I knew that with my illness my prospect of finding a husband was practically nil. And having those four children, well, that was just out of the question, wasn't it?

"Anyhow, one night I went to a singles bar. It was there that I met my blind shrink friend. He looked so helpless and alone standing at the bar by himself, shifting his weight from one foot to the other, fiddling around with his clothes, his head sort of lolling to one side, his eyes hidden behind dark glasses. I took one look at him and my heart broke for him. To live alone and in total blackness must be the ultimate loneliness, I thought. So I went up to him and introduced myself. I took him home with me." A wan smile came to her face. "He was the second man that I had gone to bed with. I was practically a virgin."

He pressed her head to his chest.

"In the morning he gave me money and I took it. He'd always paid for it and he didn't think there could be any other way for him. I felt strangely loved and needed. From then on I just sort of wandered into the business. He would send his handicapped patients to me and I would supply them with the therapy they so badly needed." She broke free of his embrace and pushed herself up in the bed, covering herself with a sheet. "My clients love me, Tony. And I love them. We need each other. They've become my extended family, and in a crazy way they have given purpose to my life."

"I guess we all have to play with the hole card that life deals us."

"That's my point, Tony. You don't. You can rid yourself of your handicap. You don't have to spend the rest of your life in the sexual underground."

"You make it sound so damn easy," he said lamely.

"It is, for you. All you have to do is to understand that we're all the products of our upbringing and then look inside yourself and see how your parents and your childhood experiences helped mold your adult life."

"You still haven't told me why the special interest in me."

She picked up his hand. "Because I love you enough to want to see you end your dependency on me. Don't you know that in order to receive love you first have to learn how to give it? When you share your life with someone you share it all, the good and the bad. You can't separate it, Tony. Your refusal to let Jane share your problem shut her out of your life. You isolated yourself from the rest of the world. And then you punished yourself by only being able to get it up with hookers. There is nothing physically wrong with you. If you can do it with me, you can do it with any woman." She screwed a finger into her temple. "It's all up there, kiddo. All you have to do is figure it out."

20

0840 hours. Monday. Eleven days had elapsed since the Gallagher/ Zimmerman hit. Scanlon was sitting in the squad room, a scone and a mug of coffee on a brown paper towel atop the desk's slide-out board. Hector Colon was sweeping out the Whip's office with a long-handled broom. It was his turn to do the morning house-keeping chores. Lew Brodie had taken the call from Christopher and Biafra Baby. They had reported on duty from the field. Brodie had made a Telephone Message and was now making a Log entry: "0800—Dets. Jones and Christopher reported on duty from the field. Re: canvass theatrical makeup stores—UF 61# 6794."

Three prisoners from the late tour were asleep on the floor of the detention cage. Their arresting officer, a cop with an altar boy's face, dozed in a chair awaiting the van that would transport them to Central Booking.

Maggie Higgins stood by the window, looking out at the sky.

Scanlon glanced over at her and noticed her forlorn look. He picked up his mug, got up, and ambled over to the urn. Bending to work the spigot, he said, "How's everything?"

When she turned to look at him he saw her red-rimmed eyes.

"Gloria and I are not going to make it living together." Her voice cracked. "The Job gets in the way."

He nodded and went back to the desk.

"*Teniente*, you got a call on four," Colon shouted from the Whip's office.

Herman the German sounded as though he were champing on a mouthful of Wiener Schnitzel. "I flew Harris on another detail."

"Thanks, Inspector," Scanlon said. "I'll keep you advised." He plunged down the disconnect button with his finger and made another hang-up call to Mrs. Gallagher. Lew Brodie came up to him and wanted to know if he still wanted him to plant on Linda Zimmerman. Scanlon told him he did. Brodie signed himself out in the Log: "0910—Det. Brodie to surveillance, Sutton Place area re: UF 61 # 6794." The van came to transport the prisoners and the arresting officer to Central Booking.

Realizing that they were at a dead end until he heard from Christopher and Biafra Baby, Scanlon telephoned his mother and promised he would try to make it to her house for Sunday dinner.

"I'll make lasagna," she promised.

Higgins began work on another term paper: "The Weaknesses of Line Inspection."

Hector Colon telephoned his girlfriend.

Scanlon remained in his office wrapped in his own thoughts. Flying Harris should unnerve him. Narcotics supervisors were seldom forced to put on the bag and flown out of their commands on uniform details. It shouldn't take Harris long to realize he was on somebody's shit list. And if he was guilty, he'd start to wonder where he made a mistake. And that was when he would become careless and do something dumb, Scanlon hoped.

Hanging up the phone, Hector Colon glanced around the squad room in search of mischief. He grabbed up the telephone and dialed Patrol Borough Brooklyn North, Uniform Force. "This is Inspector Suckieluski from the chief of patrol's office," he barked. "The chief wants the name and shield number of your borough AIDS coordinator." Pause. A mischievous grin came over his face. "Whaddaya mean you don't know? Don't you people in Brooklyn read the orders?" Pause.

Higgins turned in her seat and tossed a handful of paper clips at Colon.

Colon covered the mouthpiece and mouthed "screw you" to her. "Interim Order 8, current series, requires every borough commander to designate a borough AIDS coordinator. Well, you better. Have that Forty-nine on my desk by fifteen hundred today." He hung up the phone.

Higgins turned around in her seat, one arm hooked over the back of her chair. "Don't you think you're the funny one. Don't you know that cockroaches spread AIDS?"

Colon raised himself up out of his seat and lifted and shook his testes at her. "Wanna get into a dwarf-growing experiment with me?"

"Don't look now, Hector, but there's a nest in your brain."

The telephone message had read: "On Monday 6/29/86 at 0750 hours report to Captain Kuhn in front of the Soviet Mission to the United Nations on East 67th Street between Lexington and Third avenues in connection with demonstration to free Soviet Jewry. Uniform of the day, helmets and batons."

St. George Harris felt uncomfortable in the bag. He hated having to work in uniform. He was standing in front of the Soviet Mission along with the ten men who had been assigned to him, filling in their names, their shield numbers, their commands, and their present assignments on the UF 30, Detail Roster Assignment Sheet.

Completing the form, he thought briefly about how the Job had divided department forms according to the various branches of the Job. UF forms were for the Uniform Force. DD forms were for the Detective Division. He was a DD man. So what the hell was he doing in the bag, standing in front of this damn Commie mission, looking into the faces of ten asshole cops who were all trying to estimate just how much they would be able to get away with, and looking to get lost on him the minute he turned his back. He had flown two of his last three tours. Someone had a hard-on for him. Who? And more important, why? Herman the German? He didn't think so. He had seen the inspector this morning when he stopped by the One-fourteen to pick up his uniform and equipment. The inspector had smiled and waved at him. Scanlon? Maybe that pegleg guinea had gotten wise? Naw.

He dismissed that thought. Don't get stupid because of a few details, he warned himself.

Harris became conscious of the noise made by the demonstrators. A circle of jeering people, most of whom were carrying anti-Soviet placards, were marching behind police barricades on the east side of Lexington Avenue. Mounted policemen faced the demonstrators, the horses reined in tight.

His eyes slid over the faces of the ten cops lined up in front of him. Might as well let them know up front who the boss is, he thought. "Our post is the second line of barricades in the middle of the intersection on Lexington Avenue. No one gets past us, understand. I'm gonna be around, so make damn sure you're all out. I don't intend to go looking for anyone. If you're not out, I'll stick one up your ass. Any questions?"

A hairbag with tomato sauce on his shirt said, "You didn't assign us meals, Sarge."

"I'll do that later. Now take your posts."

Harris turned the Detail Roster in to the clerical man inside the mobile headquarters van that was parked across the street from the Soviet Mission. He wished he could get rid of the tremor of uneasiness in the pit of his stomach. I have to stay calm, he told himself, going to join his men on the barricade.

"*Abb-sah-loo-tah-mehn-teh nada*," Biafra Baby complained, slumping into a chair in the Whip's office. "It took us three days to canvass every damn makeup store in the city and we came up dry."

"Sorry, Lieutenant," Christopher said. "We gave it our best shot."

Taking in the brass buttons on Christopher's sky-blue jacket, trying to hide his disappointment, Scanlon said, "I know you did."

"Where do we go from here?" Higgins asked Scanlon.

Scanlon checked the time: 1640 hours. "We call it a day, Maggie."

The detectives slowly left for home, except Hector Colon, who lingered behind in the squad room. When Scanlon had finished signing a Five Colon walked into his office and said, "Lou, I got a problem."

"Let's hear it," Scanlon said.

"It's my girlfriend. I promised her a couple of months ago that I'd take her to an engagement party. It's tomorrow night. I put in a Twenty-eight a few weeks ago and you signed it."

Scanlon reached into one of the side drawers and took out the Squad's Diary. He flipped the pages to tomorrow's date and saw that Colon had taken three hours off at the end of his tour. "You got the time. What's the problem?"

"Well, with this Gallagher thing going down you might need me. I don't wanna leave you short-handed, so if you want, I'll pull the Twenty-eight."

Scanlon returned the Diary to the drawer. "Go to the party, Hector. We'll hold it down. Wouldn't want you to disappoint your lady love." Scanlon's expression did not betray his thoughts. A detective should know where his loyalty lay; if he didn't, then he would have to learn the hard way.

It was after 1900 when Lew Brodie ambled back into the squad room, slightly tipsy. "I might have somethin', Lou."

Scanlon was powdering his stump. "What?" he said, wondering what bar the detective had spent the past hour in.

"Around thirteen-thirty today Linda Zimmerman comes out of her aunt's apartment house and walks west on Fifty-first Street. I followed on foot. I trailed her to the Chemical Bank on Five-one and Third. She was inside for a long time, so I moseyed in for a look-see. I didn't see her, so I figured she was downstairs in the safety deposit boxes. Sure enough, after about ten minutes more she comes trudging up the stairs like an old lady and leaves the bank. I let her go, then hauled ass downstairs. Turns out that the guy who runs the vault room is retired from the Job. He let me sneak a look at her card. She rented the box on June 20 of this year, one day after her mother was killed. And, I'm willing to bet you, right after she cleaned out her mother's apartment. The vault guy told me that she comes there a lot and that she stays in the room with her box for long periods of time. Once she was inside for so long that he thought something had happened to her, so he went over to the door and listened. He could hear her talking to someone, like she was making a tape or something."

Scanlon rolled on his stump sock, leaned back in his seat, and slid his stump into the socket of his prosthesis. "I'd love to get a look inside that safety deposit box," he said, pushing his pants leg down.

"Yeah, but how? We'd need a search warrant, and we don't have any grounds to apply for one."

"Stay with her, Lew. Let me know the next time she goes there."

"You got it," Brodie said, leaving for the local watering hole.

It was a little past 2000 hours when Scanlon looked up from the report he was writing and saw George Harris standing in the doorway, watching him. The sergeant's head was cocked to the side, and he wore jeans, a blue work shirt, and cowboy boots.

I smoked the bastard out, Scanlon thought. "Long time no see, Sarge."

"I thought I'd catch you in," Harris said, moving to a chair in front of the desk. "You busy?"

"I'm plagiarizing the parameters of my semiannual Management by Objectives report from last year's plagiarized parameters." He leaned back, studying his visitor. "I reached the conclusion a long time ago that the Job is one big word blender. We keep throwing in the same words, mixing them up until they're a mix of polysyllabic bullshit."

"Ain't that the truth," Harris agreed, planting one boot firmly up against the front of the desk and leaning his chair back onto its hind legs.

Picking up the dictionary on his desk, Scanlon said, "A little game that I play with the pencil pushers in the big building. I always include a highfalutin word in the reports that I send downtown and then sit back and wait to see how long it takes some pencil pusher to steal it. Last years word was 'tableau.' It took them exactly three weeks to put 'tableau' in a department bulletin."

"What's the new word?" Harris asked, examining the tip of his boot.

"'Affranchise,'" Scanlon said. "Every member of the force has an obligation to affranchise the department from the evil influences of greed and corruption."

Harris's face remained blank. "Do the pencil pushers always steal your fancy words?"

"Yeah. Some people you can count on to always act the same way. Don't you agree?"

Harris's right eye twitched. "Maybe, I don't know. How's the case coming?"

313

"It ain't. I've got the feeling that it's going to end up collecting dust in the old record room."

"You've come up with nothing?"

"Not a helluva lot, I'm afraid."

"Did you make any tie-in with the Zimmerman hits?"

"The Nineteenth came up with a witness who saw the perp fleeing the scene."

Harris flopped his foot off the desk. "They got a good description?"

"Good enough to have a composite made." Scanlon leaned forward and took his time rummaging in the case folder. "Here it is." He pulled out the glossy black-and-white sketch. He examined the composite and then glanced from the sketch to Harris. He flattened his palm across the mouth of the man in the sketch, looked at Harris again, and said, "You know, Sarge, take off this guy's mustache and he'd be a dead ringer for you."

"Lemme see," Harris said, reaching across the desk. After scrutinizing the composite for several minutes, he tossed it back. "I guess you could say that he looks a little bit like me."

Scanlon took note of the twitch in Harris's eyes. "Tell me, Sarge, do you know anyone who owns a Browning automatic shotgun, Sweet Sixteen model?"

Harris rubbed his chin in concentration. "No, I can't say that I do. Why?"

"The ballistics boys think that was the weapon that was used to take Gallagher out."

"Are you checking the dealers?"

"There are too many of them. Besides, all anyone needs to buy a rifle or a shotgun is a forged or stolen driver's license. And the weapons were more than likely purchased out of state."

"Weapons?"

"The way I figure it, the same people took out Gallagher and the Zimmermans. A 5.56mm was used on the doctor and his wife. An assassin's rifle, capable of being broken down and assembled in a matter of a few minutes."

"What makes you so sure that the rifle was capable of being broken down?"

"Because the witness who saw the perp fleeing the Kingsley Arms stated that he was carrying an attaché case. What do you think the perp had in that case, gefilte fish?" He measured Harris. "How's Mrs. Gallagher?"

"All right, Lou. It takes time, but she's going to be fine."

"Did she return the children?"

"Yeah, she did. That was tough on her. But she decided that it was the best thing for them."

"Sounds like a strong-willed woman to me."

"She is that."

Scanlon placed his elbows on the desk and held his palms skyward. "Any chance she was stepping out on her husband?"

"No way. You asked me that once before—what made you ask again?"

Scanlon shrugged. "There is something about the lady that makes my stump itch."

"I hate to say it, Lou, but maybe you need a bath."

"You just might be right, Sarge," Scanlon said, getting up and going out into the squad room to sign out.

Harris accompanied him downstairs. Scanlon waved to the desk officer and he and Harris left the station house. A distant clap of thunder caught their attention. A radio car jerked to a stop at the curb, and both the driver and the recorder leaped out, slamming their respective doors. These were two pissed-off cops, Scanlon thought, watching the driver pull open the rear curb-side door to reveal a handcuffed man sprawled over the seat. The driver leaned into the car to take hold of the prisoner. The trussed-up man kicked out at the cop. The officer leaped back, out of the way of the thrashing feet.

The recorder of the radio car, a heavyset black cop with short gray hair, pushed his white partner aside, yanked the blackjack from its pocket in his trousers, and proceeded to beat the prisoner on the soles of his shoes. "You wanna kick a cop, haw, scumbag?"

"No more! No more!" begged the prisoner, pulling his feet away from the blackjack.

The cops dragged the man out of the car and stood him upright on the sidewalk. They took turns pushing and shoving the prisoner toward the station house. Scanlon stepped ahead of the prisoner and opened the station-house door. The black cop gave a final shove and the prisoner toppled onto the vestibule floor.

"These fucking polacks can't hold their firewater," the black cop groused, walking past the lieutenant.

"How're you getting along with Gallagher's replacement?" Scanlon asked, walking with Harris.

"I hardly see him. I came back off emergency leave and I've flown two out of my last three tours."

"There are a lot of details this time of the year—what with vacations and military leaves, there's always a shortage of bosses during the summer."

"I know that, Lou. But bosses in the junk squad never fly. Well, almost never."

Scanlon unlocked his car door and slid inside. "Maybe someone is mad at you?"

"I can't figure out why."

"If anything develops, I'll get in touch with you."

Harris nudged the car door closed and watched Scanlon bend forward to insert the key into the ignition.

Mary Ann Gallagher wore a widow's dress with black cloth buttons down the front. Around her neck hung a crucifix on a thin gold chain. She had no makeup on. On her left wrist she wore a watch with a gold link bracelet. She stood in the doorway of her Anthony Street apartment on the western edge of Maspeth Creek in Greenpoint, her anxious eyes sweeping the hallway over George Harris's shoulder. "Hello, George."

"How do you feel, Mary Ann?" Harris asked, stepping inside.

"Thank God, I'm coming along," she said, closing the door and resting her back against the portal.

Harris moved a short distance into the apartment and turned. "Are we alone?"

"The last of the biddies left a few minutes ago. But they could be back anytime."

He held out his arms, and she moved easily into his embrace, biting his shoulder right through his shirt, pressing into his body.

"I need to be inside you," he said.

"And I want you there. But first we have to talk." Taking hold of his hand, she pulled him into the bedroom and over to the bed, where they sat facing each other. "What's going on, George? I have this awful feeling that everything is about to fall apart."

"They have a witness who saw me running from the Kingsley Arms. They've made up a composite."

Her blue eyes blazed with anger, and she froze. "Does it look like you?"

"Without the mustache, yes. But the composite by itself doesn't mean a thing."

"Do you think that they're on to us?"

"No. None of them are smart enough to put it all together." He took out his pack of cigarettes, shook out a clipper, and lit it.

She fought to keep an expression of annoyance off her face. His cheapness, with cigarettes and everything else, disgusted her. He was really another version of Gallagher; like any cop he took everything he could get for free, and his idea of a present was some lousy blender that he had pried out of some merchant or a bottle of perfume that some bookmaker had given him. She fleetingly thought of the single airline ticket hidden in her hat box. Concorde to London. That was the way she was going to live. "Did you get rid of the guns and the rest of the stuff?"

"There hasn't been enough time to do it right. But don't worry. They're in a safe place where nobody is going to find them."

"Safe place, bullshit, George! I told you to get rid of them a week ago."

"I love you, Mary Ann, and I don't like it when you yell at me."

"You'll like it less if Scanlon gets wise to us."

"That dumb guinea can only think in guinea. He's no threat."

"Your dumb guinea didn't strike me as being so dumb. What about those assignments you've been getting?"

"Mary Ann, if they thought for one minute that I was responsible they'd be all over me, and I can assure you, they'd do a lot more than fly me on a few details." He stretched out over the bed and rested his head on her lap. She began to rub his forehead.

"You realize that you almost blew the whole thing by calling out 'Hey you,'" he said.

She bent down and kissed his nose. "I'm sorry, darling. I just couldn't control myself. I wanted him to look into my eyes and see who was sending him to hell. That man kept me like a fucking slave for years. I hated him and I'm glad he's dead, that miserable son of a bitch."

"You should have done what you came to do and left without

saying a word, like we planned. It was supposed to look like an attempted robbery."

"I know," she snapped. "Just don't keep harping on it. I said I was sorry."

"But because of that one mistake Scanlon realized that it was a hit and not a robbery attempt. And it would only have been a matter of time until someone thought of the money you were entitled to as Joe's widow. And that's a powerful motive. So because of you I had to run out and do the Zimmermans to throw them off the track, keep them confused. I didn't exactly enjoy doing that, Mary Ann."

"But you did it."

"Yes, I did it. I did it because I love you, because I want to have a wonderful life with you, free of any money troubles."

"I know you love me, George. And I love you too." She stopped massaging his head. "I haven't been laid in days."

"I'm really not in the mood anymore. Let me relax a little bit, first."

"I want it now, George," she said, reaching under her dress and pulling off her underpants and stuffing them under the pillow. "Here, let me get you in the mood." She reached down and, opening the top of his jeans, pushed his pants down, exposing him. She went down on him and ravenously sucked him hard. She flung herself across the bed, tossed up her dress, and gasped as he entered her body.

When she had slaked her thirst for him, she rested her head on a pillow and said, "I haven't been that horny in ages. I can relax now."

He lay next to her. "I love you very much, Mary Ann."

"And I love you, George."

"It's funny how Gallagher threw us together." Harris scowled. "It was a mutual hate society."

"If only they'd known what holy Joe was like at home."

"He used to love to put me down in front of the men. He'd countermand my orders just to make me look like a nincompoop."

"I know, darling, I know," she said, leaning over to kiss his cheek. "Let's not talk about him anymore." In a burst of gaiety, she said, "I got a check from the Lieutenants' Benevolent Association for five thousand dollars."

"That's only the beginning, my love."

"Tell me again how much."

"Close to a million dollars, practically tax-free."

"A million dollars? I can't even begin to think in those sums."

"Well, you'd better get used to thinking in those sums, because we're going to be rich."

She glanced at his contented face, a disingenuous smile pinching her mouth. "Yes, darling, *we* are going to be rich." She sat up on the bed, and her fingers rubbed his forehead soothingly. "Do you think anyone suspects that we're more than friends?"

"Naw, no one thinks of us in those terms. You're a God-fearing grieving Irish widow who thinks sex is unholy, and I'm your husband's friend. Besides, I got a girlfriend. Luise Bardwell. It's perfect."

"But you're not seeing her anymore?"

"Shit no. She served her purpose. The main thing was for Scanlon and the rest of those assholes not to connect us."

"Do you know when I first felt close to you?"

"No. But I do remember that we used to talk for hours while Joe was out doing his thing."

"It was when you first confided to me that you had never . . . you know, gone down on a woman."

He reached up and brushed the back of his hand across her warm cheek. "I remember that night."

Her voice dropped. "Did you ever do that to Luise Bardwell?"

"No, Mary Ann, I didn't. You're the only woman I've ever done that with."

"Do you enjoy doing that with me?"

A throatiness came into his voice. "I love it."

"Would you like to do it to me now?" she cooed, bending and kissing his neck. "I have all your love inside me and I'm all warm and juicy."

He pressed her face to him. "Yes."

She pushed back from him, letting his head slide off her lap. She lifted up her dress and, inching forward, straddled his face.

The prosthesis stood on the floor beside Sally De Nesto's bed. He had been watching it for the better part of one hour, once again going over his past. If he had not lost his leg, would he still have developed erectile dysfunction somewhere down the line? Why was sex so damn complicated? It had more wrinkles than the Job.

"Can't you sleep?"

He looked down at her curled-up form. "Just thinking."

"Would you like to make love?"

"I'm really not in the mood."

She sat up, hoisting the sheet across her chest. "What's the matter, Tony?"

"I'm not my own man anymore. I'm dependent on that hunk of fiberglass for mobility and on you for sex."

"Am I so terrible?"

"Terrible? You're far from terrible. You're a kind, considerate woman."

"But?"

"I need more. I need someone to love, share my life with, grow old with."

She looked down at her knees, just shapes under a sheet. "We all want to be loved, Tony. But we have to settle for what we can get. Some people get their love from pets. I've found mine with handicapped people who need me." She leaned her head against his shoulder. "If I were you, I'd go after Jane Stomer. Pretend like you've just met her. Women like to be pursued. Take my word for it. Send her flowers. Every woman loves flowers."

"I had an erotic dream about Jane. It was so real that I can remember asking myself if I was dreaming or awake. And I can remember deciding that it was real, that it was actually happening. I soiled the sheets."

"Perhaps that's a good sign. You might be getting a handle on your problem."

"Then why do I feel so lousy?"

"You gotta feel lousy before you feel better. I don't know why things are that way, but they are."

"I've also come to realize just how dependent I've become on you. It's as though I need you to give me a fix that will restore my self-confidence as a man, and enable me to get through the day."

"Everyone needs a friend now and then." She slid her hand across his chest, hugging him.

"It's time for me to start standing on my own two feet without any help. I have to try and get my act together. Can you understand that, Sally?"

"Yes I can. And I want you to know that I'll always be here for you if you need me." She hugged him. "I want to make love to you, Tony."

"I'm really not in the mood."

She worked her hand down under the sheet. "Let me see what I can do about that."

21

A warm, pleasant breeze laced with summer scents flowed through the open windows of the Nine-three Squad. The detectives went about their morning routines, checking their pigeon holes for department mail, notifications, subpoenas, love letters. Lew Brodie had called in from the field. He was on his way to plant on Linda Zimmerman's aunt's house on Sutton Place South.

Higgins had swept out the squad room this Tuesday morning and was leaning on a broom handle, staring thoughtfully at the row of file cabinets. She leaned the broom against the side of a desk and moved up to the Vulva File. She took out a Twenty-eight and filled in the pedigree information at the top of the Request for Leave of Absence form, leaving the space for the date and time of absence blank. She signed the form and took out the Vulva File, a number two department ledger. She flipped it open and wrote Valerie Clarkson's name, address, and telephone number on the next unused line. She placed the Twenty-eight between the pages along with the rest of the unused forms and closed the book.

Turning away from the file, she saw Scanlon watching her. "There are eight million stories in the naked city, Lou."

"Ain't that the truth," Scanlon said, tossing his report into the basket for the department mail.

Howard Christopher sat off in the corner watching "The Morning Show" on television, a mug of cinnamon tea resting on his knee. Scanlon noticed that Biafra Baby was among the missing. He asked Christopher if he had heard from him. "He's on the way in, Lieutenant. He called a few minutes ago to say that he'd be late. He had to drive his daughter to her ballet lesson."

Scanlon received several telephone calls. The first was from Herman the German, who wanted to know if Scanlon wanted him to continue flying Harris. Scanlon told him that he did. The CofD wanted to know if there had been any new developments. Scanlon told him that there hadn't been, and the CofD reminded him of the PC's warning not to move on Harris or Mrs. Gallagher without some physical evidence to substantiate the allegations. MacAdoo McKenzie called next and wanted to know if anything new had been developed. The last call was from Jack Fable. When Scanlon told him that there was nothing new to report, Fable told him that his detectives had developed several leads on the necrophiliac who had been using the Nineteenth as his playpen.

"An arrest is imminent," Fable said mockingly.

Scanlon hung up. He thought of Sally De Nesto's advice to court Jane Stomer and send her flowers. He picked up the telephone and dialed Frank Randazzo, a florist at the north end of the precinct. He took care of the precinct's floral needs. When Randazzo came onto the line, Scanlon said, "*Ciao, Frank, sono Tony Scanlon del novantatreesimo squadrone; come stai? E la famiglia, tutti bene? Per favore, Frank, mada una dozzina di rose rosse alla Signorina Jane Stomer all'ufficio del Procuratore Generale a 100 Center Street al palazzo del Tribunale, firma il biglietto 'Con Amore, Scanlon,' e mandami il conto qua al mio ufficio. Grazie, Frank, a Ciao.*"

Scanlon hung up and saw Biafra Baby standing in the doorway watching him. The detective strutted up to the desk. "I think that I might have something."

"Let's hear it."

"My wife is a big believer in all that family togetherness bullshit and likes to keep a running dialogue going around the dinner table. Last night as I was scooping up some mashed potatoes and telling them about how me and Christopher canvassed all them makeup stores with negative results, my wife stops cutting her lamb chop, looks me in the eye, and says as calm as shit, 'Try Bob Brown on West Forty-ninth Street.'"

"Who is Bob Brown?"

"He runs a theatrical mail-order house that sells makeup and rents stage props to theaters and schools."

"Wasn't he on the list of makeup stores that I gave you?"

"Negative. Brown isn't listed in the Yellow Pages under Theatrical Makeup. He's listed under Cosmetics and Wigs."

Scanlon slapped the side of his head.

Biafra Baby continued, "My wife is a schoolteacher. That's how she knew about Brown. Her school gets their stage props from Brown." He patted down his hair. "Then I remembered that you had told me that Gretta Polchinski had told you that Mrs. Gallagher had once been a teacher's aide. So after I dropped my daughter off at her ballet lesson, I telephoned Brown."

"And?"

"He be's waiting for us."

Scanlon lurched out from behind his desk. The phone on his desk rang. He looked at it, hesitated, and snapped it up.

"This is Thomas Tibbs, the man who saw the killer running from the candy store."

You're also the married banker from Scarsdale who is making it with Sigrid Thorsen, Scanlon thought. "I know who you are, Mr. Tibbs."

"Lieutenant, do you remember when I told you that there was something strange about the way the killer ran to the van? And I couldn't put my finger on exactly what it was."

"I remember."

"I now know what it was that bothered me. On last night's eleven-o'clock news they had a clip on the cross-county marathon in Westchester County. It came to me as I watched the runners."

"What came to you, Mr. Tibbs?" Scanlon said, motioning to Biafra Baby to take the keys for the Squad's car off the hook.

"I realized that women run differently than men. They keep their arms tucked into their sides, and their torsos have a distinctive sway when they run. The person I saw running from that candy store might have looked like a man, but he ran like a woman."

Scanlon thanked the witness for taking the time to call. He

pulled over the case folder, wrote the time and date on the inside flap, and added, "Thomas Tibbs called to state that perp who he observed running from scene ran with a female gait." He slapped the folder closed and left the squad room with Biafra Baby.

The glass sign on the door read: Bob Brown Wigs and Cosmetics. The detectives stepped into a long narrow corridor. The wall on their left was covered with autographed photos of show-business personalities wearing makeup. To their right was a counter that looked out into a work area where several women sat weaving wigs. In the rear of the work area were portable storage racks with rows of wigs set on head mannequins.

Bob Brown was a gaunt man with a flat nose and a receding hairline. "You the police detective who called?" Brown said, coming up to the counter.

Biafra Baby flashed his shield. "I called you. This is Lieutenant Scanlon."

Brown leaned out over the counter and pointed to a door about six feet away. "I'll buzz you in."

The three men sat among the wigmakers. "What can I do for you?" Brown asked.

Scanlon was fascinated by the dexterity of the wigmakers' hands. "We'd like to ask you a few questions concerning your business."

"What sort of questions?" Brown asked, taking up a wig and pushing a long hooked needle through it.

"How do you get your customers?" Scanlon inquired.

"We're well known in theatrical and educational circles. Most of our business is done by mail."

"Do you get many walk-ins?" Scanlon asked.

"A few," Brown said, pushing the needle through the skin. "But most of our customers order from our catalog."

"Then you must maintain a file on your customers," Scanlon said.

"Of course," Brown said. "That's how we know who to send our catalog to."

"Could someone call you up and ask you to mail them makeup?" Scanlon asked.

"Sure," Brown answered, "but they'd have to know what they wanted, and they'd have to send payment before we'd send out the merchandise, unless they were a regular customer."

"Don't you bill most of your customers?" Biafra Baby asked.

"Only the schools, theaters, and individuals with whom we've dealt with before." Brown stopped working and looked at the policemen. "Look, gentlemen, I've got a lot to do, so why not tell me what you want?"

Scanlon said, "We'd like to take a look at your orders for the past few years."

"Why?" Brown asked, picking up the needle and threading it with hair.

"It has to do with a case we're working on," Biafra Baby said.

"I would not want my company to become mixed up in a civil suit because I gave information to the police."

"Mr. Brown," Scanlon said, putting on his serious face, "we're working on a case of child molestation where the perpetrator dons makeup to change his appearance and then forces children to commit unnatural acts. We'd really appreciate your help."

"How disgusting," Brown said, putting down the wig and needle. "Of course I'll help."

They followed Brown through a labyrinth of storage racks containing cartons of makeup. Scanlon noticed some of the labels: Crepe Wool. Rubber Mask Grease. Creme Highlight. Shadow Colors.

Brown led the detectives across the concrete floor to his office, which consisted of two old desks fitted side by side into an alcove in the wall. He opened the bottom drawer of one of the desks and took out five bulging manila folders. He plopped them down. "Help yourself," Brown said. "These are the individual orders for the past two years. If you don't find what you want there, I'll show you the institutional orders." He left the detectives and returned to his wigmaking.

The detectives set about separating the order forms in each folder into stacks. Slowly, meticulously, they went about scrutinizing each form. They had been at it for about thirty minutes when Biafra Baby snatched a form up from one of his stacks, studying it. "Lou, does 34-16 Astoria Boulevard sound familiar to you?"

Scanlon repeated the address aloud. The detectives looked at each other. "The One-fourteen," Scanlon blurted.

The order form had been typed. A Mr. Raymond Gilligan had

ordered crepe wool, medium-gray beard stubble, adhesive stick, hair whiteners, latex, cosmetic pencils, nose putty, rubber mask grease, molding putty, and spirit gum. He had also ordered a man's wig and a walrus mustache.

Scanlon hastily signaled for Brown to join them.

"What can you tell me about this order?" Scanlon asked Brown.

The makeup man took the order form and looked it over. "Mr. Gilligan obviously wanted to make himself appear older," Brown said, handing Scanlon back the form.

"Do you have any recollection of filling this order?" Scanlon asked.

"None whatever," Brown said. "We fill hundreds of orders a month."

"What is crepe wool?" Biafra Baby said.

Brown went up to one of the storage cartons and took out a package of crepe wool. It looked like sticks of licorice. He removed the wool from its cellophane wrapping and began unraveling the fibers, spreading them apart. The wool began to curl and resemble beard hair. "It's used to make beards and mustaches." He strung the fiber over his clean-shaven face. "See, now I have a beard. It's applied with spirit gum."

"How would a person not in the business find out what to order and how to apply makeup?" Scanlon asked.

"There are a lot of books on the subject," Brown said. "In fact, I've written a few myself."

Biafra Baby pointed to the order form in Scanlon's hand. "All that makeup is used to make a person look older?"

"Most of it." Brown spread his hands. "I mean, some of that stuff has several uses."

"May we borrow this form, Mr. Brown?" Scanlon said. "It might aid us in our search for this pervert."

"Take it with you. I'm glad to help."

Scanlon went up to the packing table and tore a sheet of wrapping paper from the roller and wrapped the order form in paper. He turned to Brown. "One more favor. May I use your phone?"

The clerical man at the One-fourteen remembered Ray Gilligan. He had worked sector Henry Ida for sixteen years until he developed the Big C four years ago, the clerical man told Scanlon. "Ray went out of the picture three years ago."

Every patrol precinct in the city maintains mailboxes for its cops. Pigeonholes with three or four letters of the alphabet stapled under each hole. It would have been an easy matter for Harris to have sent the order form in the name of Raymond Gilligan and then to check the G mail slot daily for the package, Scanlon knew. He turned to the makeup man. "Can you tell me how this order was paid for?"

Brown removed an accounting ledger from the desk and flipped clumps of pages until he came to the page he wanted. He moved his finger down a column of names, came to Gilligan, slid his finger over to the numbered column, and said, "A bank money order. And there is no way I can tell you the name of the bank."

The Latent Section of the NYPD is located in Room 506 of the big building. Before going there Scanlon and Biafra Baby stopped off on the thirteenth floor to see the CofD. Scanlon asked Chief Goldberg to make a personal call to the CO of the Identification Section, of which the Latent Section was a part, and request the CO of Identification to render all possible assistance to Scanlon and Biafra Baby, who were conducting a confidential investigation under the personal control and supervision of the CofD.

Chief of Detectives Goldberg chewed on his cigar, grabbed up the phone, and, when he got connected, barked, "Harry, I'm sending two of my people around to see you. Do whatever the fuck they ask you to do, and keep your mouth shut about it, or I'll personally stick one up your ass."

Riding down in the elevator, Biafra Baby nudged Scanlon. "Goldberg's a class act."

"He's certainly a hard one to follow," Scanlon said.

The CO of the ID Section was waiting for them when they stepped off the elevator. He led them into the Latent Section, assigned a man to help them, and excused himself because he had a lot of work waiting for him. The fingerprint man who had been assigned to them had green eyes and appeared nervous.

"This is a confidential investigation," Scanlon said. "If word leaks out, the PC and the CofD are both going to be highly pissed off at you."

"Don't worry, Lou. I don't feature being flopped back into the bag. I like working days with weekends off."

"Then we understand each other," Scanlon said.

Scanlon had the fingerprint man check the name index for George Harris's fingerprint formula. Armed with the filing code, the fingerprint man was able to pull Harris's fingerprint chart from the million-plus on file. Scanlon signed the card out of file with a confidential index number. Next the fingerprint man checked the criminal and civilian name file for Mary Ann Gallagher. The dead lieutenant's widow had no record with the NYPD.

When they reached Room 506 the fingerprint man unwrapped the package that Scanlon had handed him and removed the order form with tweezers. "You're interested in knowing if Harris's prints are on this form, right?" asked the fingerprint man.

"Correct." Scanlon turned to Biafra Baby. "Better call the Squad and let them know where we are."

Biafra Baby nodded and moved off.

The fingerprint man went up to a dollhouselike contraption with an open front that sat on top of one of the workbenches. He fastened one end of the order form to one of the three clothespins that hung from the house's ceiling. He attached the other two pins to the order form. He took a tiny dish that resembled a Chinese duck-sauce bowl and dumped crystalline iodine into it. He put the dish inside the house, directly under the hanging order form. "The iodine fumes will bring out any latents," the fingerprint man said. Scanlon watched as the orange outlines began to appear: loops, arches, central pocket loops, whorls.

"All the lines are busy," Biafra Baby called over to Scanlon.

"Keep trying," Scanlon called back.

The fingerprint man unfastened the order form and placed it down on a glass plate that lay on the workbench next to the dollhouse. He picked up a second glass plate and covered the first, then sealed the edges with rubber-tipped clips.

"Why the glass plates?" Scanlon asked.

"It preserves the latents. We can also photograph them, and if we have to, at some later date, we can present them in court." He looked at Scanlon, a smug smile on his lips. "The Best Evidence Rule, Lou. Remember? Present the original trace evidence before the court."

Leaning over the plates, the fingerprint man glided his magnifying glass on a stand over the glass, examining the impressions through the eyepiece.

"I told Higgins where we are," Biafra Baby said, returning.

"Got a lot of prints here, Lou," the fingerprint man said. "And from the diversity of pattern types I'd say that many different people have handled this piece of paper."

"For now, I'm only interested in Harris," Scanlon said. "By the way, who maintains the Typewriter File these days?"

The NYPD files sample type of every typewriter that is used in the department. Each letter and character has individual characteristics that can be positively identified as belonging of a specific typewriter.

Without looking up from the linen tester, the fingerprint man said, "We maintain it."

"I'd like the type on that order form checked against the Typewriter File," Scanlon said.

"No problem, Lou," replied the fingerprint man.

A voice called out, "Is there a Lieutenant Scanlon here?"

The bank was nestled on the ground floor of a high-rise apartment building.

Lew Brodie was waiting in the corridor outside the vault room. "She's been inside for almost a half hour," Brodie said to the approaching lieutenant.

"I left Biafra Baby at the Latent Section and got here as fast as I could," Scanlon said. He looked through the security glass into the vault room. "How many people are in there?"

"We got lucky," Brodie said. "Zimmerman and the vault man. Some old guy just left."

"Let's get in there now," Scanlon said. "I want to see what she has in that box."

"Lou," Brodie said, taking the Whip by the arm, "you sure you wanna go in after her? We don't have a search warrant, and she ain't no bimbo."

"We don't have one shred of evidence, not against Harris, not against Mrs. Gallagher, not against anyone. We have a suspicion that Harris and Gallagher might be the perps, but I could be wrong about them. And then where do we go? Linda Zimmerman cleaned out her mother's apartment the day after she was killed. She rented a safety deposit box the same day. She could very well be involved in the murders."

Lew Brodie motioned for the vault man to open the door. The retired cop, a big man with a sagging neck and a pallid complexion, opened the door. "I don't want any trouble," he said to Brodie.

Placing a calming hand on the vault man's shoulder, Brodie said, "Ain't gonna be no trouble."

Scanlon looked around the vault room, his gaze coming to rest on the huge stainless-steel door. "What room is she in?" he asked the vault man.

"Number four," answered the retired cop. "No trouble, right? I'm a little nervous. I'd forgotten what it's like to be in the Job."

Scanlon motioned to Brodie and the vault man to remain where they were, and padded over to cubicle four. He listened at the door. He heard muffled sounds, and strained in vain to make out the intelligible words. Should he barge in on her, or should he wait for her to leave? He never felt any hesitation when he had to lean on a wise guy or anyone who lived on the fringe of the law. They were fair game and they knew how the game was played. Linda Zimmerman was different. Or was she? Was she a victim or was she a guileful woman involved in murder? He had to satisfy himself which it was.

A rustling came from inside the room. Scanlon turned quickly and shooed Brodie and the vault man from sight.

Linda Zimmerman gasped when she opened the door and saw Scanlon. She darted back inside, pulled the door behind her. He threw his weight against the door and pushed it open before she could lock it.

It was a cramped space with a desk built into the wall and a straight-back chair padded in green leather. She cowered against the wall, the thin green box clutched to her chest, her face furrowed with confusion. "Please leave me alone."

"Linda, I need to know what you have in that box. Knowing might help me get the people responsible for taking your family away from you."

"It's personal," she said, frantically looking around the room for an escape hatch.

"Linda, please allow me to look inside that box."

"No! I want to call my attorney. How dare you invade my

privacy?" She tried to push past him but he blocked her path. She pulled back from him. As she did, he reached out and yanked the box from her grip. She leaped at him, beating him on the head and shoulders, screaming at him to give her back her property. He pushed her away from him. Holding her at arm's length with one hand, he put the box down on the desk and with his free hand flicked the hasp off the staple.

"Don't!" she beseeched him.

He flipped open the lid. The box contained four Ziploc plastic bags filled with gray ash. She pulled away from his grip and slumped down into the chair, defeated. He prodded the bags with his fingers. He could feel bits of calcareous material. In one horrible moment of recognition his heart sank with guilt.

She was crying, talking to the bags of ash. "Daddy, they won't leave us alone."

Scanlon slapped the lid closed. "Linda, please forgive me. In my zeal...I...." For the first time in his life he was sorry that he was a cop. For the first time in his life he hated the Job. He pressed her head to him, consoling her.

"I wanted them to be safe. They were all that I had. I came here to talk to them, the way I did when I was a girl. I wanted them to be together, always."

Scanlon slid his hand behind him, reaching for the doorknob. He turned it and left the room, leaving her with her head atop the box, crying softly. He stormed out of the vault room.

"Whaddya find out?" Brodie said, hurrying beside him down the corridor.

"Nothing. Let's get the hell out of here."

"But Lou," Brodie persisted, "she must have been doing something in there."

"Goddamnit! I said *nothing*. Now let's go. Biafra Baby is waiting for us in the Latent Section."

The fingerprint man used a Pentel sign pen to rule off the points of comparison. "These characteristics match up with the ring, middle, and forefinger of Harris's right hand," the fingerprint man told Scanlon.

"We hit pay dirt, Lou," Brodie said.

"Maybe," Scanlon said, bending to examine the latent fingerprints. He noted the different points of comparison that had been ruled off on the glass. An abrupt ending ridge. A dot. A short ridge. A meeting of two ridges. The core. The delta.

Looking up from the glass, Scanlon asked, "What about the type?"

The fingerprint man said, "I enlarged and measured the writing. It was one of those check-off order forms, so it didn't present much of a standard to work with. So I had to make do with the name and address. 'Raymond Gilligan' and the Astoria address contained four A's, three L's, three I's, two O's, and two D's. I compared the characteristics of those letters against the writings in our files and came up with a match. An Underwood, assigned to the Seventeenth Narcotics District. Serial number 38J93873."

Chief of Detectives Goldberg trudged six paces ahead of Scanlon into the PC's office.

The police commissioner was standing in his sun-drenched office reading a legal brief. Not looking up from the page, he motioned the two men into chairs. "Tell me what you have, Lou," Gomez said, tossing the brief onto his desk.

Scanlon began: "I've just come from the Latent Section..." When he finished, he added, "I know that it's circumstantial, but I believe that we now have enough to move on Harris."

"I'm not so sure," the PC said. "You have no evidence linking Harris to Mrs. Gallagher. In fact, you don't have anything against Mrs. Gallagher. As for the fingerprints, Harris's weren't the only ones on that form. And anyone assigned to the Seventeenth District could have typed out that makeup order. Including Joe Gallagher."

"I'm aware of all that, Commissioner," Scanlon said. "But I'm still convinced that evidence exists that does link Harris and Mrs. Gallagher to the murders. And I want to throw a scare into them that will make them run to destroy that evidence."

"And just suppose that they don't scare, Lieutenant?" Gomez said. "And suppose that they have already destroyed the evidence? Suppose that the evidence never existed in the first place? And I want you to further suppose that we make a move on a lieutenant's widow, the widow of a decorated police lieutenant, and it backfires

333

on us, and we all end up at the other end of a civil suit. Then what, Lieutenant?"

"Then we'd be up the creek without a paddle," Scanlon said.

"Precisely my point." The PC looked at the CofD. "What do you think of all this, Chief?"

The CofD cupped his kneecaps and leaned forward. "I think that we should go with what we got. Circumstantial evidence can convict, if you have enough of it."

"If I give the green light, how would you proceed?" Gomez asked Scanlon.

Scanlon told him, adding, "I'd like Sergeant Harris to be flown on a detail tomorrow that ends around fifteen hundred hours, someplace where Mrs. Gallagher can't telephone him directly."

"Orchard Beach," CofD Goldberg said.

22

It drizzled that Wednesday morning, and was unseasonably cool. Scanlon darted into the Nine-three station house and turned to watch the rain make tiny dimples in the puddles. Shaking drops from his jacket, he looked up at the heavy clouds. Damn rain had better stop, he thought. All he needed now was for the rain to continue and the Orchard Beach detail to be canceled because of rain. It was 0747 hours. The First Platoon was on duty until 0800. Day-tour cops lolled around the sitting room drinking coffee, consulting scratch sheets, the sports pages.

The late-tour desk officer ruled off his final entry. The cop on switchboard duty yawned and stretched. The one-twenty-four man stuffed the night's mail into the mailbag. The desk officer stood and arched his back. Glancing behind him, the DO saw Scanlon reading the orders. "What are you doing in so early?"

"Couldn't sleep," Scanlon said, returning the clipboard to its hook.

"Must be an insomnia epidemic. All your people are in early. Anything up?"

"Nothing. Detectives love the Job. We can't get enough of it."

"Bullshit."

Going into his office, Scanlon rolled the blackboard away from the wall and pinned the maps that he had ordered from the Cartography Unit to its wooden frame. Yetta Zimmerman's candy store was circled in black, along with the location where the van had been found. The Gallagher residence was circled in green. Harris's official residence on Staten Island and his splash pad on Ocean Avenue were circled in brown.

Leaning against his desk, studying the maps, he ran it over in his head, how he thought the crime had gone down. Somewhere along the line, Gallagher must have mentioned to Harris or to his wife that he was delivering Andrea Zimmerman's birthday cake to her grandmother. They saw this as their opportunity to kill Gallagher. Mrs. Gallagher must have applied the makeup in the van or at home. Probably in the van on the way to the candy store. She would not have wanted to take the chance of anyone seeing her leaving her apartment in a disguise. Harris lets her off near the park and goes and sits on the candy store. When he sees Gallagher carrying the cake box, he leaves and gives her some prearranged signal.

The more he ran it before his mind's eye the more he realized that it had the right feel. And smart cops heed the feel, those moments of intuitive insight born of experience. Many times the feel for a case will go against logic and common sense. Common sense would dictate that Harris would have deep-sixed the evidence. But Scanlon knew that any chintzy bastard who clipped and saved cigarette butts and who used a tipping chart for a lousy bar tab was not about to toss expensive weapons into the drink. Besides, the cocky son of a bitch probably thought he was too smart to get caught.

Herman the German telephoned at 0820 to tell Scanlon that Harris had been flown on the Orchard Beach detail. Hundreds of thousands of people flock to the city's beaches and parks every summer. The NYPD assigns hundreds of policemen from around the city to the beaches and parks for crowd and traffic control.

Scanlon glanced out the window. "We're lucky it stopped raining—otherwise the detail might have been canceled." He asked the inspector if he had spoken to Harris.

"Just as you asked me to. I caught up with him as he was on his way up to the locker room. I told him I had no choice but to fly him out. I told him that while he was out on emergency leave connected with Joe Gallagher's death the other sergeants in the unit had all become embroiled in heavy investigations and that I didn't want to pull them off to fill summer details. So it was his turn in the barrel, I told him."

"Did he buy it?"

"He seemed to."

"Good. We'll put him at ease and then yank the rug out from under him."

"Are you sure you want me to visit Mrs. Gallagher? I was thinking that it might be better if you saw her."

"It'll be more natural coming from you," Scanlon said into the mouthpiece. "I hope she'll know how to get in touch with Harris."

"She was married to a cop long enough. She'll know."

After Scanlon hung up he played with the dial, trying to decide whether or not to call Linda Zimmerman and apologize for intruding upon her privacy yesterday at the bank. His hand slid from the dial. It was better to let time heal whatever wounds he had reopened. He wondered if Jane Stomer had received his flowers, and if she would call him to thank him. He telephoned his mother to see if she was all right and to tell her that he loved her, and to explain why he would not be able to come for dinner this Sunday. He telephoned Jack Fable at the Nineteenth Squad and went over the arrangements they had made late last night.

Three hours passed.

Higgins swept out the squad room. Christopher watched television. Biafra Baby took a shopping list from his wife over the phone, and then swept out the squad room. Brodie came up to Biafra Baby and asked him to give him a piss call at 1345, and then Brodie slipped into the dormitory to sack out.

Hector Colon telephoned his wife and told her it looked as though he were going to have to work late into the night on the Gallagher homicide and he probably would sleep in the dormitory. His wife asked him to call her in the morning to let her know that he was all right. He hung up, then telephoned his girlfriend at her cashier job at Macy's and told her he would pick her up at five o'clock. Higgins swept out the squad room again. Like everyone else she was nervous and trying to keep occupied.

At 1400, Scanlon stepped out of his office and beckoned the detectives inside.

"Let's go over it one more time," Scanlon said, tacking a map of Orchard Beach up on the blackboard. Higgins and Biafra Baby were to plant on the Gallagher residence. Christopher and Lew Brodie were to take in Harris's splash pad on Ocean Avenue. Jack Fable and two of his Nineteenth Squad detectives were to plant on Harris's Staten Island residence. Fable had received photos of Harris in the department mail.

The four anticrime cops that Scanlon had gotten on a steal from Chief McMahon, the Bronx borough commander, had been given photographs of Harris and Mrs. Gallagher and assigned to various locations in and around Orchard Beach. There were only four avenues off the beach that led to the major parkways. Scanlon had one anticrime man assigned to each of those avenues. One cop was going to follow Harris out of the parking field. As Harris drove past the exits leading onto the parkways the cop assigned to the exit would leave and join in with the other mobile unit.

Although trailing a car was difficult to coordinate, Scanlon knew from experience that it usually got the best results. That was because the bad guy was on guard, but scared. Harris would be on the watch for a tail, but he really did not want to spot one, so he wouldn't, Scanlon hoped. The cops assigned to Orchard Beach had been assigned two department taxis, one mail truck, and a tan Buick for the surveillance.

"If everything goes according to plan, and Mrs. Gallagher takes the bait, then Harris is going to try and bolt the beach detail early," Scanlon said. "And when he does, the tail men are going to be waiting."

"I sure hope these tail guys know their stuff," Brodie said.

"Chief McMahon assured me that they were the best tail men he had," Scanlon said.

"They had better be," Biafra Baby said. "Harris ain't no pussy-cat."

"I want you all to sign out radios. Make sure the batteries are charged," Scanlon said. "We're going to be using one of the closed channels. Number three. Our call letters will be Renegade." He thought a second and added, "I like Renegade—it seems appropriate for this caper." He assigned them call numbers.

"What about the men from the Bronx and the Nineteenth Squad?" Biafra Baby asked.

"Herman the German met with them last night. He assigned them their radios and their call letters," Scanlon said.

"Where are you going to be, Lou?" Higgins asked.

"Right here coordinating everything. Hector is going to be with me. But he has to take a few hours off at the end of his tour, a personal problem."

"I bet," Biafra Baby said, making an obscene plunging gesture with his fist.

A beguiling smile lit up Scanlon's face. "Any questions?" His eyes slid from face to face. There were no questions. "Then let's do it."

After the detectives left, the squad room became unnaturally quiet. Colon took the occasional call and jotted down messages. Scanlon sat at his desk listening to the static coming from the walkie-talkie standing in the middle of his desk. It was too early for anything to be happening, but he listened anyway. He powdered his stump and rolled on a fresh stump sock.

Hector Colon drifted into his office. "Lou, I was just thinking that we'd be in one helluva fix if a heavy case went down."

Scanlon snatched the roll call off the clip. Three detectives were scheduled to do the evening duty, a 1600 to 0100. He checked the time: 1450. A helluva lot could happen in a hour and ten minutes. He telephoned the adjoining detective squad, the Nine-seven. When the Whip came on the line, Scanlon asked him to have his detectives cover the Nine-three for the next hour and ten minutes. "I've got a heavy one going down and I'm working short-handed."

"You got it, Tony," Lt. Roy Benson said. "I'd just love to take my girlfriend to Monte's one night."

"Any night you want, as my guest, of course."

"Gee, Tony. You're a real swell guy."

"Fuck you, Roy. And thanks."

Herman the German rang the bell and stepped back.

Mary Ann Gallagher answered the door dressed in black, a rosary dangling from her right hand.

"I hope I'm not disturbing you, Mrs. Gallagher. But as I told you on the phone, I want to get this money to you as soon as possible."

"I appreciate that, Inspector." She turned and led him down the hall and into the parlor. They sat facing each other. He watched her finger the beads as he slid the white department envelope from his jacket pocket. "Mrs. Gallagher, this money was collected from the men and women in Queens Narcotics. There's thirty-six hundred dollars here. I know that it won't bring Joe back, but it will help you make a new life for yourself."

She leaned up out of her seat and kissed him on his cheek. "May God bless and protect you and your men," she said, taking the envelope from his hand, easing back into her seat. "Gallagher was such a good man. I miss him very much." She looked away.

He stood. "I must be getting back."

"Won't you stay and have some tea with me?"

"I really can't. I have an appointment to see Lieutenant Scanlon. It seems that the lieutenant has developed some leads on the killings."

"What?" she asked, standing up in her excitement.

"I don't have all the details, so I'd rather not say just yet. I'm sure Scanlon will contact you at the appropriate time."

"Please tell me whatever you know. I have a right to know. Any ray of hope that those people will be caught will make my day easier to face."

"I guess you got the right," he said, lowering himself back down into the chair. "It appears that the lieutenant has developed a lead to a theatrical makeup store. And he's come up with some fingerprints on some order form. He's leaning toward the theory that it might not have been just a robbery attempt."

"What? Tell me."

"That's all I know. I'll know more after I see Scanlon."

"That's wonderful news. I pray that they catch them," she said, clutching the arm of her chair.

Mary Ann Gallagher walked with the inspector to the door and waited until she heard the downstairs vestibule door open and close. She threw the rosary on the floor and ran for the telephone.

Herman the German drove to the Nine-three Squad and told Scanlon what had happened with Mrs. Gallagher. The inspector used Scanlon's desk phone to telephone the Seventeenth Narcotics

District. The operations sergeant told the inspector that a woman had just called looking for Sergeant Harris. As instructed, the sergeant had told the woman that Harris had been assigned to the crowd-control detail at Orchard Beach and had given her the number of temporary headquarters.

A woman had telephoned the headquarters van at Orchard Beach wanting to speak with Sergeant Harris of the Seventeenth Narcotics District. When she was told that the sergeant was out on patrol, she left an urgent message for the sergeant to call Mary Ann, at home.

Herman the German's face clouded. "Now?"

"Now!" Scanlon said. "Tell them to deliver the message to Harris." Scanlon went and stood by the window. The sun was out, the street below dry.

Twenty-six minutes passed before the call they were waiting for came. "Harris just threw in a Twenty-eight and took the rest of his tour off, a family emergency," the inspector said, gently replacing the receiver back in its cradle.

Scanlon picked up the walkie-talkie. "Renegade base to all units. Stand by. It's going down."

On the map in the squad room, Scanlon could see where a lagoon separated the Pelham Split Rock Golf Course from Orchard Beach. A parking area was sandwiched between the picnic grove and the picnic play area. The beach itself was a crescent of sand on the eastern end of the peninsula. Park Road wound its way across the peninsula connecting the parkway area and the picnic areas. The NYPD headquarters van was parked on the southern tip of the parking field. A number of spaces around the van had been reserved for the policemen who were assigned to the beach detail. Six rows away from the last reserved space a taxi idled, the driver slouched down behind the wheel, a portable radio on his lap.

Scanlon fingered the map of Orchard Beach. Had he covered all the exits? City Island Road leads off the beach. Pelham Bridge Road runs parallel to City Island Road. Both roads flow into the Hutchinson River Parkway, or the Hutch as it was commonly called. Renegades Two through Four were stationed at the entrances to the parkways. Renegade One was assigned to the parking field. It was One's job to tail Harris from the field onto whatever parkway the subject was going to take. As Harris and his tail passed the various entrances the unit at that particular entrance would leave and join the mobile surveillance.

Scanlon thought of something and grabbed up the radio. "Base to Renegade Two, what's the traffic like?"

"Two to Base, weekday summer traffic, Lou. Not too heavy, not too light."

"Ten-four."

George Harris appeared in the doorway of the headquarters van, uniform and equipment slung over his shoulders. Beach-weary people trudged back to their cars. Newcomers unloaded car trunks, gathering up blankets and coolers, preparing for their trek to the sand.

Harris made a rush for his Jeep.

The taxi driver parked in the parking field radioed, "Renegade One to base. Subject leaving in Jeep Comanche."

The driver of the tan Buick parked near the Pelham Bridge Road exit radioed: "Renegade Two, ten-four. No sign of subject."

Another taxi was parked on the shoulder near the entrance to the Hutch, the driver searching for a mechanical problem under the hood. He spoke into the radio that lay across the car's battery. "Renegade Three, standing by."

A mail truck was waiting behind an arbor of evergreens near the entrance of the Bruckner Expressway. "Renegade Four, standing by."

Scanlon radioed: "Base to Renegade Five, radio check, how do you read this unit?"

"We read you five by five," Higgins radioed.

"Renegade Six, how do you read this unit?"

"Five by five," Christopher transmitted.

"Renegade Seven, how do you read base?"

"We read you five by five," Fable transmitted.

Scanlon fingered the map of Orchard Beach. Damn, what was taking them so long?

"Renegade One to base. Subject passing Pelham Parkway."

"Renegade Two is leaving to join up with Renegade One."

"Renegade Three to base. I've got subject turning south onto the Hutch."

"Base to all units. Make frequent changes of close-contact car."
Scanlon paced the squad room, his radio held in front of his mouth.

Herman the German stood at parade rest in the middle of the squad room, looking down at the floor, waiting for the next transmission. Hector Colon kept looking up at the clock. He would have to leave soon. He had an engagement party to go to.

"Subject heading onto Bronx Whitestone Bridge."

"I've got 'im."

The units in the field were beginning to transmit without identifying themselves. That happens when cops have worked together a long time. They move and think as one, each recognizing the others' voices, moving as one well-trained unit.

Scanlon inspected the map. "He's going to take either the Cross Island or the Whitestone Expressway."

The tension grew. Colon slipped from the squad room and went to the locker room to change his clothes.

"He's going onto the Whitestone."

"Jack, you fall back, I'll pick him up."

"Ten-four."

"That guy is really pouring on the gas."

"He's turning south on the Van Wyck."

Hector Colon walked back into the squad room dressed in white slacks and a blue sport jacket with orange saddle stitching. He had on shiny white loafers and a maroon shirt and white tie. He sheepishly went up to Scanlon. "Lou, I don't have to go to this party. I can stay if you really need me."

"We'll manage, Hector. Go and enjoy."

After Colon had left the squad room, Herman the German looked at Scanlon and said, "I hope you remember that act of loyalty next time evaluations come around."

"Payback is always a bitch, Inspector."

The radio came to life. "He's turning west on the Long Island Expressway."

"He's making for the Gallagher house," Scanlon said. "He wants to make her rehash her conversation with you. Then he'll go for the guns." Scanlon transmitted: "Base to Renegade Five, subject is heading your way. Stay out of sight."

"Ten-four," Higgins radioed.

A short time later Renegade Five radioed that the subject was parking his Jeep on Anthony Street. "He's out of the Jeep," Higgins radioed. "Looking around, taking his time, being careful. He's moving up the steps, standing there. Now he's coming back down. Walking back over to his Jeep, taking his time, being real careful there's no tail. Now! He's running up the steps. He's in the house."

"Base to Renegades One through Four. Stay out of sight. Renegade Three and Four cover the rear of 32 Anthony Street."

Scanlon imagined the scene inside the Gallagher house. Mrs. Gallagher frantically relating her conversation with Herman the German. Harris picking up on her every word. He'd latch on to the inspector's comment about the makeup and fingerprints. There would be acrimony; heated words would be exchanged. Eventually, Scanlon hoped, Harris would be spooked and make a run to recover the guns.

"Subject is leaving," Higgins radioed. A short time later another transmission came over the wavelength. "Subject is eastbound on the BQE."

Time passed, contact positions changed.

Harris left the BQE at Queens Boulevard. When the transmission came into the base, Scanlon rushed up to the map. Examining the location where Harris exited the parkway, Scanlon cursed in Italian. Harris could not have picked a better location to shake a tail.

Queens Boulevard is a major artery that runs east and west across the Borough of Queens. The east- and westbound lanes are separated by various kinds of road dividers along the length of the boulevard. It is not possible for a driver to turn north or south at every intersection. Sometimes he must drive three-quarters of a mile before reaching a north or south turn lane. Many of the peripheral streets along the boulevard curve into other streets and avenues or dead-end into parkways or residential cul-de-sacs.

"Base to Renegades, what is subject doing?"

"Subject is double-parked on Queens and Five-eight Street. He's sitting in the Jeep watching through his sideview mirror."

"Base to Renegades One and Two, proceed to first eastbound exit and station yourself on the boulevard facing east. Renegades Three and Four, box him in."

"Renegade Five to base. Do you want us to leave this location and join up other units?" Higgins radioed.

"Negative. Stay with our lady friend in case she takes off on us. Harris could be a decoy."

"Ten-four, Lou," Higgins radioed.

"He's out of the Jeep standing on the curb, watching everything and everybody around him," one of the mobile units radioed.

"He's running across the boulevard," someone shouted over the air. "He's jumped the divider and hailed a taxi."

"Get the plate number," Scanlon radioed, a rising urgency in his voice.

"Subject got in yellow cab, license T276598. Heading north on Five-eight Street."

"Base to Renegades One and Two. Are you eastbound yet?"

"Negative. We haven't even reached a turn lane yet."

"Can any unit follow subject?" Scanlon radioed.

"That's a negative. We're all facing the wrong direction and are unable to make U-turns because of the divider." Herman the German was frantic. "We're going to lose him."

"Like hell we are. He's going for the guns and the tools. They have to be stashed someplace nearby. Someplace where he can get at them quickly. Someplace he has access to." Scanlon looked at the inspector. "We need a helicopter to search for that taxi. It takes an MOF above the rank of captain to order a chopper up."

Herman the German rushed over to the nearest desk and seized the telephone. Dialing, he said, "I hope Colon is enjoying his goddamn party. He certainly got dolled up for it."

As the inspector was telling the operations officer at the Aviation Unit what he wanted, Scanlon bolted from the squad room.

"Where are you going?"

Scanlon hollered over his shoulder, "Harris has a splash locker at the One-fourteen."

Scanlon ran from the station house and over to the radio car that had just slid into the curb. He jerked open the rear door and said to the startled crew, "Take me to the One-fourteen. Tell Central you'll be out of service—ten-sixty-one."

The driver of the radio car, a short man with the torso of a body builder, turned to look at the lieutenant. "You want the scenic route or are you in a hurry?"

"I want you to shag ass," Scanlon snapped.

"You got it, Lou," said the driver. "We'll take Manhattan Avenue up to Vernon Boulevard and Vernon all the way up into Astoria. Have you there in no time."

The car's recorder, a willowy man in his early twenties, switched on the turret lights and snatched the radio out of its cradle. "Nine-three Adam to Central, K."

"Go, Adam."

"Nine-three Adam will be ten-sixty-one to the One-fourteen on a precinct assignment, K."

"Ten-four, Adam. Advise Central when you're ninety-eight."

As Nine-three Adam pulled away from the curb, Scanlon caught sight of Herman the German running from the station house. The squealing police car sped under the massive span of the Queensboro Bridge, passed the drab towers of the Queensbridge Housing Project, and raced past the Con Ed generating plant on Vernon Boulevard.

Scanlon felt the bitter tug of frustration in his chest. He should have thought of a splash locker long before he thought about Colon's leaving the squad room to change into his partying clothes. Most cops have extra lockers in the precinct where they stash clothes and things from their secret lives. He blamed himself again and again for not seeing the possibility that Harris might have an extra locker in the One-fourteen. What safer place could there be to hide evidence of a murder than in a station-house locker that had another man's name and shield number on it, a member of the force long since retired or transferred? A perfect hiding place, a place open seven days a week, twenty-four hours a day. It had the right feel.

Scanlon asked the recorder to pass him the radio handset. The cop stretched the black spiraled cord into the rear seat.

"Switch your set to channel three," Scanlon ordered.

When the recorder complied, Scanlon radioed, "Renegade base to Renegades One, Two, Three, and Four. Base has reason to believe subject heading for the One-fourteen. Ten-eighty-five this unit at that location, forthwith."

A spate of hurried acknowledgments came over the channel.

The One-fourteen Precinct was a block away. A taxi was double-parked in front of the building. A swarm of cars gridlocked Astoria Boulevard, blocking the police car. "Turn off your lights and siren," Scanlon ordered. "Go around them."

"Lou, what's going on?" the driver asked, concern seeping into his young voice.

The radio car sped up onto the sidewalk, scattering pedestrians, and bounced back into the roadway.

Harris came running from the station house clutching a brown duffel bag.

The police car came to an abrupt stop behind the taxi. Scanlon leaped out into the roadway. "Harris!"

The sergeant was bending to get into the taxi when Scanlon's voice stopped him. He backed slowly out and stood looking at the man standing in the roadway. The two men remained motionless, as though frozen in time, glaring at each other. The crew of Nine-three Adam got out of their radio car and stood by the open doors watching the confusing scene unfold. Harris glanced down at the duffel bag. He moved around the front of the taxi and stood in the roadway facing Scanlon. He bolted for the Triboro Plaza underpass.

Scanlon yelled for him to stop and took off at a run.

Harris ran up the embankment and tossed the duffel bag over the wall. He wheeled away from the embankment and ran toward Steinway Street. Scanlon rushed up to the embankment wall and peered down onto the highway. A blue car ran over the duffel bag, and then another and another, tossing the cloth satchel across the highway.

Jabbing a finger down at the traffic feeding off the Triboro Bridge, Scanlon called out to the cops who had driven him, "Shut off the traffic." He took off after Harris.

Policemen stood on the steps of the station house scratching their heads and other parts of their anatomies and asking each other what the fuck was going on. Harris dodged his way along the teeming sidewalk. He bumped into a boy on a bicycle and stumbled. The boy and bike fell to the sidewalk. Regaining his footing, Harris ran to Forty-first Street and darted around the corner.

Scanlon careened around the corner in pursuit and came to a stop when he saw Harris leaning against the building wall, lighting up a clipper.

"Whaddaya doin' in this neck of the woods, Lou?"

Scanlon grabbed him by the shoulders and turned him to the

wall. "You're under arrest, Sergeant. You have the right to remain silent..." He informed the prisoner of his constitutional rights as he frisked him and removed his police credentials and revolver.

The One-fourteen's interrogation room was a stale cubicle, the walls of which were covered by acoustical tiles and a one-way mirror.

Scanlon and Harris faced each other across a small table. Herman the German and Jack Fable watched and listened in the viewing room, a narrow space that also contained the One-fourteen Squad's refrigerator. Harris's cowboy boots had been taken from him and invoiced as evidence. The prisoner was wearing cloth hospital slippers.

"Was it worth it, George?" Scanlon asked, toying with a De Nobili box.

"I want my boots back."

"In time. First tell me about Gallagher and the Zimmermans."

"I don't know what the fuck you're talking about. I got nothing to say to you or the other assholes on the other side of that mirror. I want a lawyer and I want to see my SBA delegate."

"You'll feel better if you tell me about it, George."

Harris laughed in his face. "You really got the balls to try one of those Mickey Mouse interrogative techniques on me? I'll feel better, shit."

"Mrs. Gallagher is talking to us," Scanlon lied. "She's giving the whole thing up. She's agreed to testify against you."

"That's nice. I hope you two have a long talk. Now get me my lawyer."

"About a dozen people saw you throw the duffel bag over the embankment. And we've recovered its contents."

Harris's eyes narrowed to slits. "What duffel bag?"

Herman the German stuck his head into the room. "May I see you a moment, Lieutenant?"

Scanlon pushed his chair back and went outside. Brodie and Christopher were waiting in the viewing room.

"The rifle and shotgun weren't in the duffel bag," Brodie said. "We've recovered the makeup, including the walrus mustache, and the tools, a crowbar, screwdriver, and a blacksmith's hammer."

Scanlon cursed in Italian.

"We had the southbound traffic shut off," Christopher said. "The men from the Bronx had already done that before we arrived. There were also two highway units on the scene. All the traffic was funneled through the chokepoint and every motorist questioned. We came up with four witnesses who saw the driver of a dark green Chevrolet swerve to avoid hitting the duffel bag. The driver stopped his car, got out, and, according to the witnesses, ran over to the bag and removed an attaché case and what appeared to be some sort of a firearm that had been broken down. He jumped back into his car and took off for parts unknown."

"He must have gotten through the chokepoint before the traffic was shut off," Brodie said.

Scanlon kicked the wall in anger. "Did anyone get a description of the car and its driver?" Scanlon asked, idly opening the refrigerator door and looking into the freezer. It was a solid block of ice.

"A thin male Hispanic with a pencil mustache, wearing a gold earring in his right ear. He had effeminate mannerisms and drove a Chevrolet that had chartreuse venetian blinds across the rear window and a pink animal with a bobbing head," Christopher said.

"No one thought to get the plate number?" Scanlon asked.

"No," Christopher said mournfully.

"Where are Higgins and Biafra Baby?" Scanlon asked.

Herman the German said, "They're still sitting on Mrs. Gallagher's apartment. I told them to remain there on the off chance that she has some evidence stashed in her apartment and might try to get rid of it. I also took the statements of the anticrime men you got on a steal and sent them back to the Bronx. I asked them to drop off the cowboy boots at the lab on their way back."

"What about your detectives, Jack?" Scanlon asked the CO of the Nineteenth Detective Squad.

"Back to command, no meal," Fable said. "No sense cluttering things up around here."

Scanlon nodded.

"Tom McCormick, the president of the Sergeants' Benevolent Association, and one of the SBA attorneys are waiting in the administrative lieutenant's office to see Harris," the inspector said.

"Where are the two cops I commandeered to drive me here?" Scanlon asked.

"They're waiting downstairs in the captain's office with their PBA delegate and one of the PBA attorneys," Herman the German said.

Scanlon looked at the inspector. "We made the lawyers' day for them. Were the PC and the CofD notified?"

"Both of them were," Fable said. "And they're both not responding to the scene. The borough commander and the duty captain were also notified. The duty captain will be here later. He's tied up in the One-oh-three on a shooting."

Scanlon said bitterly, "They're all distancing themselves from the arrest, waiting to see which way it's going to go. Which means, of course, that they think we messed it up." He opened the door to the interrogation room and motioned Harris outside.

The administrative lieutenant's office was on the same floor as the detectives' interrogation room but at the other end of the building. Walking down the corridor, with Harris in the center of the group, they passed cops who either looked away or cast their eyes downward. Policemen do not like to see one of their own under arrest.

The SBA attorney's name was Berke. He had a scabrous complexion, a red beard, and hard, cunning eyes. He was waiting in the corridor with Tom McCormick, the SBA president. Harris went into the administrative lieutenant's office with his representation. Herman the German and Jack Fable stood guard outside the door while Scanlon rushed downstairs to the captain's office.

Disgruntled policemen loitered in the muster room. The grapevine had it that the Whip of the Nine-three Squad had arrested a sergeant from Queens Narcotics. It had something to do with Lieutenant Gallagher's wife, so the word was. Hurrying down the staircase, Scanlon saw the faces of the cops looking up at him. Many of them glared their contempt up at him; some turned their backs to him and shuffled off into the sitting room.

The PBA delegate's name was Frank Fortunado. He was waiting for Scanlon outside the captain's office. "Looks like you grabbed yourself a wolverine by the balls, Lou," Fortunado said.

"Where are the two cops?" Scanlon said, noticing the delegate's iron-gray hair.

Fortunado motioned to the door. "Inside with our lawyer. Their names are Rod and Eichhorn, and they both most definitely do not want to get involved in the arrest of a member of the force."

"Your MOF is a cop killer."

"That's what you say, Lou. But we both know that that ain't gospel until a jury says it's so too, and until the Court of Appeals says it's so."

"Is the captain in his office?"

"He's on his RDO. His next scheduled tour is eight to four, tomorrow," the delegate said, chucking open the door and following Scanlon inside.

Scanlon recognized Police Officer Rod as the driver of the radio car. Eichhorn had been the recorder. The lawyer's name was Eble. Medium-tall, with wavy black hair, and an obvious penchant for expensive clothes.

The lawyer was sitting behind the captain's regulation flat-top desk. The two cops were sitting next to each other on the captain's green regulation leather couch. They appeared nervous and self-conscious.

"I have to take their statements, Counselor," Scanlon said.

"I have no problem with that, Lieutenant," the lawyer said. "Officers Rod and Eichhorn will be more than happy to answer any question put to them that is specifically directed and narrowly related to their performance of duty."

Scanlon bridled at the lawyer's use of the restrictive phrase used in the *Patrol Guide*'s procedure concerning the interrogation of members of the service.

"Counselor, your clients are not the subjects of an official investigation. So spare me that specifically directed and narrowly related bullshit. I commandeered them to drive me here. All I need from them now is a statement as to what they saw and heard when we got here."

"My clients saw and heard nothing, Lieutenant."

Scanlon hurled a withering look at the two cops, who shifted uneasily on the couch. "You didn't see Sergeant Harris run up to the embankment and toss a duffel bag over the wall?"

"I didn't see nothing, Lou," Rod said.

"Me either," followed Eichhorn.

"I suppose the other cops who were standing on the precinct steps didn't see or hear anything either," Scanlon said.

"That would be my guess," the lawyer said.

Rancor showing clearly on his face, Scanlon whirled and left the office. Policemen were still milling about the muster room. Ignoring their searching stares, Scanlon made for the staircase. He heard a rushing footfall behind him and turned. Police Officer Rod was shamefaced. "Lou, I'm sorry for what happened inside. But I had no other way to go."

"I'd like to hear why," Scanlon said.

"I've got fourteen more years to do in the Job," Rod said. "Six months from now the Gallagher case is going to be yesterday's news. But I'd be the cop who helped convict a police sergeant. No one would remember that the sergeant was tried for murder, they'd only remember that I was the scumbag who testified against him."

"Look, kid, it don't have to be that way."

"Bullshit, Lou," Rod said, sweeping his hand at the policemen in the muster room. "Look at the way they're looking at you. They don't even know why Harris was arrested. And they could care less. What matters to them is that a street cop arrested another street cop. Not some bastard from IAD whose job it is to arrest cops, but one of their own, from the trenches. No, Lou. That's a head trip I don't need. I just ain't that dedicated."

Scanlon stood by the staircase and watched Rod walk back into the captain's office. That was one of the major differences between guys who worked in the bag and guys who worked in soft clothes, Scanlon reflected. Detectives and plainclothesmen see many different sides to life. They have to understand a person's motivation and try to figure out what makes that person tick, act the way he or she does. Detectives learn early that there are no black-and-white issues in life, only different shades of gray.

Scanlon glared back at the cops, turned, and hurried back upstairs. Harris was still closeted in the administrative lieutenant's office with his lawyer and the SBA president. Herman the German and Jack Fable were still on guard duty outside the door.

"What did the two cops have to say?" Fable asked Scanlon.

"They said that they saw nothing, heard nothing, smelled nothing, and sensed nothing," Scanlon said. "There are going to be some unpleasant reverberations over this arrest. And I don't see any reason for you two to be hit by any of the shrapnel. So why don't you both sort of disappear into the woodwork?"

Jack Fable made an ugly face. "Tony, my man, I've been a detective squad commander for the better part of fifteen years. And during that time I've developed my own philosophy for dealing with these delicate situations. Simply put, I fuck 'em where they breathe."

Scanlon smiled. Fable was from the old, old school. There weren't many of his kind left in the Job. The new breed of squad commander wore a somber suit and carried an attaché case to work that contained two apples, one banana, and a Thermos of decaffeinated tea. And they wore big college rings, but still said "between you and I," and they loved to go on about how the quality of evidence was determined by the statistical concept of probability.

Herman the German bit his lips. "Gallagher was no bargain, but he was my bargain."

"We're three aging dinosaurs hanging around for that meteor to come hurling down from space and make us extinct," Scanlon said.

"I fuck 'em where they breathe," Fable said again.

Brodie and Christopher rushed up to them. "The lab boys just called," Brodie said. "Harris's boots match up with the impressions found on the roof of the Kingsley Arms. It's a positive match, Lou. And the tools found in the duffel bag were the same tools that were used to force open the roof door."

The door behind them opened, and Harris's attorney stepped out into the corridor.

"Gentlemen, I have just spoken to my clients at some length. And at this time I am officially advising you that under no circumstances are my clients to be questioned by any member of the police department."

"Clients, Counselor?" Scanlon said.

"I have just gotten off the phone with Mary Ann Gallagher. She has asked me to represent her."

23

Kings County Criminal Court is located on Schermerhorn Street in Brooklyn's once-fashionable downtown shopping district, which has been urbanized into a seedy neighborhood of hawking street peddlers, shuttered shops, and caged-in stores where customers had to be buzzed inside.

The court's arraignment part was on the first floor of the Baroque-style building. All conversation stopped when Scanlon walked into the police sign-in room. The monster had arrived. A notification tucked into the sign-in log was waiting for Scanlon: "Lt. Scanlon. After you draw up complaint see ADA Goldfarb in Rm 617."

ADA Goldfarb was a short man in his late twenties who had gone prematurely bald. He was dressed in a dark business suit and wore an orange tie. "Let's go into the conference room, Lieutenant."

Scanlon noticed that the assistant district attorney favored built-up heels. He followed the ADA into the glass cubicle.

"I'm handling the arraignment part this morning, Lieutenant. I've read over your complaint and your attending affidavits. And, I have to tell you, your case against Sergeant Harris is flimsy, at best. You are going to have to come up with a lot more hard evidence if you expect the People to win on this one." He sat down wearily in one of the two battered chairs.

"We have evidence that ties Harris directly to the scene of the Zimmerman homicide in Manhattan County," Scanlon said in mild protest.

"Ah, yes, the famous cowboy boots. But can you state with any degree of probability when those impressions were made? A week before the doctor and his wife were killed? A month? The same night?" The ADA quickly lit a cigarette. "And you have absolutely no evidence linking Harris to the murders of Lieutenant Gallagher and Yetta Zimmerman. Your fingerprint evidence is dubious — there were other prints on that form. As for the typewriter, anyone assigned to that unit could have typed out that order. In fact, I'm only going to allow you to charge Harris on the Zimmerman homicide, not on Gallagher's. The court would throw it out on the ground of insufficient evidence. I think you might just have enough evidence to hold Harris on the doctor and his wife. But nowhere near enough to get a conviction."

"Are you forgetting that I saw Harris toss that duffel bag over the embankment, and that that duffel bag contained the tools that were used to pry open the roof door of the Kingsley Arms, the same roof from where the shots were fired that killed the doctor and his wife?"

The ADA got up and started pacing the floor. "What you saw, Lieutenant, was Harris throw what appeared to be a duffel bag over the embankment and onto the highway. You are in no position to testify as to the contents of that duffel bag. Nor can you state beyond a reasonable doubt that the duffel bag that your people recovered from the highway was the same duffel bag that you say you saw Harris throw over the embankment."

Scanlon got up and felt rage growing inside him. "Are you telling me that the tools and the makeup are not admissible as evidence?"

"I'm telling you that I would not be surprised if the court sustained a defense motion to suppress them as evidence." The ADA stabbed out his cigarette. "Were Harris's fingerprints found anywhere on the duffel bag or on any of the tools or makeup?"

Scanlon sighed deeply. "No." He shook his head with disgust. "Tell me what I need for a conviction."

"A lot more than you have. Look, Lieutenant. I only handle the arraignments. I suggest you have a talk with one of our trial ADAs. One of them will be able to put you on the right track."

"Do you think we have enough to indict Harris on the Zimmerman murders?"

"Oh, sure. We can indict the Statue of Liberty. The problems come afterward."

Deputy Chief MacAdoo McKenzie stood in the center of the court's lobby, watching the ornate brass doors of the bank of elevators.

"Over here," he said, waving to Scanlon as the lieutenant stepped off the elevator.

"This Harris arrest has got the Palace Guard jumping," McKenzie said. "We're going to end up in the middle of a million-dollar lawsuit. Harris is going to walk. You and your people fucked it up, Lieutenant. Harris beat you to the punch when you allowed him to get rid of that duffel bag."

"Be advised, Chief, that I didn't let Harris do anything. And be further advised that we're going to convict both Harris and his girlfriend."

"How? You didn't even have enough evidence against Harris to arrest him for killing Joe Gallagher. And you can't even go near Mrs. Gallagher to question her. You don't have one drop of evidence against her." He wiped his neck. "The PC has directed me to tell you to stay away from Mrs. Gallagher. Don't try to question her, don't go near her. Her lawyer telephoned the PC and threatened to sue him personally if anything is said or done by any member of the department to besmirch her unblemished reputation. So from now on, as far as this department is concerned, Mrs. Gallagher is no longer a suspect."

Scanlon sneered. "Ol' Bobby Boy is a real stand-up PC."

"He's a politician looking out for his own ass, just like you would be if you were in his place."

Herman the German, Jack Fable, and the Nine-three Squad detectives were gathered in a circle outside the padded courtroom doors of Part 1A. The circle parted for Scanlon. Hector Colon said, "*Teniente,* I've contacted José Rodriguez from the Hispanic

Association. He's going to reach out to our members and ask them to have a look-see around El Barrio for the car with the venetian blinds."

Scanlon's eyes locked on Colon's. "Did you enjoy your party?"

The detective shifted uncomfortably, looked away. "It was all right, Lou."

"I've been in touch with the uptown brothers," Biafra Baby said. "They're going to be hitting some of the juice joints and number parlors."

Higgins added, "From the description of the driver there is a good chance that he's gay. I've gotten in touch with Sergeant Rogers, the head of GOAL. He's going to have some of our people hit the baths and gay bars."

"I want you all to go back to the Squad and pull out everything we've got on the case. When the arraignment is over I'll come back and we'll put our collective heads together and see if there's anything we've missed," Scanlon ordered.

"I'll have my people do the same thing," Fable said.

"Please, Jack. Speak to the detectives in your Squad who worked on the Zimmerman case. Maybe one of them scratched something on the back of a matchbook, then forgot to put it on a Five." Scanlon turned to his detectives. "And that goes for all of you. Check your notes, every scrap of paper, every matchbook, see if there's anything you've overlooked."

The echo of the detectives walking away resounded off the marble floor. Scanlon looked at Herman the German. "You going inside to watch the arraignment?"

"Wouldn't miss it for the world. I'm into legal flagellation."

An atmosphere of anxious expectation filled the courtroom. All the seats were filled. Scanlon spotted Mary Ann Gallagher, dressed in mourning black, sitting on the aisle in the middle of the room. She was whispering to the man next to her. Scanlon inched his way around the paneled wall to see if he could recognize the man she was talking to. He did. Ben Cohen, one of the criminal justice system's better-known bail bondsmen.

Scanlon was taken aback when he spotted Linda Zimmerman sitting across the room. He moved along the wall until he reached her and squeezed in next to her. "You all right?" he whispered.

Her stare was fixed on the ornate bench that dominated the courtroom. "Yes, I'm all right."

"I'm sorry for what happened in the bank."

She made no reply.

The court clerk stood in front of the bench and barked: "All rise. This court is now in session. The Honorable Florence Meyers presiding." A rustle swept through the courtroom as the assemblage rose to its feet, and then at the court clerk's signal, sat.

The first case on the arraignment calendar was called. The People against George Harris. Scanlon pinned on his shield and went up and stood before the bench. Two court officers escorted the prisoner into the courtroom from the holding pens behind the room. Harris needed a shave. Berke, the defense attorney, held an impromptu conference with his client.

The court clerk said to Scanlon, "Officer, raise your right hand. Do you swear or affirm to the truth of your affidavit?"

"I do."

"George Harris," the court clerk intoned, "you have been charged with violation of section 125.25 of the Penal Law in that on—"

Defense attorney: "Your honor, if it pleases the court, the defense waives the reading of the charges."

Judge Meyers: "So ordered."

Defense attorney: "Your honor, the defense moves for an immediate hearing on this matter, and respectfully requests that the court release the defendant on his personal recognizance."

ADA: "May I remind the court that this is a homicide case. The People have in my judgment presented a *prima facie* case and request bail be set at two hundred and fifty thousand dollars."

The judge flipped through the legal papers, scanning. "Your *prima facie* case appears to be a bit weak, Counselor."

Defense attorney: "Your honor, my client is a ranking member of the police department. He has an unblemished professional and personal record. He has a family, a home. He has roots in the community. He's not going to run. And I say now, in open court, that I fully expect my client to be exonerated of these trumped-up charges."

ADA: "Your honor—"

Judge: "Save it for the hearing, Counselor. Bail is set at twenty-five thousand dollars. This case is bound over to the grand jury. Next case."

Mary Ann Gallagher, and Cohen, the bail bondsman, got up from their pew. Scanlon left the courtroom, unpinning his shield. Linda Zimmerman followed him outside into the lobby. She caught up with him and seizing him by the arm demanded, "What the hell is going on?"

He led her around one of the marble columns, out of sight of the people leaving the courtroom. "Linda, there is a lot more to the case than you've heard on the radio or read in the papers. And I guess you have the right to know it all."

He went on to tell her about his suspicions concerning Harris and Mrs. Gallagher. As he explained to her the restrictions that had been placed on him, he could see a mounting sense of outrage in her face. He had almost finished when a sudden commotion caused them to step out from behind the column. Mary Ann Gallagher, Harris, Cohen, and the defense lawyer, Berke, were leaving the courtroom. A group of newspaper reporters surrounded them. The defense lawyer said that his client would have nothing to say at this time. Two women pushed their way through the crowd and embraced Mrs. Gallagher.

"Pat? Joan? How nice of you to come," Mrs. Gallagher said, glancing over at Scanlon and Linda Zimmerman. Harris walked away with Mrs. Gallagher. He kept looking over his shoulder at Scanlon, a smile of victory fixed on his lips.

"You," Linda Zimmerman hissed at Scanlon. "You call this justice? Harris is allowed to leave the courtroom on the arm of his whore. And you can't even arrest her."

"Linda, this is only the first round."

"You go to hell," she screamed into his face and stormed off.

Scanlon stood at the top of the steps of the Manhattan Criminal Court building watching the lunchtime flow of people entering and leaving. When he saw Jane Stomer push her way outside he was instantly aware of the perfection of her body and the lustrous beauty of her lips. He also became acutely conscious of how lonely his life had been without her.

She stopped and swept the sunglasses from her face. She glared at him briefly, then turned and pushed her way back into the building.

He ran after her, catching up with her halfway across the marble lobby. "I need your professional advice," he said, snagging her arm.

She turned. "I half expected you to show up here. The word that I hear is that you really missed the boat on Harris."

"I need your help. Let me buy you lunch, please."

"If you keep it on a professional plane, okay. Otherwise, let's just forget the whole thing."

They left the building by the rear exit. He went up to the frankfurter cart and ordered two with sauerkraut and onions, and two diet sodas. Reaching out to pluck napkins from the holder, he caught sight of her watching him.

They walked across the street and sat on a park bench. Gripping her bun with both hands, she bit into the frank's protruding end and waited for him to begin.

He spoke in an unhurried manner, telling her of his feel for the case; he spoke of how the evidence against Harris had been developed; he told her how the arrest had been made; at length he spoke of the ban against his questioning Mrs. Gallagher.

She listened, occasionally sucking soda through a straw. He noticed how her lipstick branded the tip. When he finished talking, he took a bite of his hot dog, waiting for her response. She carefully wiped mustard off her fingers. "The Brooklyn ADA was correct. The case is a throw-out. You have no corroborative evidence linking Harris or Mrs. Gallagher to any of the homicides. And you have no evidence that proves intent. The 'death-gamble' benefits aren't evidence, although they do create a strong presumption. What you have to do is prove an overt act in furtherance of the conspiracy. If you had arrested Harris with the weapons in his possession along with the tools and the makeup, you would have had a conviction. But you still would not have had a case against Mrs. Gallagher." She drank the rest of her soda. "The only way you are going to make a case against her is to turn Harris. If you can make him roll over, he'll spit her up to save his own hide. But that means a plea bargain, and Harris doing less than life."

"Any suggestions?"

"I'd go for the guns. If you can recover them, you just might be able to trace them back to Harris. Then, with the fingerprint evidence, and the typewriter, and the boots, you just might be able to make a case against him. And if the case is strong enough, he might want to make a deal."

"There are a lot of ifs and mights," Scanlon said. "What about getting the guns admitted into evidence, if I should be able to recover them?"

"If the serial numbers are still on them, and you can trace them back to their original purchaser, and that purchaser is proved to be Harris, then you might have a shot at getting them introduced."

"Anything else?"

"Canvass the banks in the area of where they live and work. That bank money order for the makeup was purchased someplace, and whoever got it had to fill out a request form. I'd also check out the libraries to see if one of them took out a book on how to apply makeup." She balled her napkin and pressed it through the hole in the soda can. "Is it worth it all, Scanlon? The frustration, the aggravation, trying to circumvent a system that just doesn't seem to care, or want to care?"

"I think it is," he said, taking the soda can from her hand and getting up. He pushed the garbage down in the wire refuse basket and came back.

She smiled and said, "Thank you for the flowers. They were lovely. But I wish you hadn't sent them."

"I read somewhere that flowers were the quickest way to a woman's heart." He raised his shoulders, let them fall. "I wanted you to know how I felt about you."

"Please, Scanlon. Don't make it any harder than it already is."

"It ain't easy being a pining middle-aged detective."

"Pining, Scanlon? You?"

"Yes, pining. To have a continuing fruitless desire."

"And that is what you have for me, a fruitless desire?"

He placed his hand on hers. "I screwed us up and now I'm trying to put us back together again. And everything I say or do seems to be wrong."

She pulled her hand away from his. "Sending flowers was the right thing."

"Then I'll send more."

"Please don't. I told you the last time, I'm involved with some-one."

"You're not being fair to Mr. Whateverhisnameis."

"Who?"

"The guy you're seeing." He started to make finger circles on the back of her hand. "I believe that you're only seeing him to get over me. I think that you're still in love with me. And that isn't being upfront with Mr. Whateverhisnameis."

"And where, may I ask, did you acquire your sudden insight into how women think and act?"

"From my shrink, Dr. De Nesto."

"You finally went to see a psychiatrist?"

"Yes, I did. I wanted to learn why I acted the way I did when I lost my leg. To help me understand why I couldn't let you share it with me."

"Was Dr. De Nesto able to help you understand?"

"Yes, Jane. I've learned a lot about myself and what makes me tick."

"I'm proud of you, Tony," she said, placing her hand on his. "It took a lot for a man like you to bare your soul to someone."

He looked down at her hands, said shyly, "I had the right mo-tivation. I realized after I had lost you just how much you meant to me. And, well, I hoped that by understanding why I acted the way I did, I might be able to win you back."

She avoided his eyes. "Was the doctor able to help you with your dysfunction problem?"

"Yes, I was helped, I think." He shifted in his seat. "I haven't been with another woman yet, so I can't be sure."

"In all this time?"

"I just couldn't bring myself to do it. The anxiety is still too much for me to cope with. I never know when or how to tell a woman that I'm an amputee. The fear of rejection can be a horror. You just can't imagine."

She ran her fingers over his cheek. "I guess I never really ap-preciated how difficult it must have been for you."

"There's another reason why I haven't been with another woman. It . . . it would be like severing the bond that I feel exists between us. I just couldn't bring myself to do that." He looked away, wishing he could muster a single tear to run down his cheek. He faced her, leaned forward, and kissed her on the lips. Without saying a word, he got up and walked alone down the winding path.

There should be fog, he thought. When he saw Robert Taylor play that scene, the actor walked away and disappeared into fog. The only mist he had for his dramatic walkaway was the debris from the stinking maw of a passing garbage truck. He didn't know what had made him come on that way with her. It must have been his cop instincts telling him to play on her sympathy, to use her maternal nature for his benefit. What the hell, he thought, all's fair in love, war, and the Job.

24

Mary Ann Gallagher was dressed in a white nightgown. She was sitting on her bed doing her toenails. The sharp smell of nail polish remover filled the air around her. Her bedside radio played soft music. The last of the biddies had left an hour ago, and she was happy and content to be alone to pamper herself and to think of Harris and everything that had happened these past days. She had known all along that Harris had underestimated Scanlon. From her first meeting with him she knew that Scanlon was a man to be wary of. She had seen that keen sense of determination in those dark eyes of his. She had warned Harris to get rid of those damn guns, but no, he had to have it his way. She could never understand men's fascination with firearms. The lawyer had told her that they had no case against Harris, and she believed him. But no matter what happened with Harris, she was in the clear. There was no way Scanlon or anyone else could ever connect her with any of it. Damn! I smudged the polish, she thought. She took a cotton ball and wiped off the polish and started over.

She had been married to Gallagher long enough to have learned that even if Harris tried to save himself by giving her up, she was safe because there was no corroboration. They'd need some evidence tending to connect her with the commission of the crime. And that evidence did not exist. She had seen to that. It was Harris who had bought everything they needed. It was he who had stolen the van and had gotten the makeup. The more she ran the whole thing over in her head the more secure she felt.

Soon she would be receiving the money from Gallagher's death gamble. And then it would be off to Europe and the good life. All those sexy European men with their heart-throb accents and trim bodies. She was glad in a way that Harris had been arrested. It would be easier now for her to dump him. She would just make up some excuse to go away by herself and disappear.

She wanted men in her life who would satisfy her needs and desires. There would be no more cops in her life, that was for sure. She was sick to death of cops and their infantile desires.

The doorbell. Oh, hell. Don't those biddies ever give up and go to bed? She screwed the brush into the polish bottle and got up from the bed, sliding her pink bathrobe off the chair. The bell rang again.

Putting the bathrobe on, she moved down the hall toward the door, calling out, "Yes, who is it?"

"It's me, dear. Pat."

Cursing under her breath, Mary Ann Gallagher unlatched the door.

A figure loomed on the other side, its hands gripping a weapon, primed to strike the moment the victim came into view. A glossy Botticelli shopping bag that had been used to transport the weapon was on the floor. The hallway was deserted. No sounds came from the other apartments. It was as though the building were deserted.

The door swung open and Mary Ann Gallagher came into view. She gasped and her mouth fell open. Before the scream could reach her lips the blade struck her neck. A horrible gurgle burst from her throat the moment the blow was struck. Smothering the wound with her hands, Mary Ann Gallagher whirled and ran down the hallway as though seeking out safety in the depths of her home. She tottered into the bedroom.

The killer put the weapon into its carrying bag, took hold of the white handles, stepped into the apartment, and kicked the door closed. The victim lay writhing on the bedroom floor, making ghastly noises. The killer moved across the room and stood by the side of the bed, watching the death throes. A cigarette was lit and the lighter carefully put down on the bed next to the Botticelli shopping bag.

Mary Ann Gallagher trembled with violent spasms; her extremities thrashed about the floor. Her body stiffened in a final convulsion and fell still.

The killer reached out and crushed the cigarette into the ashtray on top of the radio. Glancing at the body, the killer noticed that there were no underpants. A woman should be modest even in death. The corpse's nightclothes were pulled down.

The doorbell rang. The killer grabbed the shopping bag and ran from the room. Tiptoeing down the hall, the killer stood by the door, listening to the conversation on the other side.

"Mary Ann, it's us, Pat and Joan. We've come back to keep you company."

Silence.

"I wonder where she can be?"

"Maybe the poor dear went to sleep early? It has been a trying day for her, what with what happened to that nice Sergeant Harris and all."

"Why don't we come back in the morning?"

"Footsteps moved away from the door, down the staircase.

The killer cracked the door and looked out, saw no one, and slipped from the apartment, moving quickly over to the stairs leading to the upper floors.

The killer climbed to the middle of the stairs and pressed against the wall, listening to the conversation that was taking place in the vestibule, two floors below. Maybe Mary Ann was in the bathroom or washing her hair in the sink and didn't hear us. Do you think we should try once more? Yes.

Padding footsteps coming back upstairs. A hard knock at the door. The sound of a doorknob being tried, followed by the squeak of a door being slowly opened. A gasp. "Is that blood all over? Mary Ann! Are you all right?"

Peering over the banister, the killer saw the door ajar and no one standing there.

Rushing down the stairs and out into the night, the killer heard a series of piercing screams.

25

hey had done everything they could do. Now came the waiting. Waiting while banks searched their microfilm; waiting for libraries to search through old charge-out cards; waiting to hear from detective squads throughout the city. Scanlon had personally telephoned the Whips of every squad and asked them to have their people canvass their precincts for an effeminate Hispanic who drove a Chevrolet with chartreuse blinds and a stuffed animal with a bobbing head.

It was 2013 hours and they were tired and hungry.

Scanlon suggested that they go to Monte's to eat. He turned to Hector Colon. "Hector, you hold it down, will you? We'll bring you back a sandwich."

"Right, Lou," Colon said, switching on the television set.

The detectives sat at one of the large tables in the rear of the restaurant. They ate in silence for the most part. No one was in the mood for conversation. They were finishing dessert when Scanlon looked across the table at Higgins and said, "Better give Hector a call and see if anything is doing."

She returned in a few minutes with a saucy smile on her face. Rounding the table to her seat, she bent by Scanlon and whispered,

"Jane Stomer called and left a message for you to call her at home."

"Jane?"

"Hi." A silence, followed by the sound of her exhaling. "You were right, Scanlon. I am still in love with you. And I want you to know that there is no Mr. Whateverhisnameis. I made him up to hurt you."

"I'm glad you told me," he said, thinking, Thank you, Dr. De Nesto.

"Look, Scanlon, I really don't know if we can make it together. I really don't. But if you're willing to give it another try, then so am I."

"I am willing, Jane."

"I want to start off slowly, get to know you again."

"Whatever you say. I'll play by your rules. Dinner, tomorrow?"

"That sounds nice. Say eight o'clock."

"I'll pick you up." Pause. "I love you, Jane."

"Me too, Tony."

Leaving the phone booth, Scanlon felt wonderful. Better than he had in years. He felt as though he were on his way to being a complete person again. He was going to have to call Sally De Nesto and thank her, to say goodbye. He just didn't have any idea of what he would say. He went up to the bar and motioned for the waiter to give him the bill. He paid the tab and went back to the table. "We ready?" he said to the detectives.

"Let's get the tab," Brodie said.

"It's taken care of," Scanlon said.

"Lou?" Brodie said. "You don't gotta go around picking up our tabs."

"Let's get back," Scanlon said.

They left the restaurant and piled into the unmarked car.

Higgins drove. Scanlon sat in the passenger seat. The three detectives squeezed into the back. Higgins switched on the ignition. Scanlon turned on the radio.

"In the Nine-three precinct a ten-ten. Female calls for help. 32 Anthony Street. Units going, K?"

"That's Gallagher's house," Scanlon exclaimed, grabbing the handset. "Nine-three Squad on the way."

"George Henry going, Central."
"Ten-four Squad, ten-four George Henry."

Mary Ann Gallagher's two girlfriends were standing outside the bedroom screaming incoherent things at the detectives when they arrived. Scanlon rushed into the bedroom, followed by his team. He took in the body of Mary Ann Gallagher on the floor and quickly scanned the bedroom. His eyes latched on to the lighter laying atop the chenille bedspread, and then immediately switched to the crushed cigarette in the ashtray that was on the top of the bedside radio. He moved over to the bed, picked up the lighter, and put it into his pocket. Removing a tissue from the box on top of the nightstand, he snatched the cigarette butt out of the ashtray, wrapped it in the tissue, and put the evidence into his pocket.

The crew of sector George Henry plunged into the bedroom. Scanlon told the two cops to wait out in the hall and try to calm down the two women. He went back to the body and squatted on his heels. The detectives gathered around the remains. They were alone.

"There goes our case," Christopher said.

Each detective withdrew into his own thoughts.

Scanlon thought of Joe Gallagher and Yetta Zimmerman and how they had been slaughtered. He thought of Dr. Zimmerman and his wife murdered in their bed as they slept. He thought of the city's crime victims and the countless unsolved crimes and all the misery they had caused. His frustration turned to anger. Different rules have to apply to cops who turn bad. Renegade cops who murder their own. No! Harris was not going to walk away from this. No matter what he had to do, Harris was not going to walk. He looked up at his silent detectives. His face was solemn. "I'm going to take a dying declaration from her before she dies."

He waited for their response.

Brodie hunkered down next to the body. "That's a good idea, Lou."

Scanlon looked at Higgins.

"You'd better hurry before she goes out of the picture," Higgins said.

Biafra Baby grabbed Christopher by the arm. "Hurry, let's call an ambulance." He and Christopher ran excitedly from the bedroom. "Officer," Biafra Baby shouted at the cops. "One of you wait downstairs for the ambulance and direct the attendant up here. The other get in your car and go get a priest and bring him here. Hurry!"

The uniform men ran off.

"She's alive?" Pat shouted at the detectives.

"Yes," Christopher said. "She's trying to give the lieutenant a statement."

"Praise be to God," Joan said, blessing herself.

Brodie came up and stood in the doorway, hampering the view into the bedroom. Biafra Baby and Christopher stood on either side of Brodie. The terrified women stood away from the door, not wanting to look inside.

"Can you hear me, Mrs. Gallagher?" Scanlon said to the corpse. "Please try and talk louder. I can't hear you."

Higgins stuck her tongue into her cheek and made gurgling sounds.

"Mrs. Gallagher, I must ask you your name," Scanlon said.

Pressing her tongue into her cheek again, Higgins mumbled weakly, "Mary Ann Gallagher."

"Where do you live?" Scanlon asked, brushing his hand across the corpse's eyes, closing the lids.

"32 Anthony Street," Higgins mumbled.

"Do you know that you are about to die?" Scanlon asked.

"God... forgive... me... yes... I know."

"Can you ladies hear?" Biafra Baby asked the two women.

"Yes," Joan answered for both of them.

Christopher had his steno pad out, making a transcript of Mary Ann Gallagher's dying declaration.

"Mrs. Gallagher, do you have any hope of recovery?" Scanlon asked, watching the blood seep from the wound in the corpse.

"No hope... none... a priest... please... priest," Higgins mumbled, tongue in cheek.

"One is on his way," Scanlon said. "Mrs. Gallagher, will you tell me who did this to you?" He looked at Higgins, who had squatted next to him with her back to the door. "Who did this to you?" he repeated, looking at Higgins.

She took a deep breath, jabbed her tongue against her cheek, and mumbled, "George did it... George Harris murdered me...."

Afraid . . . I . . . would . . . tell . . . about . . . Gallagher . . . and . . . the . . . others. . . . We . . . did . . . it . . . together. . . . I . . . God . . . mercy . . ." She gasped. Hissed out air. Silence.

"Sweet Jesus, did you hear that?" Joan said.

Pat made the sign of the cross. "Mother of God."

Scanlon and Higgins exchanged a silent look of understanding. They stood and left the room.

"Did you get it all?" Scanlon asked Christopher.

"Yes, Lieutenant. Word for word," Christopher said. Scanlon was somber. He took the steno pad from Christopher, read what was written, passed the book to Pat, and said, "Will you ladies please read the transcript and sign it as witnesses?" He waited for them to read and sign the page, and then passed the book to his detectives, requiring each of them to sign the transcript.

One of the radio car crew rushed into the apartment with a priest, who hurried into the bedroom. Scanlon noted the time and date on the top of the transcript. The other part of the George Henry crew ran into the apartment with the ambulance attendants.

"She just expired," Scanlon told the attendants. The older of the two attendants, a heavyset man with wild brown hair, looked into the bedroom and saw the priest standing over the body making the sign of the cross. He noted the time on his watch, and began to fill in his worksheet.

Scanlon exchanged satisfied nods with his detectives. He motioned Biafra Baby aside and whispered, "Get on the horn to the One-two-three in Staten Island. Tell them to send some radio cars to cover Harris's house. And tell them to put a rush on it. I wouldn't want anyone killing him, not now."

Cassiopeia's Chair twinkled in the northern sky; crickets clicked. Sequine Avenue. Amboy Road. Outerbridge Crossing. Strange names for a strange place. An island within a metropolis. The towers of Manhattan merely a vista, not a place to live in, to raise children in. Staten Island. A frame house stood at the end of Amboy Road facing the Outerbridge Crossing. It was a dilapidated house with an untended yard; in it, a car, tireless, sat propped on concrete blocks. Harris's Jeep Comanche was parked next to it.

George Harris was sprawled over the sofa in his dingy living room, a can of beer resting on his stomach. He was staring up at the ceiling, lost in his own thoughts. He did not hear the three radio cars that glided to a stop twenty or so yards from his house. He was thinking of the duffel bag and how lucky he had been to think of tossing it over the embankment. Now the contents of the bag could not be introduced into evidence against him. He wished that he would stop having to go to the bathroom. His lawyer told him that it was a sure bet that he'd walk away from the whole thing. But he was scared.

It had all seemed so simple in the beginning. Foolproof. When it was over he was going to throw in his papers and retire. He and Mary Ann would sail off into the sunset with a ton of money. He wished she was there now to relax him. Damn, he had to go to the bathroom again.

Walking from the bathroom several minutes later, buckling his belt, he was startled when a hard knocking came at the door.

"Yeah, who is it?"

"Lieutenant Scanlon."

Harris opened the door. He looked at the detectives standing behind the lieutenant. There was real fear in his voice. "What are you doing here, Scanlon?"

"I'm here to arrest you," Scanlon said.

Harris walked back into his house, leaving the door open. Scanlon and the detectives followed him inside. Harris went over to the telephone that was on the table next to the couch and began dialing. "I'm calling my lawyer," Harris said.

"It's kind of late at night," Scanlon said.

Dialing, Harris said, "And what are the trumped-up charges this time?"

"I'm placing you under arrest for the murder of Mary Ann Gallagher."

The phone fell from Harris's hand. He gazed with shock at the lieutenant, his mouth open, his face contorting with fear, disbelief. "Mary Ann?"

"She gave us a dying declaration. In it she named you as her killer."

"You're crazy! I loved her!"

"We have two civilian witnesses to her statement," Scanlon said, motioning to Brodie and Christopher to take him.

"You set me up, you bastard," Harris shrieked, lunging for Scanlon's neck.

Scanlon sidestepped the lunge. Brodie grabbed Harris and tossed him to the floor. Christopher slapped handcuffs on Harris's wrists.

Harris struggled to get up off the floor. Brodie and Christopher hefted him up onto his feet. "You son of a bitch. You rotten son of a bitch. You set me up. I'm going to kill you. I'll kill you."

"Your killing days are over," Scanlon said.

The detectives dragged their screaming prisoner out of the house and over to the unmarked department auto. Cops from the One-two-three who had responded to cover Harris's house watched in silence. Scanlon stood in the doorway of the house, looking around the living room. He noticed the photograph of the two smiling children on the mantel. Harris's, he thought. He felt sorry for them. He closed the door and walked up to the gaping cops from the One-two-three. "You guys can resume patrol," he said.

"What's going down, Lou?" one of the cops asked.

"Somebody forgot which side he was on."

At 0900 the next morning, Tony Scanlon parked his car on the corner of Third Avenue and Fifty-second Street. He tossed his vehicle identification plate on the dashboard and got out. He stood on the corner watching four city buses gridlock the avenue. People rushed past him on their way to work. Delivery boys hustled past carrying cartons filled with coffee containers and goodies bundled in waxed paper.

Ten minutes passed before he saw her crossing Third Avenue; she was just one in a flock of scurrying people. She seemed lost, as though she were being carried along by the momentum of the flock.

Coming up to the bank, Linda Zimmerman saw him and stopped. "Leave me alone, Lieutenant."

"I had a feeling you might be coming here today," he said, moving up to her. "Mrs. Gallagher was murdered last night."

"That's wonderful. I hope with all my heart that she burns in hell," she said, pushing past him.

He blocked her. "The ME hasn't figured out yet what the murder weapon was. My money is on a spear, one of those short-handled stabbing kinds that I saw on the wall in your brother's house, or one that fell out of the closet in his office."

"Please excuse me now. I have things I want to do."

He continued blocking her path. "We arrested George Harris for her murder."

"What?"

"Yes. Before she died, Mrs. Gallagher told us that Harris had killed her. She told us in front of two witnesses."

"But I don't understand. I'm—"

"There is no need to understand, Linda. Just know that one way or the other, Harris is going to pay. The statement that Mrs. Gallagher gave us is going to put him behind bars for the rest of his life."

"There is no question of him not spending his life in jail?"

"None. I have a lead on the man who took the guns from the highway, and I fully expect to get my hands on those weapons soon."

"Those two animals didn't have a millimeter of pity between them. I'm glad they both got exactly what they deserved."

Scanlon slid the lighter he had found in Mary Ann Gallagher's bedroom from his pocket and held it up to her. "A Zippo. You don't get to see many of them these days." He opened the clasp of her shoulder bag and dropped the lighter inside, closing the bag. "Goodbye, Linda. I hope everything works out for you and Andrea."

She stood open-mouthed, looking down at her pocketbook. People rushed past them. A jumble of car horns echoed off building walls. She called to his back. "Why, Lieutenant?"

"Say hello to your parents for me," he said, making for his car.

ACKNOWLEDGMENTS

I wish to thank the following people for their help and encouragement in the writing of this book: Theodor Saretsky, Ph.D.; Irene Gellman, Ph.D.; and Carlo and Eugent De Marco of the Orthopedic Studio, Brooklyn, New York.

Detectives George Simmons, Frank Nicolosi, Anthony Tota, Robert Cotter, and Mike Albanese of the NYPD's Ballistics Squad.

Knox Burger and Kitty Sprague for always being there. Detective Milagro Markman, the NYPD's hypnotist, for showing me how it is done.

A very large thank you to Giampaolo Panarotto for translating my prose into Italian.

I acknowledge a special debt of gratitude to Capt. Edward Mamet, NYPD, who took the time to teach me about stump-sock maintenance, edema, and the true meaning of the word courage.